UNTIL THE SEA RUNS DRY

SILVER SCREEN SECRETS 2

JOANNE HO

Book Cover designed by JH Book Cover Designs

May you all find that one other who shines brighter than any movie star.

My thanks go to Candy Robosky, Tonya Gillon and Susan Johnson for helping to spot any grammar issues.

SIGN UP TO JOANNE'S NEWSLETTER!

Don't miss another release!
Be the first to hear Joanne's news, book releases, and giveaways.
Apply for her ARC teams (she has one for ebooks AND one for audiobooks) to get free, advanced copies of her books to read / listen to and review.

Plus, you'll get a free book as a thank you for signing up! What's not to like?

Sign up and join the rest of the romance fans and dog lovers at www.johoscribe.com

1

The sun shone, warming the bare shoulders of the woman as she wound the car down the familiar twisting lakeside road.

Gulls soared overhead as waves crashed against the surf below, a sound she had never heard as a child, but now fell asleep to every night.

It was a blessing, she knew, to live in this gorgeous place, with the means she now had — it was such a far cry from her humble upbringing in Oklahoma — but God seemed to give with one hand and take with the other.

It had been this way her entire life.

At just eighteen-years-old, she had known that there was more to life than what her sleepy hometown of Newcastle and devout Catholic parents could offer her.

Despite doing everything in her power to win their love, from attending church every Sunday, to the straight A's and saving her virginity until marriage, it seemed she could never please them.

It was only when she had overheard a passing conversation that she came to realize her parents had never wanted children and her presence in the world was an accident.

It would have been too shameful to have given their child away, and anything else was unthinkable. So, they kept and raised her, though she never experienced the love and warmth that was so prevalent among her friends and neighbors.

Her childhood was filled with isolation and indifference.

Though her parents were never horrible to her, she grew up questioning her value, and couldn't wait to leave this life — and town — behind.

When the job had come up to work in hospitality on a cruise ship, she had jumped at the chance. She would travel the world and get to experience all that life offered. Somewhere along the way, maybe, she would meet her handsome prince who would sweep her off her feet, and they would live happily ever after, surrounded by their many healthy children.

At least she had managed to accomplish one of those things.

Though the temperature in the car soared from the California heat, causing sweat to gather at the base of her neck, the woman kept the top of her sports car up and the AC off. She wanted nothing more than to feel the cool wind through her newly styled hair, but she couldn't afford to undo all of her stylist's good work, not after it had taken two long hours.

Today was an important day.

For what must have been the twentieth time since she

had gotten into the car, the woman glanced at her reflection in the rearview mirror.

Though she would be considered a beauty by any of the people who tossed admiring glances her way, she couldn't see it herself and always reasoned away their reactions. It was the lighting, the angles, the professionals who spent hours getting her whipped into shape.

She stared critically in the mirror, analyzing every aspect of her heart-shaped face.

The plucked eyebrows artfully framed wide eyes that were a sapphire blue in color. Only the faintest dusky pink eyeshadow brushed the corners of the lids. Her lashes were coated in a natural brown mascara — never black — that would be too harsh for her pale coloring. Not for her was the heavy smoke-eye and fake-lash look of celebrities today, which her husband lamented as trashy.

He liked her understated, but classy.

Suitably, her cupid's bow lips were coated in a sheer peach lipstick that hinted at sexuality rather than exaggerated it.

It wasn't only makeup that was kept simple; the only jewelry she wore was a platinum band encrusted with diamonds on her wedding finger that she always found impractical, as the stones loved to catch on things.

There was no engagement ring as she had been young and impatient, too desperate to be whisked away.

Too stupid to have known better.

The traffic light changed to green. Behind her, a horn blared impatiently.

People were always in such a hurry in this city. It was one of the few things she missed from back home, the neighborly manners, strangers smiling at her in the street and saying hello. Out here, only the most ambitious survived: you were either born into the right family, worked extremely hard to make a success of yourself, or you married right.

She bit her lip as the thought flew into her mind that she might have failed on all three accounts.

Stepping on the gas, she turned the steering wheel a little too fast and felt a sharp pain shooting up her left arm.

She probably should have iced it today, but there hadn't been time. Trying not to flinch, she held her car steady as the vehicle behind overtook her Jaguar and sped off into the distance.

It was her fault, she knew, that her arm hurt at all.

She should not have angered him, but she couldn't seem to help herself. Over and over, she would mess up.

Take last night. She had spent several hours cooking one of his favorite meals, a simple lemon chicken and artichoke bake served with sauteed potatoes and steamed asparagus. Technically, it wasn't a difficult dish, but she had still managed to ruin it by leaving the lid on too long, causing the vegetables to turn into a soggy mess.

When he had come home from another hard day at work and sat down at the table to discover yet another meal had been wrecked, he had been rightfully upset.

She knew how stressful it was at work right now. Nothing was going the way it should, yet he was determined to see it through — for her.

Had he not given her everything she had ever wanted? Had she not traveled the world at his expense?

Look at the house they lived in, the designer clothes

she wore. He provided everything, yet she couldn't make the effort to cook him a simple meal.

If she had been smarter, she would have apologized, and that would have been that. Instead, she'd tried to make excuses, even when she knew how much Marko hated it when she did.

Everything that had happened after that was on her. He hadn't even meant to twist her arm. If she hadn't tried to get away from him, she wouldn't have been injured.

After he'd calmed down, he'd held her, begging for forgiveness. He wasn't himself. Work was driving him crazy. He promised he'd do better by her, she just had to give him time. Time to get over this hump, and things would return to normal. Maybe they could plan a trip, visit somewhere exotic that they'd never been to?

In the morning she'd woken to a bouquet of beautiful roses, a lavish breakfast in bed, and to find that he'd booked her a day at his favorite spa as an apology.

She hadn't the heart to tell him that, when she was already injured, people working on her body was the last thing she needed.

Brooks was a boutique spa that served a VIP clientele. Only those who had deep pockets or were "someone" were allowed to become a member. She recalled how, the first time she had seen the price tag of its membership, she had choked on her cucumber water. It seemed ridiculous for a spa to not only charge a membership fee at all, but for it to be so exclusive.

But Marko had insisted she join.

She had been letting herself go lately and had put on at least two pounds — all on her hips, if he was to be believed. Needing as much help as she could get, she had reluctantly joined, and was grateful that the four-figure monthly price tag was something he took care of for her.

The day had passed by in a blur of appointments which began with a session in the sauna to clear her pores. This was followed by a seaweed mud wrap, a full body session which would cause any excess water to disappear out of her system. She was hoping she could lose enough liquid that it would get rid of those extra two pounds. To help it along, she had only drunk a protein shake all day.

After the seaweed mud wrap, she had tried their latest facial procedure, which involved hot rocks. She didn't really care for the details, had just let them decide what she needed and went along with it. Sensing that she wasn't one of their more talkative customers, the staff — though courteous — never bothered her with small talk. It was why they knew next to nothing about her other than she was polite and tipped well.

Her final appointment had been with the hairstylist. She didn't need her hair cut as she had a bi-weekly trim, and it had only been a few days since her last, but, wanting everything to be perfect, she had opted for a blowout of her long blonde hair. And since she was already there, she booked a make-up artist to work their magic too.

God knows she could never paint her face the way they did. How they masked her many imperfections was truly something.

When they were done, the staff had exclaimed over how pretty she was, but she knew that only one person's opinion mattered.

And it wasn't theirs.

Driving toward his office now, she could smell the

water as she approached. His office sat along the docks where the city skyline loomed pretty as a picture. She never enjoyed the city more than when she was at this particular dock. Something about the sound of water with that stunning view always calmed her. It made her feel as if she wasn't alone, that she was a part of this great universe.

Although she had always been a terrible swimmer and would never be able to utilize the ocean here, she was still able to enjoy it. Tapping French-manicured nails on the wheel, she glanced at the diamond encrusted Rolex on her wrist and let out a relieved breath.

Good, she had made it with twenty minutes to spare before his office closed.

She hadn't messaged him to tell him she would be coming. Wanting to surprise him for the thoughtful day he had planned, she had booked a reservation at Gino's, a local seafood restaurant he liked. She was going to prove that she too could do better, that the effort wasn't only his.

Killing the engine, she stepped out of the car on the Manolo heels she had bought a few weeks back, but hadn't yet broken in. They pinched at the front, but she gritted her teeth and tried to smile through the pain.

Marko *loved* her in heels. It would all be worth it when he saw her.

She smoothed down the black dress that clung to her body like a second skin. It was by Dior, his favorite designer, and he always complemented her whenever she wore his dresses. This particular one had been a gift for her last birthday.

He had presented it to her in a beautiful black box lined with red tissue paper. He had even bought matching lingerie to go with it. She was lucky he cared so much that he paid such attention to her wardrobe, when most men didn't even know their wife's size.

Locking her car, she shivered as a sudden gust of wind blew deep into her bones.

She glanced at the silk shawl lying in the back of the car, but refrained from reaching for it. She didn't want to spoil the effect by wearing it, even though it was always much colder here due to the proximity to the water.

If all went to plan, she wouldn't be here all that long. Once she was back in the car, she'd be warm again.

She started towards his office, situated in the back of this particular dock. She forced herself not to flinch as she balanced on her heels, wanting to appear calm and serene, hoping that it would rub off onto Marko.

As she turned the sharp corner, her husband's glass cubed office appeared. It was a modern design, sleek with minimalistic furniture, something which she had found at odds with the surroundings. She much preferred architecture that had identity behind it, and this glass modern cube seemed empty and soulless.

She could see straight inside and was surprised to find that his assistant was already gone for the day: her computer was switched off from its usual screensaver of her two children playing with their spaniel puppy. This was unusual, as he liked to keep her there to close the office.

She passed by her husband's matching Jaguar (his was a blood red while hers, a metallic bronze) so she knew he was still here.

Moored beside the office was her husband's pride and joy, the AMELIA, an eighty-foot luxury yacht with not one, but two, VIP staterooms and a master suite that could rival any found at the nearby Hilton. He loved to spend weekends sailing down the coast where they would meet up with other yachters.

Truthfully, she found it boring, and often wished she could be back on solid ground, but as it was the only thing that seemed to take his mind off the stress of his work, she kept her feelings to herself.

The boat could accommodate up to eight guests overnight in five spacious cabins. Still, it would never be used in this way. While her husband was considered the life and soul of any party, he preferred to keep his colleagues and those he called "friend" at bay, even the fellow boaters — who he never invited onboard — though they would frequently visit theirs.

He didn't like anyone to get too close. He didn't like what they could find out about him if they were to penetrate his carefully orchestrated world.

Continuing to the Amelia, she heard raised voices. Amplified by the water, though the heat level was clear, the actual words that were being said, wasn't.

Standing on the deck of the boat, her husband argued with a shorter, squatter man in a suit, though it wasn't bespoke or half as well made as the ones her husband wore. The pant legs were an inch too short, while the sleeves reached well below his wrists. His well-worn leather shoes were in dire need of a polish.

The man's face was pale beneath several days of growth. His tie was askew, and he was explaining — no, pleading — with her husband about something, hands gesturing emphatically as Marko listened with an almost bored expression, those steely eyes of his fixed on his face.

She was still walking towards them when Marko reached inside his double-breasted jacket, took out a silenced gun and pointed it at the other man.

She froze, her heartbeat slammed through her chest.

"No! Don't!"

This time, the man's words were crystal clear, soaring above his own panic and fear. The world slowed to a crawl as she sucked in a breath. Before she could think what to do, her husband pulled the trigger.

There was the tiniest whoosh of sound as the bullet shot out of the gun. Blood spurted from the man's back as the bullet tore through him. The man's eyes flew open in shock before the pain even had a chance to register.

His hands reached up to cover his heart but met only warm, sticky blood. It took a split second for what had just happened to sink in.

By the time he started falling to the ground, he was already dead.

His body hit the floor with a thud and never moved again. Without any hesitation, her husband nudged his body with his gleaming Gucci shoes, rolling the man out of sight and into the yacht. He pulled out a handkerchief, wiped his fingerprints off the gun, and set it on top of the man's body.

Her initial shock had now turned into a stark, white terror.

She had to get away before her husband looked over and saw her. Holding her breath, desperate not to make any sound, she spun but stumbled on those damn new high heels.

"Honey… What are you doing here?"

Her husband called out to her softly, yet loudly enough

that she heard him. She turned back around, willing her feet to run, but they had turned to blocks of ice.

"I... I was coming to surprise you. I finished at the spa and I'm wearing your favorite dress," she replied, unable to form a coherent sentence.

A million warnings screamed inside her mind, but she could only make sense of one of them. Even now, having witnessed Marko murder a man right in front of her, she heard her own voice berating her, telling her how stupid she was. How stupid she was for not running away.

She deserved everything that was going to happen to her.

"Come here," he said deceptively gently.

Though she wanted anything but to go to him, it was as if her feet had a life of their own.

She walked toward him, trembling with every step until she made it to the boat. Scared out of her mind, she wasn't able to stop the tears that started falling down her face.

He reached out his hand, offering it to her as he had every time she had boarded the boat before.

She took it automatically.

His hand felt cold and heavy as stone as he pulled her up toward him. Seeing her tears, he brushed them away with a fingertip.

When he spoke, his voice was deeply regretful.

"I wish you hadn't seen that."

She swallowed, trying not to recoil at his touch.

"I'll never tell anyone. I can't tell them what I didn't see. No one has to know. Let's just go to dinner. I made reservations at Gino's. They have those clams you like back in stock."

She was babbling, her voice sounded shrill and alien, but she didn't care. As long as she could keep him talking, there was a chance she might get out of this alive.

Her husband studied her silently, his dark eyes boring into her soul. When he didn't respond, she thought maybe things would work out. If they could just go to dinner, she would make a plan to get the hell away from him. She didn't need his love or security.

She only needed her life.

She stared beyond him, hoping desperately for any witnesses that might be able to stop him.

But the dock was as empty as his eyes.

He placed a hand on each of her shoulders. "I wish I could believe that, but we all know how terrible you are at keeping a secret."

And as she started to plead with him, much as the other man had done only seconds before, Marko's hands slid across her shoulders until they reached her neck.

And he squeezed.

Blinded by the pain and gasping for air, she bucked, lashing out. The diamonds on her wedding ring caught him on the cheek, drawing blood, startling him.

She felt the pressure relax from her neck and greedily gulped in a lungful of air...

But then he swung at her with a blow so hard that she dropped to the ground, hitting her head.

And then the world went black.

2

Warmth on her skin.

That's what she felt. Lying there, in the soft grittiness of the… sand?

She could feel the sun bathe her in its comforting glow. Waves lapped nearby.

She knew she was on a beach. Could smell the salt in the air tickling her nose. She must have fallen asleep while sunbathing.

That must be what it was.

She tried to open her eyes, but they felt like they were glued shut. Her tongue flicked out to lick her lips, only to feel how dry and cracked they were. She grimaced at the feel of them, which was the wrong thing to do as the skin tore.

Her tongue ran over her lip again. Tasted blood.

And then came the thirst.

The horrible, desperate thirst of someone who hadn't drunk in forever, it seemed.

She tried to gather the will to wake, though her body

seemed sluggishly slow to respond, when something small and lively crashed into her, and preceded to cover her face with wet, slobbery kisses.

She recognized that strong — and not unpleasant — smell of doggy breath and felt immediately relieved.

She liked dogs. Loved them, in fact. And this little one was super friendly.

Her eyes fluttered opened.

The hazy black spots that clouded her vision took a moment to fade, but when they did, an adorable furry face peered down at her, head cocked cutely to one side in a wide-opened stare.

He had the same features as a German Shepherd, but with salt and pepper patches to go along with the usual black and brown. His eyes were an impossible ice-blue that matched the diamond studded collar around his neck. A small silver name tag hung from the collar with the word 'LOKI.'

He was only a puppy, possibly not more than a few months old, and at the stage where his paws seemed overly large compared to the rest of him.

Her lips curled into a small smile as she tried to ignore the flash of pain that the gesture brought. Loki didn't notice her discomfort, looking down at her adoringly as if they were the best of friends already. His tiny butt shook as he squirmed with happiness at their meeting.

"This is a private beach — didn't you see the sign?"

Not quite as friendly as the dog was the masculine voice that had come from several feet away. The annoyance was unmistakable, as was the proprietary tone that had come with it.

She didn't recognize his voice, but something about the way he was talking to her was causing her heart to race.

And not in a pleasant way.

She looked past the puppy only to flinch at the sun that beat down on her. She noticed the sky next, so luminous in its brightness that it hurt to look at it.

Raising a hand to shield her eyes, she squinted towards the hazy figure of the man who was fast approaching, as Loki bounced between the two like this was a game.

The man pointed to a sign down the beach, but she couldn't see the words from her position on the ground.

What was so important that he needed her to see it?

She tried to sit up when crushing pain shot through her body. She yelped, sucking in her breath, and froze.

What was wrong with her?

"This is a private beach," came the voice again, this time with less of the annoyance that had preceded it.

She opened her mouth to answer, but the sound that came out was hoarse and unintelligible. She swallowed, but with seemingly no saliva in her mouth, all it did was make her throat feel even more scratched.

"Everything hurts," she finally managed.

As the words left her lips, she recognized how true they were.

The man kneeled down beside her, the sun against his back making it difficult for her to see his face. All she could see of him were his startling green eyes with golden flecks that gave him a feline flair. He had sandy hair that framed his face in a perfect designer haircut. There was something so mesmerizing about his eyes that she found herself lost in his gaze, but the moment was soon broken as he stared down at her in concern.

He cursed under his breath.

"What happened to you? You're really hurt."

His quick change of mood filled her with an all encompassing fear.

Stomach churning sickeningly, she stared down at herself, at her bare legs, noticing how the short, tight dress she wore barely covered them. Ugly purple bruises covered her legs and there seemed to be hundreds of cuts criss-crossing them. Stunned, all she could do was stare down in horror as the pain from her injuries hit all at once.

The world spun.

Her balance fled, and her muscles turned to jelly.

She would have sank back down if he hadn't caught her. Strong arms held her close to his warm and solid chest as his face finally came into view.

And she found herself losing her breath all over again.

He had a chiseled jaw that framed an angular face which, combined with those eyes, made him seem even more animalistic. There was a magnetism about him that wasn't due only to the broad shoulders and muscular physique that didn't have an inch of fat on it. He hadn't shaved in a while, stubble covering the lower half of his face.

Then there was that sexy smell, like sandalwood mixed with the ocean.

She bit her lip. The pain cut through whatever confusion she was feeling, until one emotion pushed through the rest.

Though he was clearly concerned, she couldn't help the flicker of fear she felt.

There was something untouchable about him, something that made him seem a world away even though she was close enough to feel his breath on her skin.

His eyes flicked up and down her body, assessing her wounds. Whatever conclusion he came to must have worried him greatly, as he softened his voice.

"I need to get you some help. What's your name?"

She opened her mouth to reply, but where her name should have been, her mind was a complete blank. She tried to shake the fog that had taken residence in her head. She was in shock. It would come to her in a minute.

But after several moments… there was nothing.

The world began to spin again. The blood pounding through her temple.

"I don't know. I can't remember."

And as she said the words, she knew with a stark, sudden terror that they were true.

She stared up at him, panic turning her blood to ice-water.

"Why can't I remember who I am?"

3

As soon as she said the words, there was a crushing fear in her chest.

Squeezing her eyes closed, she tried to picture something — anything — from her past, but where her memories should have been there was nothing but a white fog.

She couldn't see herself as a child.

Couldn't see the faces of her loved ones.

Where had she gone to school? Had she graduated? What about a job? Surely she had a career, a profession of some kind?

What of her personal life? Was she married, maybe — God — someone's mother?

They would be worried sick! She glanced down at her left hand.

No wedding ring.

No engagement ring either.

No rings of any kind.

A sudden wave of nausea forced her to lurch to one side. Her stomach heaved painfully, but nothing came out.

It wasn't only her mind: she was empty everywhere.

Loki had finally calmed down enough that he wasn't running around them in circles anymore. Instead, he darted between them, sensing their distress, yet not understanding any of it. He whined and licked her cold fingers.

"I should call the police," the man said, interrupting her rising panic.

She turned to look at him, saw he was already pulling a phone out of the pocket of his khaki shorts.

"No, don't do that!" Her words came out in one alarmed sentence.

"You need help..." he began, but she cut him off.

"I can't. Please. Not the police."

She couldn't explain why, but the thought of involving them filled her with more terror than even losing her memory had. Somehow, she had to stay away from them, and not knowing any better, she had to trust her instincts.

Right now, they were pretty much all she had.

"Then I'm taking you to the hospital. Your wounds need seeing to and I won't take no for an answer," he replied, giving no room for disagreement.

She nodded. That she wouldn't argue with.

Her response did make her wonder what kind of person would have such a response to calling the police? Only one answer came to mind.

A criminal.

Had she been involved in a crime that had gone terribly wrong?

Is that why she had washed up on the beach: had she been dumped there?

Even as the panic began anew, she found that conclusion hard to believe. She didn't *feel* like a bad person; wouldn't she know it if she was?

Her rescuer leaned over to offer his hand.

Something about that innocent gesture caused a flash of panic to crash into her mind, stunning her with its ferociousness. An icy finger of fear raced up her spine, causing her to shiver uncontrollably. She shrank away from him, as far as she could go in her current condition.

"I'm not going to hurt you."

There was surprise in his voice, but also something else. Hurt? Pain that she would react to him in such a way.

She studied his face, desperate to read his motives, but all she saw was a man — possibly the most handsome man who had ever walked the Earth — who wanted to help.

Her heart fluttered with anxiety, but she reached out and took his hand.

It felt strong and warm. His sun-kissed skin was smooth and without callouses. He wasn't in the manual trade, she could tell that about him immediately.

He pulled her to her feet, which she only just noticed were bare. The polish on her toes was chipped in many places, but had once been a French pedicure. The same chipped polish adorned her fingernails. She stared at them, trying to imagine those fingernails when they must have been freshly painted, but like everything else, the memory refused to come.

"Can you walk," he asked, looking as if he might throw her over his shoulder if she replied that she couldn't.

She wasn't sure and took a tentative step. Pain came

from all sides, though her feet seemed relatively unscathed by whatever ordeal she had gone through.

"I think so."

"My car is just over there, on the other side of my house."

He pointed toward a stunning place set slightly back at an elevated angle from the beach, probably so it could make the most of the spectacular views.

A cross between a ranch and shingle style cottage, it seemed an odd choice of a home for this man. Too homey, almost.

Which was ridiculous.

She knew nothing about him, yet here she was, making assumptions, when the only real fact she had learned at this point was that he had a lot of money.

This house with its own private beach, no less — she could finally make sense of that sign he had been pointing to — wasn't the kind of place the average person could afford, though it did not fill her with the kind of awe that was its due.

Instead, there was bitterness in her mouth.

She shook her head, trying to clear it away.

This man had shown nothing but kindness after she had trespassed on his property. What were all these bizarre reactions she was having about him?

They walked together, Loki bouncing ahead of them joyfully again, having apparently forgotten their anxiety of the moment, yapping and chasing the gulls that swooped down from the sky. Whatever fears he had picked up on, the dog was too young to remember it for long.

"I'm Logan, by the way," the man offered when they neared his home.

She gave him a weak smile. "I'd tell you my name if I knew what it was."

"Names are overrated. Take Loki." He gestured at the puppy who had found a big branch half buried in the sand and was trying desperately to dig it up with paws that seemed unwilling to cooperate.

"He'll answer to anything, though of course, when you actually want him to come, you won't see him for dust."

He was making small talk. She was grateful for the effort to take her mind off her troubles.

"How long have you had him?"

"Only a week. He was a gift and not a wanted one at that."

"A dog is a big responsibility. If you're not ready for it, you should find him a new home," she said before she could stop herself.

Apparently, she had been an animal rights activist in her previous life.

"I don't have much choice in the matter. We're stuck with each other... for now," he glowered at the dog as Loki came toward them, dragging the branch proudly, having successfully retrieved it from the sand.

"Let go of that thing! You'll get a sliver in your mouth!"

Loki's tail wagged back and forth, loving the game he now thought they were playing.

She thought it interesting that, despite apparently not wanting to have the dog, he was still concerned for his welfare.

They reached a path of sorts, created by aged pieces of driftwood set into the sand. She focused on the warmth of the wood beneath the soles of her feet.

Little details.

If she focused on the smaller things, she wouldn't become overwhelmed.

Logan led them up the short path, past several steps until they crossed a small white-painted gate and into the grounds of his home.

She was struck by how perfect it all was.

The landscaped gardens were lush, thriving with exotic flowers and plants that bloomed in cleverly designed displays, but pretty as they all were, the standout was the pool that overlooked the ocean while a rock waterfall cascaded over one end. Adjoining it was a beautiful pool house clad with a finish that resembled those driftwood steps that even from her cursory glance, seemed fit for a king.

At a fraction of the size of the main house, it shared the same shingle style cottage design, but with modern highlights that came in the form of floor-to-ceiling doors that could be opened up all the way to let the house spill into the back yard. She imagined when the sun set, this entire place would seem magical.

None of the splendor affected Loki in the least as he tore madly about the place, that giant branch gripped tightly in his mouth, but when he caught sight of a particular flower bed, he dropped the branch like it was a hot coal.

"Don't you dare…" Logan began, but the dog had already dashed over to the flower bed and started to dig a large hole in the dirt.

Logan threw up his hands but did nothing to stop him.

"Aren't you going to tell him off?" She couldn't understand Logan's reticence. If this was her home, she wouldn't let the dog — adorable or not — destroy this beautiful place.

"I've tried. All it does is get him excited again. I've learned it's best to leave him to it. Once we move away, he'll get bored and come after us."

He was right. As soon as they started away, Loki stopped digging and chased after them, barking with abandon, his face now covered with dirt.

When they finally reached the three-lane-wide driveway that was decorated with another stunning floral display, Logan started toward what she assumed was the garage. It was hard to know since it looked like another outbuilding, like the pool house. It certainly didn't look like any garage she had ever seen — any that she could remember.

Loki tossed a look her way, torn whether to stay or go, but clearly, he was devoted to his owner. He bounded after Logan, yipping at his heels.

She heard Logan curse again as Loki almost tripped him up. Impatiently, he bent down, carrying the dog in his arms so he could get to his car quicker. This delighted the dog no end as he slathered Logan's face in wet kisses.

The last thing she heard as they disappeared from view was Logan making a sound of utter disgust.

Alone, she took in her surroundings.

Remember to focus on the details…

Someone had planted white jasmines by the door. Their sweet, familiar scent drifted into her nose, causing her to grow suddenly excited. She knew what the flower was!

But how could she know that, and not her own name? What insanity was this?

The driveway itself was a sweeping river of stone flanked on either side by pristine lawns of the greenest grass. Branches heavy with the leaves of mature willows bordered the driveway, offering privacy while still letting in the natural light and some of that stunning California beach view that stretched on as far as the eye could see.

It must cost a small fortune for Logan to live here.

What on Earth did he do that he could afford such a luxurious lifestyle?

She considered whether he could be a stockbroker, though they tended to live in the East Coast by Wall Street. Maybe some other financial business: from the little she had seen of him though, he seemed too casual for the suited type. Try as she might, she could not picture him behind a desk, crunching numbers on a calculator.

Maybe he was a model — he was certainly good-looking enough. Her cheeks flamed at the thought.

She might be hurt and suffering from amnesia, yet it hadn't slipped her notice that her rescuer could have given a young Hugh Jackman a run for his money.

She consoled herself with the thought that though she might have lost her memory, she certainly wasn't dead.

A purr of a car engine caught her attention.

Logan pulled up in a gleaming platinum Porsche with tinted windows that would have obscured him from view had he not opened a door. She slid her body carefully into the passenger seat, wincing at even the tiniest movement. It was a moment before she noticed the empty backseat.

"Where's Loki?"

"Left him with the housekeeper. We haven't graduated to riding in cars yet, not since he peed all over the last one."

For a ridiculous moment, she felt lost without the little ball of joy to keep them company. He provided an easy distraction to all this uncertainty.

She reached for the seatbelt, but a wave of pain shot through her arm. She fumbled with the clasp, couldn't get it to catch. Seeing her struggle, Logan leaned over her.

"I've got it."

He came so close that she became overwhelmed by that exotically spiced sandalwood he must use as his after-shave. She could feel the heat coming off him, warming her own skin, causing the hairs to raise on the backs of her arms.

Her stomach lurched, churning at their proximity.

He had shown her nothing but kindness. She knew there wasn't any reason to be afraid of him, yet now that they were in such close quarters, in this very nice, very expensive car, she felt her vulnerability very strongly.

She squirmed in her seat, noticing how claustrophobic the car suddenly felt with its low ceiling and darkened windows.

Although cold air hissed through the AC, she fumbled for the button on the door until the dark glass window slid down, letting the comforting rays of the sun pour into the car.

"I need air," she explained, not very well.

He stared at her, his forehead knitted into a frown, clearly puzzled by her actions.

"Knock yourself out," he said, only to flinch. "Sorry, bad choice of words."

She didn't reply.

They drove to the hospital in silence, which she was grateful for. The last thing she wanted was more questions that she didn't have any answers for. Logan kept the car rolling at a smooth pace, never going near the speed limit, taking corners gently, conscious of his troubled passenger.

She would have thanked him for his consideration but didn't want to break the spell of silence. Instead, she looked over to the dashboard where a large pair of sunglasses sat beside a baseball cap, and watched pretty streets lined with glorious mansions blur past in what must be one of the most prestigious neighborhoods in LA.

It struck her that she had known they were in California before she'd even seen the street signs, though she had no idea whether that was from familiarity, or if it was just a good guess.

If not for that nervous gnawing in the pit of her stomach, and the pain from her injuries that would ebb and flow depending on how she breathed, she might have enjoyed some of the ride. But that constant uneasy nagging in her mind wouldn't go away, not until she found out who she was and what had happened to her.

Nothing, not the view or even the intriguing man beside her would take that ache away.

Recognizing that her thoughts were only going to yo-yo back and forth, she forced herself to relax, letting her head sink into the headrest. A sudden wave of exhaustion came over her, so great that her eyes started to close.

A few minutes rest was all she needed.

Maybe if she allowed herself to relax completely, her memories would return.

In no time at all it seemed, the car stopped, jolting her awake.

A concrete giant building loomed over them. They passed an embossed Cedars-Sinai Medical Center sign sitting between two neatly pruned young cherry blossom trees.

The low-key nature of the hospital surprised her.

Somehow, she had been expecting shrieking sirens and flashing red lights, but there was nothing of the sort here.

It was a dignified place, reeking of the quiet wealth of its surroundings.

By the front entrance, a family of three waited for transport to arrive. One of their members, a young child, still wearing a football uniform, sat in a wheelchair, a new cast on his legs. As Logan climbed out of the car, the family stirred to attention, noticing him immediately.

One by one, a look of astonishment came over their faces.

She wondered what it was about him that could have induced such a change. Noticing their interest, Logan helped her out of the car, steering her quickly — too quickly — inside.

The sudden speed at which he pulled her along startled her… and caused a fresh flash of pain.

"Slow down," she gasped.

What was his damned hurry?

The sunglasses and baseball cap from the dashboard were in his hands now. He slipped them on even though they were now inside the hospital.

Why was he putting sunglasses on *inside the building*?

They headed toward the front desk. Logan spoke with the receptionist there, an older woman with a stern demeanor and big blowout that must have taken hours to do.

Busy typing into her computer, she kept her eyes down

at the screen, making them wait until she was good and ready to deal with them.

"She needs help. I think she had an accident and seems to have lost her memory. I found her on the beach," Logan began, apparently not caring that she hadn't yet addressed either of them. He spoke so fast his words ran into each other.

It was as if he had become very nervous. Why would he be nervous at being seen with an obviously hurt woman?

Unless.

Maybe he was married. She looked over his hands but saw no telltale sign of a ring.

Logan's eyes glanced every which way, shoulders tensing at every person who passed. The receptionist, whose name badge said "BRENDA," pulled up a new screen on her computer, typing leisurely before finally looking up at him for the first time.

When she did, just like the family outside had reacted, she started — as if Logan was of some importance — before visually pulling herself together.

That stern expression lifted. Her lips curled into a welcoming smile.

"I need to put a name in, for reference. Can I use yours?" she asked, full of warmth now.

Logan hesitated, thinking over her question. He shook his head.

"No. I think that might not be wise."

His answer mystified her, but so, too, did Brenda's next response. She nodded, as if she had half expected him to say as much.

"Understood. The doctor will be with you shortly, could you take a seat in our waiting area?"

Logan looked to where she pointed, where several people sat waiting, one of whom, a pimply teenage kid, took out his phone and started pointing it his way. Without a care of how they might feel about it, the kid started recording the two of them on his phone.

She waited for Logan to ask him to stop. Instead, he seemed to grow more concerned beneath his baseball cap. Turning, he gave her an apologetic look.

"I'm sorry. I don't think I should be here."

She had a feeling he wanted to say more, but more cameras were now pointed their way. Without giving her any time to respond, he spun on his heel and hurried away.

Leaving her stranded.

She gaped after him in astonishment, watching his figure recede into the background. Unable to believe he was leaving her like this, the anger quickly set in, making her blood boil.

Brenda didn't seem to notice how she was feeling.

She stared at her with an openly curious smile, leaning closer as if they were acquaintances.

"So," Brenda asked in a gossipy tone. "How are you friends with him?"

It was an odd question.

Any other time and she might have noticed that. Today, however, she felt her confusion mix with a bitter disappointment that she was left alone to deal with this mess.

So much for her rescuing hero.

"Excuse me?"

"Are you friends with Logan Steel? My daughter's going to *die* when she hears her favorite movie star was here, and I got to speak to him! She absolutely *ADORES* him!"

SHE WAS SAVED FROM ANSWERING BY THE APPEARANCE OF THE doctor, a man in his fifties. Smiling, and with an air of kindness about him, he entered, followed by a team of helpers, each of them sporting caring expressions.

His name was Dr. Lewis, and he was a neurology specialist.

Promising that she was in safe hands, he explained that they would look her over to build an overall picture, before getting into the nitty gritty of what they think had happened.

They moved her to a private room and closed the blinds. She took off her dress and felt a moment of panic that clawed at her throat.

The dress was the only real thing that connected her to her past. It was her only physical link to the woman she had been before the memory loss, and to have it taken away from her like this, felt like the only security she knew was being torn away.

As if the nurse knew the turmoil that was going on inside, she patted her hand, a calm smile on her lips. The nurse had gray streaks in her hair that was pulled back into a neat bun. There wasn't a single strand that was out of place. She wasn't sure why, but that simple fact lessened some of the panic.

She was in capable hands.

The nurse helped her into a hospital gown. Her heart was listened to. Numerous X-rays performed. Blood was drawn. DNA taken. Wounds were cleaned, disinfected, then covered over with Band-Aids.

Bundled from one room to another in a whirlwind of examinations, there wasn't time to think about Brenda's comment, and whether the woman knew what she had been talking about. After several hours of being examined from head to toe, Logan was pushed firmly from her mind.

After deciding she wasn't in any imminent danger, Dr. Lewis sat her down as someone brought a tray of food. Though the bed was comfortable, she found she couldn't lean back against it. She wouldn't be able to relax until she knew what the prognosis was.

Her tongue flicked out to lick her dry, chapped lips. Feeling thirsty again — she'd already drunk what seemed like a gallon of water, but her thirst could not be quenched — she reached for the plastic tumbler of water that had come with her food.

Dr. Lewis smiled patiently at her, brown eyes crinkling with patience. Folding his hands in his lap, he waited for her to take several sips before speaking.

"I know this must be terrible for you, but other than a nasty bump on your head, and the lacerations which were most probably caused by bumping into some rocks while you were in the water, you are clinically well."

"Apart from the amnesia," she added.

"Well, there is that," he admitted. "It seems you hit your head, which has caused you to lose your memories. Now, in many cases of post-traumatic amnesia, the mind heals itself in time and you can gain most, if not all of your memory back. Unfortunately, we won't be able to give you any indication of what you should expect until we see how long your amnesia lasts."

"I don't understand, you can't just give me an estimation?" She heard the desperation in her voice and hated herself for it. Hated how weak she sounded.

"Sadly, no. The severity of your amnesia can only be determined by its duration. For example, if you only lost your memory for up to an hour, it would be considered very mild with an expected full recovery. You might experience a few minor headaches and some dizziness, but that is all. Up to seven days, however, the injury would be deemed severe and recovery could take weeks to months, and you might find that you were less capable than you were before the injury."

"What does that mean, less capable?"

"There can be some cognitive and attentional deficits. After a trauma like this, some patients struggle with concentration, for example, or they have trouble communicating things verbally."

"What if it's longer? What if I have it for a month or more?" she asked.

Dr. Lewis smiled again and patted her hand.

"Let's not worry about that, shall we? Why don't we wait and see what happens? No point worrying about things that haven't happened yet."

"That bad, huh?" she replied, trying to ignore the churning in her stomach.

A smartly dressed mixed-race man poked his head in the doorway carrying a canvas bag. He wore the white shirt, black pants, and the kind of loafers that screamed *police officer*. His skin was a dark caramel with a head of curls that he kept loose. He smiled into the room, displaying an LAPD badge that he showed to the patient and doctor.

"May I?" He asked Dr. Lewis, who rose to his feet. Giving his patient one more smile, he started out of the room.

"Yes, but keep the questions short. She's had quite the shock," he cautioned. To his patient, he said, "Detective Summers has some things to discuss with you, but he won't be long. Any problems, you just ring this bell here," he gestured to a button on the panel beside the bed, "and help will be right with you."

He reached the door before he stopped, gesturing at the bedside table.

"You may find you'll experience some dizziness or a headache. This is to be expected. I've left you pills on the side there. Take those if you feel any pain, even if it's from your wounds. But if, after you've taken them, you feel worse, or it doesn't lessen after an hour, let me know immediately."

Sitting cross-legged on the bed, she nodded at him. "I will."

He left, leaving her trying not to show her nervousness toward Summers, who made his way over. The man was here to help, yet she felt a deep weariness toward him that she couldn't explain.

"So, first thing we need to establish, since you can't remember who you are, we need to give you a temporary name. Are you happy if we go with the traditional 'Jane Smith'? I know it's not sexy, you're free to create something a little more elaborate if you'd like?"

She barely gave the name a moment's thought, though

she was grateful for his consideration. What they called her didn't matter — what mattered was who she actually was.

"That's fine. I'm good with Jane."

"Excellent," Summers said, lowering into the chair beside the bed. Taking out a leather-bound notebook, he flipped it open, pen poised over the blank page.

"Can you tell me what you remember?"

Jane paused, thinking back.

"Not much. I woke up on the beach. Everything hurt. I thought I must've drifted off to sleep as I was sunbathing, but then I saw the cuts on my body, and the dress I was wearing."

Her voice cracked from the stress of the memory. The raw shock she had felt, and the terror that had turned her blood to ice, threatened to overcome her again.

Seeing Jane grow paler, Summers gave her a moment to compose herself.

"You had no idea where you were? What state you were in?"

"No... I didn't think about that. I was just shocked at my injuries and confused about everything. But then the dog came over..."

"Ah yes, the dog belonging to Logan Steel. Must have been another shock to see a famous movie star coming your way," Summers smiled.

Jane stared at him blankly.

"I actually didn't recognize him. Should I know who he is?"

Summers gave her a half-amused, half-astonished smile.

"He's only one of the biggest movie stars on the planet. Well, he was, but he seems to have had a little trouble of late, if the gossip rags are to be believed. My other half loves everything he's done: she's dragged me to all of his movies."

"You don't like him, then?" Jane asked.

"It's not so much him: he seems a decent actor, just haven't been fond of the kind of movies he's famous for. All brawn and no brain," Summers replied. "I get enough of that down at the station," he joked.

Summers looked to be a typical cop, with the kind of confidence that came from knowing he was good at his job. He had an air of competence about him that Jane found comforting. Beneath the kindness lay a toughness of steel.

"What about your past, have you been able to remember anything? Where you went to school, maybe? Where your parents worked?"

Jane searched her mind, but there was nothing there. Only a blankness and the beginnings of a thudding headache. Rubbing her temple, she reached for the pills the doctor left.

"Sorry, I've got nothing." Frustration welled inside suddenly until she slammed her fist onto the over-bed table. Water spilled out of the tumbler, splashing onto her leg, but she ignored it.

"Outside Logan's house, I knew the flowers by the door were Jasmine. How could I know that, but not who I am? How does that make any sense at all?"

"There's no rhyme nor reason to this," Summers answered calmly. "It affects everyone differently. You need to give yourself time to heal, to get over this trauma.

As soon as I leave, I'll inform our networks and NamUs that we have you."

"What is that?"

"The National Missing and Unidentified Persons System. It's a database created by the National Institute of Justice that's accessible by law enforcement and the public. It cross-checks outstanding missing persons reports. I'm sure as soon as your family realizes you are missing, they will let us know. You just try to relax and let the memories come back to you."

"No one has reported me missing yet?" Jane asked, trying not to let the ramifications of that sink in.

"An adult needs to be missing for twenty-four hours before a report can be filed. The dress you were wearing — which is with forensics now — was a designer dress, so not cheap. Someone out there must know who you are, and I'm pretty confident that this time tomorrow, you will too. For now, you just have to rest."

Jane sank back against the pillows, reassured by Summers's conviction. Summers got up from the chair, snapping his notebook closed.

"That's probably all I need from you today. I promised the doc I wouldn't take much time."

"You don't need anything physical to ID me with? I probably have a birthmark somewhere," Jane offered, twisting herself so she could examine her arms and legs.

Summers waved her back down. "I can get all that from the doctor. They would have looked for any identifying marks during your examination. They're trained in cases like yours," Summers replied.

Cases. She was a case now.

Jane tried not to shudder at the shiver his words had given.

"When you feel up to it, we'll take your prints down at the station."

Her face must have frozen as he smiled reassuringly.

"It's just procedure. What usually comes up for most is a parking violation, but if it did, we'd at least know who you are."

Taking out a card from his wallet, he left it on the side table. "If you remember anything, or even if you just want to talk, here's my card. I'd rather you call me than sit here worrying."

He flashed a sudden grin at her. "After all, that's what *I'm* trained for." Summers reached into his bag and retrieved an assortment of goods.

"And these are some things I picked up for you. We've got chocolate and fruit, some gossip mags that my wife reads in case you don't like anything on the TV here, a toothbrush and toothpaste. I know it's not much, but it should help to ease your stay," he finished.

Feeling a wave of gratitude, Jane gave him a grateful look. "Thank you, I appreciate it."

Summers flashed her one last smile and exited the room.

Alone, the sudden silence was as heavy as a blanket.

Moving gingerly off the bed, Jane stepped into the bathroom that connected to her room. Overhead lights flickered on, set off by her movements, bathing her in a harsh light.

For the first time, Jane could see her reflection... but a stranger stared back at her.

She noticed the eyes first, so shockingly blue that they

looked like contacts. Next to that, her blonde hair seemed pale and uninteresting.

Though her body was covered in injuries, none were too severe. Her face was mostly untouched, save for a cut on her right brow. It hadn't required any stitches, and the young attendant who had been dealing with her wounds had thoughtlessly commented how lucky Jane was to have escaped from her ordeal to be rescued by a movie star!

As if that small fact could make up for losing one's entire life.

She stared at herself, moving her eyes down her body, hoping that any of it would be familiar.

Despite the loose fit of the green hospital gown she wore, she could see she had the kind of curves that were considered enviable. Her bare feet with the chipped nail polish — cold now from standing on the hospital floor — were attached to long, toned legs. Her stomach was flat, her butt high and perfectly pert.

Jane knew this body hadn't come by naturally. It had come through hard work in a gym and frequent dieting.

Running her hands over her body, she tried to feel something…

Anything.

But it was as unfamiliar as a stranger.

Tears sprang to her eyes as she wondered if she would be a stranger to herself for the rest of her life.

4

Logan gunned the car all the way home.

He felt like a jerk for leaving her, though he really didn't have much choice.

As soon as he was recognized, as soon as those phone cameras were pointed his way, he knew he'd had to get out of there, or the place would turn into a zoo. Paparazzi would have descended upon the hospital, trying to sneak pictures of her for the tabloids. She wouldn't have gotten a moment's peace.

Given everything that had already happened, it was the last thing she needed.

While his motivation for leaving was to protect her, he also could have done without the added complication their story would bring.

It was only that very morning when his team of managers, agents, lawyers, and publicists had drummed in their message in a three-hour emergency meeting that had almost caused his head to explode.

One more strike.

Just one more scandal.

And he would lose the only job they had managed to secure for him in the past year. He would lose all of his properties. The investors for Steel Pictures, his fledgling film company — the one he'd created in order to give himself better material than the mindless action movies that came his way — would pull out. And he could forget the fleet of luxury cars that sat in his garage: he'd be lucky if he could afford regular Ubers.

He would be dumped by his agency, and likely his long-suffering manager, Trevor, too, even though the two had clawed through the trenches together until they had reached their starry heights of fame. Trevor was the only real friend he had in the industry, yet even their relationship was getting strained from all the recent crap he'd had to deal with.

When the crash had come, it was stunning how quickly it had happened.

After slogging his way through weekly acting classes only to be told that his kind of talent was best suited to non-speaking roles, Logan had plowed on with determination, eager to prove his teachers — all bitter actors, themselves — wrong.

He had guest-appeared on one bad soap after another, and cheap commercials that were only shown in budget stores, until he'd finally had the kind of break that every wannabe actor dreamed of.

It was due in no small part to Pinnacle Studios CEO, Mack "Stonewall" Rockefeller, taking a chance to hire the cocky unknown who blew the other actors out of the water with his stunning audition.

Protect and Serve became Logan's first film. He played

a hardworking cop and a single dad, fighting to stay clean when all around him, others were playing dirty. The movie became an instant international hit, propelling him into the stratosphere of movie stardom.

Following that, Logan was offered the lead in a new action-movie franchise, which went on to break box office numbers. While the films were not exactly high art, they were entertaining, and their success afforded him the kind of luxury he had always dreamed of.

The only thing that was missing from the perfect picture was his love life.

Logan couldn't move without a woman throwing herself at him, and while it had been fun at first, to change bed mates faster than he'd changed clothes, the cheapness of it all soon grew old.

It didn't help that this was the one area of his life where the media scrutinized him relentlessly. It was as if they were more interested in who he was sleeping with, rather than his work.

When he met Ellie Godwin, it had seemed a no-brainer to get involved. She was the most successful television actress in the country, with a popular long-running sitcom that had turned her into the nation's sweetheart. And, with the kind of killer curves that made men sit up and take note, and a sweet, wholesome personality, Logan had fallen into his first real relationship since he'd become a big star.

The world went insane for their coupling. However famous they each had been on their own, once the two became an item, they couldn't breathe without having it splashed across the tabloids.

Things had been good at the start.

Ellie was fun to be with, and they were the guests everyone wanted, but it soon became clear that Ellie wasn't the nice girl she projected into the world.

In reality, she was scheming and spiteful and completely self-absorbed. That girl-next-door persona that had made her so successful had been created by her team, polished until only those unlucky few who really got to know her, discovered the truth.

And by then, it was usually too late.

His phone rang. CAA calling flashed onto the screen in the car. He ignored the call, not wanting to deal with his agents right now.

He wondered if the news had gotten out already.

Had he been linked to the woman he'd helped?

An image of her face came into his mind, flooding it with her startling beauty that had made his breath catch. There was something so fragile about her that, despite his best intentions, his protective instincts had kicked in.

And that was even before he'd noticed her wounds.

It wasn't only her beauty that had captured his attention. There had been such fear in her eyes that it had cut right through the clutter in his mind.

His hands gripped the wheel as he thought of the only woman he had ever truly loved. She, too, had looked at him with that same feral fear that even now, more than two decades later, he still hadn't been able to shake the memory.

It was probably the reason he had listened to her plea not to call the police.

Something terrible had happened to her, and while he wanted to learn her story and make sure that she was being taken care of, it wasn't wise to get involved.

No more scandals.

In particular, that meant no more women.

Especially ones that caused his heart to skip a beat.

Still, if it hadn't been for those cameras and the people at the hospital, he wouldn't have left quite so unceremoniously.

Logan was many things, but he wasn't the unfeeling jerk the media painted him out to be.

Pushing aside the image of her face, he drove, wondering what in the world had happened to her. He comforted himself in the knowledge that at least she was in good hands now.

5

Hours had passed since her talk with Detective Summers.

After some time examining every inch of her face and body only to not have learned anything new about herself, Jane had given up and crawled into bed.

There, she tugged the blanket over the top of the head, and in the blessed softness of her cocoon, shut out the world, the uncertainty and fear, and fell asleep.

When she woke, the sun was preparing to set against a purple-orange sky. Jane started, blinking at the sky, surprised to see how late it was. She had slept for an entire day.

Staring at the unfamiliar room, everything came crashing back.

Waking on the beach. The terrifying condition of her body. Losing her memory. The puppy. Then Logan, and how he had left her so abruptly.

Her eyes were drawn to the clipboard hanging from the end of her bed. The chart attached to it was neatly filled with signatures and timings. Though Jane had been fast asleep, the staff had kept their eyes on her, checking her status around the clock.

This should have filled her with assurance, but the idea of strangers entering her room, watching and assessing her while she was unconscious, left an unpleasant taste in her mouth.

Her head started to thump.

What had the Doctor said yesterday… to watch out for headaches? Did this qualify as a concern?

She pondered the thought when she noticed how thick her tongue felt, how dry her lips had become again.

Most likely she was dehydrated. She couldn't remember when she had last had a drink.

She sat up, but the very act caused every muscle to shriek. Jane flinched, her lips thinning into a tight, thin line.

Not exactly the best start to the day.

Catching herself, a mirthless laugh came out. However badly she felt now, it was a good sight better than yesterday. She should stop feeling sorry for herself. At least she was safe here. She reached for the jug of water that someone had considerately left, filling the tumbler beside it to the brim.

She gulped the cool water down, marveling at how quickly it seemed to kick her body into gear. Almost instantly, she felt less groggy, more clear-headed — like she could finally begin to think about her current predicament.

Possibly.

She poured herself another glass. Drank that down, too, before she stopped, quenched for the moment at least.

Setting the tumbler down, she swung her legs to the edge of the bed — wincing from the various cuts that needed more time to heal — and stood up to peer through the window.

The Hollywood hills loomed in the distance, though the famous sign was half-hidden under a layer of smog. An ambulance with its flashing red lights pulled into the parking lot below. Though she was five storeys up from the ground, she could see the patient, strapped securely to the gurney, as the ambulance crew rolled them out of the vehicle and into the hospital.

Across the Los Angeles skyline, the bustling city prepared for another busy night. Everywhere she looked, there was movement. People rushed below, getting in and out of their vehicles, while across the horizon, streetlamps flickered on as the glow of headlights streaked across the motorway.

People hurrying home to their families and loved ones, while her own life was a complete and utter mystery.

Pressing a hand against the glass, Jane stared down at a couple walking hand-in-hand as a wave of crushing loneliness hit.

Everywhere she looked, it seemed that she was the only one who was alone. Tears welled in her eyes. An ache tugged at her heart.

No!

She would not sit here crying and feeling sorry for herself. She was alive, and that was something. The rest would come naturally.

Hating the silence that gave the room an oppressive feel, Jane reached for a remote control and pressed on. The large flat-screen television on the wall opposite her bed flashed onto a movie channel, where a black and white comedy played.

While she wasn't interested in watching a movie, she studied the actors joking on the screen and tried to place them. Should she know who they were?

But just as Logan's had, their faces drew a blank.

Maybe something current would be more helpful?

Flipping through the channels, she tried to find one that looked interesting, something that might jog her memory.

Maybe there was a show she liked to watch regularly?

Jumping from channel to channel, she grew increasing discouraged when all that seemed available this time of the day were reruns of sitcoms, and a BBC nature show, which though beautiful, she couldn't focus on.

She set the remote down.

Her eyes slid over to the chair, at the bag of provisions Summers had bought. She tried to remember what the cop had said was in it, but she hadn't been paying much attention at the time: hadn't really cared what products were in the bag, her mind on other, more worrying matters.

With nothing else to do, she grabbed the bag on her way back to the bed. Sitting cross-legged, she tipped the contents onto the bed.

Various snacks and toiletries slipped out, all of which she pushed aside. She'd check them out later, but right now, she needed something mindless. Reaching for one of the gossip magazines, she started reading. It didn't take long for her to grow annoyed.

Almost every page was dedicated to how a woman looked. The magazine seemed only interested in selling products that promised to make any woman look like one of the supermodels inside its pages, which Jane knew was complete nonsense — you were either born that way, or you weren't.

Of course there were things a woman could do to help her look and be her best, but most of the products being peddled would only burn a very large hole in their wallets.

Turning the page, she saw candid shots of an actress climbing out of a car. The paparazzi had caught her in an awkward position, but that hadn't stopped the headline from screaming that the woman had unsightly cellulite.

Why would anyone read this nonsense?

It would only make a woman feel bad about herself, like she wasn't good enough. Worse still, it could make the act of criticizing other women the norm.

She turned the page… and stopped.

It was a double-page spread on Logan Steel.

With all her mixed-up emotions, she had almost forgotten about him, but seeing his face again, she was taken aback by his rugged good looks.

If possible, he looked even more appealing in the picture than in real life.

It was another candid, taken when Logan hadn't been aware of the camera. He wore a baseball cap — a different one to the one she had seen yesterday — though his movie star looks couldn't be hidden away.

He oozed masculinity and sex, and looked like the kind of man your mother wouldn't want you to date, knowing that he would be trouble.

Jane stared at him, trying to place the movie star with

the man she had met, the one who had seemed to let his puppy call the shots.

She read through the article, which detailed his troubled personal life. Learned that Logan had been dating America's sweetheart for the last two years. From even their first date, fans couldn't stop speculating about how beautiful their future children would be.

Their romance had enchanted the world until, quite suddenly, the two had broken up a year ago. From then on, it seemed Logan's world imploded.

The fans who had previously worshipped him, now blamed him for the breakup: he must have cheated, as sweet Ellie would never do anything to jeopardize their relationship. Stories were written up about Ellie, desperate to start a family with him, but Logan had been too much of a womanizer to commit.

Though they didn't know him in real life, many of his fans took the breakup personally, turning against him.

Then Logan's latest movie had tanked.

Whether fans were just upset about his broken relationship, or it being an unfortunate coincidence, for the first time, Logan's movie had fallen far below expectations.

There was speculation that Logan's home run was over, that his betrayal of Ellie had caused his downward spiral. It wasn't helpful that Ellie appeared in numerous spreads, looking wan and shaken, giving interviews hinting at his playboy ways.

Jane poured over the words, taking in everything the article had to say about the mysterious man. After some very loose logic, the spread ended with a few facts, though it wasn't very complimentary with its information.

Following a string of flops, each progressively less

successful than the one that preceded it, Logan was due to start his next movie later that week. The article couldn't help pointing out that it would be the first where he would be the co-star, and not the actual lead.

Rumor had it that this role would be different from his previous ones, that it would require actual acting rather than simply smoldering into the camera. Was Logan really the man of the steel, or would he sink from the weight of another crippling failure?

Jane closed the magazine with a snap of her wrist. She found the whole angle of the article distasteful — were there really that many people who liked to read about the misfortune of others? Yes, Logan was rich and famous, but that didn't make him any less of a person. It didn't make him immune to feelings. She couldn't imagine what it must feel like to have the world rooting for your downfall.

He flashed into her mind — not the man from the magazine, but the one she had met. She saw the sun shining behind his head, framing him with a golden halo as he peered down at her, eyes crinkled with concern.

She remembered the soft feel of Loki's tongue as the puppy had made their acquaintance. For a moment, before she had realized the awful truth… their meeting had seemed like a meet cute from a movie itself.

His hand had felt so strong when he had helped her up, and, despite being a little cool and obviously annoyed at the squirming bundle that was his new puppy, Logan had shown her much kindness by taking her to the hospital when he could have put her into a taxi…

Why, then, had he left her without a word?

A flicker of irritation cut through the warmness she had started to feel.

She was only a hiccup to his day: she hadn't meant anything to him in his big, important world. Still, surely even a movie star could have managed a little more sensitivity. If nothing else, he could have faked it.

She wondered if Summers had any news on her real identity yet. How long did forensics take to investigate a dress? What exactly was she hoping they would find? Surely everything would have washed off in the ocean?

Jane rubbed her head.

So many questions with no answers in sight. She would have to be patient. If Summers had news, he would be in contact.

Her stomach rumbled. She rubbed at it absently. It must have been a while since she had last eaten. She leaned toward the "call" button the doctor had shown her when she caught sight of her filthy hands.

Dirt was caked over the knuckles. There was even sand beneath her nails. She noticed the ends of her hair next, dry and gritty.

As hungry as she was, she couldn't eat without having a shower first. She was filthy and would feel better once she was clean.

Moving to the bathroom, she shut the door, turned on the shower, then reached up behind her to unfasten the hospital gown.

Testing the water with a hand, she stepped beneath the spray and let the water rain down. The hot water massaged her aches and pains, washing away the remains of the beach that, until now, still clung to her. She watched the tiny grains of sand and grit mingle with the soapy water, swirling between her toes and down into the drain.

By the time she emerged from the bathroom, a cloud of steam behind her, she saw the tray of food that had been left on her table. She recognized the dish instantly — Chicken Parmesan and spaghetti Alfredo. Next to the plate of pasta, there was also a piece of apple pie for dessert, a juice box, and a small bowl of fruit salad.

Saliva flooded her mouth as she hurried to the food and dove in. The pasta was overdone, the chicken a little dry, but it wasn't a bad effort. Despite those small issues, it tasted like the best meal she had ever had in her life. In no time, she had finished everything. Embarrassed at what a pig she had been, she pushed the table away.

Her eyes found the phone beside her bed. Picking up the handset, she looked at the buttons, hoping her mind would recall a well-used number.

Home, maybe? Her parents? Work?

The numbers stared up at her blankly.

She all but slammed the phone down as a flash of irrational rage came over her. What the hell was she supposed to do? Just sit here until something came back to her? What if it never did?

What if she never remembered who she was at all?

Footsteps sounded in the hallway outside, followed by the appearance of a woman in her thirties. It was a nurse, but not one she recognized. She had brunette curls that she kept tied back in a high ponytail. Coming into the room, the nurse gave her an approving smile, her ponytail swinging from side to side.

"Good, you cleaned the tray. Are you still hungry? I

could get you something else?" She had a warm, friendly voice.

"It was you who left the food?" Jane asked.

"Yes," her nurse nodded. "I heard you were in the shower and knew that you'd be hungry. You slept clear through breakfast and lunch, and I saw on your chart that you came in yesterday afternoon."

"Thank you," Jane answered simply as the nurse started to gather up her empty plates and tray. "Has anyone left a message for me?"

The nurse looked up. "A detective Summers said he hasn't found anything yet, but not to worry as these things can take a while to go through the system. He called for you earlier, but you were asleep," she added by way of explanation.

"No one else called?" Jane asked, feeling suddenly disappointed even though she already knew the answer.

"Not that I know of. Were you expecting someone to?"

Jane shook her head. "No. I just wondered."

Why would Logan have called? He was long gone by now and had probably forgotten all about his little rescue.

The nurse headed to the door, carrying the tray with the empty plates.

"Dr. Lewis will come by to check on you tomorrow. He's stuck with back-to-back emergencies today and sends his apologies, but he wanted you to know that the best thing you can do right now, is to try to take it easy. Don't do anything strenuous and don't beat yourself up if you find there are lots of things you don't remember. In most cases, the memory comes back a little at a time. Give yourself time to heal up and recover from your ordeal."

Jane shot her a grateful smile. "I'll try. I have already learned one thing about myself today, though."

The Nurse beamed at her, flashing pearly white teeth. "That's fantastic! What is it?"

"I don't much like gossip mags," Jane replied.

"You and me both," the nurse said, smiling. "My name's Karen, by the way. If you need me, just push that button. Now, before I take these back to the cafeteria… are you sure you don't want anything else? I'm heading there, anyway?"

Jane didn't want to impose, but the thought of more food was welcoming. She had only made a dent in her hunger.

Catching the expression on her face, Karen grinned.

"I'll bring you back a few things so you can snack on them through the night."

Winking, Karen left.

Settling back into the bed, Jane tried the television once more until she landed on a hospital drama.

Maybe it was all the carbs, or the hot shower, but within moments of watching, her eyelids became so heavy that she could barely keep them open.

Her last thought as she fell asleep was that she had seen the episode of Grey's Anatomy before.

6

The next few days passed by in a blur.

There were mental exercises that the staff took her through, including common sense questions, general knowledge, and IQ puzzles. All were designed to gauge the health of her brain.

Jane felt as if she was back at school and taking her SAT exams. At least, what she thought it must have felt like to take them — she didn't have much to compare it to.

The bruises had faded from the vivid black to an ugly yellow and green. The cuts and scratches were beginning to heal with any pain that came from them taken care of with painkillers.

Her body was improving at a daily rate, though Jane couldn't say the same for her memory.

She'd watched reruns of Grey's Anatomy in the evenings, in the hope that it would spark up more in her subconscious other than the fact that she had seen the show before, though yet, nothing had come to mind.

This was now her fifth day at the hospital. Detective

Summers would be swinging by within the next hour to talk to her.

Jane had hoped to pick up a clue on whether the detective had any news on her identity or family, but Summers had kept the phone call informing her of his impending visit, brief and businesslike: she wouldn't learn anything until the man showed up at the hospital.

She stared at her reflection in the bathroom mirror for what must have been the millionth time since she had woken up on that beach.

Running a brush through her hair, she tied it into a ponytail as a knock sounded.

"Jane? Can I come in?" Dr. Lewis asked.

"Yes, I'm decent." Jane emerged from the bathroom to see his kindly face smiling at her.

Although she had only known him a short while, she was confident that he truly cared about her well-being. She felt safe under his care that he would do everything in his power to help her through this ordeal.

"How are you today? Anything new to report?"

"No. I've read everything I can get my hands on. The magazines in the nurses lounge, whatever they bring to me. I've watched television until my eyes turned blurry, but I've got nothing. Nothing is coming back to me."

Just saying the words had panic welling up inside her chest again. As he had instructed her to do before, she took several deep breaths until the thumping of her heart began to slow to something more manageable.

"We said this might happen. Worrying about it is not going to make your memory return any sooner. Your brain has suffered quite the shock. It needs time to mend itself. You've already remembered that you like to watch that show so, believe it or not, we are making progress already. It may only seem like a small thing, but that actually means your memory is starting to come back — no matter how slow. If this was the worst case of amnesia, you would not remember anything at all, so we need to take this as a positive sign."

Jane nodded, although she couldn't quite force her lips to smile. Crossing to the armchair by the window, she sat down, folding her hands in her lap.

"So, what kind of fun and games do you have for me today?"

She tried to muster up some enthusiasm, though another day of testing was the last thing she wanted. Stuck inside the room and hospital, several floors above the ground, she was beginning to get cabin fever.

"Actually, were done with the tests," Dr. Lewis revealed. "Your vitals are good and your wounds healing nicely. Barring your memory loss, there is nothing physically wrong with you that you need to be in a hospital so... you are being discharged today."

Of all the things she had expected to hear, it wasn't that.

The panic she had managed to clamp down returned with a vengeance. She shot to her feet so fast that the world swam. She had to hold out her arms to steady herself.

Seeing her distress, Dr. Lewis crossed the room. She gripped onto the hand he held out for her.

"But... where am I supposed to go? I don't have any money, no identification. What's going to happen to me?"

He sent a reassuring smile her way.

"Detective Summers is on his way. He will explain

your options to you, but you don't need to worry: you will be taken care of."

His cell started to ring inside his pants. He pulled it out of his pocket and checked the screen. "I'm sorry Jane, I'm needed urgently."

He detached himself from her grasp, edging toward the door.

"I know you must have many questions, and I understand the concern you must be feeling, but Summers will be able to answer all your questions, unless you have anything health related you need to know?"

Jane could barely hear above the pounding of her heart.

Other than the few people who had been taking care of her, there was no-one else that she even knew. It seemed impossible that they were turning her loose into the world so unprepared. So vulnerable.

"I'm right here," he continued. "If you have any concerns or questions, or you start to feel differently, call or message any time and I will get back to you as soon as I can, but I really do have to go right now. I'm so sorry."

He hurried away, answering the call on his phone. He had disappeared and was around the corner before Jane could even think to ask him how she could call him without a phone or money.

"I see the doctor has given you the good news," Summers commented wryly from the hallway. Jane turned to see him looking the same as the last time she had seen him. He could even have been in the same outfit.

"I can't believe I'm being discharged when I have nowhere to go. I don't have access to money or a home.

And, I'm guessing that no one has come forward to claim me or you'd have mentioned it already."

Summers face twisted with apology. "No, not yet. But it's early days. I'm hoping we'll have information soon. In the meantime, getting to leave the hospital… it's not bad news, is it? After all, the food can't be all that great."

He was doing his best to make light of the situation. Jane appreciated his attempt even if she couldn't feel it herself.

"From where I'm standing, I'm about to lose the only bed, food, and shelter I've been offered."

Summers extended her the courtesy of not lying.

"Traditionally, in this kind of case, the state wouldn't be able to provide much help as there aren't enough resources to deal with a situation like this. You'd go into the system and be handled that way, though luckily, that won't be happening to you. It seems you have a guardian angel, so you will not be homeless after all. In fact, I'd wager you'll be very well taken care of."

"A guardian angel? Who?" Jane couldn't think who this secret benefactor could be.

"I don't get to give good news very much in my line of work. Since I'm taking you there right now, can you humor a cynical cop and let him play fairy godfather for once?"

Summers seemed so excited that she cast her initial objection aside and the questions she had been meaning to ask died a death on her lips. It didn't really make any difference. She certainly had no choice in the matter, so she might as well let the man have this moment while he could.

The drive to her new home took less than twenty

minutes, even with the Los Angeles traffic. Jane spent the time staring out the window, eyes eating up every person, every sight that passed by, in the desperate hope that something would spark up a flash of recognition. It wasn't until Summers' car started down a familiar winding driveway that she gasped.

"Logan is my guardian angel?"

Summers let out a low whistle. "Got it in one. I know he hasn't been to see you at the hospital, but he has called me at the station to hear your progress. When I told him you were about to be released with no real support set up for you, he was pretty outraged. Got very creative with his curse words."

"How did he go from outraged to inviting me to stay in his home? That seems a stretch."

Jane didn't want to knock her good fortune, but the question had to be asked, particularly when she considered how he couldn't wait to get away from her at the hospital. He certainly hadn't seemed all that concerned then.

"Well, you're not staying with him in his house exactly. Best I understand it, he is offering you his pool house. He has more room than he knows what to do with, and since you will be separate from the main residence, technically, you don't even have to bump into each other if you don't want to."

He must have seen her frown.

"It's an incredibly generous offer and one I have never heard in my lifetime, so I would take it at face value."

"I'm not trying to sound ungrateful. I just can't wrap my head around any of this."

And she couldn't. Things were moving so fast that she felt as if she were being left far, far behind.

Summers eyes turned dark with sympathy. He got out of the car and waited for Jane to do the same.

"If you're not ready, we can give this a moment."

Now that they were here, Jane was curious to see Logan again. Would things be different now that she knew who he was? She couldn't imagine that would be the case. For whatever reason, the thought that he was a movie star hadn't caused the butterflies in her stomach. However, picturing his face did make her knees go a little weak.

She squared her shoulders, determined to push aside her conflicting emotions. If nothing else, she needed to thank him for saving her life, and now, for taking her in too. With a great deal of apprehension that she couldn't explain, she nodded at Summers.

"I'm ready. Let's go."

7

A petite Asian woman around fifty-years-old opened the door.

Her smile caused deep dimples to show. She bowed the head full of silver hair that she wore in a neat bun.

"I'm Kitty, Mr. Steel's housekeeper. You must be Jane and Detective Summers. Please, come inside."

She stepped aside so they could enter.

Almost immediately, they were tackled by a yapping ball of fluff as Loki sprang at Jane, overexcited to see her again. His mouth was gripped around something brown and made of leather. It wasn't until he stopped jumping at her that she saw it was a shoe.

A very expensive looking shoe.

She crouched down to stroke him, a delighted smile on her lips.

"I guess you remember me, then?"

In response, Loki threw himself at her feet, rolling over to expose his soft, white tummy as he squirmed, waiting for her to tickle him, though he never let go of that prized shoe.

Summers laughed at his antics. "This must be the dog who found you on the beach. You should get him some treats."

"You could, though he seems to prefer my shoes," Logan sounded irritated as he approached the group.

Gone was the relaxed man she had met before. In his place stood the movie star. Dressed in a tailored shirt that he'd paired with designer jeans, there was a magnetism about him that caused her heart to flutter.

His hair was wet, as if he'd just stepped out of the shower. He wore a pair of leather sandals on his feet. At his appearance, Loki released the shoe that had been in his mouth and dove for his sandals, snarling and snapping at them as if they were an animal.

"Stop it, you mutt! You've already ruined several pairs, already!" Logan attempted to move his feet away only for Loki to attack them with renewed fervor. Trying to ignore him, he shook Summers' hand.

"Good to meet you in person at last."

Summers flashed a grin at the other man. "My wife is going to lose it when I tell her about today. Figure, it'll buy me several years of conversation at family functions."

"I think you've vastly overrated their interest in me."

Logan turned his attention to Jane.

She squirmed, unsure what he must think of her, while she was unfortunately aware of her own reaction to them. Under his intense gaze, her body was growing warm, and she had to resist the urge to fan herself.

Logan was having his own reaction to seeing her again.

In the days since he'd left her, he hadn't been able to

keep her out of his mind. Her face kept popping up at the most random moment, distracting him from work, which was a problem as he was knee-deep in pre-production on his new movie.

Despite how full his days had been with fittings, physical training, and rehearsals, he'd still found time to check in with Summers on her progress. He could have called her himself, but each time he'd picked up the phone, his mind had gone blank. He couldn't think what to say. Then some other urgent business would preoccupy him. By the time he remembered, it was always far too late into the night.

When he'd learned of her imminent discharge, and the lack of support that would be offered her, something primitive had woken. There wasn't anything he hated in the world more than injustice — and he'd experienced plenty of that growing up.

It seemed obvious to offer her the use of his pool house, though the decision hadn't come easily.

As he'd been concerned with, several pictures of his visit at the hospital with Jane did surface, though his team had made fast work of having them taken down. A stern call from Summers had helped proceedings.

His team were furious for having to retract them, however. This was exactly the kind of publicity he needed to reverse public opinion of him. They couldn't have engineered a better story, and it had landed in his lap — for free.

But Logan had refused to use Jane's misfortune to further his career.

Instead, he'd paid a pretty big sum to keep the owner

of the photographs quiet, incurring the wrath of those around him.

With that incident still so close, he could only imagine the implosion that would occur when they were given the news that, not only had he forced them to sit on the story, he was now bringing the girl to his home to live.

Then there was his attraction to her.

Even just the sight of her was causing his brain to misfire.

There was something about her story, her very demeanor that brought out the protector in him. His very soul cried out to care for her, yet he also wanted to explore what lay beneath the baggy T-shirt and skirt someone had given her to wear.

The two conflicting thoughts competed for space in his head.

How was he supposed to stay away from scandal and women — this woman in particular — if she was living across the back yard from him?

He couldn't worry about it now. What was done, was done, and she was standing in front of him, waiting for some form of greeting.

"Hello Jane. You're looking much better."

Smooth. Women always loved to be told that.

"I probably couldn't have looked much worse," Jane replied, only to wonder where that had come from. How she had looked upon waking on that beach shouldn't even be an issue. As the heat of embarrassment stung her cheeks, she hurried to continue. "But, thank you. I'm very grateful for everything you've done."

"It's nothing. I have all this room and the pool house has never been used."

Summers shook his head, apparently not reading — or possibly ignoring — the tension in the room. "That's a line I'll never be able to say in this lifetime."

Kitty took the small break in the conversation to offer everyone a drink, but both Jane and Summers declined. Unable to stop Loki from attacking his toes, Logan hissed a sigh of exasperation and passed Kitty the puppy as the doorbell rang. Logan glanced at the Bvlgari watch on his wrist.

"That's my driver. Sorry to cut this short, but I'm due at the studio."

"You're leaving?"

Jane couldn't stop her surprise from showing. While she hadn't expected fanfare, this rushed meeting didn't seem enough time to acquaint herself with the man whose home she would now be living in, pool house or not.

He didn't seem to pick up on her nerves.

"Yes, but Kitty here will help you with anything you need."

He shook Summers' hand again, nodded at Jane and left without saying goodbye. His seeming disinterest in her stung.

Kitty set Loki down and gestured into the house.

"If the two of you would come with me."

Summers didn't move, shooting a smile at Jane. It took her only a moment to read the apology in it.

"Do you have to go, too?"

He nodded. "I actually thought Logan would be here to help the transition. We're short staffed at the station due to the flu that's been going around, and I've already been gone for most of the day. Much as I'd love a tour, I should head back. There's a mound of paperwork on my desk that's taller than I am."

Jane tried to quell the rising disappointment. For whatever reason, the thought of being left on her own was inducing no small amount of panic.

"I understand. I've taken a lot of your time, already."

"Oh, it's my pleasure, believe me. After what you've gone through, this is the least I can do. Now, you have my numbers. If you remember anything that you think might be of use, drop me a line. I'll be in touch when I have news my end. Try not to drive yourself crazy in the meantime."

His eyes turned soft.

"I mean it, Jane. Relax, enjoy this nice place. Oh, before I forget." He retrieved a handful of leaflets from his jacket. "Here's some information about memory loss with some websites that might prove useful. Have a look through these."

"Thank you."

She took them, though her hands felt frozen to the touch. She wanted to beg him to stay, to help her find a way through all of this, but she swallowed the pleas. She was a grown woman and not a helpless victim. There was nothing to fear about this place or the man who had shown such kindness.

He squeezed her shoulder. His touch warmed some of the ice she was feeling. "You'll be fine. After all, you've got Kitty and Loki here to keep you company."

Kitty flashed a smile at them. "Yes. And Loki brightens up everyone's day but Logan's," she joked. "He's not really used to having a pet just yet, is he?"

She addressed the question to Loki, who tilted his head

as he listened to her, causing his big ears to flop adoringly to one side. The shoe he'd discarded in Logan's presence was back in his mouth.

"Take care of yourself, Jane. We'll speak soon."

And then he was gone too.

"This way, Dear."

Kitty led the way through the house, though Jane could barely take in the stunning design of the place. She felt as if she was outside of her body, living in a dream that wasn't hers.

She noticed only the details as they came at her: modern artwork that stood on white plinths lit by their own spotlights; the giant log fires that seemed to form the centerpiece of every room; marble floors with matching columns that held up the thirty-foot ceiling; and lush modern furniture that seemed as if they had never been used.

On and on, the luxury was never-ending, though Jane hardly registered the sights at all.

It wasn't until they arrived outside the pool house, that anything akin to pleasure went through her body.

Bathed in the mid-afternoon sun, it was even more lovely than she had remembered. Having followed them there, Loki charged into the pool house, dove onto a pristine white leather sofa and ran from one end to the other, barking with delight, almost as if he'd forgotten about this place and had rediscovered it all over again.

"I didn't have much time stock it as well as I wanted to, but you should find much of what you need here," Kitty said. "The kitchen has a range of foods that should suit most diets, and in the bedroom, I managed to have some clothes arranged for you in a variety of sizes."

She smiled. "Logan wasn't very helpful at describing what size you might need."

"That is more than enough, thank you." Jane couldn't believe the effort she had gone to for her — that both of them had gone to.

"If I have missed anything, I'm just a phone call away," Kitty explained.

As lovely as this all was, it was starting to feel overwhelming. This house, Logan, her entire situation. A wave of exhaustion caused her to sway on her feet. Kitty took hold of her elbow, looking aghast, steering her inside.

"You need rest! You've had far too much excitement for the day. Why don't you sit? I can make you some tea if you'd like?"

Jane shook her head. "I think I might just need some time alone, to take all this in. My head is a little overwhelmed."

Kitty looked immediately contrite. "Of course. I'll get out of your way. I'll take Loki and we'll leave you to acquaint yourself with your new home."

She started for the dog, but Jane stopped her. "Do you mind leaving him? I wouldn't mind his company."

"Are you sure? He can be a handful?" Kitty's expression was dubious.

"If he's too much, I'll let you know."

Kitty nodded, happy with her answer. "Press 9 to call me any time, day or night. I live in the house with Logan."

"Thank you. I will."

Alone with only the puppy, the sudden peace calmed her racing pulse, and the exhaustion she had felt turned into curiosity for this wonderful house. She went off to explore, joined by Loki — and that ever present shoe in his mouth — who seemed thrilled to be left with her.

The wooden floor had a pale varnish that let the richness of the oak shine through. Her shoes — a pair of used Crocs that a nurse had given to her at the hospital — clicked softly on them as she wandered into the vaulted room that served as the living area.

Light shone in through the floor-to-ceiling doors that, when closed, formed the walls on three sides of the pool house, giving direct views onto the extensively landscaped grounds beyond. Numerous skylights revealed more of that crystal blue sky above.

The furniture was as tasteful as the house itself, chosen for its shabby chic style where distressed wood and heritage colors met wrought iron metal.

In almost every corner and surface, plants and flowers provided bursts of color to what was an otherwise white landscape. The whole effect was an oasis of calm, yet one couldn't deny the luxury that abounded.

Despite the expensive furnishings, it was a comfortable place, where large fabric sofas and armchairs were placed strategically around the room to make the most of those sumptuous views.

As beautiful as it all was, Jane found it difficult to take in.

For every item she looked at, she couldn't resist the urge to see if it would spark up a memory of some kind, which made this Cinderella moment lose some of its appeal.

A giant television fixed to the wall above the fireplace caught her eye. Maybe some television would be good?

She turned it on, but as soon as the sound came out from television, she knew it was too much. She didn't want to turn it off, however, needing whatever comfort it provided.

She pressed the mute button and immediately felt better.

She crossed to the fireplace, saw several framed photographs on the mantelpiece, but they were of commercial images instead of the personal ones she had hoped to find.

The lush greenness of a tropical rainforest loomed out of one, where an impossibly colored parrot sat amongst the trees. Another depicted a spectacular horizon of a distant mountain range, so tall that clouds hid the top of the mountain from view.

Studying the mountain range, Jane could tell immediately that they were located in China. She was as sure of this as her previous love affair with Grey's Anatomy.

Possibly she had been to China in her past? It seemed she knew something of geography. Could she be a teacher? Neither thought rang any bells right now, so she filed them away, hoping they would be of use in the near future.

Bored with the sofa now, where Jane was obviously not joining him, Loki bolted to her side as she moved to a sweet-looking office space where a laptop waited. She recognized the logo on the rose-gold colored metal and traced her finger over the apple that was embossed on its case.

Opening it, she pressed the on button and sat down,

waiting as it powered to life. Loki pawed at her knee, wanting up on her lap. She obliged, setting him on her lap, wrapping her arms around him. He curled against her happily, that shoe clasped between his paws as he started chewing on it.

When the Google screen appeared, she was struck by an overwhelming need for information. She wanted to visit the websites that were mentioned in those leaflets Summers had left with her, but she had left them somewhere and didn't want to wait to find them.

Pulling up the search bar, she typed the words "missing people in the USA" and hit return.

Thousands of hits flooded the screen.

Frightening articles appeared with statistics containing the kind of numbers that made her eyes go wide. She clicked on the most promising sounding site: missingpeople.org.

She read over the general introduction for how to use the site and found the tab where she could input details in order to search the database.

She filled in as much information as she could. The physical details were easy: hair and eye color, height, even weight — these were relatively simple, but when she came to the age box, she stumbled.

She had no idea how old she was.

What had they said at the hospital during her initial examinations, which all seemed much of a blur now? Twenty-five to early thirties, the staff had decided.

They hadn't pulled the number out of thin air, and had come to it by examining her teeth and bones, and calculating it from there.

She checked the corresponding box to say she was ready and hit submit.

A wheel spun on the screen as the results loaded. When the individual hits started loading, Jane figured she'd see a handful of people matching her description. But, as the side scroll bar grew longer and longer, she saw that there were hundreds of women matching her description alone.

Swallowing, trying to contain her horror, she clicked on one.

An attractive blonde with a sunny smile appeared on screen. She sat at a crowded ball game, waving into the camera with no cares in the world.

No idea that her life was about to take such a dark turn.

The woman had gone to work one day only to vanish into thin air. She lived with two other girls in a house share in Chicago. Her roommates had become concerned when she hadn't returned home at her usual time.

As far as they knew, she wasn't dating anyone. She wasn't one for going out on work nights so it was very out of character for her not come home, even more so to not tell her roommates why: both of whom were good friends of hers.

By the next evening, when they still couldn't reach her, the girls knew something terrible must have happened.

She had been missing now for over three months. Jane's eyes read over that last sentence again.

Three months.

How could someone disappear for three months with there being no sign of them?

A shiver ran down her spine. Suddenly cold, she

curled herself closer to Loki. He squirmed, making sounds of delight, leaving the shoe alone for a moment as he attacked her face with kisses. She hugged him close, taking comfort from the simple act of having him near. He went back to his shoe, chewing it as if it were the tastiest thing he'd ever eaten.

She clicked on Megan Brown from Pittsburgh.

Megan was happily married with two young children and a stay-at-home mom. By all accounts, she was the kind of woman that other mothers wanted to be. Megan kept a beautiful home, was a devoted wife and patient mother, who was loved by everyone who knew her.

After dropping her kids off at school, she went to get her daily groceries, but her husband never heard from her again. They found her car across state lines a day later with signs of a struggle inside. Despite a thorough investigation, police had no clue what had happened, or where she had gotten to.

Megan had been gone over eight months.

Jane's stomach started to churn.

On and on she read through stories of numerous women who disappeared one day only to never be seen again. She read through each name carefully and studied the photographs until their faces seared into her mind.

She read until her eyes grew tired, and the churning in her stomach turned into a growl.

By now Loki was upside down and fast asleep. His bright pink tongue hung out of the corner of his mouth. Every now and then, his oversized paws paddled the air, but he didn't wake.

Carefully, so that she wouldn't disturb him, she carried him to the sofa where she set him onto a wool throw, arranging the cushions around him so he wouldn't fall off if he were to startle awake.

Moving into the kitchen that overlooked the living area, she took in the butler sink and a giant gas stove set into a strategically placed island. A large bowl of fruit of seemingly every type sat on the island, as well as a basket of fresh bread beside another stunning flower display.

She opened the fridge to find it stocked completely with food. The bottom drawer contained a wide variety of meat and fish, from wagyu steaks, to fresh caught tuna. There was even a lobster if she felt so inclined.

She didn't — much of what she was seeing seemed far too rich and fussy. She moved to the crisper with its rainbow of vegetables. There was a shelf of deli meats and cheeses, tomatoes and peppers marinating in garlic oil, and a row of fresh, cold-pressed juices.

And those were only the raw ingredients.

There were also two full shelves of ready meals, but she didn't recognize the label: it looked as if the meals had been freshly prepared by a chef. The range was extraordinary.

Behind her, there was a wine rack filled with quality picks.

Her stomach rumbled again, not as impressed with the array of food on display as she was. Nice as the choices were, she only wanted something very simple. She decided on eggs.

Quick, simple, fast.

She thought it a sensible choice. Considering that she wasn't sure if she even knew how to cook, it seemed the best option.

Finding a cast-iron pan, she set it on the stove to heat as

she cracked open an egg into a bowl before she had to stop.

What *kind* of eggs did she like?

Guess there was no time like the present to find out.

Breaking two eggs into a bowl, she whisked it up while a knob of butter melted in the pan. She scrambled the eggs quickly and assuredly. Just before they were cooked through, she took them off the heat and let the heat of the pan finish the eggs. Without bothering to dish it up, she ate a forkful, then another.

While the eggs were cooked very well — they were soft and creamy, still glistening with moistness — she wanted to see if there was another style she liked better.

Dumping the rest of the uneaten scrambled eggs onto a plate, she rinsed the pan and started again. She made a plain omelet while she set a pot to boil.

She liked the omelet much less than the scrambled eggs.

When the water was ready, she whisked the water until a whirlpool formed in the water. Then she dropped in an egg as the swirling water wrapped the wispy strands of egg around itself until the poached egg was done. Next, she tried frying eggs over easy, medium, and hard. When they were done, she hard boiled another.

By the time she was finished, the counter was covered with ten styles of egg.

She tried a little of each only to come to two conclusions: one, the assured way in which she'd handled herself in the kitchen revealed that she could definitely cook. And two: her favorite eggs were actually the first ones she'd made. She liked them scrambled with butter, on a low, low heat until they were only just done and still creamy.

Having made far too many eggs, she couldn't finish any of them. Not ready to face the clean-up, she left them and wandered into the bedroom to find an oasis of white and calm.

The pretty King-size bed was covered with white French linen. Feeling suddenly tired, she kicked off her Crocs, took off the clothes that still had that hospital smell attached, and went into the walk-in closet.

The shelves were filled with beautiful satins and silk. Dresses in a variety of colors and lengths were suspended on the rail. There were Merino sweaters and cardigans, and leather jackets for those colder moments. A rack of shoes of all types, from flip flops to stilettos, covered the length of one wall, while another contained different bags and purses.

Jane gasped at the sheer volume on display, stunned that anyone would have gone to all this trouble for her.

Unless, of course, Logan always had these clothes available for his female visitors. That seemed a more likely explanation.

Picking a simple white cotton nightdress, she changed into it. It fit her so perfectly it could have been made for her.

She left and climbed into the bed and was instantly hit by how much more comfortable this bed was compared to the hospital one.

A whine sounded from the floor.

She looked over the edge of the bed to find Loki staring up at her, his tail wagging from side to side, back to carrying that shoe again. His hopeful expression tugged at her heart until she found herself lifting him onto the bed with her.

"Just this once, then, OK? But that shoe is staying on the floor."

She wrestled it from him and dropped it on the floor. He looked at the shoe, wanting to retrieve it, but when Jane laid down, he yipped in excitement and dove under the covers. He investigated this new world for a while before finally settling down. His warm body pressed against her thigh as Jane allowed her eyes to close.

Thirty minutes later, she was still wide awake despite how weary her body felt. A sigh hissed out of her. Knowing that she couldn't just lie there, she brought the laptop onto the bed and went back on the missing persons' site.

She read story after distressing story until she was dizzy. Needing a change of pace, something light and inconsequential, she found her way to a gossip site and typed in Logan's name.

She clicked on the most recent article.

Logan was being interviewed on his breakup with Ellie Godwin. Pictures of the two accompanied the article. They were two of the most beautiful people in the world and their coming together seemed like a fairytale.

Even the manner they had met was like something out of a movie: it was at a mutual friend's wedding and by all accounts, the two couldn't keep their eyes off each other so when the split had come, there were rumors of Logan's cheating, and even hints that he suffered from an abuse problem.

Logan was quizzed about Ellie's revelation that she'd tried to save him from himself, but he sidestepped the question, leaving the reporter to make up their own story.

Ellie had found love again now with a sports star, a

football player, while Logan had been single since their breakup.

Jane poured over the photographs.

When she finally fell into a deep sleep, it was with Logan and his beautiful ex-girlfriend on her mind.

8

Something was wrong.

Something was very wrong.

Her eyes were open, but there was nothing except the hazy blackness that surrounded her.

She tried to move forward, but felt a current of resistance that seemed to force her down. She was sinking lower and lower into the depths of this blackness, where only emptiness lived.

And it was cold.

So cold.

Pimples raced up and down her arms as an increasing pressure built. Like a clamp was squeezing her chest, her breathing became tighter and tighter. The pressure grew until she could no longer hold it. She had to release it.

The air burst out of her mouth and lungs.

Only then did she realize she was underwater.

Drowning underwater.

Forcing her eyes skyward, she caught a glimpse of the

light on the surface. She knew she had to get up there if she was to have any chance of surviving.

Panic coursed through her body. She willed her arms and legs to move, but they were numb and felt as if they were strapped down against her body.

Were her arms tied?

Was she restrained?

She didn't know, but as the fire began to burn inside her lungs again, she kicked her feet with renewed vigor and was rewarded with the tiniest movement.

A glimmer of hope flared inside, only for her body to be sucked down further than where she had begun.

She had to get the surface.

She had to breathe if she was to have any chance of surviving. The icy waters seemed to have lulled her body into a strange state. Though her heart pounded, she was light-headed, and the world seemed to be fading away from her.

She sank further into the murky darkness as her eyes began to close.

The sound of rushing water filled her ears…

Jane eyes flashed open as she found herself staring at the white ceiling above the bed.

She could hear the splashing of the water as if she were still in its grasp. Forcing herself up, she pressed a hand against her chest to feel her racing heart.

The nightmare had felt so real that she could swear that she could feel the water in her lungs. The dream was likely a flashback to whatever had happened to her. It was no wonder that the distress she'd been feeling was so real — her body couldn't tell the difference.

Blinking away the sleep from her eyes, she felt beside

her for Loki, but there was no sign of the puppy. A happy yip sounded outside, followed by more of that splashing which was actually coming from outside.

She got out of bed and padded toward the sound. It didn't take long to discover the source of the commotion.

Logan cut through the pool, swimming length after length in super fast time. An overexcited Loki ran beside him, following each length, apparently too afraid of the water, yet wanting to partake of this fun exercise. His tail whipped behind him in a frenzy.

Occasionally, Logan would glance over at the dog to make sure that he was OK, but other than that, his sole attention was on this morning swim.

He slid through the water like a seal as Jane marveled at how easily he made it seem. If she had been able to swim half as well, maybe she wouldn't have ended up on the shore in the state that she had.

She wasn't aware how long she stood watching him, but she must have made a noise as Loki's attention was suddenly diverted to her. He stopped chasing Logan and started tearing toward her.

He was so excited, he wasn't aware of how slippery the area around the pool was and halfway to reaching her, he skidded headfirst into the pool.

"Loki!" Jane cried out, trying to get Logan's attention. But he hadn't heard as he continued obliviously — swimming away from his puppy.

Without the second thought, Jane sprinted toward the pool and launched herself in. As soon as the water hit, she gasped at the sudden cold even as a memory of her nightmare filled her with a fear that sent shivers down her spine.

She forced her fear away, kicking and paddling to stay afloat as she searched for Loki. Finding a speck of dark gray underwater, she swam toward it, reaching him in a few strokes. She grabbed at the squirming, panicking furball, winding her arm around his body. As soon as his snout came above the water, he started whining, frantically scared at what had just occurred.

Logan must have finally heard as he stopped dead in the water, spinning around until he located the two of them. His eyes assessed the situation quickly as he swam toward them with almost inhuman speed.

"He fell into the water when you weren't looking," Jane explained between gasps, the impromptu exercise and coldness of the water hitting her hard.

"Give him to me," Logan commanded. He took Loki from her, climbed out of the pool and set him down. Loki shook himself, splashing him from head to toe. Logan waited to see if he needed more assistance.

"Are you OK?" He asked the puppy.

Loki whined unhappily, pressing against him for reassurance, his tail between his legs. Logan crouched and stroked his head until the puppy's tail raised and started to wag.

"I think you're OK. We should probably keep you away from the pool until you've had a few swimming lessons."

Loki barked in solid agreement.

Jane half swam, half paddled toward them. When she reached the side, Logan was on his knees with his hand outstretched toward her.

"Here," he offered.

Relieved to be getting out of the pool and that awful

water, she took hold of his hand as he lifted her out of the water.

His eyes looked her up and down and grew very wide. Turning away quickly, he grabbed his towel from the lounger and offered it to her.

"I'm fine," she started.

"Your dress is white," was all he said as he averted his eyes.

The comment was so bizarre, she didn't know what to make of it. Wasn't this a strange time to criticize her clothing? It wasn't like she'd had any time to go shopping. She wore what had been left for her — a nightdress that she'd thought was very nice, actually. What was his deal with it right now?

She looked down at herself only to see that she wasn't wearing anything underneath, and having just jumped into the pool, Logan was being greeted with his own version of a wet T-shirt competition.

She snatched the towel from him, wrapping it around herself, cheeks flaming.

"I'm so embarrassed."

"Don't be. I barely saw anything," Logan responded.

Truth was, he hadn't been with a woman in some time and the glimpse of her perfect body — and it really was perfect — was stirring up some mighty strong emotions in him.

Which was mortifying, as the last thing she needed was him leering at her.

Get a grip, Logan. The woman needs your help and nothing more. Remember, you are on your last strike.

No women. No trouble.

Nothing.

Jane made sure her modesty was concealed before speaking again.

"I didn't mean to interrupt your workout. I saw him fall in and it looked like he couldn't swim." She was annoyed at how nervous she sounded.

Logan glanced back at Loki, who seemed fine. The puppy snarled at the water that was his mortal enemy now, giving it a wide berth.

"I'm glad you came when you did. I didn't hear him falling in."

He looked as if he wasn't happy about that. Once again, Jane was confused by him. He didn't want the dog, apparently didn't like him too much either, but he took care of it and consoled him when he was scared.

The man was a riddle she didn't know if she'd ever find the answer to.

"I haven't really had a chance to say thank you for everything you've done," she began, trying to say the speech she had been working on only to find that her mind had melted into a jumble by the sight of his glistening body.

"It's nothing. The pool house was just sitting there. It was the right thing to do."

She tried to ignore the flash of disappointment his answer caused. His decision wasn't personal at all. Just a Good Samaritan helping out his fellow human being. She could have been anyone else and he would have done the same.

"I'm very grateful. This is an incredibly nice thing you're doing," she finished.

He fixed his eyes on her face, picking up on the tone

she had thought she had disguised. "You sound surprised."

"I am."

"Why?"

"It doesn't seem like the sort of thing you'd do."

She knew the second the words were out that she'd said the wrong thing. His eyes narrowed and the easy going air that had been there a second ago vanished in an instant.

"You can't believe everything you read."

She had touched on some kind of nerve. The last thing she wanted was to insult the man who had gone out of his way to help her, but she could see it in his expression that the warmth between them had gone.

She felt a great deal of embarrassment for not only visiting those gossip sites yesterday, but then allowing them to color her judgment of him.

So much for thinking she was better than that.

She wondered how she could repair the damage when Loki escaped Logan's clutches and sprinted headfirst into the pool house, leaving a trail of water in his wake.

"Get back here, you little..."

Whatever he was going to say was cut off by the sound of something smashing inside the pool house.

Logan cursed and started inside. Jane followed closely behind.

More crashing sounded as they heard Loki scrabbling inside, having a whale of a time as he tore through the place, destroying everything that came across his path in what he thought was a game of chase.

"Stop it, Fleabag!" Logan shouted. Loki was standing on the white sofa now, soaking it with his paw prints.

Every shout from Logan only caused his tail to wag harder.

When Logan refused to move, Loki suddenly lowered onto his stomach, looking for all the world as if he were acquiescing to Logan's commands.

Jane knew it was a ploy but didn't have a chance to warn him.

As soon as Logan got within an arm's reach, Loki shot off the sofa, skidded through Logan's legs, and scrambled to Jane, hoping to bring her into the game.

Logan vaulted over the sofa, sprinting for the dog as Loki bounded toward her. Jane dropped into a crouch as the puppy suddenly launched himself at her.

She caught the squirming bundle in her arms and was instantly smothered by puppy kisses that sent her into peals of laughter.

"Don't let go of him. I'll get some towels to dry up this mess before he wrecks anything else," Logan instructed, disappearing off and returning moments later with a couple of towels, one that he wrapped around his midriff like a sarong.

Logan took Loki and dried him off, which the puppy didn't find quite as much fun, judging by the struggling that ensued.

"Did we wake you?" Logan finally asked when the silence was beginning to grow awkward.

The nightmare flitted into her mind before she pushed it away.

"No. I was getting up."

"I didn't want to wake you, but only two things ever get me going in the morning. A swim, then a coffee. And what with this new movie I'm working on…"

She heard the stress in his voice, though he had tried to disguise it.

"It's not going well?"

He considered her question. "It could be going better. I've got a dictator for a director, and a co-star gunning for me to fail. It makes for a not so pleasant experience."

"I'm sorry," Jane replied automatically, as if this were something she often said.

"This is what it's always like now. Still, it's nothing compared to what you're going through. Scummy actors, I know how to deal with. I wouldn't have a clue what to do in your shoes."

Jane shrugged her shoulders. "My problems don't supersede yours."

He studied her beneath dark lashes, his expression curious.

"It's been a long time since I've met someone who thought that."

"Maybe you should talk to some normal people for a change," Jane replied. "Not me, of course. Someone who knows who they are."

She softened her words with a smile that he echoed. That small change lit up her face and made her seem years lighter. It was nice.

He wished she would do it more.

Loki whined in his lap, fed up with being restrained. He was as dry as Logan could get him, so he let him go. The dog looked for something to amuse himself, then suddenly started chasing his tail. He went round and round until he caught it in his mouth, at which point, he froze, not sure what to do next.

They laughed as he started for them, still with his tail in his mouth.

Logan sniffed the air. "Do you want a coffee? I could do with one."

Jane hadn't set the coffee maker so the fact that the air was filled with the unmistakable rich aroma was surprising.

"Must have been Kitty," Logan supplied. "The woman is a miracle worker. I don't know what I'd do without her."

"Let me get you a cup," Jane offered, heading into the kitchen.

He nodded, following her into the kitchen. Jane poured two steaming cups, only to find Logan staring at the remnants of those half eaten eggs lined up on the counter.

Her face grew hot, and she knew she had to explain herself.

"I wanted eggs yesterday, but I felt like Julia Roberts in that movie, the one where she didn't know which kind she liked, so I made one of each variation I could think of."

Her explanation sounded a little crazy, but his response surprised her.

"It wasn't that she didn't know what she liked, it was more that she made herself like whatever the current man in her life liked. What she needed was to discover who she was on her own without a man in order to be able to find the right one. And, as part of that process, she also had to learn how she liked her eggs cooked. The eggs were a metaphor," Logan explained.

Jane didn't immediately respond, surprised by the sensitive explanation. It seemed very insightful. Hands around her cup of coffee, she considered the man in front of her.

"I gather there hasn't been any more news on your identity?" He asked, eyes flicking to the wounds on her arms. It was good to see how much they had already healed. A few more days and there would only be the scars left to deal with.

"Nothing yet. Summers seemed to think it isn't that unusual in these kinds of cases. Said it takes longer to resolve these situations."

"It must be difficult to know that someone has actually disappeared unless you live or work with them. I imagine there is a procedure to follow, and that it takes some time."

She appreciated his effort to make her feel better, even if she couldn't get her mind over it all.

"I just don't know how someone can not know that I've disappeared for almost a week? Don't I have a family or a boyfriend? Friends? How can no one have noticed?"

Frowns appeared on Logan's forehead. "Even if you lived with someone, it's possible they could have gone away with work. It would explain why he doesn't know you're not home."

"I know I had money; that dress I was wearing is expensive. I just wish I knew something. Anything would be better than this empty space I have inside."

She caught herself. She was complaining too much, and to the one person who had helped her. "Sorry. I don't mean to concern you with all this. You have enough on your own plate."

"I understand. That's why I..." His eyes darted to one side suddenly, a look of exasperation coming over his face. Setting down his coffee, he jumped up.

"Loki! Put that cushion down!"

The dog had a very expensive embroidered cushion in his mouth and was dragging it across the floor like a security blanket. He looked so much like a child that Jane smiled.

"He doesn't know what he's doing. He's just a baby. And those are just things. I'm sure you can afford to replace them."

Logan shot her a funny look that had her regretting her words.

Why had she said that? What money he had was none of her business. She couldn't believe that she had been so crass. She focused her attention on a safer subject.

"Loki," she called in an enthusiastic and friendly voice. "Why don't you put that cushion down and come play with me." She patted her knee to emphasize her point. Loki forgot about the cushion completely and bolted to her side, skidding across the waxy floorboards in his haste. She caught him before he shot past her. At her touch, he flopped over.

"Oh, you want a tummy rub, do you? I guess I'd better give you one." Jane laughed, enjoying her moment with the lovable puppy.

Logan watched them silently before turning his eyes to the clock behind Jane.

"My driver will be here soon to take me to work," Logan explained as he started for the door then stopped. He looked at Loki lying before Jane, a puddle of delight.

"You're really good with him," he commented.

He was right. Jane was completely comfortable with the dog — it was the only time she had truly felt comfortable since she had woken up on that beach. She was obviously used to being around one. Maybe she had her own dog out there somewhere.

If that was the case, she hoped to God he or she wasn't starving, waiting for her to come home.

She shook the morbid thought away.

There was nothing she could do about it either way. Whether her imaginary dog was dying without her was something she probably shouldn't think about, not if she ever wanted to sleep again.

"I must have experience of being around them," she said simply.

"What do you have planned for today?" He asked.

She hadn't given it much consideration. "I guess, spend the day on the internet, to see what I can find out."

He mulled over whatever was on his mind. "Do you want to come with us?"

"To where, your work?"

"I need to take Loki to the set, but I don't have time to be keeping an eye on him. You could help look after him while I'm being fitted for my costume."

"I could just do that here though, if he's going to be trouble at work?" Jane offered.

"Loki has to come with me today. My publicist has arranged a photographer to grab some candids of us on set so I need him there. You'd be doing me a huge favor if you came," Logan replied.

She could hardly say no, given her current situation. Despite the flutter in her heart, she nodded.

"OK."

"There's just one thing. I don't think people would be very understanding about our arrangement. A lot has been said about me recently that hasn't done my reputation any good, so I'd rather not give the gossip rags even more to print about me. Do you mind if we keep how we met, and the fact you are staying with me, confidential?"

It was half true. Mostly, he wanted to keep things confidential so that he could protect her.

"Of course."

There was a lot about his world she didn't understand, but his request had seemed simple enough.

Why, then, was there a sense of foreboding so great that it made her shiver?

What could possibly happen by agreeing to help look after his dog?

9

An hour later, driven by a chauffeur in a smart gray suit, their car pulled into Universal Studios.

Known as the "Entertainment Capital of LA," it was one of the oldest studios still in use. Jane wound down her black-tinted window, marveling as they drove past the streets of New York City, complete with brownstone houses and their stoops.

It looked so real that she found it hard to believe that it was a set. It was only when the city block receded into the distance that she saw the wooden planks and metal beams that supported the sets.

The magic of Hollywood was on full display.

They drove down an avenue flanked on both sides with soaring palm trees that reached into the cloudless sky, slowing only to let a golf cart pass.

In the back of the cart, her chestnut locks flowing, Jane recognized the stunning woman in the skintight peach evening gown and satin gloves that went up to her elbow, but couldn't place her. The woman's eyes landed on Jane without interest and looked past her into the car. She started, her Merlot-painted lips, parting.

"Logan? Is that you?" She gasped, her bust suddenly heaving from the apparent effort of saying those four words.

Logan cursed as he signaled for the driver to move on, but the woman had already stopped her cart and gotten out of it — directly in the path of their car, stopping them from continuing.

"Sorry, Boss," Daryl apologized. "We're going to have to wait until they pass."

The woman sashayed toward them, hips snaking with practiced ease as she peered in, revealing a lot of cleavage that she pressed against the window. A whiff of sickly strong perfume assaulted Jane's nose, making the back of her throat itch. She leaned back to get away from both the smell and that cleavage.

"I thought I recognized that steely profile," the woman laughed, loving her own play on the words.

"Sheena," Logan nodded. He couldn't bring himself to fake enthusiasm or interest at the sight of her.

"I was shocked to hear about you and Ellie. You must be devastated," she purred, not the least bit believable in her concern. Her words were directed at Logan, though her eyes openly assessed Jane from head to toe. Jane had the distinct feeling the woman was memorizing every detail so she could relay her impression of her later.

"The end of a relationship is always sad," Logan replied in a bored toned. He must have repeated this exact same phrase many times before.

"But worse still when one partner moves on so quickly. I know Ellie feels terrible about finding love again, and so soon after your breakup."

If there was an award for insincerity, this woman would have won it.

"She doesn't like to waste time." There was a bite to his comment. A bitterness that came with the words.

"Ellie's not one to hang around, that's the truth," Sheena laughed coyly. "Anyway, I saw you passing, and I couldn't help from stopping. I just wanted to check up on you. I know the last few months have been very rough on you…"

Logan gave her a level stare, knowing his welfare wasn't of any concern to her. "Don't believe everything you hear. I'm just on my way to a fitting now, actually—"

"Oh, yes, of course. I remember hearing about this one. You're taking a lesser role." Her heavily made-up eyes glittered with malice. Jane shrank back into her seat, unconsciously wanting to keep away from the negative energy the woman exuded.

"It's a co-starring role," Logan muttered through gritted teeth. "The shorter time constraints allow me to work on multiple projects."

But Sheena had moved away from the window, done with the conversation now that she had gotten her jabs in.

"Oh Honey, you need to get a better publicist. That line is as overused as my plastic surgeon."

With another laugh, Sheena swanned back to her cart and left, waving grandly at the two of them.

"Can you roll up the window?" Logan requested quietly.

"Of course." Jane jumped to do his bidding. When he

didn't expand on that meeting, she couldn't stop herself from asking, "Not a fan of yours, I gather?"

Logan turned to stare out of his window. "She's a friend of my ex. She's always been a bitch. Seems to live for other people's misfortune. I don't think she's ever said a nice word about anyone."

"Not even your ex? They are friends after all."

"I'm sure she talks about her behind her back."

It was on her mind to ask more when the car stopped in front of a white square building. Pretty flower boxes sat on every window. If not for the framed poster that hung beside the front door, Jane would think this any other office block — plain and uninspiring.

"We're here." Logan climbed out of the car. Loki shot up, scrambling after him, all thought of strokes gone from his head. Whatever Logan might think of his puppy, the dog was besotted with him.

Jane followed them into the building, immediately noticing how people going about their way, suddenly stood up straighter, seeing the movie star in their midst. Their eyes became fixed on Logan, and all had a smile or greeting for him, even those he clearly had never seen before in his life.

Loki bundled along by his feet, drawing admiring coos though he didn't get half as much attention as his master. Walking along behind them, Jane garnered the odd questioning look, as if they were wondering what the relationship between the two were, much as Sheena had done.

"Logan! Great job on your last movie! Loved it!" A man in a designer suit with slicked back hair and impossibly white teeth congratulated him.

"Thanks," Logan replied as the suit handed him a

card. "I work for United, if you want to jump ship, give me a call. I'm sure we can work out a better deal than the ones you're currently getting."

Logan took the card, slipping it into his pocket then continued only to be stopped several more times before they reached their destination, a room with a small plaque inscribed with the words "WARDROBE."

Without a second glance at the cards he had collected on the short walk there, Logan tossed them all into the nearest trashcan. Catching Jane's look of surprise, he shrugged.

"I get hundreds of unsolicited business cards a day. That's where they all go."

"Why don't you just say you're not interested?" Jane asked, thinking it far too wasteful.

"It's better not to engage, or I'd never make it anywhere."

"There he is!" A woman of sixty appeared, long skirt swishing across the floor.

She was as thin as a rail and dressed solely in black. Her only assent to color were the bright triangular earrings and jangly bangles that went up both arms, reaching almost to her elbow.

Jane wondered how the woman could do anything with them on.

"Helena, how are you?" Logan smiled at her, kissing her fondly on the lips. It was Logan's first genuine greeting of the day. She cupped his face in her hands, rolling her eyes skyward.

"I am well, though the same can't be said of a certain someone." Her nose wrinkled on the word 'someone.' "Nothing is going to plan today, it seems. *He* was hoping that the location for the grand finale would be finalized. But we can't get into the building as the master key isn't working. And Jackson isn't happy with his trailer as the TV isn't big enough for him — of course, the fact he shouldn't have time to watch any television while on the job seems to have escaped him. Movie stars! Who would love them?!"

A grin spread over Logan's face. Turning to Jane, he explained, "She's talking about our director, Venger. He can be somewhat... highly strung."

"A jerk. That's what he can be," Helena corrected. "Worked with him twice already and the man drives me up the wall. Can't deny his genius, however. Such is the way it always seems to be with the talented ones. Only this one behaves himself." She nodded at Logan, causing a look of momentary embarrassment.

"I can't help being good around you. You inspire us to do better."

Helena cackled loudly and ducked her face, diverting her attention to Loki so Logan couldn't see the pleased expression his praise had created. "And how is my favorite puppy, today? Just as gorgeous as usual?"

Loki's tail whipped from side to side, a slip of pink tongue peeking out. In his mouth he carried a chew toy (Logan had refused to allow him to leave the house with any of his shoes). The toy squeaked as Loki bit down onto it. She scratched his chin. "Of course you are! Look at that face. I could eat you up!"

Logan gestures at Jane. "Helena, this is my friend Jane. She's here to help keep an eye on the mutt while we work."

Helena straightened, turning appraising eyes on Jane,

though the smile she offered seemed genuine enough. "Hello, Dear. Welcome to the madness."

"Do you need me and Loki to leave you alone?" Jane wasn't sure what her new role as his helper required, but she felt in the way. People were constantly rushing in, then out, their faces lined with concentration as they went about their work.

Helena waved a hand her way. "You both are fine to stay. I'll just need you to keep him away from us — I have lots of fun-looking but dangerous gadgets of the trade that he'll probably find interesting. The last thing we need is for him to swallow some pins."

"I'll try my best," Jane answered, though she wasn't filled with confidence. The dog had already spied an open metal case brimming with clips. Jane got to him just as his teeth tried to clamp down on something shiny and metallic.

Scooping him into her arms, Jane crossed to the other side of the room, but as soon as she let him go, he darted back to Logan, snapping at his ankles, at the one shoelace that had unraveled.

Logan lifted up his foot, hoping to shoo the dog away, but it was the absolute wrong thing to do as Loki clamped his jaws around it, refusing to let go even when Logan had lifted him clean off the floor.

Suspended by the shoelace, Loki didn't seem the least bit bothered. The spark of annoyance that flashed from Logan's eyes, however, told a different story.

Shooting them both an apologetic look, Jane grabbed hold of Loki and gave him a firm tug until his jaws released the shoelace.

"This isn't going to work. Why don't I take him for a walk until you are done?"

"Here's his lead," Logan replied as Helena gestured for him to strip. Without pause or any kind of self consciousness, Logan unbuttoned his shirt.

The sun chose that exact moment to move out from behind a cloud, showering him in a halo of light that only seemed to highlight his athletic frame.

Used to the sight of half-naked Adonises around her, Helena was all business. When Logan started on the zipper of his pants, Jane realized that she was gawking at him. Snapping her mouth shut, she focused on the lead that she took from him and spun around, hoping that no-one had noticed her reaction.

"Jane?"

She had taken several steps away before she remembered it was her name now.

"Yes?"

"The photographer will be by at noon. Be back with Loki by then."

He removed his watch and offered it to her. "Take my watch."

Jane took it, noting how heavy it was. Fixing it onto her wrist, she read the label engraved on the watch. "Bvlgari... this must have cost a fortune?"

"You know watches?" Logan asked, his surprise not any less than Jane's.

"I guess so. I recognized the brand as one of the luxury ones. I wonder how I knew that?"

Helena snorted loudly. "People who know money, know Bvlgari. Me? I just use my phone. Of course, if someone were to *gift* me one of those watches, I wouldn't say no."

Logan's eyes turned incredulous. "What would you want with one? You'd never wear it."

"Of course I wouldn't!" Helena agreed. "Spending that kind of money on a watch is obscene. I'd sell the damn thing and put down a deposit for a house. Or at least, a new car."

"It's not like I paid for the watch…" Logan trailed off, only to regret his words as Helena arched a perfectly painted black brow at him.

"Why do the richest people get given the most things? Isn't it strange how our society works?" Helena directed the question at Jane.

Feeling the need to leave before the conversation turned to something she didn't remember — and opening up that can of worms which she had promised to keep secret — she left.

She moved down the twisting corridor, careful to memorize her way back. Loki strained at his leash, impatient to get away, but Jane knew not to take him off it, not if she wanted to keep the dog in her sights.

Production staff raced by, speaking a mile a minute into phones or radios. Everywhere she went, people moved past, busy with their frantic lives. A wave of wistfulness came over her as she wished she could have a purpose — one bigger than only keeping Loki entertained.

They spent the next few hours ambling through the studio, taking in the sights and sounds wherever Jane was allowed to go. No one ever stopped or bothered them, as if it was the most normal thing in the world for a woman to be walking her dog in a studio.

Suspended on the walls were posters of the movie Logan was currently in pre-production with. It struck Jane as amazing: the movie hadn't even started filming, yet there were posters advertising it.

She passed by a large studio where a set was being constructed. Trees for a snow-covered forest were being built. Despite that it was fake, Jane still shivered. It seemed much colder here, as if the snow was real.

Loki tugged against her, desperate to play in the fake snow. Knowing that he would eventually get the better of her if they stayed here, she took him outside, following the signs that pointed to "The Village."

Expecting an actual village, Jane was surprised when she came upon a quaint cobblestone courtyard formed of popular retail stores. There was a Starbucks, Borders, Walgreens, Whole Foods, as well as a juice bar specializing in cold-pressed beverages, and a make-your-own salad bar.

She took in the bright pictures in the window displays, analyzing each and every item on offer, hoping for it to spark a memory. Other than learning that she could get a great-looking Caesar salad with a drink for less than ten bucks, however, her brain failed to comply.

Loki ambled ahead of her, stopping when he reached the entrance to the book store. He cocked his head, asking for permission to go inside.

"Go on then," Jane replied, half expecting him to go the other way. He surprised her by walking into the store, as if he had understood her.

She followed him quickly, worried about the possibility of toilet mishaps — she hadn't thought to bring any baggies with her — when she spotted a young sales assistant nearby.

Her low-slung jeans paired with a tiny cropped top revealed an enviably toned stomach. Blonde and perky, Jane would have placed her as having been the high school prom queen. Head cheerleader, too.

A crate of hardcover books sat beside her that she was arranging onto a shelf. Chewing loudly on a piece of gum, her eyes turned round with delight when she caught sight of Loki.

"Oh, what an adorable dog!"

"Is it OK for him to be in here?" Jane hadn't seen any signs saying otherwise, but it was always better to check these things.

"Of course! We love all pets here. Are you looking for anything special?"

"Just browsing." It was true. Having seen the selection on display, she had the urge to peruse the aisles. Maybe she'd be able to find information on her condition. Failing that, she might at least recognize some of the titles on the shelves. That would give her some sense that she had been in this world before.

"Everything's pretty clearly signposted. If you need any help, give me a shout." She blew a bubble with her gum, then went back to stocking the shelf.

Jane looked down at Loki, sniffing the corners of a large pyramid created entirely of the latest bestsellers, and whispered nervously, "Do not have any accidents in here."

He looked up, those icy-blue eyes of his trying to understand her words. The expression on his face was so comical, she had to stroke him, which of course, led to a round of tail-wagging that almost toppled the display.

She dragged him toward the non-fiction section.

Names and faces peered out from the covers. Smiling faces with positive titles such as "Living Your Best Life," and "From Rags to Riches." Jane recognized one of the authors as the celebrity chef, Mason Wild. His current hit "Cooking Your Way To A Better Life" was being turned into a movie, a gold banner across the top of the cover exclaimed. Jane had to hide a laugh.

Only in Hollywood would a chef's memoir be made into a movie.

Her eyes scanned over the book covers. Some she recognized, though she couldn't recall having ever read any of the books.

That familiar sense of frustration was starting to rear its ugly head. She crossed into the psychology section and picked up a book about memory loss, though the headings might as well have been written in Chinese, filled with scientific terms that went straight over her head.

Loki whined, which she took for his way of saying they should try another section.

"Good idea."

She found herself by the new releases.

Glossy titles with impactful covers competed for attention. Thrillers seemed popular — a majority of the books depicted people being hunted or chased.

None of those appealed. Ignoring the books with the loudest, noisiest covers, her eyes found their way to a book half hidden behind a tall pile, almost as if it was there as an after thought.

A silhouette of a man in a wheelchair looked out over an orange horizon as two young children were torn away from his desperate hands.

Even though she hadn't wanted anything sad or stressful, she couldn't tear her eyes away from that image. There was something so powerful about it, that she found herself reaching for the book and turning it over to read the synopsis.

The book was based on a true story and was about an ex-army vet who, crippled by a war he didn't believe in but fought for anyway, came home only to find himself in a battle of a different kind when his wife dies in an accident leaving him to fight the state for custody of his two children.

My Blood, My Right, was the debut novel of a young author whose grandfather was the vet in question. She opened the book.

The words leaped out at her, hard-hitting and descriptive, yet filled with a poetry that sent her emotions into a tailspin.

She didn't know how long she stood there, reading the book. bored with the store by now, Loki had curled up by her feet and was quietly playing with his chew toy. Every now and then it squeaked, but even that didn't draw her attention from the story.

"I've heard that's a good book."

Jane looked up. Her eyes had to take a moment to adjust to Prom Queen.

"Haven't read it myself. It's not really my thing, depressing stories. Who wants to read about sad people, right?"

Jane didn't know how to answer since apparently, she was one of those people the girl didn't want to know about.

"Do you want me to ring that up for you?"

Having noticed how long Jane had been reading for free, this was her way of asking her to pay or giving her a gentle nudge to leave the premises. It wasn't a library after all.

As she must have done a million times before, Jane reached for her purse before remembering that she didn't have one.

"I'm sorry. I don't have my purse on me…"

Prom Queen gave her a knowing look that made her feel about two feet tall. Loki flopped to his side, stretching out his too-big-for-his-body paws. The name tag on his collar dangled down, giving them a perfect view of it.

The girl's eyes went wide.

"Wait… Is that… Loki? Is that Logan Steel's dog?!"

Her question came out in a rush. She started breathing quickly, almost as if the man himself was there instead of his dog. Hearing his name, Loki sat up.

"I should have noticed straight away. I'm a huge, huge fan of his!" Prom Queen clutched her hands to her chest, overcome with excitement.

Jane observed the girl, whipping herself into a frenzy for the dog of a famous movie star.

The girl started talking, rambling about which of Logan's movies she loved the most and why, going into so much detail that Jane would have been overwhelmed from the sheer volume of words gushing out of her mouth if she had actually been listening to any of it.

Instead, she was trying to understand this strange phenomena of fandom.

"You can have it," Prom Queen said suddenly, thrusting the book at her.

"Excuse me?"

"Take the book! Give it to Logan… as a gift from me!"

Her eyes went even wider as a thought came that almost made her lose her mind.

Grabbing a black marker that sat beside the till, she tugged off the cap with her mouth, opening the book to the title page. She had already started writing on it when she stopped, her eyes sliding across to Jane.

"You're not seeing him are you?"

Jane answered, "No. Not at all."

Prom Queen flashed a relieved grin, then scribbled the name CLAUDIA in letters so big that a blind person could have read it. Beneath that, she wrote her phone number and "CALL ME!" — not concerned in the least by how presumptuous she was being.

Adding enough xx's and oo's to cover the page, she finally presented the book to Jane with a flourish.

"I'm going to have to dock the price of it from my wages, which isn't much anyway, so please make sure that he gets it. And don't forget to tell him how much I love him."

So much light flashed out of her feverish eyes that Jane wasn't able to say what she was truly thinking. It felt wrong to diminish her excitement, no matter how ridiculous she found the entire thing.

"I will… Thanks. Come on, Boy," Jane gestured to Loki, tugging gently on his leash as they started out of the store. Before they even reached the exit, Jane heard the girl tapping into a phone.

"OH MY GOD, you will NEVER guess what just happened!"

10

Helena hovered around Logan, a row of pins clamped in her lined mouth.

"Who's the girl?"

Barring his mother, Helena was the only woman who ever spoke to him so directly. He considered it a curse with age; the older a person got, the less they worried about such small things as boundaries.

"No one. She's just looking after the dog."

"Hmmm," Helena replied. "She's very attractive for a pet sitter."

"Is she? I hadn't noticed."

"There are lots of things that are wrong with you, Logan, but your eyes have never been one of them."

Logan had to quell the sigh of exasperation the conversation was causing. "She's just someone I'm helping out. There's nothing more to it."

But Helena was like a stubborn dog who wouldn't let go.

"Why does she have all those scratches? On her arms.

She's tried to cover them with that top she's wearing, but I saw them anyway. What have you gotten yourself into?"

Logan gave her a level stare. "I don't know."

She hissed out her own sigh as she folded a section of the shirt he was wearing and pinned it in place.

"You know I love you, but just don't hurt her. She seems like a nice girl. Nothing at all like your usual type."

At that, Logan took offence. "Firstly, I like nice girls…"

To which Helena issued another of her snorts.

"And secondly, there is nothing going on!"

Helena shook her head at him. "The fact that you don't know how appealing you are, only makes you more appealing."

Logan threw up his hands.

"You missed your calling, you know. Forget costume designer, a fairground fortune teller spouting nonsense is what you should have been."

Helena peered down her long, fake lashes at him. "You may protest now, but I've known you for far too long. Be careful, if not for her sake."

JANE HAD BEEN OUTSIDE, PLAYING WITH THE PUPPY IN THE SUN for another half an hour or so, when an older man approached with a warm smile.

A camera was slung around his neck and there was some form of identification pinned to the breast pocket of his blue shirt. Even from where she sat on the grass, Jane could read the bold red print of the press badge.

The photographer who seemed to be in his fifties, sipped from a cup of coffee before he spoke to her in a rich, velvety voice that put her instantly at ease. "Excuse me, I believe you are Jane, correct?"

Jane nodded. "Yes?"

"I'm Karsten," he replied swigging down the rest of his coffee. He tossed the empty cup into a nearby trashcan. "I work for the studio recording behind-the-scenes footage. I've got an appointment with Logan for some pictures, and I'd really like to grab some of him with that cute little guy over there," he said, bending down to give Loki a big grin.

Loki barked his own welcome and ran toward the arms Karsten had opened for him.

"Where did you want to do the pictures?" Jane asked, wishing she had more of an idea of how these things work. Were they supposed to stage a play session out here? She felt uncertain, stupid. How could she not know something so simple? More importantly, why hadn't she asked Logan before she'd left?

"We're to bring the puppy to Logan. Apparently, his costume's just about finished, so this will be a great chance for us to see them in action. People will lap it up, the movie star and his dog. Adele sure knows what she's doing," he added begrudgingly.

Jane got up from the grass and dusted herself off. "Adele? I don't think I've met her yet." It hadn't escaped her notice that Logan seemed surrounded by women.

Karsten gave her a smile. "You'll know when you meet her. She's a force of nature, that one."

Jane ran through everything that had passed between her and Logan, but she couldn't recall him ever having mentioned an Adele.

They headed back to wardrobe, though Loki kept straining at his leash, due in no small part to Karsten, who kept encouraging him to play which only caused him to grow overexcited. When she was at risk of having her hand pulled off, Jane picked him up. He squirmed, not completely happy about being restrained, though that didn't stop his tongue from working over her face.

"He adores you, how long have you been looking after him?"

"Oh, not that long."

She fell silent, not sure what else she could or should say about the matter.

A few feet from the room, Loki must have caught Logan's scent as he perked up and alerted.

A whimper of excitement left his lips as he tried to escape her arms. He was such a ball of energy that she couldn't hold on to him any longer. He kicked off her chest, tumbled through the air and landed on his feet and ran into the room, yipping a mile a minute.

Jane tore after him.

Inside, Loki was running around as fast as he could, dragging his leash on the floor while Helena and one of her assistants, a girl in her twenties, snatched up the end of several costumes that were hanging over a long table.

"The scissors! Watch out!" Helena gestured at a pair of wickedly sharp scissors that were balanced precariously close to the edge of the table.

Not understanding the danger, Loki charged for that same corner.

The girl — Eden — tried her best to get to the scissors before him, but she was no match for the tiny dog. He was like a rocket, barreling full speed toward that table. When he crashed into it, the scissors flew off and up, windmilling in the air toward the dog with unnerving aim.

Jane could only watch in horror until, quick as a flash, a figure darted across the room and snatched up the dog just as the scissors impaled the space where both had been only a moment before.

The man — Logan — glanced toward her, looking equally stunned.

"That was too close for comfort," he said as a flash bulb burst in his face followed by a stream of clicks. The photographer, Karsten, had caught the entire thing on camera.

"That was amazing!" Karsten exclaimed with barely concealed excitement. "The action star saves the day!"

"No no," Helena exclaimed, moving toward Logan waving her arms outs. "Put the dog down! No fur on the clothes!"

Logan set Loki down, but Jane caught the flash of annoyance he sent her way. She only had one job to do, yet she had failed spectacularly. A voice sounded inside her head — a male voice — filled with a red-hot rage that raised the hackles on her neck.

The voice, which she couldn't place, lamented her use to the world, causing a wave of shame to wash over her. It was gone in an instant, leaving her confused and a little shaken.

Someone was talking to her.

Another man… Logan.

As he approached, she saw him in his costume for the first time. His hair had been slicked back and gleamed from the wet-looking gel that had been applied to his head.

His face held a layer of make-up, nothing too overt, but enough that she could see the difference from his natural appearance. He was dressed all in black in an impeccably tailored suit.

He looked incredibly handsome, his rugged good looks and toned body shown off to perfection in the suit which must have been the cause of her suddenly sped-up heartbeat. She could feel her pulse racing, her heart thumping in her chest like a drum.

Logan was still saying something to her, but she couldn't hear him above the sound of her own heartbeat.

There was a rush through her head that made her light-headed. The room began to sway. Her vision seemed to grow darker around the edges until all that was left was Logan. And even then, his face seemed to be fading with the rest of the room until there was only an outline of him.

But that suit…

That suit remained clear as crystal.

Her breath started coming, faster and faster until she was gasping for breath. She couldn't breathe. Why couldn't she breathe?

A concerned voice was talking to her. A woman. But what was she saying?

Something about her breath… That she was having a panic attack. Her voice sounded so far away that Jane couldn't be sure she'd heard correctly.

Nothing was real right now except for her inability to breathe and that tightness inside her chest.

And the man with no face, in that suit, who had filled her with such chills.

"Give her some room," an older woman commanded.

Dimly, she knew it was Helena taking charge. There was a click click click sound in the background that she didn't like. That click signified intrusion into this already stressful moment.

"Sweetheart. You are having a panic attack, but you will be fine. You just have to keep breathing in and out," Helena said firmly.

Jane felt someone take hold of her hand.

"I am here," Helena assured her, her voice sounded right beside her now.

"Just keep breathing. In, then out. In, then out."

Jane forced her mind and body to focus on Helena's simple instruction. In and out. That's all she had to do. Breathe in, expel out.

A few breaths later, and the edges of the room had started to become clear again. The faceless man in front of her reverted back to Logan. She blinked, unsure why she was in a heap on the floor while four concerned people, and one whining puppy, loomed over her.

"What happened?"

Though she directed the question at the room, it was Logan who answered.

"Something triggered you into having a panic attack," he answered softly.

"But, nothing happened? I don't understand."

Still on her knees beside her, Helena patted her hand. "First, you must recover. You can worry about what might have caused the reaction, later."

Her head inclined toward Karsten, recording everything in the room. Jane sent a silent prayer of thanks her way. It had been on the tip of her tongue to mention the man's voice she had heard. Instead, she fell silent.

"Do you need a medic?" Logan asked.

"No. I don't want another doctor."

There was more panic in her voice than she'd intended, but the last thing she wanted was more examinations. She'd had enough of those to last a lifetime.

"Maybe you should go home. I'll get my driver to drop you and Loki off."

Jane wasn't sure if the uncertainty in his voice was concern or annoyance. He was probably regretting his offer for her to accompany him, already. It was no wonder he wanted to send her home. It was a mistake for her to come here in the first place. She didn't belong here.

She didn't belong anywhere.

She hugged Loki close as Logan called his driver. All in all, this day hadn't turned out how she had hoped it would at all.

11

ONE WEEK AGO

THE WATERS WERE CHOPPY AS MARKO STEERED THE YACHT into the ever-increasing expanse of the sea.

He could smell the iron in the rain that had just started to fall. The air held the unnatural silence that always preceded a storm. Normally, he'd never dream of heading out on the water on a night such as this, but these were extenuating circumstances.

He hadn't time to check the weather forecast before he'd left, and there was no service on his phone out here — it was one of the very reasons he had chosen this particular spot for his needs. He hadn't even had time to change out of the tailored black suit he wore.

Tonight, his plans had gone very awry.

His eyes flicked down to the two still figures lying side by side on the deck. They glossed over the man with barely concealed contempt. A local restauranteur, Marko had protected Devito's business for years only for the man to renege on their deal.

For the past twelve months, he'd been late with his monthly security payments, citing a dramatic downturn in business. Then it had been a sick kid and mounting hospital bills. On and on, the excuses had come, but when Marko had been smart enough to investigate the truth for himself, he'd discovered the man had developed a gambling addiction that had spiraled out of control.

Everything Devito had told him, all those tears he had cried… they had all been a lie.

Marko had no real choice in the matter, not when the man had shown how little he could be trusted. While he could — and often did — forgive a great many things, loyalty was something he took very seriously.

His eyes slid over the man's still figure to his wife.

He took in the delicate tilt of her chin and that graceful neck he had kept adorned with jewels throughout their marriage.

Unconscious, she looked so beautiful and peaceful, like an angel living amongst this earth. He had thought that about her from the moment he had first laid eyes on her, almost seven years ago.

She had been twenty at the time.

They'd met on a cruise ship. She'd tended the onboard gift store. He'd noticed her extraordinary beauty first, but her verve for life was what had drawn him in. While the other staff had acted as if they didn't want to be there, she was so happy to be working, he'd been drawn to her like a moth to a flame.

He'd visited her daily, buying tacky souvenirs he knew he'd dump the second they made it to shore, all to have those little interactions with her that were the highlight of his day.

When the ship had docked in Italy for the day, and she'd gone off to explore as wide-eyed as a child, he'd followed. He'd watched from a safe distance away as she had smiled and talked to everyone around her with such joy, he'd wondered how the world couldn't see how special she was.

When she'd stopped to devour a gelato, Marko had engineered bumping into her. From there, it had been natural for the two to explore the city together. He encouraged talk of herself as she tentatively opened up about her childhood and the restrictions that had been put upon her early life.

He listened attentively, filing everything away.

Before they had even returned to the ship, he knew that she would be his.

In a world so tainted with ugliness, she was as untouched as a newly blossomed rose, and Marko was excited to be the one to expand her horizons.

He couldn't wait to show her all the wonderful things she hadn't yet experienced. He would take her to his favorite restaurants, where they would dine on Michelin-starred cuisine. He would dress her in the best designer gowns so she wouldn't keep wearing those terrible clothes that weren't fit for her.

He would get her hair styled properly until she looked like the princess he knew lay beneath. And he would teach her that chewing her nails was not something a lady should do.

She was a diamond in the rough that he would polish until it gleamed.

If only she hadn't turned up as she had that night.

He wasn't one for surprises and had thought that she had known this about him, though apparently, the fact had slipped through that pretty little head of hers.

His mouth twitched with irritation.

A flash of lightning streaked across the horizon, lighting the sea of black and the line of rocks that jutted out of the water.

He had arrived at the right spot.

He killed the engine and hauled Devito's body across the deck.

It took all of his strength to toss him over the side. It seemed it wasn't only gambling the man had been addicted to if his girth was any indication. Marko didn't bother to hide his disgust as Devito's body flopped into the water and was dragged down by the weights he had attached to him.

He couldn't stand anyone who didn't take care of their appearance.

As far as he was concerned, they were a waste of space and didn't deserve to share the air he breathed. He had done Devito a favor really, since the man was eating himself into an early grave, and that was if the loan sharks hadn't got to him first.

At least this way, he had only suffered for an instant.

He tossed the gun he had used into the water, watching as that, too, disappeared without a trace.

Now what was he going to do about his wife?

A sound behind him caught his attention.

He spun around to find his wife standing shakily on the opposite side of the yacht.

Her eyes were wide with fright. Her hair — immaculate at the marina but now a mess of tangles — blew in the wind that had suddenly picked up.

Her feet were bare, the Manolo heels having fallen off when he had carried her onboard. Her dress was twisted around her hips, riding high, revealing much more leg than was decent.

"You killed him," she said, her tone laced with horror, but it was the underlying accusation that upset him.

"You don't understand, Dear. This is how my business works." Marko thought his response calm and controlled, all things considered.

"You work in insurance?" She replied, confusion clouding her eyes.

He didn't bother to set her straight, focused on calming her instead. There was a wildness to her eyes he didn't like.

"He wasn't a good man."

"That doesn't mean you can kill him." She gaped at him, stunned by his reaction.

"You have no idea how many lies that man has told, how many lives he was ruining with his actions. He doesn't deserve your sympathy."

"That still doesn't give you the right to do that! How can you be so calm about this? You just murdered a man!"

His hope that she would understand him were fading by the second. Her face turned a whiter shade of pale.

"Unless… was he not your first?"

Marko didn't say anything, wondering how he could frame his answer in a way that she would accept it.

Maybe he should just lie? He'd be doing it to spare her, of course. She never could take much stress.

A light appeared in her eyes, the light of dawning realization.

"You are a monster. I don't know how I didn't see it before, but it's as clear as day now."

Her words cut into him with the sharpness of a knife. The yacht rocked unsteadily as another flash of lightening tore through the sky, followed by the crack of thunder directly overhead.

Fear had turned his blood into a freezing river of ice.

He was losing her.

He could see it in the way her lips had curled with horror.

In all the years, throughout each of their disagreements, she had never looked at him as she was doing now.

He had to win her back.

There must be something he could say, something he could do to make her forgive him.

"This is just a hiccup. We can move beyond this. Let me take you home, and we can talk things over."

She took a step back but bumped into the side of the yacht. The crashing water below filled him with unease.

"Look, I didn't want to spoil the surprise, but I've booked us on that trip to China you've always wanted to go on. Five-star hotels and flights, even a visit to a panda sanctuary. Move away from the side and I'll get us home. Everything will be all right once we get home. You'll see."

There was nowhere for her to run, and she must have known that by the acceptance that came into her eyes.

She looked down at the churning water, at the storm that was beginning to whip around them, and back to him. There was a defiance in her eyes he had never seen before that caused an uneasy flutter in his stomach.

"You've already taken far too much from me. I won't let you take my life too."

Before he could start toward her, she jumped over the side.

"NO!"

Terror leaped in his throat.

He sprinted for the side, leaned over it, but it was impossible to see anything other than that crashing surface. He scanned the water for any sign of his wife, but it was as if she had never existed at all.

A crack of thunder as loud as the pain in his heart threatened to tear him in two.

The floor beneath his feet lurched so violently that he almost fell. He couldn't stay out here, not with those rocks so close, not if this storm were to get any worse.

"EMILY!"

Another clap of thunder was the only response to his cry.

Casting one last, desperate look over the ocean, Marko sailed home, barely able to see through the blur of his tears, as he left his wife to drown.

12

Jane woke from another troubled night.

She couldn't remember anything clearly, but it seemed she must have suffered with another nightmare as she felt barely rested at all.

Half expecting another repeat of the Logan and Loki swimming show, she was disappointed when the pool was empty.

Something small and bright caught her eye outside the front door.

She made her way over to find a lovely gift basket sitting on the ground containing a selection of breakfast muffins, waffles, and a bottle of fruit infused syrup with a Post-It note stuck to it.

Jane read over the message that had been left by Kitty, who had heard that she'd been upset yesterday. The breakfast foods were so she wouldn't have to trouble herself with cooking in case she didn't have the energy.

She felt a rush of gratitude. The woman really was a Godsend.

Carrying the basket into the kitchen, she nibbled on a blueberry muffin while sipping on coffee that she brewed. Wanting to give Jane her privacy, Kitty hadn't come inside the pool house that morning.

She located the phone, only to notice another note from Kitty. This one helpfully explained that Jane had her own phone line here, what the number was, and how she could check her voicemail.

There was a message from Detective Summers that had come within the last hour. This surprised her. Had she been that exhausted she'd slept clear through it?

Summers didn't have much to report. It seemed more a courtesy call, and her initial excitement at hearing his voice quickly dissipated. Jane thought back to the first moment she had woken on the beach. By her count, it had been just over a week since her new life had begun.

How could no one have reported her missing, still?

Didn't she have anyone in the world who cared about her?

The thought struck her with a sudden terror. She glanced at her reflection in the polished steel of the table where the phone sat, wondering what had happened in her life to have led her to this moment.

Not wanting to start her day being so negative, she dialed '9' as Kitty had instructed. Within three rings, the other woman picked up.

"Good morning, Jane, how are you feeling today?"

Her warm and familiar voice made her feel immediately better.

"Better for finding those treats on my door. Thank you, Kitty. You are so thoughtful."

The other woman tutted, but sounded pleased. "It was nothing. Have you tried anything, yet?"

"The blueberry muffin was delicious."

"Oh, that's the one I like the most too. If there are any other flavors you prefer, you just let me know and I'll remember it for the next time. Now, was there something I could help you with?"

"No," Jane replied. "I really only called to say thank you."

Kitty made a sound of delight. "You are very welcome."

"I won't keep you, I'm sure you must have a ton of things to do." She wanted to speak with her longer, if only for some company, but she couldn't occupy Kitty's time like that.

"I do have a busy day today," Kitty admitted. "But if you need anything, anything at all you just let me know. Call or come by the house if you prefer."

Jane promised she would, hung up the call and went to take a quick shower. The pulsing hot water and the conversation — however short it was — had rejuvenated her spirits.

Her eyes slid over to the laptop, charging now, since she had used up the battery when she'd returned from the studio yesterday only to search through endless websites that had left her drained.

She couldn't face another day of the same again.

What she needed was a day off. Something to take her mind off her troubles.

One of the key points that had stuck through her research was that a person with amnesia should try to go about their lives experiencing every day things in order to jog the memory.

While staying home might feel like the safest thing to do, it wouldn't be productive, and would only cause the sufferer to take longer to recover from the entire ordeal.

She needed to go around the neighborhood. Visit the grocery store. Simple, everyday things.

Emboldened by her decision, she left the pool house. She walked through the gardens, enjoying the fresh air and the cheerful rays of the sun until she came to a curved stone path lined by rosebushes which opened up into the main residence.

The back of the house had a large terrace with a fire pit and a circle of comfortable-looking chairs surrounding it. A long, banquet style table with an outdoor kitchen overlooked a white rock wall, which at first glance seemed a strange feature, until she saw the projector hidden in the beams of the roof.

The wall was an outdoor home theater, and she imagined, a stunning place to entertain in the evening. An ancient wisteria tree hugged the back of the house with its branches, as clumps of purple flowers trailed down.

She could see straight through the folding glass doors that opened into the living area beyond. Out of the folded doors came a bundle of energy as Loki greeted her with exuberant excitement, barking, yipping, and whining, all at once. She caught him in her arms, almost knocked over by the full force of him.

"Glad to see you're in a good mood as usual."

"He's too young to know any better," Logan said behind her.

He was glad to see she had more color in her face

today, though she still had that initial edge each time he spoke to her. He'd noticed it when they had met again, for the second time, though she wasn't aware of it herself.

It was almost as if something about him made her unconsciously wary.

He'd put it down to one of the odder reactions famous people could receive, but it didn't ring true in her case, especially as she hadn't even known who he was initially.

"How are you feeling?"

"Better, thanks. I'm sorry for the trouble I caused yesterday."

"There was no trouble. You don't have to apologize."

She tucked a strand of hair behind her ear. "I'm not sure what happened, but I'm sure it won't happen again. I probably hadn't eaten enough."

He didn't think a lack of food would induce a panic attack, but he left it alone.

"If you're not happy with the selection Kitty left for you, you can always request whatever you need."

Jane's eyes went round. "Are you crazy? That fridge is full of amazing food."

"That you are apparently not eating." He pointed out the obvious.

"I've actually just inhaled two giant muffins, and they were delicious, so you're wrong about that."

He laughed, suddenly. A loud, booming laugh full of life.

"Well, good. It's what it's there for."

"I was actually thinking of going out today. I have some things I'd like to get."

He frowned, looking concerned. "If Kitty has made a

mistake or gotten things that aren't suitable, you can just let her know and she'll fix it."

"Kitty has been amazing. Everything in that closet is stunning. It's just, as beautiful as it all is, I just feel like I would like to choose my own clothes. I know this might not make much sense, and I don't want you to think I'm being ungrateful, but… I didn't choose any of it. I'm not sure why that is important to me, but it is. As ridiculous as it seems, I'd really like to go out to a store and buy a few things for myself."

She waited for the inevitable blowout her suggestion would cause, knowing that it was coming. How could it not when he must have spent a small fortune on her already?

Logan thought over her question, wondering why picking her own clothes would be so important, when it suddenly came to him.

She had no memory of who she was. She didn't even pick her name. But she could certainly choose her own clothes.

"Of course. I should have thought of that, myself. You'll need money."

He took out his wallet and handed her some bills. "Sorry, I don't carry much cash on me."

Jane tried not to gape at the wad in her hand. There must have been several thousand there.

"Thank you. I don't know how, but I will pay you back every cent that you've spent on me," she said, and meaning every word.

His eyes pinned her to place. She couldn't read the expression in them, but he stared at her so intensely, sweat started to gather. Finally, he simply shook his head, ignoring her comment.

"Do you know what store you want to go to? I'm leaving for work in a minute so I can't drive you myself, but I can drop you off. Daryl should be here in a few minutes."

"I was hoping that I could borrow a car? Whatever is the cheapest one that you have?"

Her question threw him. "Are you sure you're ready for that? How do you even know if you can drive?"

She had already given this some thought.

"There's only one way to find out."

A FEW MOMENTS LATER, SHE SAT BEHIND THE WHEEL IN HIS SUV.

It was the cheapest car he owned, though that wasn't saying much. It was clearly not an average SUV, not with the kind of specs it came with.

And it was made by Rolls Royce.

Just the cabin alone — a cocoon of leather, wood, and gleaming metal with deep-pile lambswool carpets — was enough to make Jane take stock. She didn't need to know anything about cars to know that this was top of the range luxury.

She was starting to regret her decision to borrow it, not wanting to be responsible should anything go wrong.

"What is this car?"

"It's a Cullinan."

"And *this* is the cheapest one you've got? Just out of interest, how much was it?"

"They gave me a discount. I think it came in at just under $300k in the end."

Jane swallowed drily. "A bargain, then."

He flashed a grin at her. "I thought so."

In the time that she had known him, he hadn't smiled at her much. The big grin he bestowed on her now created butterflies in her stomach.

"I hope you've at least used it a bunch of times."

"This will be my fourth, I think."

"Right. I don't suppose you have an Uber account, do you?"

"You'll be fine. If something should happen, I have several other cars left."

Sitting in the passenger seat, he looked less confident when Jane took a while to familiarize herself with the mechanics.

After shifting the seat around until she was comfortable, she checked the wheel, the gears, and the dash — for what, Logan wasn't sure. "Are you sure you know how to do this?"

"Not at all," Jane replied with her own grin as she turned the key that he had already slipped into the ignition.

The engine roared to life, purring beneath her feet as she put the car into drive. She checked the mirrors, then eased the car out of the garage and onto the drive as easily as if she were walking. She didn't even think about the action of driving: it was all coming naturally.

Excitement washed over her.

She was doing this! She could remember how to drive.

"Why don't you take us around the property for a test run?"

Jane shot a look at him. "Isn't that your driver arriving now?"

Yesterday's sleek black Mercedes had pulled up alongside as the same driver — Daryl — stepped out of the car, nodding a greeting at them.

"Good morning, Sir. Ma'am."

Logan nodded back a greeting. "I need a moment, Daryl."

"Of course." Daryl got back into the car to wait.

He turned back to Jane. "He's fine to wait a few minutes."

She was touched that he was setting aside this time for her, especially when he was needed at work, but only a moment later, she started feeling stupid. Despite his assurances, this wasn't about her. He was concerned that she would crash his expensive car and probably wanted proof that she was a capable driver.

Needing to prove that she was, she took the car around the property, proud at the way she controlled the vehicle. They arrived back beside the Mercedes as Logan unsnapped the seatbelt she hadn't noticed him putting on.

"Did I pass?"

He smiled. "Yes. But be back before midnight," he joked, flashing that famous grin of his that made women all around the world weak at the knees, and found, to her annoyance, that she wasn't exempt from it.

"Why, does it turn into a pumpkin?" She quipped before she could stop herself.

As small as the drive had been, it had done her the

world of good. The tension that she carried on her shoulders had lessened. Even those worry lines that seemed permanently etched across her forehead had gone. And now she was making a joke. Logan liked this change in her.

He shook his head. "No, most of the staff will be gone by then and I'll be asleep."

"OK."

He got into the other car. Before he could go, Jane called out the window to him.

"One last thing… Do you know where I should go for clothes?"

He laughed as if she'd said something funny. "In Beverly Hills? Rodeo Drive, Baby."

A flash of a scene entered her mind. She saw two women, one with bright red curls, and the other, an exotic-looking brunette having the exact same conversation.

"Wait, I know that line… that's from Pretty Woman! I remembered something!"

"That's great, Jane. You're starting to get your memory back." His smile grew wider, knowing what this meant for her. "And it seems like, you had a thing for Julia Robert's movies."

"It does seem that way, doesn't it?"

He started toward his car, but she had to stop him again.

"Sorry, one more last thing… where exactly is it, Rodeo Drive?"

Instead of answering, he leaned in through the window, so close that tantalizing scent of him seemed to fill the car, causing her to hold her breath.

Having no idea how his closeness was affecting her, he typed the address into the GPS.

"Have fun."

And with that parting remark, he left.

WIND BLEW THROUGH HER HAIR, THE SMELL OF SALT WATER tickled her nose.

Jane drove down the winding road from Logan's estate as cautiously as possible without being a menace to other drivers, knowing that a timid driver was as bad as a careless one.

Before she had gone, she had popped in to see Kitty. The woman had been overjoyed, approving of her plans to go out for the day. She had offered to babysit Loki, though Jane had declined. Though she and Logan hadn't discussed the issue further, she felt that Loki was her responsibility. Plus, she happened to adore his company, so it wasn't a hardship to take him with her.

Her eyes flicked over to the small bundle of fur by her side. On getting into the car, he had circled the seat several times. He'd looked out of the window, yipping at the scenery flying by with such extraordinary excitement, only to have passed out, dead to the world, after just ten minutes.

A smile tugged at the corners of her lips when she heard the whisper of his breath hissing out from the gaps in his teeth.

There was something comforting about the little sounds he made. Whenever he was with her, she felt less alone in the world, and wondered if all pet owners felt the same way.

Her thoughts turned to Logan. There was something

unreachable about him that was at odds with the kindness he displayed. He could be somewhat aloof at times, but he didn't seem the awful person the world said he was.

She pushed the thought away from her mind.

It didn't really matter what anyone thought of him. What mattered was how he treated her and so far, that was better than anyone else.

She drove through luxurious neighborhoods, each more extravagant than the last. With driveways that were as wide as an entire street, and imposing front doors that seemed designed with giants in mind, she lost count of the water fountains that welcomed any visitors who might have set foot on the properties.

It wasn't until another fifteen or so minutes, when she approached the South side of the neighborhood, that the homes became more modest. Single-family dwellings with terracotta roof tiles littered this new area. Along with it came a different scent in the air. Warm spices that tickled the back of her throat, warming her all the way down to her toes.

She felt a pang of longing in her chest as she drove past the homes and wondered where it came from. Did these houses remind her of her own house?

That familiar frustration began to build. A weight pressing down on her chest that constantly reminded her that she wasn't a whole person.

Loki whined in his sleep, possibly picking up on her turmoil.

Considering how well known Rodeo Drive was, it wasn't as wide as she expected, consisting of only four lanes divided by a central reservation of white flowers that ran the entire length of the main strip.

But what it lacked in size, it more than made up for in appearance.

Lush palm trees with their trunks wrapped in fairy lights flanked both sides of the street, giving it a boulevard feel. The pavement itself was spotless — if any litter or gum was dropped here, it was removed almost immediately.

All around her were some of the flashiest cars ever produced, most of which she wasn't familiar with. There was one car whose sleek, almost futuristic body she recognized as a Lamborghini. She was pretty sure she couldn't have owned one of those since they cost several million dollars. That she knew that surprised her. Logan's extensive car range hadn't filled her with any kind of interest. It seemed likely, then, that her knowledge of the car might have something to do with the previous man in her life.

She pushed back into her mind, trying to picture him, but as usual, there was only a black fog where her memory should have been.

She studied the glistening shop fronts with their sumptuous displays. Names like Ferragamo, Chanel, Valentino, and Vera Wang flashed past. She recognized all the labels, and could even have listed them in ascending order of the most exclusive.

Perhaps she was affiliated with the fashion industry?

Fueled by this new thought, she started pulling the car into a spot that opened up ahead of her when a bright yellow Hummer blasting hip hop music cut her up, stealing the space, almost causing them to crash.

The driver who couldn't have been more than twenty, had the nerve to scream at her as if she were the one in the wrong.

She opened her mouth to snap back a sharp retort of her own, one that would leave a searing mark on his skinny, little head…

But only the faintest whisper of a word came out and even then, she was horrified to find that it was, "Sorry."

Why on earth would she *apologize* to him?

Her reaction to the jerk shocked her almost as much as his attitude had.

A million responses ran through her mind, a million other ways that she could have — and should have — responded. All manner of stinging retorts that would have put the little punk in his place, if she hadn't been such a coward.

The music from the hummer woke Loki, who yawned, then stood up to see where they were. Jane looked out past him, to the Gucci store they were parked by, and saw the pristine sales assistants in their sky-high stilettos, marble-smooth faces, and salon-styled hair as a lead weight sank to the bottom of her stomach.

She knew she wasn't bad looking, that she would possibly be considered pretty by some, but she looked nothing like these carefully presented women. She wore no make-up and her nails were as chipped as the moment she had woken up on the shore.

Maybe coming here in her condition hadn't been the wisest of choices.

"Hold on, Loki. We're not staying."

He yapped at her, not understanding a word yet excited non-the-less. Lifting his wriggling body off her lap where he had now climbed onto, she set him back onto the passenger seat, curling his leash around the seat belt.

When he was calmer, they set off again.

13

Jane drove around aimlessly, taking in the sights and sounds, as she attempted to familiarize herself with the city when the friendly sight of The Grove caught her attention.

The retail complex housed many stores as well as a thriving farmer's market that seemed appealing — and far more approachable than Rodeo Drive had been.

"Loki, we have a winner."

He pulled at his restraints and whined, but the wagging tail revealed there wasn't any hard feelings about his current predicament.

"I know we've been driving a lot, but we're almost there."

She found a space near the market and parked. With Loki's leash wrapped firmly around her hand, and the money Logan had given in the pocket of the linen pants she had decided to wear today, they headed for the farmer's market.

Despite being the middle of the day, the place was alive

with people milling around, trying the different foods that were available. A white clock tower stood off to one-side revealed it was a little after twelve-thirty.

Loki pranced by her feet, overflowing with excitement. His pink nose pointed in every direction, overwhelmed by the smells on display.

She caught a snatch of something delicious that made her mouth water. Her feet headed in the direction of a busy stall serving freshly fried donuts dipped in cinnamon sugar. The stall owner, a pretty Black girl with glowing skin, smiled at them.

"Your dog is so cute."

As if he understood the sentiment, Loki danced on his paws before sitting down, tilting his head up at the girl. His tongue was hanging out so much that it was amazing it was still attached to him. Whining loudly, he scooted forward.

"Thanks. I think he is working you right now, though."

She laughed, rubbing her cheek, leaving a streak of sugar on it.

"You want some? They're really good, even if I say so myself."

Jane shook her head. "I shouldn't..." she began automatically, but stopped. It wasn't as if she had an issue with weight — far from it.

"One or two isn't going to kill anyone. Besides, what's the point of living if you can't treat yourself now and again?"

"I've already eaten two muffins today," Jane answered, slightly ashamed.

"When was that?"

"For breakfast."

"Well, it's lunchtime now, so…"

"You do speak a lot of sense," Jane answered, caving rapidly. "I'll take one."

"You won't regret it," the girl beamed back, handing her a still-warm donut wrapped in a napkin. Paying, Jane thanked her and started toward another stall. Having smelled the heavenly thing in her hand, Loki began doing figure-eights around her legs. Within moments, he had twisted the leash all around her feet so that any more movement would have been at her peril.

She detangled herself and fed him a piece of donut. He practically swooned with delight. She was reasonably sure that, though not the healthiest of food she could give him, donuts were safe enough.

She ate the donut faster than was reasonably polite to do so. Dusting the sugar from her fingers, she headed toward a stall that specialized in mushrooms. Button, Porcini and Chanterelle mushrooms spilled out of wicker baskets. Beside them were their lesser-known cousins, the alien-looking Enoki, Shiitake, and Morel.

Able to identify them by sight, she squirreled the knowledge into the mental file she was building for herself.

Knows various edible mushrooms… check.

She perused the food stalls for fun, though refrained from purchasing anything else.

A bell peeled close by, causing Loki to bark. Jane spotted a bright and cheerful two-decker trolley approaching, driven by a smiling, uniformed driver.

The trolley was built from a 1950s Boston street car, a nearby sign revealed. Powered electrically, it took visitors on a ride throughout the mall. When the trolley stopped right by her, Jane got on.

Going slowly, it allowed them to take in all the sights the place offered. When she caught sight of the Nordstrom sign, she felt a flutter in her chest.

This was where she wanted to shop.

Helping Loki off the trolley, Jane spied a pretty green print midi dress in the window display that she instantly loved. Heading inside, the store was a large white space with strategically placed racks and displays of gorgeous clothing.

Loki tugged at his leash, keen to play among the fun looking mannequins. A buff security guard who must have been at least six foot five tossed a look their way. Jane steeled herself for the inevitable ejection that she felt was surely coming, but his eyes glanced past her with disinterest.

It seemed dogs were as welcome as their two-legged owners in many of the stores in this city.

Having felt surrounded by a heavy, dark cloud, there was now excitement at the prospect of feeling normal again. And what could be more normal than trying on and buying clothes?

She walked past a section that was in the middle of being arranged. Several mannequins lay on the floor, their limbs in a pile beside the bodies still waiting to be attached. She maneuvered Loki past and spotted the dress she wanted. Making sure Loki was preoccupied with the chew toy they had brought with them today, she reached for the dress but stopped short of taking it.

She had no idea what size she was.

She no idea what size she wore — for anything.

She should have paid closer attention to the items in her closet, but her daily dressing routine had consisted of grabbing whatever didn't seem too ostentatious. She had never once glanced at the labels inside.

Instead of shoes, her feet were encased in generic flip flops. She slipped her right foot out of one, hoping to see a size, though it only revealed an "M" which wasn't particularly helpful.

She took hold of the collar of her shirt, twisting the collar around, but it was impossible to see what the label said.

A sigh of irritation hissed from her lips. Shopping was going to be a lot more difficult than she'd thought if she didn't know what size she was.

"You look like you're in need of a little assistance."

The warm voice that greeted her belonged to a sales assistant with startling emerald green eyes. Her hair was a glossy almost-black, and she was wearing a summery off-the-shoulder dress that showed off creamy bronze skin. If it wasn't for the nametag pinned to her chest, Jane would have thought her a customer.

"What gave it away?" She smiled back ruefully.

Clare — for that's what the name tag read — smiled wryly at her.

"Well, the adorable dog wrapped around your feet for one. If you take a single step forward, I think you'll find yourself flat on your face. And the fact that you were looking at the rack like it was an alien creature."

She had a nice, easy way about her that seemed completely natural, almost as if she were a friend and not a sales assistant interested in only her money.

"I need some things, but I don't know what size I am."

Clare blinked at Jane, confusion clouding her eyes.

"Has your weight fluctuated recently?"

"No..." Jane hesitated, unsure exactly how she could explain herself. Should she go for a variation of the truth, or would a lie be easier?

"I lost my memory recently. I woke up on a beach with nothing but the dress I had on. I can't remember anything of my life before, including my name or what size I am."

That wasn't at all what she had expected to say. It seemed she needed to talk to someone about her ordeal, and poor Clare was going to be the victim.

To her credit, Clare's immediate response was to take a moment to let her reply sink in. Jane felt terrible. What a thing to spring on the poor woman. She only wanted to sell her some clothes!

Mortified at blurting out her story, she fumbled an apology. "Sorry, I didn't mean to just blurt that out..."

Feeling the sting of tears, her embarrassment turned to horror. Seeing the onset of them, Clare took her by the shoulders and steered Jane onto one of the velvet gray pedestal seats dotted around the store. Gently, she tugged Loki's leash from her numb hands.

Jane sank onto the seat, laughing humorlessly. "I don't know why I said that. It's unprofessional of me. You don't need to deal with this..."

Clare tutted and gave her a reproachful look.

"Honey, you are having a moment, that's all. We all get them, even without the horrific thing you just told me. Let yourself feel whatever you're feeling and just breathe through it all. I'm fine. You don't have to worry about me. I just want you to feel better again."

She exuded such kindness it made Jane want to cry… which was ridiculous.

She couldn't have a meltdown in this store, of all places.

"Would you like some water?"

Jane shook her head, reaching out to grab the woman's hands.

"No… thank you. Give me a second… I'll be fine in a moment."

Clare squeezed her hands. "You take all the time you need. I'll be here, playing with your pretty dog."

Loki sat a few feet away, his expression concerned, sensing her distress. He chuffed and shuffled closer, laid his paws over her feet. She reached down to pet him. As soon as her fingers felt his warm fur, some of the panic she felt began to fade.

True to her word, Clare played tug with Loki, dangling the chew toy in front of him, giving Jane the space she needed to compose herself. When she felt able to continue, she stood up.

"All better?" Clare asked.

Jane nodded. "I'm sorry—" she began only for Clare to stop her.

"You need to stop apologizing. I've said I'm fine with it, so let's move on. Now, do you want to talk about what's happened to you, because that's fine with me? Or would you prefer that I help you with clothes first? I'm honestly happy with either, but I don't want you to feel stressed or upset if you don't want to talk about it. You tell me what you'd like to do."

Jane picked the easiest option. "Clothes first, I think."

"Excellent. So, what do we need to get you?"

"Everything."

Clare blinked at her again. "Everything, everything?"

Jane nodded. She didn't bother explaining about the clothes that waited for her back at the pool house, not sure she would understand.

Clare cast a professional eye over her. "What you're wearing, it's not a bad fit, but we can do a little better."

She walked a ring around her. "I'd say you were a size six with maybe a 38inch chest. What kind of dresser do you think you are?"

"I don't understand the question," Jane replied.

"Are you conservative or hippy? Do you prefer casual and comfort, or is style the priority?" Even as the words left her mouth, Clare knew she'd made a mistake. She winced, seeing the expression on Jane's face.

"You probably don't know any of that, do you? Well, then this is a first. You'll try on everything until we figure out what you like.

She rubbed her hands gleefully. "Oh, this is going to be so much fun. I swear I've waited for this moment my entire life."

Sending her a beaming smile, Clare bustled away, humming to herself as she perused the racks and shelves, rifling through the items on display until she returned with a lovely v neck burned orange floral dress that she held up to Jane. "Do we like?"

Jane nodded immediately. "It's beautiful."

"And, it should suit you perfectly. Go try this on before I pull any more outfits for you. I'll wait here with… Loki, was it?"

Jane nodded, taking the dress into the nearby changing room. Moments later, she emerged with the dress draped over her like a second skin. It clung to her curves, showing them off, yet managed to not be overtly sexual.

In a word, it was perfect and Jane's expression said as much.

Clare grinned, a smug smile on her lips. "If everything looks as good as that on you, this will be even easier than I thought."

Jane couldn't resist a twirl in front of the mirror.

"This is a keeper, then?"

"Absolutely."

"Fantastic!" Clare clapped her hands together, delighting Loki, who barked. Jane tried to settle him back down immediately. She had wedged the end of his leash under one of those gray stools, using the weight of it to keep him in place.

"I'll be back with more."

And she was off, a mini tornado whirling through the store with a sole purpose in mind. She grabbed then rejected clothes here and there. When her arms became overloaded, she dropped by with her latest choice, then disappeared off to find more.

Jane slipped into a million different outfits — at least that was how it seemed. From other floral dresses, each with a different design and cut, to thin cashmere tops and skinny jeans that showed off her long, toned legs.

Every outfit Clare bought fitted her well, so it was only a case of which ones she wanted to keep. It didn't take long before Jane didn't bother looking at the clothes before trying them on, trusting Clare's impeccable taste.

Which was how she found herself staring dubiously at her reflection in a leopard-print catsuit that channeled the eighties with padded shoulders that almost reached her ears. She emerged from the changing room looking highly unimpressed, wondering how Clare could have gotten it so wrong.

"Really?" Jane said, only to find the other woman in a fit of giggles, collapsed over a stool.

"My God, you're actually wearing it!"

Her reaction wasn't what Jane had expected. Clare had to gulp in air to stop herself from laughing long enough to speak.

"We haven't been able to get anyone to try that thing on — I honestly don't know what they were smoking when they decided to stock it. We've had a running bet in the store about which of us would be the first to get a customer to try it. You've just won me fifty bucks. Thank you!"

"I'm glad to be of service," Jane replied, feeling utterly ridiculous.

"Would it help if I said that if anyone can pull it off, you do?"

"Not particularly."

Jane started back into the changing room, only to be stopped by Clare.

"Wait! I need physical proof of this or they won't pay up."

Clare snapped a photograph, not the least bit concerned by the glower Jane gave. Jane spun on her heel, heading back inside with all the dignity she could muster when her heart stopped.

"Where's Loki?"

"He was right here." Clare gestured to an empty space on the floor only to look immediately worried.

"LOKI?!" Jane called out, as panicked as any parent at losing her child. "LOKI, COME HERE!"

His answering yip was reassuringly happy and close by. They heard the unmistakable sound of four paws running toward them as he shot out from beneath a display of long dresses, carrying a mannequin arm in his mouth like a trophy. Seeing how proud he was, they laughed.

"No, drop that!" Jane commanded. Loki growled playfully at her though his tail wagged harder.

"Oh, he's fine. His teeth won't make a dent on that thing."

Jane looked at the limb dubiously. "Are you sure? What's it made of, titanium?"

"No idea," Clare laughed. "And they don't pay me enough to worry about it."

After the clothes, Clare returned with handbags and accessories. Both seemed to be where her heart lay. She modeled one stunning piece after another until Jane had to beg her to stop.

There wouldn't be enough room in the car to get all of this home.

"Where are you living now?" Clare asked innocently, not understanding how loaded the question was.

A deal was a deal, and she had promised to keep their arrangement confidential, but she didn't want to mislead Clare either. She decided to skirt close to the truth.

"The man who saved me… he took me in."

Clare's eyes went wide. "Are you sure that's safe? I mean, who is he? What do you know about him?

Jane thought it sweet that her only concern was for her safety.

"Enough to know that he won't hurt me. He's a… successful businessman. And I'm not staying in his house exactly: he's given me the pool house so I have plenty of privacy."

Clare's eyebrows rose several notches, her concern turning mischievous.

"The pool house? Just how successful is he? Wait, is he the one paying for all these clothes? Is he married? Engaged?"

Before Jane could even answer, Clare fired off another question.

"If you tell me he's gorgeous, I will literally die right here. Please tell me he's as ugly as sin."

"He is not unpleasant to look at."

Clare faked wiping sweat from her brow. "So he's hot, he's rich, and he saved you? That's quite the fairytale ending you've found yourself in."

"We're not… there's nothing between us. He just has extra space and felt sorry for me. There's nothing more to it than that."

A snort burst out from Clare. "Of course there isn't. People take complete strangers into their homes all the time. I mean, I can't count the amount of offers I've had to field off. It gets exhausting."

There was a twinkle in her eye.

"I'm just saying, this will make a wonderful story to tell your grandkids, that's all," she finally finished with a grin.

Jane wanted to laugh — the woman was incorrigible — but something stopped her. Though her comments were meant as a bit of fun, she couldn't ignore the thought that had crept into her mind.

What if she was already someone's partner?

She could be married or engaged. In which case, it would be wrong to be attracted to Logan. Not wanting to put a dampener on Clare's mood, she kept her thoughts to herself.

"I don't think that's going to happen. As kind as he has been, he makes me nervous."

Clare grew suddenly serious. "In what way?"

Jane shrugged. "I don't know. He's very intense, I guess. And I don't really know what he's really thinking about anything. I can't make him out. He confuses me."

"Better that than he bores you! I'd take confusion over boredom any day. Then again, it's been so long for me, I'd probably take any man at this point."

Jane looked at Clare, at her vivaciousness and beauty and the funny, warm personality she had displayed.

"I find it hard to believe that men don't throw themselves at you."

Clare laughed. "You're too kind, but after you've been burned like I have… Well, that's a conversation for another time. Let's just focus on you today."

The two sorted through their favorite outfits and enough underwear to keep Jane covered for at least two weeks, and they were finally done.

Clare helped carry the items to the cashier where Jane paid in cash. Her eye twitched from nervousness when the balance flashed up. The price was a lot higher than the five bags that sat on the counter looked like they should have cost.

"Let me help you to your car," Clare offered, cutting into her thoughts.

The two loaded the bags into the Cullinan as Clare gave the car the side-eye.

"Your businessman must be *very* successful to own this car. I've only ever seen a few of these passing through the city."

Jane thought it best not to comment.

After three hours cooped up in the store, Loki couldn't wait to go outside to relieve himself. When he was done, Jane had to wrestle the mannequin arm from his mouth and settle him into the car.

When he was strapped in, Jane turned to Clare.

"I didn't actually expect to enjoy myself today, but you've turned what was a stressful chore into something fun."

Clare smiled, flashing white teeth at her. "I'm so glad to have helped. And listen, LA can be a big and lonely place when you don't know anyone. I know you have your buff businessman to talk to, but if you need anyone else, or just want to grab a cup of coffee, here's my number."

She handed Jane a business card from the store that she had scribbled her details onto.

"I really would love to see you again, not only to make sure you're OK, but I liked your company too."

Jane took the card, surprised by the rush of happiness Clare's offer of friendship gave.

"Thanks." She tucked it carefully into the new handbag slung across her shoulder.

"Call me, OK? I mean it."

Climbing into the car, Jane wound down the window. "I will. I promise."

"And if your businessman has any friends…" Clare

wiggled her eyebrows suggestively, making Jane laugh. Giving her a bright wave, Clare disappeared into the store, leaving Jane smiling at the first friend she had made in this town. Looking across at Loki, she grinned.

"Well, that wasn't as horrible as we thought it was going to be. Maybe, it's going to be a good day after all?"

14

Cars screeched by. Horns blared, their drivers glaring through their windows at Jane with barely concealed annoyance.

As if any of this nightmare was of her making.

She'd been driving along, happy for the first time in days, when the car had started spluttering. Not knowing what to do, she had pulled off to the side — it was just unfortunate that she had been on a narrower stretch of road than usual when the problem occurred.

After some twenty or so minutes trying to find what was wrong, she had given up and was now trying to figure out how to call for help.

She didn't have a phone, and with only Summers' number — safely squirreled away in the pool house — and Clare's, it seemed too much to burden her for help when they had only just met.

Loki whined, unhappy with being stuck in the car. As was becoming the norm, he picked up on her anxiety and was not liking it one bit.

"I know, Buddy, I don't like this any more than you do."

She considered her options. But, with only the cars streaking past, there wasn't a break in the road for miles.

If it wasn't for Loki, she would have risked leaving the car and walking until she could get to a phone or flag down assistance, but he was only a puppy and jumpy from all the commotion. She wouldn't be able to get anywhere safely with him, and it was out of the question to leave him there alone.

She leaned back in the driver's seat, arms wrapped around him, unsure who was calming who. All she could do was wait and hope that someone would take pity on her and stop.

But this wasn't a city known for its neighborly ways.

Cars raced past, the occasional driver scowling their displeasure as they talked on their phones. She hadn't been in LA long, but already she was starting to see how the people here were always in a hurry, multitasking even when at the wheel.

A woman drove past, touching up her makeup — and not only her lipstick. She dabbed eyeshadow onto the corners of her eyes and had even looked directly at Jane, all while at the wheel of her car. She had seen her plight, but it hadn't been met with any sympathy.

When the sun started sinking lower, and the skies became awash with red, sirens screamed into the fast-approaching night. A police cruiser appeared and slid up alongside. A policeman with salt and pepper hair emerged from the car and gestured for Jane to wind the window down.

It might have been the hostile expression on his face, or

the way he swaggered toward her as if he owned the world, but something about his presence made her uneasy.

"Ma'am, can you step out of the car?"

Looping Loki's leash around the steering wheel, she got out and closed the door firmly behind her to stop any thoughts of escape the puppy might have.

Despite how unthreatening she must have looked, he kept one hand on the gun strapped to his hip, and barked, "You can't stop here. You pose a serious risk to yourself and other vehicles who might not see you until it's too late."

Thanks, Sergeant Obvious. She hadn't thought of that.

"I was having car trouble. It started making a strange noise, so I pulled over, but now I can't get it to start again."

He stared at her beneath a pair of bushy eyebrows. "Why haven't you called for assistance?"

"I don't have a phone," she answered truthfully, squirming under his gaze.

He didn't speak for several moments, pinning her in place with those eyes that clearly found her version of the story wanting.

"I can radio for help for the car, but I'll need to see your license first." He started toward her, hand outstretched as he waited for the requested item.

A sudden dread came over her at his request.

She had been so desperate to feel even one iota of control that a license had completely slipped her mind. Even college kids knew better than to drive without a one. What a stupid, stupid thing to forget!

The blood drained from her face. She found herself stammering a reply. "I don't have one on me…"

His eyes turned flinty.

Forty years on the job and he still couldn't believe how the rich behaved.

They pulled all kinds of stunts knowing their lawyers and limitless bank accounts would bail them out. As soon as he had pulled up, he'd spotted the expensive bags on the backseat of that overpriced, splashy SUV which someone would only ever buy if they had more money than sense.

Once he'd taken note of those factors, and what looked to be a designer dog on an equally designer leash, he'd had this woman made. And if she thought she could play the helpless victim and bash her eyelids at him, she had another thing coming.

"If you are driving without a legal license in your possession, that is a criminal offence which I can arrest you for. You could go to prison for this, did you know that?"

Terror had turned Jane's blood cold. "No… I didn't. I can explain…"

From the curl of disdain on his lip, it was clear he wasn't interested in hearing what she had to say. "Hand over your ID. I need to call this in."

Jane shrank under his gaze, her voice barely a squeak. "I don't have that either."

His eyebrows rose into his thinning hairline. "You're telling me that you have been driving with no ID *or* license? Ma'am are you in any way a criminal or fugitive?

It was on the top of the tongue to reply that she was neither, except, she didn't really know if that was true, that unhelpful voice in her head provided.

She had to do something before the situation spiraled out of control. An image of her being handcuffed and dragged away to prison flashed into her mind, leaving a bitter taste in her mouth.

"Detective Summers!" She cried out.

"My name is not Summers," His brow knotted, causing thick lines to furrow on his forehead as he considered the possibility that the woman was on drugs.

"If you call him, he can explain who I am. He's in the downtown office. Please, call and tell him it's Jane Smith."

"Jane Smith?"

His incredulity was palpable. Not for nothing, Jane already knew that it was the most common — and most anonymous name they could have picked for her. At the time, she hadn't given it much consideration, though right now, every bone in her body wished she'd spent a little longer creating her new alias.

The cop hesitated, fighting an internal tug-of-war as he contemplated what to do. He must have thought there was some truth to her story as he returned to his car.

It took a while for him to be connected to Summers, and Jane could only hear snatches of the conversation above the roaring traffic. Summers must have waved his magic wand as, shortly after, when he returned to Jane, the frosty demeanor that had been present before, had gone.

In fact, he seemed sympathetic now.

Almost friendly.

It was a complete U-turn.

"I understand it has been a difficult few days but you can't go around driving without a valid license — understand?"

Jane nodded, relief surging through her body and down to her frozen feet that felt like blocks of ice. "Is someone coming to fix the car?"

She hoped they would arrive soon. This was too much excitement for her, and she needed to get Loki back. She could see him eyeballing her new handbag like it was a juicy steak.

"Eventually, but you don't have to worry about that. Your ride is on the way."

He looked excited by this. A light had come into his eyes. There was even a pep in his step.

"Summers told me about your rescue. The damnedest thing being rescued by a movie star. You couldn't make up a more outrageous story."

Jane was starting to recognize what might have caused the change in his manner. It had been the same with the girl in the book store. His eyes held the light of fandom, that feverish glow that signaled more questioning was about to come — and none of it about her.

She steeled herself for the onslaught.

"So, what's he like then? I've seen a lot of his films. He likes to play the hero, doesn't he? He's had a bad time recently, what with that famous break-up and his movies tanking. Is he as difficult as they say he is?"

He waited for her to answer with bated breath.

"I don't know him very well. We only really just met," Jane began, hoping that his questions would stop. While his attitude might have changed, she hadn't forgotten the way he had made her feel. He hadn't shown any kind of understanding toward her until he learned of her affiliation with Logan.

The fakeness of it all turned her stomach.

"But you're living in his house, aren't you? You must know some things about him?" He leaned over, coming in so close that she could smell garlic on his breath.

Loki growled a warning from the car, paws planted on the seat defiantly. Believing that he was encroaching on her space — which he was — he was letting the man know he should back off. He seemed to have no idea how small he was compared to the stocky man. No fear or hesitation. He only wanted to protect her.

Jane's heart swelled with affection for the little guy.

Either the cop didn't pick up on his warning, or he simply ignored it. He moved even closer. She backed away until her butt hit the side of the Cullinan.

"He took me in and gave me a place to stay in his pool house. That's all I know," Jane offered unwillingly, hoping that the small bit of information would satisfy his curiosity.

He pointed a finger at Loki.

"I don't believe that for a second! Isn't that his dog? You can't read a paper without seeing the two of them around. You must be closer than you're admitting if he's letting you look after his dog."

His eyes took on a hard glint again as he studied Jane.

"I'm telling you, that's the truth. I don't have any more information to give you."

The fact she was having to explain herself like this struck her as harassment. Her blood started to pound, that sick feeling in her stomach growing by the second, her fight-or-flight instincts kicking in.

He's just another fan, she tried to tell herself.

Just another person who wanted to share some of Logan's limelight. But her nerves were starting to scream, and the hairs on the back of her neck were raised.

He was so close to her that she could see a vein pop in the middle of his forehead. She noticed small details of his face: a missed spot where he had shaved that morning, and the scars that criss-crossed his face after a bout of what looked to be chickenpox.

Loki strained against his leash, stretching it taunt. Jane's eyes slid behind him to the passing traffic. Drivers peered at them with morbid curiosity, but no one stopped. No one wound down the window to see if she was being harassed by this cop.

No one thought she was in any danger.

Her pulse was racing now, and there was a strange pounding against her temple. The cop was saying something to her, but the pounding in her head was so loud that his words were disjointed. He might as well have been underwater for all the sense she could make of it.

Icy fear coursed through her body. Jane flinched, pressing herself against the car. The cop reached out to touch her.

Loki's yapping turned into high-pitched barks as he tugged and twisted against his restraints. Her heart was slamming inside her chest now. She almost didn't see the black limousine until it screeched up beside them.

The passenger door flew open as a powerful figure leaped out of the car. "Take your hands off her!"

The last thing Logan had needed was the distress call that had come through Summers. Thanks to Jackson's meddling, he'd fumbled his new lines and had barely gotten through an entire scene. Subsequently Venger, their director, had spent the day screaming about his incompetence.

When he'd rushed off to help Jane, the last thing he'd heard was Venger kicking over a chair as he threatened to have him replaced. Still, his work issues had taken a backseat when he'd seen Jane, pressed up against his car, with that cop looming aggressively over her.

All the color had gone from her face. She looked as frightened as a child.

And something primal in him had been activated. He didn't stop to think about his actions. He only knew that he had to get her away from him.

He had to stop that look of utter fear that had come over her face.

He'd shouted at the man, his voice carrying so much authority that it seemed he was the one in charge and not the policeman, whose hands dropped from Jane's shoulders like stone. An ugly red flush crept along the sides of his neck. He jumped back.

"Mr. Steel! I... I was just asking your friend about her relationship to you."

Logan's eyes were as hard as the steel in his name.

He looked angry, furious even, his fists clenched down by his sides. There was the faintest residue of make-up on his face, as if he hadn't had time to clean it all off before he'd arrived here, though he was dressed in his own clothes.

The drivers who had been passing by, disinterested in her predicament, slowed their cars. Some pointed their phones at them, recognizing Logan.

"Her relationship to me, or lack of it, isn't any of your concern. What is, though, is why you have stopped her in the first place? What exactly has she done?"

Under Logan's burning rage, the cop was losing some of his bluster.

"You have it mistaken. I didn't stop her. I found her here with the car pulled over in a very dangerous situation. It was only as we were talking that I recognized your dog. As it seemed unlikely that you would let a stranger have him, I wanted to establish her reason for having him."

His blatant lies caused outrage to flood through Jane, turning her blood hot.

"Is that true?" Logan turned those intense green eyes to her.

"No. I was trying to explain that I was having car trouble, but he wasn't interested in that. He just kept asking questions about you."

The angrier Logan became, the more his eyes glittered like diamonds. Rather than explode with rage, his voice grew quieter, something that made both the cop and Jane, nervous. She shivered, wrapping her arms around herself.

"How did he find out about me?"

"He called Summers to confirm my identity. Summers is the one who must have mentioned you."

"Mr. Steel, far be it from me to interrupt what is obviously a lover's quarrel, but there's a bigger problem at play here: she was driving without a licence which is a criminal offence in California. I should arrest her right now."

Logan closed his eyes, unable to reconcile the day he was having. His shoulders tensed. For a brief moment, he looked like a beaten man who had been shoved into a hole, but was trying to claw his way out.

And he found his way in one simple word.

Jane had heard it too, the opening that Logan jumped at.

"You said you *should* arrest her. Is there is something I

can do to persuade you to drop this? This is a unique situation after all."

The cops eyes turned shrewd. "Give me a moment." He went back to his car and made a call.

Jane wrung her hands, compelled to both explain *and* apologize.

"I wasn't thinking about a licence. I just wanted to do something for myself. I had no idea it was going to end like this. I'm sorry for any inconvenience I may have caused."

"It's not your fault. I didn't think of it either. I should have, though. Then we wouldn't be in this mess."

His words were clipped. She wasn't sure if he was angry at himself or her. With the kind of life he lived, she wouldn't have thought much was out of his control, yet he was genuinely worried. Before she could make any more of it, the cop returned, a jaunt to his step. His small eyes narrowed into slits.

"It's clear this boils down to an unfortunate state of affairs. While I am sorry for the recent difficulties you have faced, a crime has been committed today. Question is, what are we going to do about that?"

Jane frowned. "I don't understand what you are asking."

A snort of disbelief shot out of Logan.

"I think I do."

He turned to the policeman. "What can I do that would be a suitable gesture of appreciation for dropping the charges?"

The cop smiled at Logan pleasantly, as if the two were exchanging pleasantries as opposed to the blackmail that was going down.

"Well, now, my missus is just the biggest fan of yours. It's coming up to our twenty-fifth anniversary. I think she would just about die if I were able to take her to one of your movie premiers. You know, a big one, with lots of other celebrities in attendance?"

There was a lazy half smile on Logan's lips, though his eyes were so cold, it was a miracle the cop didn't freeze under their gaze.

"Give me your details. I'll have my manager send you a pair of tickets for my next movie."

The cop beamed, white teeth glinting. "That is mighty kind of you, mighty kind. Of course, there will be an overnight stay at a five-star hotel too? That would finish off the night like no other."

Logan didn't bother to speak, managing only a curt nod.

The cop opened up his notebook, scribbled down his details and handed them to Logan. To his credit, Logan didn't screw up the paper like most would have, folding it into his hand instead.

He was able to hide his contempt well.

There was nothing in his eyes or his expression that revealed how he felt about him, but it was just something about his demeanor, the very energy pouring off him that told Jane how much he resented being put into this position.

And it was all her fault.

Great way to repay him for all of his kindness.

"I think that's all for now. See that you don't drive without a licence again. You won't get this lucky, twice."

He got into his car, leaned out of the window, grabbed Logan's hand and started pumping up and down.

"Mr. Steel, it was truly great to meet you. Thank you again. My wife won't believe me when I tell her what just happened."

Logan extracted his hand, surreptitiously wiping it on his pants, but the cop had turned away. Sticking a hand outside the window, he waved and left.

The silence between them was as wide as a gulf.

Feeling awful about what had just taken place, Jane reached out to him.

"You didn't need to do that. You should have let him arrest me. I did commit a crime after all."

The words stuck to her tongue. She couldn't believe how stupid she had been, and that this was the result.

Why was she so dumb?

Logan stared at her with a strange expression.

"I don't think jail is a suitable course of action."

He was being kind, but Jane knew she didn't deserve his kindness.

"I can't believe you'll have to pay for my mistake."

He laughed a laugh as bitter as a lemon peel.

"This is LA. This is how things work around here. Nobody does what's right. Every one does what benefits them."

The words had barely left his mouth when a flashbulb popped in their faces, blinding them. Jane shrank back as black spots danced in her eyes.

"What the hell…?" Logan spun around, searching for the culprit as more flashes popped, followed by the sound of a camera clicking.

A low growl rumbled out of Logan as he spotted the paparazzi hanging out of his jeep behind them; he must have followed him from the movie set.

"Come on!" Logan yelled. "Can't I get one moment of peace?"

The photographer, a normal-looking man in his forties with a balding head and round face, shot him an apologetic smile. "Sorry Logan, it's just my job."

"Then you should get a new one. One that doesn't piss people off so much."

The man shrugged, set his camera down and drove off. Jane attempted to break the sudden silence his absence had caused.

"Are you going back… to the set?"

"Yes."

She tried not to flinch at the anger in his voice, knowing she deserved worse.

"What about the car?"

"It's already been taken care off. The tow truck will be here soon."

He couldn't look at her. It was obvious he was sick of the sight of her.

"Loki and I will wait here for them then. You can go back to work."

His jaw clenched. He looked down at her. She became acutely aware of how much taller he was, at least a foot and a half. She felt so small in his shadow, and it had nothing to do with his fame.

The seconds ticked past. When he finally spoke, it was through gritted teeth. He pointed to the limo.

"Get in. We'll drop you both home and then I'll go."

Jane opened her mouth to object but stopped at the look he gave.

"Just get in the car, Jane. Please."

Jane got in the car.

15

Streets flashed past the window. Their sight usually offered a comforting familiarity, though tonight, nothing could get through his growing sense of unease and the resulting anger that never seemed too far behind.

All day he had had to deal with his co-star — an up-and-coming comedian — throwing it in his face that he was not the main attraction of this movie.

Logan had never been much of a diva, but he was used to the kind of respect afforded him for being the star of each of his last ten movies, so to have been demoted like this — and to a comedian who owed his newfound fame to his father-in-law's clout in the industry and not, through any talent of his own — burned like a ring of fire.

It was nepotism at its ugliest, something Logan had come across time and again and which never ceased to amaze him how the outdated practice hadn't only become accepted, but was now the norm.

He was pretty sure the practice had led to the recent decline of the box office and the subsequent spat of terrible reboots. It was probably those same people who greenlit movies about emojis, of all things. And toys.

He missed the days when toys were made of movies, and not the other way around.

Even with the crap Jackson had been dealing, he had been determined to shut up and do the job to the best of his ability when his manager had called, sounding more stressed than he was comfortable with.

He'd been stuck in the middle rehearsing a tense scene, comprised largely of chunks of dialogue, something that would have caused even the most prepared actor concern, but Logan had an additional issue.

Since he was young, he had known that there was something different about him. While friends at school found classes easy and blew past homework like it was nothing, Logan struggled… a lot.

It wasn't that he wasn't smart — everyone knew he was — from his school teachers, to the mother who had single-handedly raised him, there was just something about the act of reading and writing that proved problematic.

It didn't matter how many times he read over a sentence, the words and letters seemed to move around. It wasn't until he failed several classes in a row that his favorite teacher investigated his situation. Once she had spent one-on-one time with him, she quickly realized what the problem was.

Logan was dyslexic.

Despite learning he had an actual condition that would make it more difficult to read and write, Logan never wanted it to hold him back. Having seen his mom return home day after day, heavy shadows under her eyes, and with all kinds of ailments from the three jobs she held down, he was determined to do right by her.

His mother's sacrifices would not be in vain.

It took years of constant effort to get a handle on the dyslexia, staying home to do the required work, watching as his best friend — and next-door neighbor — went out on dates and had a good time.

When acting came into his life, one of the unexpected bonuses had been how little physical reading was involved with it, and how there were other ways he could learn the scripts; some that didn't even require reading.

Many of the most successful movie stars didn't bother to learn their scripts, preferring to have someone feed them their lines during each scene. This wasn't something that interested him, however.

Part of the joy of acting was getting into the head of a character, to breathe life into them. How could he do that with someone feeding him lines in the moment? There would be no spontaneity, no playing around and playing off his co-stars.

While that kind of laziness wasn't for him, Logan discovered he could pay for an assistant to record the script into audio files that he would listen to — much like his favorite audiobooks — and memorize his lines that way.

He'd tried this method on occasion, but preferred to keep it as a last resort: there really wasn't anything like reading a script organically and letting the words imprint into his head.

Of course, after his string of recent flops, this particular job had become his most difficult to date. And with

Jackson egging him on, it was getting harder to stay on his best behavior.

This kind of competition was par for the course: friendly, even not-so-friendly camaraderie, was normal on a film set. He couldn't get along with everyone. Most times, he didn't even want to. Sometimes, he just wanted to be left alone to do the work.

Instead of using his time productively today, he had been forced to go out here and bargain with that idiot cop. Technically, he could have sent his manager to handle it, but Jane was his responsibility and for whatever reason, he needed to keep her safe.

He needed to protect her.

And that worried him greatly.

They had only known each other a few days, and much of that time, they hadn't even spent together. It would be easy to blame it on the memory loss, but seeing her in that fragile state on the beach, with those vivid bruises and cuts that criss-crossed her legs, added with that vulnerable manner of hers, he'd felt the overwhelming need to take care of her.

Worse still, he'd been attracted to her, which in the moment, had felt all kinds of wrong.

A quick glance at the Cartier watch he wore today revealed it was almost five now. He'd been gone from the set for almost three hours.

Three hours that would be billed to him if this downtime wasn't covered by the movie's insurance. Three hours where several hundred people would have nothing to do, but wait for his return as they bitched about him.

What a great way to begin a new job.

The annoying thing was, this was exactly the kind of

behavior people expected of him. They expected him to be a bad boy. It was precisely why he made great pains to be the opposite. He wasn't one of the movie stars who liked to inflate their ego by deliberately turning up as the last one on set.

Defending himself wasn't sexy, however, and it was something his PR team had been very against, so for better or worse, Logan had gone along with his reps's advice.

For years he had done everything they advised — after all, he was paying a lot of money for their expertize. When a case of mistaken identity created a bad boy image for him, they had run with it, explaining that the average housewife and mother secretly dreamed of being swept away by a rugged, bad boy movie star.

Logan hadn't been interested in the games, thinking the entire thing ridiculous. He'd wanted his work to stand up for itself, only to be told that no one really cared who he was as a person.

Movie stars were like rock stars and supermodels: they weren't real people. They were beautiful but untouchable, to be revered or despised — and nothing in between. If you fell in the middle of those camps, you were as good as dead.

All publicity was good publicity.

His phone vibrated with the arrival of an email. Half expecting a message from his irate director, he scrolled to his inbox only to notice that Jane had been speaking.

He'd been so lost in his thoughts, he hadn't realized. He considered apologizing when his eyes took in the subject of the email that had just been sent.

It wasn't from his director, as he'd suspected, but Trevor. And the heading for the email from his manager said URGENT!!! That much, he could read straight away.

He itched to open the email. Feeling Jane's eyes on him, he decided it could wait a few moments. They were already pulling into his drive.

The car had barely stopped moving before she flung open the door.

"Thank you," she said, though this directed at his chauffeur. Daryl smiled a little sheepishly through the rear-view mirror, having picked up on the uncomfortable vibes in the car.

"Of course, ma'am."

To Logan, she simply stared. Waiting for him to say something, anything.

He wished he'd been paying attention to her and he was about to admit as much when his phone blew up with messages and calls.

Something was going on.

"One second," he asked Jane, even as her face took on an irate expression. He listened to the voicemail from Trevor and cursed loudly.

He considered not telling her the news.

She likely wanted to put the day out of her mind, but it wasn't done with either of them yet. He squared his shoulders.

"That photographer who followed me from set? He has already posted those pictures of us by the car. It's all over the web that I was arguing with my new girlfriend when she had broken down by the side of the road."

Jane's eyes were round disks of shock. *"Girlfriend?"*

"Girlfriend," Logan confirmed. "This day keeps getting better and better."

"I can call the sites and clear this up," Jane began, unable to believe that things could have been taken so much out of context. And so fast, too.

"That's a terrible suggestion."

He didn't have time to explain what he meant by that. The seconds the words left his mouth, Jane got out of the car and took her bags from Daryl.

Keeping her head high, even though she could feel the sting of approaching tears, she tugged on Loki's leash. Loki tossed him a sad look as the two disappeared inside the house.

16

Logan watched her figure retreat into the giant house and he knew he couldn't leave it like that, not least because Armageddon was about to occur, judging by the amount of messages he was suddenly receiving.

His phone was ringing off the hook, and Logan didn't need to look at the screen to know that most of the calls were coming from Trevor. Wanting to hold off on whatever the crisis was, he hit decline and got out of the car.

"You want me to wait for you?" Daryl asked. Daryl had been with him for years and was one of the few people he trusted with the daily ins and outs of his life. Daryl wasn't the chatty type and barely spoke two words. Logan liked this about him. He liked the calmness the man exuded, which is why he'd kept him on his service for almost the entire time he'd been in the movies.

"I'm not sure yet. Can you wait and I'll let you know when I do?"

Daryl nodded. "Of course."

Logan's phone started ringing again. In the short time

their conversation had taken ten more notifications of missed calls and voicemails had appeared.

This was going to be bad.

Trying to ignore the wave of dread that was creeping up his spine, he finally answered the phone. Trevor didn't wait for a greeting before launching into his tirade.

"Maybe, we weren't clear enough when we said our priority was to work on repairing your damaged reputation. That meant, being a good boy, not getting into trouble, certainly not being seen abusing your new girlfriend in front of a policeman. None of that is what we discussed Logan, did you not get the memo?"

"Of course I got the memo Trevor, I'm the one who created it. This is another misunderstanding. And for your information, we didn't have a fight, and she's not my girlfriend."

"So not only have you abused a woman in front of the law, now you're going to deny her importance to you?" Trevor's voice had risen an octave.

"Why would I lie about something like this? She's the woman I saved on the beach."

"The one you wouldn't allow us to run a story on, the story, might I add, that would have absolved you in the public eye, turning you into a hero again. *That woman?*"

"Her name is Jane..." Logan supplied helpfully.

"I swear to God, Logan..." Trevor paused to take a breath, fighting the urge to reach down the phone to throttle his client and friend.

"It wasn't anything big. She went out for a drive but forgot that she doesn't have a license right now..."

"Let me get this straight. She was driving without a license. In California, in your car?" Logan could almost hear the thoughts running through Trevor's mind as he tried to weave a narrative that the public might buy.

Logan's footsteps echoed in the hallway as he made his way inside. "She knows how to drive. I'm sure she had a license before she lost her memory. It's not her fault she doesn't know who she is."

Trevor's thunderous silence spoke volumes. When he spoke again, his voice was pained. "I think you're going to have to start from the beginning. And don't leave any detail out."

Thirty minutes later, Kitty opened the front door to a barrage of people.

Behind them, an array of expensive cars littered the driveway. She showed them into the living area where Logan sat, waiting, nursing a whiskey.

Without greeting him, they started talking over one another.

"What have I told you about not doing anything without running it by me first?" This had come from a tiny Asian woman with an equally tiny waist and a fake weave of long black hair that she wore in a sleek ponytail that reached down to her butt.

Her face was covered in make up that emphasized her almond-shaped eyes and the sharp planes of her face. Not even five-feet-tall, she wore towering stilettos that boosted her up. Her ponytail whipped from side to side as she stormed up to Logan, glaring beneath dramatic false eyelashes.

"Adele, lovely as always to see you."

His publicist folded her arms across her chest, red talons glittering dangerously. "Shut up."

To Kitty, she said something in their native Cantonese.

However hard Adele was on the people around her, she was always respectful to Kitty, recognizing the life the older woman had experienced. Logan couldn't be sure, but it seemed the two might even have been friends outside of work, though the thought often instilled panic in him — even if he didn't think she would betray his trust, the thought of Kitty revealing his secrets to Adele made him break out into a cold sweat.

Several more people came in after Adele.

Logan spotted his assistant, a nice girl in her early twenties called Vicky. Originally raised in Iowa, she was as wholesome as they came and refreshingly different from the girls who usually flocked to this city. She flashed him an apologetic smile, knowing he hadn't called her there as the last person arrived.

Trevor wasn't a tall man, maybe two heads shorter than Logan on a good day. He worked out fairly frequently in the gym but hadn't been able to shift the extra weight he carried around his stomach that he could never quite hide, no matter how expensive the designer suit he wore.

Logan had been his client for the past decade. Trevor had stuck by and mentored him when no one else in town had believed in him. The two had a solid relationship, and he was the closest Logan had to a best friend.

"I see the gang's all here," Trevor commented wryly.

"Why don't you all make yourselves at home," Logan directed at the room. His sarcasm wasn't even acknowledged. Kitty took drinks orders from the assembled group, trying not to appear flustered by the unannounced company.

"I don't have any food or snacks ready." She seemed mortified that she was letting him down.

"It's fine, Kitty. None of them will be staying long," Logan replied firmly.

Adele raised a thinly plucked brow. A smile came over her lips that never quite reached her eyes. "It's cute that you think you're in charge of this meeting." She sat down and crossed one leg over the other, a high-heeled foot swinging daintily.

Logan knew better than to tackle her head-on.

Overexcited by all the new people, Loki made his way around the room, introducing himself to each of them. Vicky beamed when he came her way. She played with him until Adele's swinging shoe caught his attention. He stared at the sharp point of the heel, mesmerized.

"I understand you're all concerned; I am too. But this whole thing is a mistake, and we just need to figure out a way to fill in the press while respecting both mine and Jane's privacy. This doesn't have to be a big deal."

"Of course it is!" Adele snapped, unable to hide her irritation any longer. "You have been single by design! When the time was right — when *I* decided it was right — we were going to reveal your new relationship to the world. I have spent months vetting suitable candidates. I don't give a rat's ass who you screw in private, but who you mess around with in public, that's on me. Have you any idea how much of my time and effort you have wasted with this stunt of yours?"

Adele tapped her stiletto on the oak floorboards. The sound of it rattled his head though it had a different effect on Loki. The puppy hunkered down until his stomach pressed against the floor and stalked that swinging foot.

When he was only inches away, his jaws opened wide to snap around her heel…

Adele jerked her foot away. "Don't you dare!" She hissed at him. Startled by the tone in her voice, Loki backed away from her like she was something terrible, then ran behind the sofa to hide. Logan gave his dog a level stare.

"Oh, but you'll listen to *her*?"

Loki's only response was a sad bark before retreating to a fluffy dog bed that sat in the corner of the room. He circled the bed and laid down, staring at the rest of them like a wounded soul. Ignoring his theatrics, Logan addressed Adele.

"I already told you that you don't need to do that. I can find my own girlfriend. I don't need you auditioning a love interest for me."

"And you've been in this industry for how long?" She rolled her eyes as if she was talking to an idiot. "Your next relationship was planned to coincide with the launch of this new movie, but now all anybody wants to talk about is the ordinary woman you have fallen in love with. Speaking of which, why isn't she here? She is the cause of all this."

Logan shook his head. "Oh no. You'll terrify her. Jane is not a part of this madness. She's an honest victim. We have to leave her out this."

Trevor's his eyes held an apology. "I don't think that's going to be possible. Her face is already plastered everywhere. If she doesn't hear of this soon, it's only a matter of time.

The woman herself chose that moment to step into the room. Her eyes looked wild, like a trapped animal. She'd obviously seen the news. At the sight of them all, she stopped dead.

"I was looking for Logan, but I see I'm interrupting."

"Actually, we're here to talk about you so you might as well sit for this."

Confusion shone from her eyes. "Me?"

"Well, you are the mysterious woman of the hour, are you not? It's Jane, isn't it? We need to have a discussion about how we're going to deal with this catastrophe."

"Maybe we could take this down a notch or two?" Trevor chided, taking pity on Jane who looked almost ready to pass out. "Jane, please, take a seat."

She perched on the end of Logan's sofa, wondering who on earth these people were? Logan introduced them all.

"I don't understand why this is even in the news. Can't you set them straight?"

Adele looked at Jane with a half exasperated smirk.

"You want us to tell the public that Logan found a woman with amnesia on the beach and brought her home out of the goodness of his heart?"

Jane was bewildered by the question. "But that's what happened?"

Adele continued. "Has it ever occurred to you how that might look to the average person? There are plenty of haters out there, people who spend all day sitting behind their computers, waiting to spew hateful remarks about anyone and everyone, but they leave their most vehement vitriol for the rich and famous because they represent everything that those people will never have."

Her small hands waved in front of her, emphasizing her point. "And what happens when we see people with things we don't have? We resent them. We become jealous and filled with envy."

She pointed at Logan. "These people don't need any more excuse to hate him. Nobody is going to believe the truth, and if they did, they'll only twist it into something it isn't. It is amazing what madness people will come up with, and it's my job to handle that madness, even if it means spinning the truth into one that will be easier to swallow."

Kitty hurried in with a tray of drinks. Several glasses of champagne were handed out from his extensive wine cellar. It didn't slip Logan's notice that even in this stressful situation, his team were of sound enough mind to pick one of the most expensive brands he stocked.

There was one drink that stood out among the sea of champagne flutes. A simple cup of tea that Kitty handed to Jane.

"I made this for myself, but I think you'll be needing it," Kitty revealed.

Jane smiled her appreciation and held onto the tea as if it was a lifeline.

"We'll fix this," Trevor commented. "She is right, though, much as I hate to admit it."

The curve on Adele's lips grew wider.

"I know how to fix it. It's pretty simple, actually. We need to pretend the two of you are in a relationship, a very happy one. No one can mention where she came from. I'm assuming there's not going to be an issue with her real identity? As far as I've heard, they've had no real leads on it."

Logan wasn't sure why he wasn't surprised that Adele

knew that: the woman had contacts everywhere. It was partly why she was so good at her job.

"We'll make up the background details, nothing you won't be uncomfortable with. We need to run this until the movie comes out and is a success. Then the two of you can part ways. I'm sure Logan will help you, Jane, so that you'll be well taken care of."

She meant money. Adele was suggesting that they fake a relationship in return for financial compensation. Jane set her mug onto the coffee table, almost spilling it in her haste to put it down.

"We can't do that. It's a complete lie. And what if I'm already married, but I just can't remember?"

Trevor nodded, looking troubled. "That's a good point. She could be married already. The last thing we need is her actual husband turning up."

As much as he loved his manager and his team in general, Logan could kick them all right now. "Real people's lives are affected. Maybe a little more tact and consideration could be shown."

The general tone and chatter quietened at his request. Jane's eyes met his across the sofa. She seemed to be silently pleading with him to end this madness. He wished he could.

Trevor turned his attention to Jane. "I know this must seem very strange to you, but this is how business is done in Hollywood. You've been caught up in this unfortunate mess, but Adele's suggestion is probably the easiest one for us to work with. I know this must be hard: you've been through so much. But since you're already staying here with Logan, and the rumor mill is already spinning out of control, do you think you'll be to help us with this? It shouldn't be for too long."

Jane knitted her hands together. "I don't know. What if I'm asked questions about me, about who I am?"

Seeing a crack in her armor, Adele smiled with encouragement. "The beauty of this is, you can be whoever you want to be. We can work with you to create a background you are comfortable with."

Jane swallowed drily as several faces stared back at her, waiting for a decision.

Logan's chest seized. She looked like a rabbit caught in the headlights while a pack of wolves descended. She had no one to protect her, no one to stop them from feasting on her vulnerable body.

"Guys, this is too much to ask of her. You need to come up with another solution."

Her eyes slid to Logan, so blue they reminded him of the ocean he lived by.

"I want to help. I'm just uncomfortable with having to lie to so many people, and to fabricate a life for myself when I already don't know who I am. This is a lot to take in."

"Oh, don't think because of the way I come across, that I don't understand how tough this must be for you," Adele replied. "Contrary to what some might say, I have feelings too. We won't be asking too much of you. You just have to go on a few public dates with him, do some photo shoots. Most women would die for this kind of opportunity."

She had said the wrong thing. She knew it the instant Jane's eyes turned hard.

"Most women haven't lost their memory."

"I think that's Jane's way of saying a polite no," Logan started only for Jane to correct him.

"I will help you. It's the least I can do to repay you for your kindness. But can we please not do anything too elaborate? Even if this is the norm, it's not my norm."

Trevor clapped his hands together, startling the room.

"Excellent. Thank you so much, Jane. Logan and the rest of us, the whole team, we really appreciate you stepping up like this. I'll get the contracts drawn up, you'll have them by the evening. Now, why don't we get out of their way. Adele, have your team come up with a couple of profiles that we can run through with Jane in the morning."

Adele nodded, typing into her phone. "Already on it."

"Jane," Trevor continued. "If you have any questions or if you are not happy with anything, you just call me. Logan will give you my details."

He looked to the others. "OK. Let's go. We've all got work to do."

They exited en masse, leaving Logan and Jane, the latter looking like she wasn't quite in her body.

"I know they can be a bit much, but they mean well."

She looked so frozen that Logan had to do something about it. He took hold of her hands in his. They were ice cold, but the heat that came out of her eyes at his touch could have scorched them both.

His heart began to race. What was it about this woman? He took a moment to compose himself before he spoke again.

"If you need more time to think things through, or if you change your mind and want to call the whole thing off, it's fine. My team are always pushy, but they work for me, so if you want out, you just tell me and I will let them know."

Sincerity shone from his eyes. Jane lost herself in his gaze. His hands felt so warm that she could feel their heat all the way down to her feet, it seemed.

This moment meant a lot to her.

That he would take this time to ensure she didn't regret her decision… it let her know that she had come to the right choice.

"Thank you." She said simply.

He squeezed her hands as they stared at each other. The air was alive with electricity.

"Oh. Sorry," Kitty apologized, lowering her eyes to the ground as a blush stained her cheeks. "I came to get their glasses."

She went to leave. Logan let go of Jane's hands and stood up.

"Go ahead. I should get back to work."

Nodding at Jane, he exited the room.

17

Logan returned to the set, steeling himself for the fallout his long absence had likely caused, while Jane retreated to the serenity of the pool house, taking Loki with her.

Her mind was a whirl with this new "relationship" she found herself in.

Having seen her face splashed over the entertainment news channels, she had changed to a radio channel, deciding she didn't need that kind of information in her face.

Time came and went until she had to eat or she'd be no good to anyone. She decided something more substantial than eggs was needed. It was time to see how well she really coped in a kitchen. If nothing else, it would help to take her mind off the day's madness.

Rummaging through the fridge, she settled on grilled chicken breast, asparagus and potatoes, marveling at how easily the art of cooking was coming back to her.

She peeled the potatoes, slicing them thinly to bake.

She seasoned and marinaded the chicken breast in a simple lemon butter. Jazz played from the hidden speakers in the walls. She hummed along to a tune. It was halfway through the song before she realized that she knew it.

She started on the asparagus, washing then trimming the ends on the chopping board…

A memory rushed into her mind, startling her into dropping the knife. It clattered into the sink but she ignored it, focused on what she could see in her head.

Her long, elegant hands rinsed a colander of white asparagus under a chrome tap. What she could see of the kitchen was modern in style, with black graphite counters and mahogany cupboards. There was jazz playing in the memory too, though a different song. Pots sat on the stove, steam misting the air. She lifted her gaze from the hands, hoping to see something of the house that could give her a clue of its location, but the flashback vanished.

She was back in the pool house.

A relieved smile spread over her face. Her memory was finally starting to come back to her. She was hit with the compulsion to tell Logan, but in his absence, she ran over to Loki instead. He lay on the sofa, demolishing what looked to be another shoe of Logan's but at her approached, he sat up.

"Loki! I'm starting to remember things!"

She grabbed his paws and started to dance with him. Caught up in her excitement, Loki barked and spun around on the sofa until he grew dizzy and fell. She celebrated with him a while longer before returning to finish cooking her meal.

When it was all done, she ate by the roaring fire. The

dancing flames healed her soul and provided comfort to Loki, stretched out in front of it.

She cleaned up the kitchen, enjoying the simple domesticity of the task, and was sipping from a glass of wine when footsteps approached. Not the light quick steps that she'd come to associate with Kitty, but the weary tread of a tired man.

When Logan's face came into view under the string of garden lights draped over the terrace, she was taken aback by the vulnerability she saw in him. For the first time since she'd known him, he looked like a normal man — still as handsome as sin — but one in need of a hug.

Bathed by the warm, flickering light of the fire, wearing a white dress, she looked almost like an angel. Logan's breath caught and had to swallow. Seeing that she was staring at him, his shoulders came up and he injected an energy that he didn't feel into his voice.

"Am I disturbing you?"

She swung her bare feet off the sofa, intending to get up.

"Don't get up on my account. I'm not going to be long."

Loki woke from his slumber and ran to greet him, tail wagging a mile a minute. He jumped into the air, desperate to nuzzle Logan's hand only to keep missing it. A whine of frustration burst out of him. Taking pity on him, Logan petted his head, sending the dog into a frenzy of barks.

A hint of a smile appeared on his lips that he tried to hide. Jane wondered why he thought he couldn't show affection for the puppy, given that it was the natural outcome of spending any time with one at all. After a few moments of play, he pulled away from the dog.

"I remembered something tonight," Jane volunteered tentatively. She had been bursting to tell him, but now that he was actually there, she wasn't sure if he'd even want to know.

"From your past?"

She took comfort that he sounded interested. "It wasn't much. I just remembered a song on the radio. Then I saw myself washing asparagus at what must have been my home."

"That's good news, and a great sign that your memory will probably return with time."

The smile he gave softened his face, taking away the edge that was normally there and made her stomach flip flop. "So, what brings you here?"

She didn't know why she had asked, only that she'd had to say something so it wouldn't look so obvious that he was having an effect on her.

It must be the wine.

"I'm actually here on business."

The flash of disappointment his words caused filled her with surprise.

"This is for you."

He handed her a thick white A4 envelope.

"It's the contract Trevor drew up."

"Already?"

"I think he has a couple of standard ones ready to adapt for any scenario," he replied. "He likes to be prepared for all eventualities."

Jane tested the weight of the packet in her hand. It weighed more than a few sheets of paper should have.

Opening it, she took out the paper-clipped document that must have been at least 50 pages long. Logan caught her shocked look and quickly explained.

"Is mostly just legal jargon. There shouldn't be anything in there of concern."

Her eyes skinned over the unfamiliar legalese, the words swimming through her head like a black cloud.

"I thought it was just going to be a simple memo that would say we both agreed to this, and maybe a confidentiality clause. This is much more than I expected. I don't even understand what half of it means?"

"Do you need me to get you a lawyer to talk you through it? Trevor assured me that there's nothing out of the norm in there. He said this is the usual type of deal that gets shopped around for things like this."

"You'll have to give me a moment to read through it."

She expected Logan to leave, but he headed toward the kitchen. "Go ahead. Do you have any coffee left?"

Jane pointed to the coffee machine, her eyes already focused on the contract. She read through the pages as fast as she could, trying to make sense of the complicated terms while Logan drank coffee and played with Loki, to the puppy's unending delight.

When she was done, she felt as if her head would explode.

"This is crazy. Do you know what you can do to me if I break this contract? Look at this passage here." She showed him the paragraph that particularly concerned her. "See what this says?"

Logan barely looked at the words before glancing away.

"I would never come after you if something happened.

This is just Trevor, looking out for my interests. It's what he's paid a lot of money to do. Please, don't take this personally. This is just... "

"Business," Jane finished for him.

"Right."

"But if Trevor is looking out for your interests, then who is looking out for mine?"

At least he didn't try to brush that remark away, though she was taken aback by the lack of interest he showed in the actual contract itself. He'd not bothered to read the section she'd pointed out to him.

"If you're not happy with it, or the sum of money suggested, we can forget the whole thing. I can call them right now and tell him the deal is off. Just say the word and I'll make the call."

To make good on this, his finger hovered over the call button. Any other person and she would have thought he was full of bluster, but there was something in his eyes that made her believe him. Then there was the undeniable fact that he'd already gone out of his way to help her.

"I trust you. Do you have a pen?"

"You don't have to sign right this minute, Jane. We can wait until the morning..."

She shook her head. "I'd rather just get this over and done with. Besides, I literally have nothing to lose."

He handed her a Mont Blanc pen that weighed almost as much as she did. She signed the contract and handed it back to him.

"What now?" Jane asked. "What happens next?"

Logan tucked the contract into his pocket.

"I suspect Adele and her team will be in touch tomorrow. She'll likely rehearse your story with you in case you are stopped by anyone curious enough to ask where you came from. There'll be interviews of course, though we'll arrange those when you are ready."

A jolt of shock sent her teeth chattering. "Interviews? There wasn't anything about interviews in the contract."

"It kind of comes with the territory, but we won't do any that you are not fully briefed on. We'll make sure to get questions from the journalists ahead of time so that we can prepare the answers. We won't let them ask anything we haven't agreed prior. I'll handle all this. You just have to come along for the ride."

He made it sound so simple and easy.

Why did she feel as if she had just made a deal with the devil?

18

Everywhere she looked, people hurried around like bees.

Bright lights beamed down, artificially illuminating the New York city set that Jane stood in.

It was so surreal.

She had seen the wooden planks and fittings of the unfinished back side of the brownstone buildings yet, from the front, she could swear that the tree-lined street was real.

She touched a leaf from a branch that dangled overhead. Plastic. There was no life in the thing, no energy or that feeling of groundedness that came with a living tree.

It was all as fake as the tarmac beneath her feet. Only the cloudless blue sky was real, that and the endless bustling of the film crew.

Loki, her trusty companion, strained against his leash, stalking a fluttering piece of paper that danced in the breeze caused by a giant wind machine. She loosened her grip on him, letting the leash go slack. With a cute wiggle of his butt, Loki leaped forward and caught his victim between two fluffy paws. He whined excitedly, snapping his jaws at the piece of paper which Jane now saw was today's call sheet.

She had seen them everywhere, but it was only when she had asked a production assistant that she was told what it was. Put together by the assistant director, it was the daily schedule detailing what scenes would be shot that day, where they would be shooting, and what cast or specialist personnel or equipment might be needed for it.

"Can I see that before you destroy it?"

Making a game of it, she stole the call sheet from right under Loki's nose. He took it with good form, tail thumping on the ground as he waited for her to play some more.

"You can have it back in a minute."

Her only answer was another whine of excitement, followed by the lowering of his two front paws while his butt pointed toward the sky as he found a leaf to chase after.

She scanned over the details, trying to make sense of them. There was a lot of information on the page: from the weather, expected time of sunrise and sunset, when they would be breaking for lunch, as well as the two scenes that would be shot. There wasn't much cast listed today, only Logan and two others. She wondered what the scenes would entail.

A group of men walked past, all manner of tools clipped to the belts that were slung around their waists. The most commanding of them, a silver-haired man with a pencil tucked in his ear, held up what looked to be a drawing of the interior of the Statue of Liberty. Their passing conversation drifted over as they calculated the measurement and work involved with creating such a set.

Someone hurried past, speaking into a radio, guiding extras dressed in twenties style clothing. The movie was a period piece based on the true story of a crime lord who almost took down New York. She didn't know much about it, just that it was supposed to have a great story.

The door to a large trailer, opened.

"Jane? Do we have a Jane here?" A production assistant called out in a voice loaded with impatience.

Jane had to fight the ridiculous urge to raise her hand. "Yes, that's me."

"Logan will see you now."

She rushed off, radio chattering, leaving the door open for her.

Inside, the trailer was covered with lush cream carpet. *So impractical.* She'd hate to be the cleaner.

Long leather couches, mahogany surfaces, and discreet lighting gave the car a sophisticated yet comfortable feel. A 65-inch television overlooked the seating area where a glass coffee table was covered with a thick script printed on cream paper.

A rainbow of notes had been stuck to the script, the handwriting on them large and clear. Surprisingly, there were also tiny drawn pictures on the notes among the sentences. At a laugh from the end of the trailer, she glanced over.

A makeup area had been created in what might have been a bedroom prior. Logan sat in a swivel chair in front of a large mirror lit with bright bulbs. His hair was expertly styled by an ultra slim man with blue hair and a pencil mustache that made Jane think of the villain in old cartoons.

Seeing Logan, Loki barked and bolted for him, tugging the leash from her hand. He launched himself into his lap, but only made it half on. His back legs paddled the air comically, though the stylist didn't seem too amused.

"I can't work if you insist on bouncing around like that!"

But Loki didn't care about him, lavishing love on Logan's face until he had to force him down.

"I liked it more when you didn't have the fleabag."

"You and I both, Federic. You and I both," Logan responded with a wry shake of his head. Though his words seemed harsh, he softened them with a stroke of Loki's head. Loki sighed happily when his attention was caught by a pair of his shoes that sat on the floor. His ears pricked up, his mouth already opening in anticipation.

"No, Loki! Those are for the movie!"

Jane had been prepared for such a moment. Opening her bag, she took out one of the shoes Loki had already been using as a chew toy.

"You don't want that one, Loki. You want this tasty shoe that you've already started on." She waved it at him in a tantalizing manner, causing him to drool at the sight. He bounded to her, snatched the shoe out of her hand, then promptly went to work demolishing it, the other shoes completely forgotten.

"It worked." No one was more shocked than she was.

A giant smile of welcome spread over Logan's lips.

"Perfect timing. You always know what to do with him. How was your ride, Darling?"

He strode toward her covering the distance in three quick strides. Taking her hands in his, he kissed the tops of each before entwining his fingers with hers.

Jane blinked, shell-shocked by the greeting, unprepared for how happy he was to see her. Her mouth curved into an answering smile as she bathed under the warmness of his gaze.

"It was… uneventful."

Turning so his back was to Federic, Logan's smile dropped, eyes turning down with apology. It took a moment for her to understand, but then it became clear.

This was what she was being paid to do.

This act, their contracted "relationship," it would all be beginning now.

As if to confirm her thoughts, Logan's eyes flicked briefly, but pointedly, to his hairstylist, before returning to her. In that small motion, he had made it very clear that this was their coming out, and that his stylist would likely be a terrible gossip.

Forced to match his familiarity, Jane stepped into him. "How has your day been so far?"

She almost flinched from her bad acting. She'd have to do much better if they were going to pull this off, particularly with Federic side-eyeing them so closely.

"Much better now that you're here."

His arms slid around her, drawing her so close that her nose almost touched his.

Even though Jane knew — just like the set — that none of this was real, that he was an actor, she couldn't help the sudden rush of pleasure that went through her body. Under his intense gaze, she lost herself.

His smile grew wider. Electricity cackled between them until she had the irrational thought that he was going to kiss her.

And yet… she didn't pull away.

She raised her face so close to him that she could smell whatever heavenly product his hairdresser had put in his hair. Heat spread from Logan, his eyes turned smoky with desire until the world was quickly forgotten.

With her face tilted up at him like that, those bow-like lips quivering with anticipation, it was all Logan could do not to taste them. Drawing on every inch of professional power, he forced himself not to act on what he was feeling, knowing that it wasn't real, and more importantly, it wasn't the right thing to do.

Jane was vulnerable, a victim. She'd been thrown into his world and dragged into this sham of a publicity stunt. She didn't understand how this all worked, and he couldn't complicate matters by crossing the line, no matter how much fun the two might have in the process.

She wasn't like the other women he'd dated.

She had gone through a terrible, and very recent, trauma. There were so many unanswered questions, he couldn't take advantage of her. He came back to his senses, and a wall came down.

The door to the trailer blew open as Adele, towering on a pair of leopard print platform shoes, came thundering in. The two of them jumped apart, leaving Jane startled by the moment that had come between them.

"Jane, you're here? Well, it's nice to see the new lovebirds, right Federic?" She aimed the question at the hairdresser who looked startled at being caught openly staring. Federic ran a hand through his streaked blue hair.

"Yes, it is. You didn't tell me you were seeing someone," he chided in an affronted voice.

"Didn't know I had to," Logan replied smoothly.

As if he ever told him anything.

"Just wait until everyone hears about this new lady in your life. The make-up girls will be *devastated.*"

"No more than usual," Adele commented in an amused voice. She explained, "Every single production Logan has worked on, the make-up girls have fallen madly in love with him, so they will be very disappointed to learn of your existence. You're the only one who isn't famous that he has fallen for. I'd almost think he was changing his playboy ways."

It was all being said for Federic's benefit. He lapped it up like a dog.

"I hate to be the bearer of bad news but," Adele paused dramatically. "There'll be another photographer around set today. He's working on an article the LA Times are running. He was scheduled for later in the week, but there was some kind of mix-up. I'm afraid we've had no time to ready you for this."

Jane's heart plummeted. "But you said you'd rehearse with me…"

Adele issued a curt nod. "And we will. This isn't an interview, luckily, just some candids he's been brought on to shoot. It's normal procedure. Some shoots have a permanent photographer, some actors hire their own so they can flood their Instagram feed with images. This production seems to only employ them on an ad hoc basis. You won't even have to pose for them. Just go about your day as normal and be your normal loving selves."

Easy for her to say.

She didn't have to pretend to be a whole new person, in a relationship that wasn't even real, with a man she was starting to develop real feelings for.

"Yes Ma'am." There was only the hint of an eye-roll from Logan. While they might have to participate in this role-play, he didn't like or believe in it.

This was a very strange business they were all involved in.

"Is that what you're wearing?" Adele suddenly turned to Jane, a hand on either hip. Her eyes flicked up and down the length of her and apparently found her wanting.

Jane glanced at her reflection in the mirror. She wore a simple duck-egg colored top that covered her arms — and the wounds she had sustained — a pair of jeans and strappy leather sandals.

"I didn't think I needed to dress up."

"This will be the first time the public will meet you. We would have thought this whole thing through better, then again, we weren't informed of the press today."

Frustrated, Jane gritted her teeth. "But I like this outfit."

She might as well as not replied. The woman was long past hearing her.

Adele dialed a number faster than the speed of light and was on a call before Jane could blink. "It's me. I may need help. Do you have something chic but not too dressy? I'm thinking daytime Jessica Alba style. No, not Nicole Kidman, we want femininity *and* warmth. Like your pretty fourth-grade teacher."

"Isn't that what she's already dressed like?" Logan's voice cut through the madness. "I happen to think she looks wonderful as she is." His smile seemed more genuine, as if this wasn't for Federic's benefit this time. "Leave her alone. She's fine. Let's not turn this into a stunt."

Adele shot him a dirty look that would have made lesser men cower.

"I know you'll find this hard to believe, what with your big movie-star-ego-brain, but I actually do this for a living and I do it well. Maybe you should listen to me, it is after all, what you pay me for."

"Jane doesn't belong in our circus, Adele. She didn't ask for this. How about we let her make her own decisions? I'm sure she's more than capable of them."

Jane shot him a grateful smile. Adele shook her head, unswayed by anything but her own certainty. The room waited for Jane to answer.

"I'd prefer to wear my own clothes, but maybe Federic can do something with my hair? I never know what to do with it."

The stylist fell over himself to help. "Of course, Sweetie! Come, sit in my throne. Logan's about done, anyway."

Giving them the stink eye, Adele spoke into her phone.

"Apparently we're fine... but pull some clothing and leave it on a rack in case we change our minds."

She glanced at the slim wristwatch that dangled from her wrist.

"I've got to sort out my other A-Lister now. She seems to have gotten herself in a little trouble last night and I need to bail her out before the press catch wind of it. Jane, I suggest you hang out around here. We can bring you magazines or movies to watch, food, drink, whatever your little heart desires. But stay close to the trailer. And keep Loki with you. We want to see the three of you together, one big happy family."

With a wink, she left, taking all the air with her. Without her, the trailer seemed suddenly lifeless. Catching the expression on her face, Logan laughed.

"You'll get used to her. She can be a bit abrasive, but she has never let me down."

Federic turned her chair toward the mirror.

"What're we thinking? Nothing too fussy, right?" His long slim fingers slipped through her hair, pulling it away from her neck, cleverly creating several styles as she watched.

"You know, I think I'll just add some volume at the roots, maybe do a waterfall braid to the left of your face. She wants Jessica Alba so we'll give it to her. Simple, but chic."

Jane didn't have a clue what any of it meant, but she nodded, relieved not to have to think about her appearance anymore. It was exhausting, and not particularly interesting. Still, once these photographs were released, there was always the hope that she would be recognized. The lack of contact from Summers was disturbing, though she tried not to think about it too much.

Say what you wanted to about Federic, but the man worked miracles — and fast. In no time, he stood back with his comb to admire her. "Gorgeous!"

It wasn't even a question as far as he was concerned. Jane had to admit the style was a good choice. The braid showed off her delicate features, enhancing her graceful neck. She was thankful her face hadn't suffered much, and what marks and bruises there had been, she had already covered up.

"I'm being called to set. Are you ready?" Logan asked, offering a hand to her.

"I'm not staying here?"

"Not when I'm not here, no. You'll come to set with me. In-between takes, we'll come back."

"Oh. OK." She took his hand, surprised by how easily it was coming to her. She drew from his strength as they stepped out into the world, Loki at their heels.

Immediately, a flood of faces greeted Logan. He was polite with them all, but kept his focus on her. Leaning close, he whispered into her ear. "Just smile. We'll be there soon."

Jane attempted to smile, but the sudden onslaught of attention was shocking. Where moments before, no one had paid her the least bit of attention, now the entire world stared.

Some smiled, though several frowned when they saw the woman whose hand he held. Much like Adele had, they looked her up and down, looking almost annoyed that Logan had chosen her.

He gestured at a golf cart. Their young driver stood to attention as they drew close.

"Afternoon, Mr. Steel. Miss. I'm going to be your driver on set today," he flashed a big grin at Jane, revealing white teeth and dimples. He had an honest way about him that she liked.

"Call me Jane."

He waited until they were seated before taking off. They drove through the studio, past a sea of crew setting up tall lights and heavy looking cameras until they arrived at a set of an Italian restaurant.

As soon as Logan set foot on the ground, he was whisked away by the scowling 1st AD. Logan said something to him and the man stopped, tossing a look back at her.

"You can watch by the monitors over there," he gestured to a line of monitors. A group of people were already gathered there, mostly dressed in the casual gear of the film crew, though a few wore suits. "Someone hook her up with sound so she can hear."

Almost immediately, someone approached with a small electronic pack that had headphones plugged into it. "Here you go."

"Thanks," Jane started to reply, but the sound guy had already gone.

She looked down at Loki. "I guess we're on our own. Try not to make any sound."

He scratched his head with a back leg and shook his head. It was only then that Jane noticed that he didn't have the shoe anymore. He must have left it at the trailer. She looked into her bag and the jumble of toys she had brought with her today to keep him occupied and fished out a rubber bone that they'd never played with. He took it with a big yip of delight.

If anyone thought it odd that she was there — and with a dog, no less — no one said a word.

The suits didn't bother looking at her, huddled together, discussing the scene ahead… and rather heatedly. Only the woman with a folder jammed full of notes spared a moment to smile at her. Toned, with weathered skin that spoke of a lifetime working in all elements, the only other sign of her advancing age were the gray streaks woven through jet black hair.

"First time?"

"On a film set? Is it that obvious?"

The woman tucked her pen into the top of the folder, which Jane could now see contained the screenplay. "I'm Gayle. Script Supervisor."

Jane shook the hand that was offered to her. "Jane."

She knew she should have used the "girlfriend" label, but the word tripped on her tongue.

"And this is Loki."

Gayle laughed as Loki nudged her in greeting. "He's a stunner. Yours?"

"He belongs to Logan. Apparently, you're the only one in the world who doesn't know that."

Gayle didn't understand the comment. She raised a brow in question.

"Oh, nothing. It was a joke."

There was movement by the restaurant. The director, a thirty-something man with a mohawk and ripped jeans who wouldn't have looked out-of-place working at the Apple store, spoke with Logan, waving his hands animatedly.

Logan listened, taking in his direction. Jane could see the focus he was drawing into himself, how his eyes clouded over, face growing slack. It was as if, at the switch of a button, the rest of the world had ceased to exist.

"Quiet on set! We're going for a rehearsal!" The AD yelled out.

A hush fell over the area. Busy as they were, the crew stopped chatting, even moving slowly so that they wouldn't make any noise as they still worked. Jane sucked in her breath as "action" was called.

Channeling his character, Logan became someone else entirely, even speaking with a different timbre to his voice. The effect was both electrifying and mesmerizing. She couldn't keep her eyes off of him, and it seemed neither could anyone else.

All eyes were pinned on Logan, playing out the emotional scene, displaying the kind of emotion she had never seen him show.

"And... cut!" The AD suddenly yelled out, startling her. She'd been so invested in the scene that his cold call to reality was a jolt to the system.

"He's good, huh?" Gayle commented. "Didn't know he could act like that. Nailed all his dialogue, too. Didn't miss a single thing."

Jane glanced down at the screenplay in her folder. "Is that what you do, make sure he says all of his lines?"

Gayle nodded, eyes gleaming. "One of the things, yes. I also ensure the continuity is right, that, for example, he has the right clothes on for this scene. If he was drinking something, I'd make a note of what level the water was at in the glass. The devil's in the details."

"That sounds like a lot to be thinking about."

"It is, but I don't keep it all in my head. I note everything down here," she nodded at the folder and script.

"We're going to go for a take," the AD yelled out. "Quiet, please!" He waited a few seconds for the noise to die down before calling, "And... ACTION!"

Once again, Logan morphed seamlessly into character, doing an even better job than before if she was any kind of judge. Jane watched, enthralled by the artistry he exuded until the scene was over.

A make-up girl rushed to him, dusting the shine from his forehead as he looked around the room. When their eyes met and held, Jane felt a spark deep within her bones. His lips curled into a sexy smile, the full wattage of it directed at only her.

And just like that, her heart began to thump.

19

The afternoon flew by.

Although she had watched take after take of Logan performing the scene, she never grew tired of seeing how he would tackle each one with a new approach.

She had seen him inject the kind of fury that would terrify most. Then he'd swapped to a seething, but quiet rage, punctuating every word of the dialogue like a knife. When that was in the can, he became desperate, needy almost.

It was astonishing how many ways he could play the same scene.

They were moving onto the second scene of the day now, taking place on a different set. It was close enough to walk, but Logan had been taken by the golf cart. When he had looked for her, Jane had gestured for him to go without her.

She would head there with Gayle. The older woman

had been a Godsend, explaining things to her when she hadn't understood a terminology or command.

Gayle was busy deep in conversation with the director. Not wanting to interrupt, Jane strolled behind them, making a game of it with Loki, who, by the way he was tugging and pulling, was beginning to get bored from being stuck here. She wished she could let him off the leash, but she just couldn't risk it.

There was a lot more that had to be ready for this next set. The director had moved on from Gayle now, but she was engaged in a conversation with several others. Finding herself in everyone's way, Jane tucked herself into a corner beside a pile of messily stacked props.

A group of attractive young women stood by, holding makeup brushes and combs. Standing behind a large screen, Jane was hidden from their view. She heard their energetic chatter, however, as they gossiped about the crew.

"Naomi said he's terrible in the sack, only cares about himself," said one.

"To that, I say pot calling kettle," answered another, wryer voice. "How you are in life is how you are in bed."

"True. What about Logan then? What do you think he's like between the sheets?"

Jane tensed at the conversational turn, her ears pricking up.

"Passionate. Wild. Dangerous," swooned one of the girls. "I'd die to get the chance to bed him."

"Have you seen that woman around here today? She's looking after his dog."

"The stiff looking one? Yeah. To be honest, I'm kind of

shocked that he's seeing her. Can't imagine what the attraction would be myself. She's so boring looking."

"Right? And no where near as pretty as Ellie. What a step down."

"He's probably still heartbroken over her. This one looks like she'd be low-maintenance, which, if what everyone is saying about him is true, she'd need to be."

Jane was growing smaller by the second. While their relationship might not be real, it still hurt to hear how little these women thought of her. Feeling the need to leave, she started moving away.

Loki barked loudly at a piece of string that hung off the side of the set. He dropped his rubber bone, readying to attack this new threat, unaware of Jane's mortification.

A hush fell over the women. One by one, their faces appeared around the screen. Caught red-handed, the women did the only thing they could think of. They each shot her a big, fake smile.

"Oh hi. Didn't see you there. I love your outfit."

"Right? So cute, very sweet."

"Hey Loki," the one who seemed to be the ringleader said, reaching out her hand for him. Loki snapped his attention away from that string, revealing sharp fangs at the girl, growling, not liking her in the least.

Jane couldn't have been prouder of him.

The girl snatched her hand back. "I guess he's testy with everyone."

"Only those he doesn't like," Jane replied, relieved to have found her voice.

The girls looked at each other, guiltily.

"I think we're needed on set," the Ringleader lied.

They hurried away, pretending to have received some unspoken call to work. Jane gave Loki a big fuss.

"You are the world's best boy, aren't you? My little hero."

Loki leaned into her, lapping up the attention. Wishing she could get out of there yet knowing she couldn't until Logan was finished for the day, she resigned herself to the fact that she would just have to cope with being uncomfortable and judged unfavorably.

Somehow, she had become one of those women she had seen in those gossip magazines.

Looking across the way, she met Logan's eyes. He must have picked up something from her expression as he started toward her only to be stopped by the AD, calling for another take.

It was an intense scene that involved his co-star, the lead of the movie who looked the director's double. They were around the same age, reeking of the kind of cockiness that spoke of privilege and wealth.

Jane instantly disliked both, though she had no real reason to. While Logan became still, drawing the emotions needed for the scene, his co-star, Jackson joked around with the director, playing the fool until she wished someone would tell them both to behave.

"ACTION!"

The scene began, the two of them sparring off each other. Logan's character was having a disagreement with his co-star about a woman they were both in love with. Their words and tension spiraled into a tsunami of rage when Loki ripped his leash out of her hands and tore across the set to that piece of fluttering string that had gotten him so worked up.

"Oh no," Jane said under her breath, shocked beyond belief.

The weight of his leash bounced over the wooden floor, echoing loudly with the sound of his scrabbling paws.

Everyone turned to look.

"CUT!" The AD yelled. One of the suited men Jane had seen earlier, turned on her.

"What the hell is that dog doing here? Do you know how much interruptions like this cost the studio? What kind of idiot brings a dog to the actual set?"

He spat the questions, eyes bulging from his head.

"What's the matter with you, can't you speak?"

A million faces watched her terrible faux pas. She opened her mouth to defend herself, but the words wouldn't come. Instead of replying to his barrage of questions, she heard a voice in her head.

Say something, you idiot! What the hell is wrong with you? Tell him who the dog belongs to.

But faced with the heat of his anger, Jane found herself shrinking.

She was afraid of him.

To her horror, her shoulders started to tremble. Unable to look at him, she dropped her gaze to the ground. Having heard his shouts, Loki stopped chasing the string and padded back to her, his tail between his legs, somehow knowing that he had done something wrong.

"Remove them from the set. Now!"

Logan had been lost in the moment, swallowed by the depths of his character and the torture he was going through, having to restrain himself from pummeling the punk of the man in front of him who dared to love the same woman, yet treat her quite so badly. The script didn't call for a physical fight — it was stronger without one — though it was all he could do not to punch his co-star in the face.

And he couldn't put it all down to being in character.

The scene had been reaching its crescendo when somewhere, from the far reaches of his mind, he had heard the dog barking. He'd assumed it was his imagination, some trick of his mind, but when the irate voice shouted after it, he'd known with a sinking stomach.

Loki.

And the person, the woman the voice was so aggressive against, had to be Jane.

It hadn't been that long ago when Logan had started at the bottom rung of the ladder, and he was well acquainted with being of a lesser status than everyone else. But seeing Jane's pale face as she took his abuse… saying nothing in return, sent him into a spiral of his own rage.

He had seen another woman like that once, one he worshipped with all of his heart, and it had almost broken him then.

There was no way he would allow this now.

As a minion rushed to do the bodiless voice's bidding, Logan's own cut through the silence like a knife. "Touch her and you will live to regret it!"

The minion froze, unsure who to obey.

Logan sprinted to Jane, daggers flying out of his eyes at the suit who had dared to shout at her.

"She's my girlfriend and that's my dog. I told her to bring him, so if you have a problem with that, then I'm the one you should be talking to."

Seeing him so close sent Loki into another round of barking. He jumped up at Logan, delighted to see him.

POP!

A flashbulb went off, blinding them all. The photographer pointed his camera at the commotion, recording the moment with wicked speed as his ID swung from the chain around his neck.

The reaction by the man in the suit, who had started this, was stunning. The rage he had exhibited only a second ago vanished in the blink of an eye. He laughed uproariously, as if this was all a big joke.

"Only a man in love could have taken me so seriously!"

He waved the confused crew member away, smiling at Logan and Jane, who, Logan was relieved to see, seemed to have come out of her shock. The color was returning to her face. That stone gray visage had gone.

"Of course, we won't be throwing anyone off the set. I was being facetious and I apologize if my words were taken literally." He reached out, started pumping Logan's hand. "Ira Cohen, VP of the Motion Picture Department, Cerberus Studios. Great to meet you. There's no problem here, Logan. I'm a big fan of yours. Big fan."

The look Logan gave him was usually reserved for something he would scrap off the bottom of his shoe. Cohen acted as if he couldn't see it. He turned to Jane with a toothy, shark-like grin. "Your lady — what's her name?"

Neither Jane nor Logan intended to reply, but the answer came from behind them.

"Jane Smith. Her name is Jane Smith." Stomping forward on those terrifying heels of hers, Adele appeared holding a phone in each hand. To the photographer, she informed loudly, "They met several weeks ago on a beach and have been inseparable since."

"Which beach?" The photographer asked, noting it for the upcoming article.

"A private one."

So much for having time to approve her story. The whole thing was turning into a circus. Picking up on Jane's uneasiness, Logan took charge. "Can you give us a moment?"

He addressed the question to the director, though it was meant for everyone around them.

"Two minutes, then we're back to work," the AD called on the director's nod.

Steering the photographer away, Adele filled him in on the backstory she and her team had devised for them, sticking as close to the truth as possible. Cohen followed after them, eager to get away from Logan's glare.

"I couldn't stop him. I'm sorry for disturbing the filming! I guess we'd been here too long, and he got bored. I'll take him out right now. It won't happen again."

She started to leave when Logan's hand landed on her shoulder. The heat of it singed her skin beneath.

"It was an accident, Jane. I'm not worried about that."

"You look angry…"

And he was.

"At that idiot, not you. When he was talking to you like that, why didn't you defend yourself? Why didn't you stand up to him? You should never let anyone talk to you like that."

"I don't know. When it was happening, all I could think was that it was all my fault. It never even crossed my mind to deny it."

His eyes grew troubled. She could drown in the dark depths of them.

"We're almost done. Are you OK to wait or should I have Daryl take you home?"

Warmth spread through her body. He cared about her! Her heart did a dance when she noticed the many faces still staring at them.

Of course, this was still part of the act.

And maybe even this chivalrous turn was all for their benefit, for the article to go with those pictures.

And she had almost fallen for it.

"I'll wait in your trailer."

He knew the second she pulled away that something had happened. One minute, they were making a connection only for that shadow to have crept into her eyes.

The AD sent an impatient look his way. Logan knew time was up.

"Yes. Wait for me there, after, we'll do something fun after."

"Fun? What kind of fun?"

God, she was suspicious. He almost toyed with her, but for her obvious wariness.

"Why don't I cook for you?"

She blinked at him slowly, as if he'd spoken another language.

"You can't cook?"

"Says who?" Logan challenged, amused by the confusion in her eyes.

"The magazines haven't mentioned anything about you being able to cook."

A slow smile stretched over his lips. Unable to help herself, Jane found herself drawn to them.

"So you've been reading up about me again?"

A delicious blush spread over her cheeks.

"Only to find out who you are since I couldn't remember anything about you."

Logan mimed stabbing himself in the heart.

"The lady doth maim with her words."

"Logan! We're ready." The AD called, apparently all done with waiting.

With a wicked grin and a flash of mischief, Logan sprinted back to the set.

"That one is trouble," Gayle said, coming up behind her. "You've got your work cut out for you there."

Jane had a sinking suspicion that the older woman might be right.

20

What should have been a simple shopping trip at the Whole Foods store turned into an exercise in patience.

Having finished the day's work, Logan had kept his promise — or threat — as Jane liked to think of it. Accompanying him to the fresh pasta section, she fought to keep Loki from investigating every product on display and possibly knocking it over in the process.

Smelling something delicious, the puppy darted forward to the source, but Jane was ready for him with an iron grip. She tugged his leash gently, getting the dog's attention.

"No, Loki. No pulling."

At her calm but firm voice, he stopped struggling. Pleased that he was finally starting to learn, she smiled down at him.

"That's right. Good boy."

"He's really taken to you," Logan observed her beneath

the shining Ray-Bans that seemed glued to his face the second they were in public.

She wanted to tell him he needed a better disguise. Though they might have hidden his eyes from view, they did nothing to disguise his star power if the slack-jawed gawking of the other shoppers was any indication.

"We don't have to go through with this. There's plenty of food in my fridge already. We can just cook something from that."

The Ray-Bans tilted until his eyes peered over the top of them.

"A man is nothing without his word."

She had to force herself not to roll her eyes. The man was full of drama.

"Since you insist on this exercise tonight, what are you making for dinner?"

He sniffed a bunch of basil. "Only the best lasagna you'll ever have this lifetime."

"Lasagna?"

The hand with the basil lowered. "You sound surprised?"

"It just seems so… normal. I thought you'd go for something elaborate…"

"It can't always be lobster and caviar. Much as I like both, nothing beats a home cooked lasagna, and I'm in the mood for something other than protein shakes and steamed chicken breasts."

The skepticism must have shown on her face as he continued, "Most women would be thrilled to have me cook for them, yet you act as if it's going to be torture."

She was starting to sound ungrateful. Her mouth

twisted with an apology. "I just didn't see you as the cooking type."

"Hard to picture an action star bent over a stove? I'll have you know that I learned from the best."

"You've trained with a Michelin chef, haven't you?"

He shook his head, amusement making his green eyes sparkle.

"Better. Keep guessing."

Jane wracked her brain. "A celebrity one?"

He snorted, enjoying the game. This might be the first time she had loosened up in his presence, and he found this version of Jane — the one who talked to him about normal things while they shopped for groceries — quite appealing.

"Why would a celebrity chef be better than a Michelin-starred one?"

Jane shrugged her shoulders. "I think I might be bad at guessing games. I give up."

"My mom," Logan revealed, his eyes lighting up at the thought of her. "She cooked everything from scratch when I was a kid. I helped prepare all of our meals. When I was younger, I considered it such a chore — what boy wouldn't? But as I got older, I came to appreciate the love and care she took in creating every dish. She was at home in the kitchen. It was her happy place. I guess she passed that on to me."

"You've not mentioned her before," Jane commented, pleased that he was opening up to her.

"She's amazing. Kind, caring, the hardest worker I know. Obviously, she's the most beautiful woman in the world too."

The love that poured out of him at the simple mention of her name made her smile. "Of course she is. And your dad?"

His smile froze. Those green eyes took on a hard glint. "The less I say about that loser, the better."

Just like that, their conversation was cut short. Jane hadn't known what a short fuse he had for the topic of his father, and she wished she hadn't gone there. That tension he carried so often on his shoulders was back again.

What she had read of him hinted of a tough childhood. She even remembered reading that he was estranged from his father, but in the moment, she had forgotten, and had put her foot right in it.

A plump woman wearing a sunny dress pushed a shopping cart inside which sat an equally plump baby. Her face did a double take as she stopped dead in front of Logan, clearly recognizing him. When he caught her watching him, it was as if their conversation hadn't sent him into a dark place.

He flashed her a high-wattage smile that sent the woman's knees knocking.

The woman grabbed his arm.

"Can I have a picture of you with me and the baby? I'd love to be able to show it to her when she's old enough to understand."

"Of course."

Throwing his arm around her, he smiled into the phone she pointed at them.

"Oh, thank you! Thank you!"

Overjoyed, she went away, staring at the picture of them, more taken with the proof of their meeting than of the movie star who still stood in front of her.

"They ask for a picture and just leave?" It seemed incredibly rude.

He reached for a pack of lasagna sheets, studying the label. "At least she asked first and thanked me after. A lot of people forget to do either."

He said it so matter-of-factly that Jane was flooded with sympathy.

"That's pretty crappy."

"People get excited. Anyway, I don't mind a bit of rudeness. It's the crazies you need to watch out for." The sheets went into the basket he was carrying, along with two boxes of heirloom tomatoes and a couple of cans of Redpack plum tomatoes.

"Aren't you going to go for the San Marzano tomatoes? They're the best."

Logan cocked a brow. "I actually prefer this home-grown brand. It's cheaper too."

"I wasn't aware that thriftiness was a word you understood judging by all the cars gathering dust in your garage."

"I haven't always been rich. My mom worked three jobs to keep us afloat. Some things stay with you regardless of what zip code you now live in."

She felt suitably chastised.

"That wasn't nice. Sorry."

"Don't apologize. Just don't do it again." He softened the words with another high-beam smile that made her grow warm.

She had to wrench her gaze away or risk falling under his spell. She studied the incredible amount of cheese on display.

"I'm assuming you want parmesan? I'm guessing

you'll be bypassing the ricotta to make a bechamel sauce?"

She had spoken without thought, but Logan picked up on what she hadn't.

"Correct, pass me the Parmesan."

She reached for the Parmigiano-Reggiano. "This is the real stuff. Did you know that a lot of the Parmesan that's sold in the US is fake? The real stuff only has three ingredients by law."

"I did actually, but look what you just remembered too. You know a lot about cooking."

"I guess you're right. Maybe I should be the one cooking tonight?" She flashed her own grin at him.

"Next time," Logan replied smoothly.

Inside, his stomach did a tango.

What was happening here? Was he becoming a method actor, or were they actually getting along and enjoying each other's company?

"Um, Logan? Can you sign this for me?"

A box of cereal and a pen were thrust at him. He took both automatically.

"Of course, who shall I make the Special K out to?"

SIZZLING PANS FILLED WITH TANTALIZING AROMAS WAFTED IN the air, making Loki, sprawled over the chaise lounge beside the kitchen, salivate.

Jane couldn't blame him. Despite this being the king of comfort foods, what Logan was cooking was anything but simple.

While she chopped onions and garlic, he had fried

cubes of seasoned pancetta in a cast-iron pan with butter. With that browning, a heavy-bottomed pot heated on the stove with both the tinned and chopped heirloom tomatoes simmering inside. She'd watched as he'd added herbs, salt and pepper, stock, and a liberal glass (or two) of a rich red wine.

"Is that done?" He gestured to the chopping board where a mountain of onions sat. Her eyes stung from their acidic breath. Without thinking, she reached up to wipe them.

The instant resulting burn was terrible. Welling with tears, she fumbled for a towel.

"Here, let me."

He dabbed at her eyes with something that smelled strongly of him, surprising her with his gentleness. When her eyes stopped streaming, she sent him a sheepish smile.

"Thanks. Forgot how much they can hurt."

He rolled up the damp sleeve he had used on her.

"Why didn't you use a kitchen towel? Now I've soaked your shirt."

He shrugged, not bothered in the least, throwing a pound of ground beef and Italian sausage meat into the pan. "The towels are great for cleaning up spills, but not soft enough for your face."

His thoughtfulness created another pull in her stomach that, if she wasn't careful, would cause her to do something stupid.

Washing her hands to give herself something to focus on that wasn't him, she almost jumped when his voice spoke close to her ear.

"Have you heard from Summers?"

At the mention of the detective in charge of her case, her face clouded over with concern. "No. I haven't had any messages on the phone here."

Stirring the meat in the pan, he let everything brown. "What about your cell?"

She gave him a funny look. "I don't have one."

The hand holding the wooden spoon froze. "Yes, you do. One was bought for you a while ago. Kitty must have forgotten to give it to you."

He frowned over the stove, stirring the pan more vigorously. Jane jumped to the woman's defense.

"She has such a lot to do around here, and she's been so great at looking after me. Please don't make a thing of it."

He stopped stirring. The spoon sat in the pan.

"She's been with me for a long time. Short of committing a crime, I would never fire that woman. She's been through a lot."

She picked up the sadness in his voice. "What happened to her?"

He took the pan off the heat, drained the fat and poured everything into the pot of simmering sauce. "Hang on, let me get this on. Can you pass me the milk and butter?"

She fished both from the fridge and handed them to him.

"These are my secret weapons. The milk tenderizes the meat, while the butter adds another layer of richness and depth."

She watched as he added them and covered the pot with a lid. Setting down the wooden spoon, he wiped his hands on the towel that was slung over one shoulder and poured two glasses of wine, one that he handed to her.

"She came over from Hong Kong about forty years ago, when she was just a child. Her parents wanted to make a life for their family in the US and they invested everything they had into a carpentry business but not one year into its opening, her father had a stroke that left him paralyzed on one side. Her mother, could only find work in what was essentially a sweat factory. Since her father couldn't do much physically anymore, and with medical bills mounting up, she slaved away."

Jane took a sip of her wine, trying to picture what that life must have been like.

"When Kitty was old enough, she got her own job as a cleaner in a hotel. Although she worked hard, she kept being bypassed for promotions."

"Why?"

Logan shrugged. "She never had time to socialize with her workmates, always having to rush home to look after her parents. She was always overlooked. I guess it's like any industry, promotions and jobs tend to go to the most popular employees."

Steam bubbled up from the pot, a slither of the sauce spilled over the side, scorching the stove. He turned down the heat.

"She was working at the hotel when I lived there on location for a movie. I was there for two months and she took care of the mess I made on a daily basis with no complaints. I'd left money, expensive watches, all sorts of things strewn around, but she never took so much as a dime."

"One day, I came back early from the set to find her sobbing in the bathroom."

He paused, his jaw clenching from the memory.

"Her mother was becoming more and more forgetful and Kitty had come home the night before to find that they had been burgled. What little money they'd had, had been stolen. They were going to be evicted, and she didn't know what she was going to do."

"So you hired her and the rest is history?" Jane didn't mean to sound glib. Her heart hurt from all of Kitty's family struggles. She wanted for their happy ending to come into play.

"Something like that. I gave her the guest house. She and her parents lived there until her father passed away. Her mother developed Alzheimer's but she lives in a really great care home not far from here. Kitty sees her every weekend."

The question was on the tip of her tongue and she almost stopped herself from asking it, but that warm and bubbling feeling was back.

And it needed an answer.

"It must cost a small fortune to keep her in a home around this area?"

"It's all taken care of."

The graceful way he didn't take credit for paying for Kitty's mother's care left her breathless. He had a history of looking after needy women. In return, they stuck to him loyally.

She wondered if the same would apply to her.

The rest of the lasagna cooked slowly over several episodes of Frasier, which Jane discovered she loved almost as much as Logan. They laughed, sitting on the sofa, Loki between them, as the snobby brothers were continually bested by those around them.

When the buzzer announced that dinner was ready, Logan set a sizzling slice of the Italian dish in front of her and waited, a boyish look of expectation on his face. He picked up a forkful, bringing it to her lips. Her lips parted…

Sending ungentlemanly thoughts through his mind. How had he not noticed how sweet her lips looked before? Maybe because she usually looked anxious, as if she was second guessing her every reaction, hoping that it was the right one.

But right now, this was the most relaxed he had ever seen her.

Under the fairy lights that twinkled around them, with a glass or two of the wine having taken off those sharp edges of hers, she radiated warmth.

The fork slid gently into her mouth, and she sighed a sigh of happiness.

"That is… delicious. The meat melts in my mouth, the sauce is delicate yet punchy with flavor. It's the best lasagna I've ever tasted."

He rumbled a low laugh. "That you can remember."

Grabbing her own fork, she dug in. "I'd remember if there'd been a better one. This is stunning, Logan. So, so good."

He puffed up his chest, standing a foot taller. Forget the fame, money, and notoriety: apparently all it took to feel this good was the appreciation shining from her eyes.

There was something about her satisfied look and the

sighs of breathless appreciation that had heat rushing through him.

He hadn't felt this way about a woman for a while, not since his last disastrous relationship.

Yes, there had been women after her, but they were short flings, some physical fun. He never had feelings for them that lasted more than the heat of the moment.

But Jane had thrown his emotions into turmoil from the moment he had met her.

Seeing her on that beach, those injuries lashed over her delicate skin… and that vulnerable way she had looked up at him when she couldn't remember who she was.

It was like he had been sucker-punched in the gut.

She reminded him too much of that other woman he had lived his life for.

His mother.

Yet, looking at Jane, it was like a string had been plucked in his heart.

She devoured several mouthfuls before noticing he hadn't touched the food himself. Hadn't moved at all in fact. His eyes had become dark with tension, the air fizzling around him.

Her hand with the fork lowered.

The intensity in his eyes left her breathless. Drawn by a magnetism that she couldn't deny, she moved closer until her face was only inches from his own.

A storm was brewing inside her chest, but she couldn't stop the pull of him. He was everywhere. That scent of sandalwood mixed with the musky natural smell of him sent her senses on fire.

When he bowed his head and pressed his lips to hers, it seemed the most natural thing in the world.

She tasted as sweet as honey, those soft lips yielding beneath his own. She kissed him tentatively, as unsure as he was of what was happening here, yet with such a need that it had him fighting to control himself.

She wasn't like any of his regular women.

She wasn't a fan, or one of the savvy women in the industry who knew what it would be like to hook up with a celebrity.

She was delicate and pure.

And she had no idea who she was.

The shock of the thought was a bucket of ice on his heat. He jerked away, and had to fight the urge to crush his lips to hers again, when he saw the dreamy look on her face.

He knew he couldn't pursue this.

Especially now, not when her history — and possibly her mind — wasn't clear. Not when he was filming the most important movie of his career and his world teetered toward implosion.

Confusion clouded her eyes. She picked up the fork again, hoping that her hands wouldn't shake and belie the churning in her stomach.

Her very core was shaken. She didn't know what to do next.

A million questions ran through her mind, dazzling her with their urgency.

Had he meant to kiss her?

Women threw themselves at him all the time, and while Jane knew she wasn't an eyesore, she certainly wasn't perfect like most of the women in LA. She had many, many flaws, and that was even without the obvious issue they couldn't escape.

She saw the turmoil behind his eyes. He seemed to be fighting an inner battle.

A spark of hope flared in her chest, pushing back the fear rapidly wrapping its claws around her heart.

"Aren't you going to eat? I was thinking of putting on a movie. We could watch it together?"

She blurted the question out, but immediately regretted it. What was she doing? Why was she glossing over that kiss when they should be talking about it like adults?

She waited for his answer, sweat forming at the base of her neck.

"I have to go. I need to go over my scenes for tomorrow."

Whatever hopes she'd had of them spending time together sank like a stone.

"Oh."

She didn't trust herself to say anything more.

His brow furrowed with thick lines. He regarded her with an unfathomable expression.

"I'm sorry about the kiss. I shouldn't have done that."

She reeled at the sharp sting of his words. This was stupid, it was just a kiss that shouldn't have happened. No big deal. She needed to get a grip on herself.

"It was nothing, don't worry. I'm a big girl."

She forced another forkful of food into her mouth. She couldn't taste the food that now felt cloying and heavy, but she'd be damned if she'd let him know that.

Logan wanted to say more, but in the end, he lowered his gaze to the dog that was staring up at them.

"Enjoy your dinner. Loki, come. Let's leave Jane in peace."

He reached the doorway and paused.

"Adele will be here in the morning. She's arranged something for us tomorrow night. I should have mentioned it earlier, but it slipped my mind."

If she tried to speak, Jane's voice would betray her feelings. She gave a curt nod of her head and held her breath.

By the time she let it out again, he was gone.

What a fool she had been to think he would be genuinely interested in her!

She was nothing but an employee, like Kitty. Sure, he cared for her, but it was only the kind of care that any decent person would have for someone in her position.

It was possible he just felt sorry for her. She had nothing and no one, after all. She was about as empty as they came.

She put down her fork, her appetite gone.

She cleared up the mess in the kitchen on autopilot. Washed the dishes, pots and pans by hand, even though there was a state-of-the-art dishwasher she could use. Put away the leftovers, then took a bath.

When she emerged and went to the kitchen to make a cup of tea, she spotted another one of those Kitty gift baskets sitting outside the front door.

She brought it in to find the latest iPhone inside with an apology from Kitty for forgetting to give it to her earlier. The phone had already been activated for her.

She checked the call log. No messages. No missed calls.

No one in the world who was missing her.

She changed into her nightdress and got into bed. However kind Logan had been to her, it was clear she didn't belong here.

This was just a fairy tale, but it would be over as soon as soon as she regained her memories or their contract was up. If she was going to protect her heart, she had to learn who she had been, as fast as possible.

Before Logan had a chance to break it.

21

"Are you going to tell me what it is I'm actually doing tonight?"

Jane asked, wondering why, with all the people running through the house to get them ready, no one thought to brief her on the day's events.

An impatient sigh hissed out from bright red-lipsticked lips, one high-heeled boot tapping on the marble floor of Logan's office.

"It's just a small event to kick you off. A charity ball to raise money for the Make A Wish Foundation. You'll go, eat, dance a little, smile nicely for the cameras, then come home. There's nothing to it."

Jane perched on one of the leather sofas as Adele — dressed today in a skintight jumpsuit with a heavy golden chain wrapped around her dainty waist for a belt — blew through the room.

"A shortlist of outfits have been pre-selected for you and will arrive within the hour. You don't have to worry about a thing. It's all been done for you. You try them on and go with the one you look best in. Hair and makeup will be here a few hours before Daryl arrives to take you both there. Then the two of you grin, hold hands, maybe even a chaste kiss if you're so inclined and boom. We're done in time for you to catch The Late Show… so why are you trying to make my life more difficult than it needs to be?"

The question was directed at Jane.

After another sleepless night plagued by a nightmare that she couldn't remember, the last thing she wanted was to deal with tonight's events where she would have to fake a relationship with the man she had tried to have a real connection to last night.

Still smarting from his rejection, it had taken everything she had to turn up for this meeting seemingly composed.

Inside was a different matter entirely. Her gut churned with a tidal wave of emotions.

Logan leaned against the window, the sun slanting in behind him, emphasizing the ripples on his body. He hadn't said much other than to enquire about her sleep. She'd almost think he had been affected by their kiss if it wasn't for the way his eyes were glued to his phone.

If he didn't give a damn, then so wouldn't she.

"I don't need someone to pick out my clothes for me."

Pouring a glass of champagne into a tall flute (who had champagne at ten in the morning?), Adele shot a look at her. "This is how things are done."

Jane fixed unwavering eyes on the other woman. "Things will go a lot more smoothly if you at least pretend to consider my opinion. I may not know who I am, but I can pick my own damn dresses."

The words exploded out of her, surprising her with the depth of her emotion.

A slow, approving grin stretched over Logan's lips as he finally looked over his phone at her. Their eyes met across the room, sparking off a bolt of electricity that fizzled the air.

Jane tore her gaze from him. Rather than the anger she'd expected, Adele only shrugged, her acrylic nails tapped busily on the iPad in her hands.

"Since this means so much to you, I'll set up an appointment at select designers across town. You can try on their dresses to your heart's content."

Stunned at how easy that had been, Jane nodded. "Thank you."

She turned the iPad to her. There was a page of dresses displayed on the screen. "Scroll through this and stop when you see ones you like."

Jane didn't know why she was being asked to do this, but she figured she shouldn't push her luck. Adele looked like she was itching to do some damage with those wicked talons.

The dresses were stunning creations. The detailing was exquisite, and she fell in love on every page of the screen, but was finally able to narrow it down to one particular designer, the reason for this exercise.

When Adele saw Jane's choice, the frown that seemed her default expression twisted into a nod of approval.

"Armani Privé. Smart choice. "

She typed up a quick email and fired it off. "They'll be ready for you in an hour. I'll have a car take you there."

"You made the appointment... *already*?"

Adele peered at her, lips pressed in an exasperated

line. "You understand that Logan is a big deal, right? You haven't forgotten that?"

Jane's cheeks turned hot. "Of course, not."

"Then we are done here." She turned her attention to Logan. "You're all sorted?"

He saluted her smartly, earning a flinty glare.

"I'll see you both later. Try not to mess anything up until then."

Logan cleared his throat against the sudden silence.

"Are you clear on what's happening? If not, I can have my assistant walk you through it?"

So this was how it was going to be. No mention of that kiss or the feelings that had come with it.

It was all work.

She nodded. "I'm going to call a friend to see if they will be able to come with me to the store."

He frowned. "I thought you didn't know anyone here?"

"It's a new friend." The call was answered within a few rings. "Hello… Clare? This is Jane. We met at your store the other day."

The other woman's voice bubbled down the line.

"Jane! I'm so glad to hear from you, how are you? Any news?"

"Not yet."

Sympathetic noises came down the line.

"Give it time, I'm sure they'll figure it out. Are you free to grab a coffee sometime? I hope that's why you're calling. I haven't stopped thinking about you since we met."

"Actually, I need help with something that I thought you'd get a kick out of it."

"What is it? I'm all ears."

"I need to pick out a dress for a charity ball… but I'd like your professional advice if you are able to come? It's late notice, I'm sorry to say, but I was only made aware of this myself, late last night."

She shot a look at Logan. He looked briefly guilty and made no effort to hide the fact that he was eavesdropping on the conversation.

"I'd love to help! When and where were you thinking of going?"

"Well, that's the thing. The appointment's for an hour's time. It's at the Armani Privé store."

Clare's gasp of excitement could be heard clear across the room.

"Are you kidding me?! Oh my gosh, I've driven past so many times but never been inside. But, an hour?"

"I know. It's crazy, I shouldn't have called. Who gives people an hour's notice? It's so tacky of me." What a way to ruin what could have been the start of a great friendship.

"Hey, that's fine. I'm surprised more then anything. Luckily, I not at work today. I do have a hot yoga class, but I can easily cancel that. So yes, I can meet you there. I'm so excited. Thank you for thinking of me, Jane!"

"It's me who needs to thank you for doing me this favor."

Jane was ready to ring off when Logan tugged on her arm. "One second, Clare." Covering the phone, she asked, "What?"

"How did you meet this woman?"

"At the store, where I bought my clothes the other day."

Logan's brow arched high. "In the Grove? She's a

sales assistant you met in the Grove? How do you know you can trust her?"

"Are you serious? She's lovely."

"I'm sure she is, but how do you know she's not after something?"

"Because she knows the situation. She knows I don't have anything."

"You told her about me?"

His concern was starting to make sense. "No. I didn't tell her you were you — I'm not that stupid. I told her you were a successful businessman."

"But that doesn't mean anything. You said I was successful. And you'd spent a decent amount of cash at her store…"

She laughed, not quite believing what was happening here. "Clare is a good soul, Logan. I know you've been out here a long time, but there are still decent people in the world."

"I think I'd like to decide that for myself."

There wasn't anything he could have said that would have shocked her more.

"You want to meet her?"

"Yes."

"But…"

"I'll drive you myself. If we leave now we should get there before the traffic hits. Come on."

LESS THAN AN HOUR LATER, THEY WERE PARKED OUTSIDE THE polished frosted glass windows of the imposing three-storey high building where two white columns held up the entrance.

Jane sat in Logan's Rolls Royce, safely behind the blacked-out windows that covered all of his cars. They had left Loki at home since this — she had been assured — would only be a short trip, as he too, had things to ready before the ball that night.

"This is ridiculous. I'm a grown woman. I don't need you to vet who I spend time with."

Wearing those ever-present Ray-Bans, Logan continued his inspection of the faces that passed outside.

"Be that as it may, this is happening."

There was a stubborn tilt to his chin that she hadn't noticed until now. Clearly, despite how ridiculous this was, nothing would dissuade him from this exercise. Among the sea of sharply dressed shoppers whose wealth shone from the glinting rings and watches that adorned their bodies, one woman stood out from the crowd.

Even from inside the car, that warmth that seeped out of her made Jane smile. She hadn't known how nice it would be to see a friendly face.

"There she is! Clare!"

Jane left the car and waved. Logan's head craned round to the woman.

On first inspection, she seemed pretty normal.

She had a good figure beneath the white blouse and jeans she wore, but chose not to be flashy about it. She wore flats on her feet. No jewelry on her hands that held onto an oversized Boho bag. She did seem nice — and out of place on Rodeo Drive. But if Logan knew anything about this town, it was that looks could be deceiving.

Clare went up to Jane and gave her a warm hug. "It's so good to see you again, Jane. You look fantastic."

Jane glanced down at the simple gypsy dress she had chosen before she had known about this shopping trip.

"Thanks. You too."

Clare laughed, a self-conscious smile on her lips. "I probably should have made a bigger effort considering where we are, but I ran out of time, so they'll just have to take me as I am. Hopefully, they won't throw me out of the shop."

"You look perfect. And if they're going to be jerks about it, they can toss me out too."

A shadow fell over the two of them as Logan approached. Jane flinched inwardly, hoping he wasn't going to do anything that would upset her new friend.

"Hi there, I gather you're Clare?"

Completely unaware, Clare turned to him with a smile. "Yes. You must be the businessman Jane mentioned..."

Her voice trailed off, her eyes turning very wide. "Has anyone told you you're the spitting image of that action star, Logan Steel?"

Jane could feel her cheeks turning hot. Clearing her throat, she smiled apologetically. "That's because it actually *is* Logan."

Right on cue, Logan flashed that mega wattage smile of his, taking Clare's hand in his. "Good to meet you."

Clare allowed him to shake it, swapping gazes between the two of them. "I'm not sure what's going on here?"

"I just thought I'd come and meet this new friend Jane has told me about. So, I hear you work in Nordstrom?"

"Yes." She laughed. "Not very glamorous compared to you, I'm sure, but I like it."

"I take it you live in the city, then?"

"Born and raised." She smiled at them both, surprised by the interest he was showing in her.

"What area?"

"Nowhere as nice as you, I'm guessing."

Logan slipped off his sunglasses but didn't reply. Clare started to feel uncomfortable under his intense scrutiny.

"Palms, West LA."

"And do you live there on your own?" Logan asked with such directness that Jane winced. If it wasn't for the scene it would cause — and no doubt, the subsequent publicity issues — she would have told him to get lost. This kind of macho whatever-this-was, wasn't welcome.

Clare blinked up at him, those green eyes of her cloudy with confusion. "I don't see what my relationship status has to do with anything?"

Clare turned to Jane to see if she could shed some light.

"Given everything that Jane has gone through, I'd just like to know who she's spending the day with," Logan replied.

Embarrassed, Jane gave Clare an apologetic look.

"Well, if you must know, I'm not dating. Haven't dated in two years now, not since my fiancé cheated on me with one of his groupies."

Jane gasped, a hand flying to her throat. "I'm so sorry, Clare. How awful."

Catching the doubtful expression on Logan's face, Clare's eyes lost some of their softness.

"We were high school sweethearts. Artists, both of us,

but we couldn't both go after a career as a painter — one of us needed to pay the bills — so he decided that I should get a job to support his career… and like a fool, I agreed. As soon as he became successful, he didn't want me anymore. That's pretty much all there is to know about me. Happy now or do you want my social security number, too?"

That question was directed at Logan. He stared down at her, the two of them facing off, until the corners of his mouth began to twitch.

"I apologize for my rudeness. I just wanted to be sure you weren't a serial killer. I'll leave you to it."

He strolled back to the car leisurely, stopping twice for selfies and an autograph, as the two women looked on.

"The man is impossible," Jane spluttered. "I told him it wasn't necessary to vet you, but he's as stubborn as a mule. I'm so sorry. I completely understand if you want to call this off."

Clare waved a bronzed hand at her, a twinkle in her eyes. "Don't you dare! This is the most excitement I've had in a long time."

"You're not insulted?"

Clare laughed. "He only grilled me because he cares about you. How can I be insulted by that?"

Jane wasn't so sure that was the case. "He's a confusing contradiction of a man."

Clare linked an arm through Jane's. "Aren't they all? That's what makes it so thrilling!"

Her enthusiasm was contagious, and Jane soon found herself relaxing in her company. "But was it all true, what you told me about being rescued on the beach and losing your memory? The businessman was actually Logan?"

"Hard to believe, I know, but yes."

Clare clutched her hands to her heart, swooning. "My God, it's so romantic, like something out of a movie!"

If only, Jane thought to herself, casting a last glance at Logan's car as it roared off down the street.

If only.

22

Arm in arm, Jane and Clare strolled through the doors of the Armani store to be met with two black-as-night Art Deco styled metal staircases that formed a diamond around a display of gorgeous gowns.

Nothing else of the store could be seen, hidden by three storeys of frosted glass. Ambient music played, relaxing the mind yet seeming to energize it at the same time.

Clare's shiver of excitement vibrated through to Jane. "Once we go up those stairs, life will never be the same again."

Jane laughed, feeling her girlish excitement.

"Then what are we waiting for?"

They ran up the stairs as fast as they could. At the top floor, their way ahead was blocked by a set of double doors made of more of that frosted glass.

Jane pressed a bell on the wall. A pleasant voice enquired from the intercom, "Welcome to Armani Privé. Can I have your name, please?"

"It's Jane Smith... and Clare. We're supposed to have an appointment—"

Her next words were interrupted by the swoosh of the doors opening inward. A beautiful red-haired girl with impossibly long legs in a halter-neck top and high-waisted culottes greeted them warmly.

"Hello. I'm Fiona, and I'll be assisting you together with my team."

Beyond her stood a line of equally stunning girls, any of who could have come straight off the catwalk.

"We've been fully briefed and have already selected some gowns that we think might be suitable. If you follow me, we can start the process off."

Fiona swept her dead-straight hair off one bare shoulder and led the way to a room with deep-pile carpet and a circular sofa. Crystal lights dangled from the ceiling, providing a bright yet intimate setting.

"Please, sit, relax," Fiona gestured to the sofa as one of the other girls appeared with a platter of fruit, cheese, and nibbles, as well as flutes of champagne and a bowl of chocolate dipped strawberries.

"Would either of you like something else to drink? Maybe some tea or coffee?"

Grinning from ear-to-ear, Clare picked up a glass of the champagne. "I'm perfectly good with this, actually. Jane?"

"Same here." They clinked glasses, took a sip of the champagne.

"This is quite possibly the best day I've ever had, and we haven't even begun yet," Clare sighed.

Fiona smiled, brilliant blue eyes shining. "Well, you

should see what we have lined up for you. It seems, you are a very lucky lady."

Jane nibbled on a strawberry, savoring how sweet the fruit was. Her eyes grew wide as six gowns were presented to them — each with their own assistant.

"Oh my. These are extraordinary." She admired the first dress, running her fingers through the silky material, watching as the sun glinted off the tiny pearls that studded the neckline.

"Are those real?" Clare gaped, champagne forgotten for the moment.

"Yes. Over five hundred pearls — all hand sewn, of course."

"Of course," Clare repeated, shooting an impish look at Jane.

Jane glided toward a misty pale dress of silver, drawn by the stones that shimmered each time the material moved.

"The changing room is over there," Fiona pointed. "Hannah will bring the dress in for you and help you with it too, if you require?"

"Thank you," Jane answered, feet already moving of their own accord. "I'll see you in a minute," she told Clare.

"Sure thing," Clare replied, though her eyes were busy sizing up a dress of their own.

"That would look wonderful with your figure," Fiona encouraged. "Why don't you try it on?"

"I'd love to, but this is all for Jane. There's no way I'd be able to afford a dress like this. It's way, way out of my ballpark." Clare deflated a little, embarrassed by the very admission.

Fiona refused to accept her answer. Her chin tilted up stubbornly. "You're here, anyway. Who knows when you'll come back again. It's no problem for me if you try the dress on. I don't work on commission." She winked, letting her know that she meant it.

"You're sure that's OK?" Clare could feel herself caving. The dress was just so beautiful. When would she ever get a chance like this again?

Fiona escorted her to the changing room. "Here you go. I can't wait to see how you both look."

Inside her own changing room, Jane stripped down to her underwear and slipped into the dress. It fell over her body like a ripple of air. Though the dress covered her in all the right places, she felt as if she wasn't wearing anything at all.

There wasn't a mirror in the changing room, which must have been by design.

She stepped outside. The end of the short hallway spilled into that lounge area where mirrors abounded. She went there now, wondering if the dress would even suit her. Wouldn't she look ridiculously out-of-place wearing something so luxurious?

When Fiona saw her, she drew in her breath.

"Oh, Jane. Sensational. Just sensational."

Jane stared at the woman in the mirror, shock radiating through her body. The comparison she had made in her mind to air, was perfect. The dress caressed her body in such a lover's embrace that it was almost impossible to see where the dress ended and she began.

She turned to inspect herself from all angles. Every curve, every line of her body was on display.

Though maybe a bit too much.

There wasn't an inch of her that wasn't exposed: the dress left nothing to the imagination.

Trailing skirts and bare feet padded behind her until Clare's reflection came into view. Jane's mouth fell open.

"Clare! You look wonderful!"

And she did.

The emerald green silk dress she wore really showed off her curves, and the color made her bronze skin seem as if it glowed. Clare beamed, pleased by the compliment, a rosy flush on her cheeks. Stepping around her, her eyes widened when saw Jane full-on.

"I'm sorry. I was expecting to see my friend, Jane, and not this sexy model who could give Marilyn a run for her money." She circled her, taking it all in. "I don't know how you're wearing that thing? It doesn't even look real."

She made a curvy gesture with her hands. "It is very va va voom. Methinks, Logan — and just about every man in the universe — will lose their minds when they see you in that."

Far from being pleased by her comment, there was an anxious flutter in Jane's stomach. "You don't think it's too revealing?"

"You can't see through any of it. It just lets everyone know what a gorgeous body lies beneath the dress," Fiona jumped in.

Jane inspected her reflection, still with that flutter. "I'm not sure I want to be exposed like that to the world."

"But... a body like yours needs to be admired. I'd kill to have curves like yours."

Fiona twisted her slim, manicured hands, thinking that Jane was out of her mind to not show off her every asset.

"I believe Jane might be less Instagram Kardashian and

more Oscars red carpet, am I right?" Clare addressed the question to Jane who nodded, surprised for the moment that she even knew who the Kardashians were from memory — and quite a bit so, as the dangerously sexy and heavily made-up Kim flashed into her mind. But she had not recognized Logan that first day.

The irony wasn't lost on her.

"Yes. I'm sorry, Fiona. I'm just not comfortable revealing so much of myself. I don't want to be that kind of spectacle."

Fiona did an admirable job of swallowing her disappointment. "No fear, I have many more dresses for you to try."

"I guess I'll just have to keep you company then." Clare pretended to sigh. "Can't have you feeling lonely, even if this dress needs to come home with me — I for one, have no problem letting the world see my fabulousness!"

Jane shot her a grin that lit up her whole face. Reaching over, she squeezed Clare's hand. "I'm so glad you're here with me."

Clare matched her grin with one of her own. "Anytime."

The rest of their time at the store passed in a flurry of activity.

Dresses were tried on and discarded. Champagne was drunk, strawberries devoured, all as the two talked and laughed, thoroughly enjoying their time together until Jane finally saw the one dress that left her breathless.

As luck would have it, it was last on the rack.

An off-the-shoulder mermaid gown the color of blush, with a jewel-encrusted waist that sparkled when it caught the light, it slipped on like a second-skin, cascading into a pool of misty material by her feet.

The dress whispered when she moved, swishing like liquid-silk. Wearing it, Jane felt as if she was an ethereal being sent from the heavens, but it was when she saw herself that she knew this was the one.

The color of the dress emphasized the creaminess of her skin, giving it a glow that would have put the moon to shame. The dress felt right: it lent her a beauty and grace that she did not feel. Even she had to admit what difference a good dress could make.

"You're making me think I could bat for the other side," Clare pretended to leer at her. "If you don't choose this dress, you are a mad, mad woman."

"I have to agree," Fiona stepped forward. Taking hold of Jane's long hair, she twisted it expertly, holding it high on her head. "You must wear your hair up, like so. See how this shows off the delicateness of your neckline?"

Staring at her reflection, Jane could barely recognize herself. This was why people paid for the best — so that they could work miracles like this.

She stared at her face, at her eyes that seemed more blue than usual. Was it the lighting, or had she always had those dark flecks in her irises?

Suddenly, her reflection changed, morphing into that of another Jane.

This other Jane looked like her, but for the terrified expression she wore. Her ghost-white face stared back at her, her mouth opened in a silent scream that only she could hear.

When Jane blinked, the vision had vanished. There

was only her current reflection in the mirror, but the shock of whatever she had seen left her trembling.

"Jane? Are you alright? What is it?"

"Is the dress too tight?" Fiona fussed. "Can you breathe?"

Catching herself, Jane took a deep breath in. "I'm... I'm fine. The dress is fine, too. I'll take this one."

"But what happened? You look white as a sheet." Clare hovered over her. "Come," she took her hand, leading her to the changing room. "Let me help you out of the dress."

When Jane was back in her own clothing, Clare patted her hand reassuringly.

"It could have been a memory, or maybe your mind playing tricks on you. You've had to deal with so much in such a short space of time. Did the doctor warn you that something like this would happen?"

Jane tucked a strand of hair behind an ear as she hung the dress onto a hanger.

"No. I guess this must be normal. The shock of the old mixing with the new."

"If it happens again, you should call the doctor."

Jane chewed on the end of a nail. "I don't think it's worth bothering him about it."

"You suffered a head trauma. Those things are worth worrying about. Promise me you'll see a doctor if it happens again, and you have another reaction like that. I'll even come with you."

Jane hugged her, overcome with feeling. "You are a wonderful person, Clare. Has anyone ever told you that?"

Clare snorted, though her eyes grew brighter. "Only every man who has ever wanted to get me in the sack."

She elbowed her. "You do realize my comment earlier was just that, right? I don't really want to jump your bones, no matter how hot you look."

Laughing, Jane picked up the dress. "Let me get this wrapped up. We've probably spent far too long in here. I'm sure Adele is having a fit. The woman is like a tiny drill sergeant on speed."

The dress was carefully packed into a box filled with tissue paper, then into a smart Armani bag, but as they went to leave, Clare was also presented with a box by Fiona.

"Oh no, like I said, I can't afford anything in here. Probably not even that bowl of strawberries we demolished." She laughed, but there was embarrassment in her eyes that she couldn't quite hide.

Fiona smiled warmly. "It's all been taken care of."

Clare gasped. "But how?" With trembling fingers, she lifted the lid of the box to see the sea of emerald green inside.

"That was the dress you liked the most, wasn't it?" Fiona asked.

"I'd get married in it if I could, but I don't understand?" She looked to Jane, who was equally bemused.

"It's a present from Mr. Steel. An apology for the way he treated you earlier, but also a thank you for keeping Jane company today."

A warm feeling came over Jane.

Logan did this?

"I thought he didn't approve of me?" Clare spluttered.

"I guess you were mistaken," Fiona smiled at them both. "He's a wonderful client, a great man. I hope you have fun at the ball tonight. And Clare, I hope we'll see you again too… and if you do happen to get married in that dress, you'll make a stunning bride."

They left the store as Jane spotted Daryl waiting outside for her. He tipped his hat at her.

"I can't believe he did this, especially when he grilled me like that." Clare couldn't stop staring at the box in her hand, as if it would dematerialize if she looked away.

"I haven't really figured him out yet," Jane admitted.

"When you do, I suggest you hold on to him," Clare winked. "That one's a keeper… and if you meet any eligible bachelors at the ball, you know who to call."

Daryl took Jane's bag from her. "I'll be in the car when you're ready to go."

She nodded to Daryl. Spotting an empty soda can on the sidewalk, Jane picked it up and tossed it into a nearby trashcan. "I can't stand it when people litter."

"Preaching to the choir," Clare agreed.

"Especially when there's a trashcan right beside it," Jane continued. "I mean, how much of a jerk do you have to be?"

She hugged her new friend. "I had a blast. Thank you for coming, and at such short notice."

Clare waved off her thanks. "Are you kidding me? Look what I got out of this… a new friend, a grilling from a movie star, and a to-die for dress! I've not had this much excitement since I tossed my fiancé to the curb!"

"I hope you find an occasion to wear it soon."

Clare looked confused. "What do you mean? I am going to live in this thing. I can't wait to see what they think when I turn up to work in it. Have a great time with Mr. Movie Star. I look forward to seeing your faces splashed all over the place."

"I thought you don't read the gossip columns?"

"That was before I knew someone famous. From now on, I'm going to be living vicariously through you. Twitter, sign me up!"

Her energy was contagious. Climbing into the car, Jane wound down the window. "Let's hang out again, and soon."

"Absolutely. See you!"

She was off, sashaying down the street, hugging the box to her chest as if it was the most precious thing in the world.

"What next, Daryl?"

Her driver looked at her through the rearview mirror.

"Home, Miss. Jane. Miss. Adele has a team of stylists waiting for you."

"Of course she has," Jane smiled.

23

The lines on Logan's script blurred.

Letters shifted, rearranging themselves before his very eyes. He blinked and scratched his nose with annoyance.

It had been three hours since he'd dropped Jane off at the store. Despite the army of people that waited to prepare them for the night ahead, he'd needed to set aside time for the big scene that was filming at the end of the week.

It was the culmination of his character's story, the moment where everything — including his motivation for killing a man — rested. It was the revelation that would, if done correctly, send shock-waves rippling through the audience.

There were only two twists that had gone down in the history books prior, two that were referenced over and over again: that of Chinatown and The Sixth Sense, but with this, it was hoped that there would be a third.

It was for this scene that Logan had signed up for the movie.

But the work was proving more troublesome than he had anticipated. His focus was off, and if he were to be honest with himself, he knew where it had gone.

To a woman who knew nothing yet was twisting her way around his heart.

He had acted ridiculously this morning, when he'd demanded to meet her friend and proceeded to interrogate her as if she were a criminal, yet he hadn't been able to control himself. He'd needed to know that Clare wasn't anything other than she had appeared to be.

He'd been rude, he knew that, but it wasn't until she had revealed her fiancé's betrayal, and saw the hurt that still stung her eyes, that his concerns had been set aside.

With it, the guilt had come.

It seemed the least he could do after causing that unexpected upset was to gift her a dress as an apology. He'd had no real choice: it would have been adding salt to the wound if Clare had to spend the morning trying on clothes (he'd known she would — what woman wouldn't, put in the same position?) only to leave with nothing.

A smile tugged the corner of his lip when he pictured their faces as they learned of his surprise.

Jane had been cool to him today. It was that damn kiss and his reaction afterward that had drawn her frosty ire. Didn't she understand that he was trying to protect her? Trying to do the right thing?

Her coolness had disturbed him and made him retreat into his own shell.

Movie stars — in particular male action stars — had it drilled into them that they could never show any weaknesses or discomfort. He had to be strong at all times. When she'd blown past him that morning with barely a look tossed his way, he'd pulled out his phone and pretended to focus on it, despite not being able to make out a single line of any email.

There had been too many people in the room for him to be able to talk with her, and by the time they were on their way to the store, it seemed the moment had passed.

He didn't like how much she was getting under his skin. There was so much at stake here that she wasn't even aware of.

A vein throbbed in his temple and he closed his eyes, blocking out the words that were the bane of his life. Without even trying to, an image of Jane came into his mind.

He saw her at the store, standing in a sea of dresses, laughing with the kind of wild abandon he had yet to see in her tightly controlled movements.

She was an enigma.

So many of the things she said, even the way she moved, seemed at odds with each other. He saw the openly delighted way in which she had tasted his food, and the outburst she'd made at Adele this morning when the other woman had overstepped her line. But then a flash of her trembling body and white face reappeared. He saw that lowlife executive yelling at her in front of the entire crew — and how she hadn't said a word to defend herself.

It was almost as if she were two people.

One who yearned to be free, while the other kept a tight rein on her emotions and words. He had spent years studying body language with some of the most renowned teachers in the world, and her conflicting behavior was a puzzle. He wasn't convinced he could put down those conflicting sides of her to the memory loss.

There was something else going on with her that he was determined to find out.

And it was going to start with tonight's ball.

Tonight, he would get to know the real Jane who hid beneath the layers of protection she wore around herself.

HANDS WERE TOUCHING HER ALMOST EVERYWHERE, IT SEEMED.

Wearing only the stunning silk lingerie that someone had thrust at her (Jane shuddered to think how they knew her exact size), she laid on a leather recliner as her hair was expertly washed by an Amazonian woman with the gentlest touch. Her skin was buffed and her hands manicured in the spa that formed an entire wing of Logan's house. Though she had already been here a while, she still couldn't wrap her head around it.

The man had his own indoor spa.

The room was carved out of marble and divided into sections. On the far side sat a pair of matching massage tables, an array of oils and candles on a stone stand beside them. Another contained the make-up area. A rainbow of products waited in an easily accessible tiered display for someone to play with them. Lightbulbs protruded from the mirrored wall behind them. Across the room stood the nail bar and hairdressing salon.

As soon as she had arrived home, she had been whisked into this section of the house — which she hadn't even known existed. A part of her wanted to see Logan, to thank him for the kindness he'd extended to Clare, but she hadn't forgotten the awkwardness of the morning, or the tension of last night. Either way, the decision was taken off her hands as he'd been locked in his office, working for most of the afternoon.

She sank into the recliner, letting out a deep sigh as the team worked over her body. There was a minty aroma in the air, from all the creams and oils they used that relaxed her. The tension faded from her shoulders, massaged away by those magic fingers.

Energy sparkled from the team that were prepping her for the night's ball. There were six girls, all wearing conservative white dresses and pumps. They tackled their jobs with such enthusiasm, it would be easy to think that they were the ones who would be going out.

"You are frowning, am I doing this too hard?" Her hair washer asked with a Russian accent.

"No, no. It feels heavenly. I'm just not used to so many people fussing over me."

"You are Mr. Steel's lady now, you should get used to being pampered."

If only you knew.

Hoping to avoid further talk, Jane closed her eyes and tried to let the alien sensation of strangers touching her body fade away. Hopefully, the process wouldn't take too long…

It was almost four hours later when they finally announced that she was ready.

Once they had washed her hair, someone else had dried it, while another lotioned her body — ignoring Jane's insistence that she could do it herself. A Chicken Caesar sandwich was brought in, which she gratefully devoured, causing the girls around her to recoil in horror.

It was unheard of for a woman to eat carbs… and at *lunch* of all times!

Her face was artfully made up: light on foundation as Jane's flawless dewy skin didn't need much, the barest of eyeshadow and liner, and a deep red lip for drama. Her hair was put into a French twist made special by shifting it to one side as artfully arranged wisps spilled down to frame her face.

When she slipped into the dress and the strappy diamond-encrusted heels, Jane had to admit that the entire effect was dazzling. She stared at herself in the mirrors, unable to believe that the polished and composed woman reflected in them was her.

The girls' chatter and sighs of appreciation silenced at Logan's arrival.

The look on his face was electric.

His jaw turned slack, his mouth opening into an O. But it was his eyes raking over her body, turning hooded with a deep lust that sent her heart pounding in her chest.

And he wasn't the only one affected by the other's appearance.

Wearing a dark silver tuxedo that perfectly showcased his rippling muscles, and the toned body beneath, Logan looked every inch the movie star. His walnut hair had been styled with a textured pompadour blowout that added almost two more inches to his already tall frame. Cleanly shaved, his tanned skin glowed. His very presence seemed to have sucked all the air out of the room.

Jane drew in a sharp breath.

He was dangerously, lethally handsome. She forced her hands that had become clammy down to her sides.

Sensing the undercurrents in the room, the team of staff left, leaving the two alone.

"You are stunning, Jane. Truly beautiful."

He crossed the room to her, long legs striding as if he couldn't reach her fast enough. The fingers that lifted her chin were cool to the touch, yet conversely, they seemed to scorch her skin.

She fought to stay calm even as her stomach did flip flops.

"I had not noticed how graceful your neck was before. Like a swan," he murmured. His fingers glided over her skin in a light caress that sent chills shooting up her spine, the nerves seemingly heightened after hours of being handled.

"A shame then, that your look isn't complete."

It took a moment for his words to sink in. She watched in a daze as he pulled a string of diamonds from his pocket.

The stones dazzled under the lights, glinting like a thousand stars.

She gasped, drawn to the sparkling jewels. He reached up behind her to fasten the necklace.

"This is only on loan so don't become too attached," he warned.

His breath caressed the back of her neck. In response, her knees trembled, and she had to force them together to stop the knocking sound she was sure they would make.

"What will happen if I do?"

"It usually comes with its own bodyguard but since I

use the Harry Winston label quite often, they trust me enough not to run away with their goods."

"Are you kidding, about the bodyguard?"

"No."

"But that's..."

"Crazy?" He offered, finishing her question. "Not when you learn how much these things cost."

"I was going to say, silly. If a necklace costs that much than maybe no one should ever wear it."

"But what would adorn this lovely neck of yours, then?"

When had a neck or a woman enticed him as much? His fingers shook so much, he struggled with the clasp.

You've jumped across buildings, dangled out of helicopters and swam with a sea of sharks, so you can damn well work a clasp!

Finally, the thing was on, but he couldn't remove his hands from her. They slid down her neck, holding onto the space between her shoulders. He wanted to peel away that dress with his teeth until he exposed every inch of her creamy skin.

"What are you doing to me, Jane?" He asked, his voice, husky with desire.

Jane was drawn into those green eyes of his, drowning in the moment. She couldn't think of her fears or worries. But then she remembered last night, the way he had pulled away.

The man blew hot and cold so much, she had no idea what was going through his mind. He was definitely flirting right now, using those lethal charms on her, but to what end?

It occurred to her that this could just be part of their

act, but none of the makeup girls were here anymore, so who would benefit from this?

"I'm glad to see the lovebirds are getting hot and heavy, but save it for the cameras," Adele's imperious voice came from behind them.

They jumped away from each other like a shot.

"What terrible timing you have," Logan growled, scowling with the kind of anger Jane would find intimidating. Adele waved it off with a tiny hand.

"The car's waiting outside, but can I say, you two do look the part."

She had also changed for the occasion and was wearing a skintight Hervé Léger bandage dress that didn't leave anything to the imagination. If she wasn't as petite as she was, the dress would have looked vulgar on anyone else, but Adele somehow managed to pull it off. She looked dainty and perfect, a lynx in blood red with nails to match.

Pivoting on her heels, she stalked off ahead of them.

Placing a hand down the small of Jane's back, Logan nibbled on her earlobe, sending shock-waves rocketing her world.

"Duty calls, but it doesn't mean we can't have any fun while we work."

Jane sprang away from him.

"Don't do that!"

His laugh boomed around the high-ceilinged room.

24

Against the setting sun and a purple and black sky, they arrived at a majestic Art Deco mansion.

The stretch limousine that had brought them there stopped beside a red carpet that rolled out from a set of stone stairs. Spotlights shone down, illuminating the sea of celebrities that posed for the cameras lining each side of the carpet.

Lights flashed, white teeth beamed out of the night. Adele, who had ridden with them, got out of the car. "Showtime folks. Jane, it's time for you to shine."

Logan emerged to cheers (and a few boos) from the crowd. He reacted as if he had only heard the encouragement and waved at the gathered spectators.

He took hold of Jane's hand and gave it an encouraging squeeze. She stepped out and was immediately blinded by cameras. Voiceless faces shouted her name.

"Jane! You look great!"

"Over here, please."

"This way, Jane!"

The attention was deafening, the flashing lights and the crowd, overwhelming.

"Try to relax," Logan advised. "They only want to see how stunning you are."

Though he must have said this to every date he'd ever taken to something like this, Jane found her courage building. This was such a special event, she should try to savor each moment as she might never be a part of again.

If she had any family out there, surely they would see these pictures? She was comforted by the thought until another took over her mind: as soon as her family learned where she was, she would be back to her old life, and Logan… all of this, would be gone.

The sobering thought forced her to stand straighter. She had to live for the present, enjoy every moment she had with him as it could soon be all gone.

She turned to the cameras as they captured the excited smile on her face. Hand in hand, they walked up the red carpet, stopping now and then for more pictures. Occasionally, Logan would move to the barriers that held the public at bay, and pose for selfies or sign autographs. Some of the fans even wanted Jane in the shot, which she gladly obliged. The worship that came along with the fame was a heady mix: she could see how easy it would be to lose yourself to it if you didn't keep both feet on the ground.

Inside, the now black sky formed a dramatic backdrop against the domed glass ceiling. A big band played popular songs that even Jane recognized in a jazzy style. Dancers swirled across the floor, a kaleidoscope of color and motion. There was laughter, chatter and merriment everywhere she looked.

"Logan Steel! So good to see you again, my love," a redheaded woman with curves so dangerous that she should need a license to weld them, purred. An equally attractive, strong-jawed man stood smiling beside her.

"Mandy! Didn't think I'd see you here tonight," Logan kissed both her cheeks, shook her husband's hand.

"I had to meet this mysterious woman who has stolen your heart." To Jane, the smile offered wasn't as sultry, though it was genuine. "Lovely to meet you, Dear."

Jane returned her smile, taking Mandy's elegant hand in her own. "I'm Jane."

"I starred in one of Stonewall's movies a few years back. Stonewall's the CEO of Pinnacle Studios. He bankrolled one of my first movies," Logan explained.

"Yes, and we should talk about the possibility of another venture together," Stonewall offered. "If you'd stop running off to make all these action films, anytime you want to do something more character based, call me."

"None of that right now, gentleman. No business tonight, not when you have two lovely women waiting for a dance," Mandy interrupted.

"Of course. How is Lexi these days? It must be awhile since I've seen her. Is she still as strong-willed as I remember?" Logan enquired.

Stonewall raised a brow. "Worse. She is madly in love with the bodyguard we hired to protect her."

"After that kidnapping scare?"

"Yes."

"I remember seeing him at her birthday party. Tall, lethal looking. Is he the one who saved her?"

Stonewall nodded. "Let's not forget, he also let the

man take her in the first place. No one seems to ever mention that..."

Exasperated, Mandy sighed. "Honey, stop. You've got to let that go or Lexi's going to take real issue with you."

Logan studied his expression but couldn't read him. "I can't tell if you approve of him or not."

Stonewall sighed the long-suffering sigh of any parent. "I don't approve of her being in love or any of the things that go along with it... but, as a man, he's probably the best I could have hoped for. He dotes on her. They're even engaged now."

The word "engaged" seemed to cause him physical pain.

"He's an ex-marine," Mandy revealed to Jane. "A real-life hero. And he has the most incredible dog who should have his own movie franchise if you ask me." She elbowed her husband, this being a conversation they must have discussed, many a time.

"Now who's talking work?" Was his smooth reply.

"Maybe we should ask them to help us with Loki," Jane suggested. "Logan's dog is adorable, but he hasn't a clue how to train him."

"I'm sure something could be arranged," Mandy smiled. "Kane actually trains both dogs and their handlers for the security firm he works for."

Stonewall frowned at Logan. "I seem to remember you saying that you weren't one for pets?"

"I wasn't. He was kind of sprung on me. I didn't have much choice in the matter."

"Lexi's going to be upset that she couldn't convince you to adopt one of her dogs," Mandy commented. Their daughter worked at PAWS, a local animal shelter with a no-kill policy.

While they chatted, paparazzi surrounded them, their cameras working overtime, taking shot after shot of the group. The constant name calling and vying for their attention was becoming hard to ignore.

"Shall we give them the money shot so they'll go away?" Stonewall asked.

With the women in the center, the four smiled into the cameras for the shot that would become the cover of all the newspapers in the morning.

It seemed that Jane was introduced to the entire entertainment industry. Everywhere she looked, celebrities and VIPs greeted them, though none with the same warmth as Mandy and her husband. Behind their smiles, their eyes glittered with self-importance, and barely concealed malice in a few cases.

There was one particular moment of unpleasantness.

Spotting them from across the room, a man with a ruddy complexion barreled rudely past the guests until he reached them. Without waiting for Logan to finish speaking to his audience, he interrupted.

"I guess they let anyone in nowadays."

Jane felt herself freeze, sure that the comment had been meant for her, but the man's gaze was on Logan. Logan excused himself from his current conversation, his eyes a study in impatience.

"It would appear so."

"Touche," the man yanked at his bowtie, loosening it. The scotch he held in one hand swished around his glass. "Then again, I might have made more of myself if you hadn't stabbed me in the back."

Logan sighed, a long-suffering sigh. "Each time we bump into each other, we have another of these unpleasant meetings. When are you going to move on and let sleeping dogs lie?"

"That's easy for you to say. You hadn't risked your entire career and fortune — even your marriage — on that movie. You walked away from it at the last minute, tanking the entire deal and destroying my life."

"I've said this before, Jon, but I'll say this again in the hope that my answer will finally get through that dense head of yours. It wasn't personal. It was a business decision. Unfortunately, you had personal stakes involved — which, in fairness, anyone could have told you was a bad idea — but you gambled hard, and lost. You need to face up to that instead of blaming me, as frankly, I'm getting tired of this bullshit."

Jane hadn't said a word, watching them over the top of her glass of champagne. The air was charged with intensity. She didn't like this man and wished he would go away. She took a step back, only to draw his attention.

"Honey, I'm not the one you should be worrying about," Jon sneered. His face loomed close, large and threatening. She could smell the alcohol on his breath, feel the anger seeping through him.

"Step away from me, please."

She hated the tremble in her voice and how scared she sounded. This man was likely full of bravado and drink. There wasn't anything he was going to do to either of them, yet she couldn't stop the irrational dread that had taken hold.

Seeing her face turn the color of chalk, something

snapped inside Logan. He stepped in front of her, blocking her from Jon.

"If you don't leave by the time I finish this sentence, I will have no problem tossing your sorry ass out of here. This is a charity ball *for kids,* for Christ's sake. Get a hold of yourself."

His voice was raised now, his words carrying over to the guests partying close by. Faces turned to stare, pinpointing Jon — with his flushed face and unsteady hand spilling scotch over the floor — as a troublemaker.

Knowing he was making a spectacle of himself, Jon straightened, trying for some semblance of dignity.

"As if you'd ever lift a finger, Steel. You'd only get your team to do your dirty work, but no amount of publicity is going to stop your fall from grace. Enjoy swimming in the cesspool with the rest of us."

Knocking back what remained of his drink, he shoved his way through a group of chatting guests. Logan didn't care what the idiot had to say, concerned with only one thing. He took Jane by the elbows.

"You've turned very pale. Are you OK?"

She gave a small laugh. "I'll be fine. I'm just being ridiculous."

He eyes burned with intensity as he looked at her. "Jon is an ego maniac who loves to play the victim, but he's harmless. He's just flexing his balls because he feels so inadequate here."

His words were so descriptive that a picture of the man struggling to squeeze snooker balls that kept slipping through his tiny hands had her laughing. When she explained, his eyes danced with mischief.

"I thought the 'tiny hands' part of your vision most telling. You know what they say about them, of course..."

He raised a brow, happier now that color was coming back to her cheeks. For a moment there, she had seemed as if she might faint.

"Tiny hands, tiny... gloves." She shot him an impish look that made him weak at the knees.

There.

There was the woman he was hoping lay beneath the walls of protection she built around herself.

She was always so careful, tip-toeing around everyone, hesitating before she ever spoke as if to second guess herself. She might not have her memory, but Logan was beginning to get an insight in who she might have been before they met.

But he would wait to discuss those thoughts with Detective Summers.

Tonight, he was going to give her the best night of her life. Filled with the kind of intention that had brought all of his success, he wrapped an arm around her waist, noting how right it felt to have her nestling into him.

"I don't know about you, but I could sure do with some of that feast over there."

Her eyes turned wide at the banquet that lay before them.

They drank champagne, nibbled on Hors d'oeuvres of Miyazaki wagyu beef skewers, lobster-stuffed hibiscus, black truffle pot stickers and the caviar, sea urchin and scallop tartare that was cradled by an ice sculpture of an angel, in an homage to the children's charity that funds were being raised for. Individual pot pies, Kobe beef steaks, and baked sea bass were the mains to choose from.

Dessert came in the form of French macarons inspired by popular ice-cream flavors, red velvet brownies shaped like angel wings, and Matcha cake pops that Logan fed to her, using his thumb to brush away any crumbs left lingering on her lips.

When their stomachs were full, he took her for a spin around the dancefloor. Under the crystal lights, he twirled her round and round until she was giggling, breathless and dizzy.

"I'm going to fall."

He swooped her down grandly. "Then I'll simply have to catch you."

The smile he gave her could have stopped time.

She couldn't hear the music anymore or the sounds of the other revelers. There was only him and those eyes that she was sinking into. The air was electric. She had to speak or risk losing herself completely.

"This is some night."

It was a lame comment, designed to break the intimacy of the moment. But Logan wasn't phased for a second, having expected just as much.

Slowly, he helped her to straighten, tucking her face against his chest so closely that she could feel the beat of his heart. Laying his chin on the top of her head, he whispered into her hair.

"If you think this is good, just wait until you see what I have planned for the rest of the night."

A shiver ran through her. There was no doubt in her mind what he had meant by that... the only question was, whether he meant it or if this was all part of the show they were putting on.

She was so confused.

They were having such a wonderful time that she knew she was falling for him. But that was a dangerous, reckless, ridiculous thing to do. She was no one, and he was out of her league. She had absolutely nothing to offer him, not even her history.

But that winning smile that had set millions of hearts on fire was now directed at her.

And she was helpless to resist.

Wrapping her arms around his neck, she held onto him tightly, hoping that they could stay this way, forever.

SEVERAL HOURS LATER, WITH HER FEET BEGINNING TO HURT from the shoes, they sat by a water fountain under the light of a thousand twinkling stars. Jane kicked off her heels and massaged her sore toes.

"I've never really understood how feet can be erotic, but looking at you rubbing yours, I'm beginning to change my mind."

She stopped immediately, a blush staining her cheeks, and stared at him, uncertainty in her eyes.

"Relax, I'm not going to jump you right here… unless you want me to? Could get messy."

As he made no move toward her, she knew he was having fun at her expense.

"You're terrible," she finally replied.

"On the contrary, I've been told that's not true, but since this is clearly making you uncomfortable, I will be a gallant gentleman and change the conversation. Let's see... ask me anything and I'll tell you the truth."

She gave him a level look.

"Are you sure you want to play this game? I could run off and sell your story to the highest bidder tomorrow."

"I trust you. And you're also under contract, so I'm not particularly worried."

"Well, in that case... Have you always known you wanted to be an actor?"

He nodded. "Yes, since I was a kid. It's all I've ever wanted to do."

She thought for a while. "Why have you kept Loki if you're not particularly fond of dogs, or didn't even want one in the first place?"

"That's on Adele. She thought the public would like me more if they saw me as a responsible dog owner. She gave him to me so we could have lots of photoshoots of us together."

"Surely, you could just as easily do the photoshoots without actually keeping him?"

Logan blinked as if the thought had never crossed his mind. "Well, he was already with me. It's not like I don't have the space or time to take care of him, and, outside of the shoe thing, he isn't the worst company in the world..."

He trailed off, embarrassed by the admission. Jane had to hide her smile. The man had clearly become attached to his puppy, even if he didn't want to face the fact himself. She waited a moment, wondering if she should ask the real question that was on her mind.

"How many women have you truly loved in your life, and who were they?"

If he was taken aback by the question, he didn't show it. With a knowing smile, he answered, "One. So far, she has been the only woman to have completely stolen my heart. Not only is she beautiful, she's strong and fierce where it counts, but soft and gentle despite suffering many bitter disappointments in her life. She is, to this day, an angel amongst men, and I worship the very ground she walks on."

The love that came from him was palpable, as was the sudden, jealous knot in her stomach. She had asked, needing to know if he was capable of such love, but now that she had her answer, she didn't feel quite as she had expected.

"Are you talking about Ellie Godwin, your ex?"

Logan almost choked on his tongue from laughing.

"Why on earth would you think that?" A knowing look fell across him. "Wait, let me guess. Those magazines you keep denying that you read."

She shrugged, unapologetically. "You can't blame me for thinking that. They said you were head over heels in love with her…"

"Until I cheated on her?"

There was that raised eyebrow again. She was starting to think it might be his default expression.

"Ellie and I were in a real relationship, but it was never based on anything other than lust and fun. We met, and with all the chemistry flying around, things happened. But, she isn't the sweetheart the world thinks she is. That's the result of a carefully orchestrated campaign by her people. We broke up because I discovered she had cheated on me many times over. She also has several substance abuse problems."

"But, why did they say you were the cause of the

breakup, that it was you who cheated, you were the one with the addiction problems?"

"Because it suited their narrative better." Logan laughed, a hollow laugh that didn't meet his eyes. "This industry, hell, this entire city is built on them. Why else do you think so many co-stars 'fall' for each other during the press tour, only to break up the moment the movie comes out? Half of the relationships in this town are nothing more than publicity stunts."

"Like ours?" The question slipped out before she could stop it.

He lifted her chin with his fingers, forcing her to look at him.

"Ours may have started like that, but I think we can be adult enough to acknowledge that something real is happening here now. You do things to me, Jane, things that no other woman has done before."

"Not even the love of your life?"

Dammit, there was that spark of jealously again. She wished she could get a handle on it before she acted like a complete fool. A slow, knowing smile spread over his lips.

"I hope not, that would be far too disturbing." Seeing her confusion, he finally came clean.

"I was talking about my mom, Jane. She's the only woman I've ever totally and completely loved. Oh, and for the record, my mom never liked Ellie either. Couldn't stand her, actually. Thought her vapid and fake."

The resulting relief and the boost to her mood was troubling. She needed to steer this conversation to safer waters. "If you're not careful, Logan, you might develop a heart."

His eyes fixed on hers, intensely dark under the pale moonlight.

"If I'm not careful, you might steal mine."

She drew in her breath as a warmness seeped into her veins. Was this real? Could he really be falling for her?

"There you are," Adele called out from the night. "I've been looking for you everywhere. What're you doing out here?"

Logan rolled his eyes. "Trying and failing to have a quiet moment."

Adele heard the pointedness in his comment and, as usual, chose to ignore it.

"You can be as quiet as you'd like when you're dead or D-list. Until then, work calls."

"What's going on?"

"Stonewall Smith mentioned that he was serious about doing something with you again. He'd like to have a quick chat with you while Mandy is preoccupied. You've got about ten minutes before she extracts herself from the clutches of our host. The two of them are singing a number with the band, which will no doubt turn into one or two more. Go work your magic. He's hiding by that statue over there."

She gestured at the figure who they could only see from the glowing tip of his cigar.

Adele turned to Jane. "We'll have to do this conversation without you. It'll put him in a better bargaining position."

Jane waved them away. "I'm fine here, resting my feet. Go, network or whatever it is you need to do."

Bowing grandly to her, Logan flashed a quick grin before heading to his clandestine meeting with Adele.

Alone in the peace and quiet, Jane had a moment to admire her surroundings.

The house was beautiful, all lit up like a set from one of Logan's movies. She could hear the luscious voice of a woman singing sexily with the band which could only be Mandy Gray, who, Jane she suddenly realized she *could* remember.

Excited by the memory, she tried to place what movie she had seen her.

There was that one where she had played a single mom who could barely afford to feed her kid, but through her own tenacity, she'd managed to put herself through law school and went on to become the highest paid cooperate lawyer in the country. Jane was pretty sure there had been an academy award nomination for that performance, if not the actual award itself.

If only she could place *where* she had seen the film.

Closing her eyes, she tried recalling an image of the movie in her mind. Mandy's face appeared, all sultry wanton sex. Her hair was loose over one shoulder and pin-straight — quite different to the wavy style she wore tonight. Instead of a dress that clung to every curve, the Mandy in her mind's eye wore a pant suit, but the shirt was unbuttoned almost down to her navel, revealing a tantalizing glimpse of the lush body that lay beneath.

It was a look that had won over a generation of men and women alike and had left a lasting impression on her. She couldn't wait to tell Logan she'd had another memory! She sighed happily, hugging herself.

"I wouldn't look so pleased if I were you," a male voice sneered close to her ear. "He's probably off shagging some chick in the bushes."

Her eyes flew open.

She jumped, senses on full alert at the hostility from the man who had just spoken to her. With a jolt of wariness, Jane saw the face of Jon, the man from Logan's earlier altercation.

The hours hadn't been kind to him.

His bowtie, askew and loosened before, was now absent altogether, as was his jacket. His sleeves had been rolled up at some point, but now dangled messily around his wrists, while remnants of whatever he had eaten stained his shirt.

He lurched drunkenly on his feet, bristling with self-righteousness.

Jane knew she had to tackle this head-on. Replaying Logan's comment in her mind that he was bitter but harmless, she forced herself to stand taller. She would not cower to this bully.

"I don't want to talk to you, please leave." She was proud of how firm and in control she sounded, with not a hint of the nervousness she felt.

His face turned as hard as stone.

"*You* don't tell *me* what to do. What, do you think you're one of *them*?" He gestured at the guests in the distance. "If I can tell you don't fit in, you can be sure those pompous asses can."

The flutter of nervousness was churning now. She glanced around her, noticing how isolated she was. She could see Logan, but he was out of earshot, his back to her, talking animatedly with Stonewall and Adele. None of them were looking her way. No one was.

She was alone with this man.

Chilled, she wrapped her arms around herself, forced herself to speak again.

"If you don't leave, I will have someone remove you."

The ultimatum was meant to give him pause, instead his face grew redder.

"You don't threaten me, girl. Not when I know who you are." Spluttering with anger, spittle flew out of his mouth when he spoke.

There was nothing he could have said that would have shocked her more. She froze like one of the stone statues around them, eyes wide open.

"What do you mean?"

His eyes slid suggestively up and down her body, making her feel as if she was naked. Despite her best intentions, she found herself withering under his gaze.

"You're clearly new to the scene but tell me, what agency are you with?"

Jane had no idea what he was talking about, but she had decided he was full of it and she wasn't going to stick around to hear any more. She started away, not bothering to pick up her discarded shoes. She only needed to get away from him.

He followed.

"You're very good at playing innocent and coy… then again, maybe he's paying you more for that."

Suddenly, he lunged and slipped an oily hand around her waist. His grip was surprisingly strong. Pulling her into him, he hissed into her ear.

"How much do you charge for an hour, maybe we can work out a deal?"

His words struck panic into her, but it was nothing like

the terror that took over as a forgotten memory flashed into her head.

Water… there was water all around her, but Jane wasn't in it. She was leaning over the side of a boat?

No…

It was a yacht.

She wore a bikini and a sarong, her head sheltered from the beating sun by an oversized straw hat. She stared out at the endless blue ocean when she was grabbed from behind.

And suddenly, the calm she had been feeling morphed into sharp daggers of fear.

The memory vanished as quickly as it had come, but the terror remained…

And so had his arm, which tightened around her, squeezing the air from her lungs.

"Get off me!" She managed to gasp, but it was no use.

His hold on her was vice-like.

She glanced over at Logan, but he was still deep in conversation and oblivious to the danger she was in.

She twisted wildly, trying to escape his clutches when he started pulling her behind a tall hedge…

25

Fear constricted her throat, making it impossible to speak.

This couldn't be happening to her, not here.

Not now.

Yet it was.

With a strength that belied his five-foot-ten stature, Jane was being dragged into the shadows where nothing good was going to come of it.

She bucked, flailing her arms, trying to reach up and maybe stab him in the eyes with her fingers, but he was ready for this, dodging to avoid them.

Heart on fire, she sucked in a deep breath.

"LOGAN!! HELP ME!"

She cried out into the night, hoping her voice would carry over to him. She didn't know if it had, as she couldn't see anything but the dark, oblong shapes of the hedge that now surrounded them.

She twisted and bulked, making it as difficult as

possible for him to move her, when footsteps crashed toward them as a figure hurtled into view.

She caught a glimpse of his face as it flashed beneath the light of a lamp.

Logan!

His fist smashed into Jon's face. Jon's head snapped back, pain clouding his vision. He released Jane immediately, cupping hold of the nose that must be broken. Jane stepped quickly aside as Logan threw Jon to the ground, straddled him and held him there by the shoulders.

Fury blazed from his eyes as he glared down at him.

"You don't ever touch her!"

He punched him again and again as Jon started sobbing like a baby. More footsteps crashed toward them, someone big and heavy-footed, without any of Logan's grace.

Stonewall.

His eyes assessed Jane quickly, but when he found her uninjured, he turned his attention to Logan and the cowering Jon.

"Logan, you can stop now."

But Logan was far from hearing, driven by the terrible rage that laced his heart at seeing Jon's hands on Jane, knowing he'd intended to do more than just grab her.

Lights flashed, illuminating the pair, as guests rushed over to see the commotion. Stonewall grabbed Logan by the elbows and physically hauled him off Jon.

"She's fine, Son," Stonewall said into his ear, the voice of reason. "You need to stop. You have an audience."

It was another moment before he was able to see straight. With the threat now curled into a ball, wailing like a baby, Logan staggered to Jane, who fell, trembling, into his arms.

She felt as fragile as a bird.

Her face was drained of all color, even her lips. Some of her hair had escaped the French Twist and now fell around her in clumps. She looked disheveled and shell-shocked...

And it had taken every ounce of willpower not to kill Jon.

He hadn't thought about what he was doing, wasn't really conscious of it. All he knew was he had to save her and finally put that maniac in his place — even with all those cameras pointing at him.

He didn't care about his reputation anymore. In that moment, only Jane's safety mattered.

Blocking her from their view, Logan took hold of her hands. They were like ice.

"Did he hurt you?"

She managed to shake her head, tearing her gaze away from the figure on the ground who had caused her such terror. In Logan's arms, she was safe. She leaned into him, taking comfort from his strength.

So many lights flashed in her eyes that they blinded her.

"Show's over, people. How about we head back inside? I hear the celebrity auction is about to begin and you're not going to want to miss who you could get a date with."

It was Adele, doing what she did best. She attempted to wave the gathering crowd away, but they mostly ignored her. What was happening here was far too juicy to ignore.

Logan needed to get Jane home to safety. He had to get that panic-stricken look out of her eyes. He tugged gently on her hands, but she didn't move. There were too many people, too many cameras pointed at her. Her chest rose and fell worryingly fast. She was on the brink of another panic attack.

One that, he knew, would be recorded by the spectators here.

His mouth thinned into a line. No way in hell would he allow that to happen. He picked her up in his arms.

"Give her some space!"

No one moved, the guests crowding around them, each thinking his words hadn't applied to them. A low growl burst out of him as he half jogged, half elbowed his way to their car. The last thing he heard was Adele's voice demanding that the crowd stop filming them.

When they arrived home, Logan didn't bother asking if she could walk. Scooping her into his arms, he carried her into the living room. Any protests she might have uttered were ignored. He settled her onto the sofa, covered her with a wool blanket.

Excited yapping drew close until a bundle of fur hurled itself at the two of them. Loki's face shone with love at their return. He barked and licked and squirmed as Jane came out of her icy stupor to stroke him, his fur warming her frozen hands.

Logan set Loki on her lap and watched as Jane's arms went around him automatically. Just being with the puppy was helping her to come back to herself.

"I'll be right back," he said.

"OK," she replied. It was only two syllables, but it was more than she had said since they'd left the ball. He returned moments later with a tray of peppermint tea, a jar of honey, and a cup.

Pouring a cup of the tea, he stirred in a spoonful of honey and handed it to her. The smell of the mint cleared her mind, helping her come back to herself.

"Thank you."

"I've never seen anyone go into shock like that. Are you sure you don't want a doctor?"

"I'm fine. I was just scared."

"I should never have left you alone." He ran a hand through his hair. His jaw was clenched so tight, veins popped up from his skin.

"You weren't to know he would come back."

"But I should have known he'd try something. He all but warned me earlier, but I was too cocky, too sure of myself." Reaching over Loki, he took her free hand, entwining his fingers with hers. "If anything had happened to you, I'd never forgive myself."

His concern brought a lump to her throat. Her hand felt so small in his, like he could protect her from the world. Her heart was beginning to melt and there was nothing she could do about it.

She sipped the tea. The drink soothed her soul, chasing away the cold the attack and her flashback had caused. "This is good. Will you thank Kitty for me?"

He looked vaguely insulted.

"You think I can't handle making a pot of tea? First you question my cooking ability — which I clearly proved

— and now this." He shook his head at Loki. "I can't win, can I?"

Hearing the sad tone in his voice, Loki lifted his nose to the ceiling and howled, earning a tummy rub from him. Jane laughed.

"The two of you are incorrigible."

Loki shoved his nose into her leg, encouraging her to join in with the petting.

Letting go of Logan's hand, she obliged. The dog fell onto his side, rear leg lifting, peddling the air in utter bliss.

They were interrupted by his vibrating phone, sliding around the leather sofa, the name Adele flashing insistently. Logan declined the call only for the phone to ring again, this time, Trevor. He rejected that call too and switched the phone to silent.

Jane set her tea onto the glass coffee table. "This entire night was meant to give you some good publicity, not make things worse. Are they very angry?"

"I can deal with the fallout tomorrow. I only have one thing on my mind right now, and that's you."

She acted as if she hadn't heard him. "I'm so sorry, Logan."

"Why are you apologizing? You didn't do anything wrong."

Her gaze dropped to the carpet, her shoulders hunching over. "I shouldn't have antagonized him."

"There was nothing you could have said to him that would have justified his actions, Jane."

Her brilliant blue eyes filled with shame. "But I told him to go. I commanded him, actually. That's what set him off. He didn't like taking orders from me."

Logan had heard enough. He would not let her

shoulder any more blame, not for a second longer. "If anyone's to blame, it's me. I made light of him and didn't think him a threat. I wouldn't have left you alone for a second if I had known he would attempt something like this."

He fell silent, hoping that his words would sink in.

"At least some good came out of today. I had two memories, I think."

She filled him in on what they were. When he didn't respond straight away, she wrung her hands. "I'm sorry. I shouldn't have said anything."

Logan cursed under his breath. "Stop apologizing! Why do you keep thinking things are your fault?"

Her eyes were round discs. "I know I've made things ten times worse for you. And after all you've done to help me. I know I'm only a job, a contract."

Her words sent him reeling. "Is that all you think you are? We had a connection tonight, Jane. At the ball."

"I thought that was for show."

"You flatter me, but I'm not that good an actor."

His words were crushing, his eyes brittle as glass. She'd hurt him with that comment. It was the last thing she'd wanted to do, but her mind was a jumble of confusion.

"What about that night, our kiss?"

"What about it?"

"I invited you to stay, but you left. You pulled away and only came back to talk about the job."

"Is that what this is about?" The pieces finally fell into place. He couldn't believe that was what had been bothering her.

"That wasn't about you, Jane. I have dyslexia. Pretty

badly, actually. And I needed to work on my lines for the next day's filming, to make sure I had them memorized. I didn't want to leave you that night."

She didn't know what to think, blindsided by the revelation. "Dyslexia? Then how do you read your scripts?"

"Very slowly. I have to break down each sentence, and I have my own form of shorthand, diagrams and such, that I note in my scripts."

She recalled the bloated script from his trailer. "The Post-It notes?"

"I use those when I run out of space on the margins. Vicky, my assistant, also reads the script aloud, and records it for me, though I try to use that as a last resort."

"Why didn't you mention this before?"

He rubbed the stubble that was starting to show on his chin.

"It's something I'm not particularly proud of having. I understand it's not my fault, but I still feel lesser because of it. I suppose it didn't help that my team decided to keep it under wraps: it was felt that it didn't add to my action hero persona. Only a handful of people are aware I have it."

Since he was finally coming clean, there was no going back. He had to say the very thing that had been on his mind almost from the second they had met.

"That wasn't the only reason I left that night. I've been attracted to you from the start, but you were traumatized. A victim. Added with the memory loss and it didn't seem right for me to take advantage of you like that. And, as you've since discovered, I do have a tendency to be protective over helpless women. I had to know that what I was feeling was for you, and not because of my hero complex."

Jane felt as if she wasn't in her body. "I might not know who I am, but I can decide who I want to become involved with. How could you think you'd be taking advantage of me?"

He peered at her beneath dark lashes. "You're staying in my home. You could have thought you had to reciprocate, even if you didn't want to, or risk angering me."

She would never have thought that of him, though she understood why it might have been a concern of his.

"You would never do that."

"But, you didn't know that."

She shook her head, her eyes softening. "I do, actually. I know enough about you that I trust you more than anyone else in this world."

His smile was rueful. "So, out of the five people you know, then?"

She gave him a look that clearly showed that was not what she meant.

"So, you really did want to stay with me that night?"

Though he'd already explained his feelings for her, she still seemed to doubt them.

She would never believe anything he had to say about the matter. Whatever had happened to her in the past, something — or someone — had done a real number on her confidence. Whether she could remember that or not, it seemed obvious to him now.

He would just have to show her.

Leaning in, he kissed her with a passion that left her breathless. Wrapping his arms around her, he pulled her in close. Only Loki, still lying between them, stopped him from crushing her to him.

Her lips yielded beneath his as he tasted her sweetness. He nibbled and teased, enjoying the shiver his actions caused. She trembled in his hands even as she moved into him more.

Her body felt so right in his hands, he had to fight the urge not to tear off her clothes then and there. This night had to be savored. He stood and scooped her into his arms again. Her hands went around his neck and he caught a hint of the delicious citrus scent that covered her skin.

Still kissing her, he started toward the bedroom as Loki bolted off the sofa after them.

When he laid her down onto his bed, Jane wasn't even aware how they had gotten there, caught in a wave of desire so strong. She barely noticed the bed that faced the wrap-around windows that overlooked the ocean, or the roaring log fire that sizzled in the corner, adding to the heat that could already be felt.

Loki made a leap for the bed, but it was too high for him. He whined, but when there was no assistance from the two of them, he moved to the fireplace and settled on a pair of Logan's slippers.

With her hair fanned around her, her chest heaving with desire, and those lips plump from their kissing, Jane was a vision.

Logan kissed the neck that had been teasing him all night, luxuriating in the silkiness of her skin. She tasted of cream and honey, and smelled of some heady concoction that sent blood rushing through his veins. He reached behind her to the zipper as she turned onto her side to grant him better access.

That small movement that signified her eagerness for him rocked him to his core. He slid the dress off her, drawing in a breath at the miracle of her body which, until now, he'd only had glimpses of.

Lowering his lips to hers again, his hands explored her body. She gasped into his mouth, her hands reaching up as she undid his shirt.

She fumbled with the buttons, struggling to concentrate when his mouth, his hands were doing delicious things to her. Finally the shirt came off, and she saw just how beautiful he was. Her hands laid against his chest, fingers curving around the smattering of dark hair that was there. They moved down to his navel. He shivered. She loved that she was the cause of it.

She undid his belt buckle, fingers trembling until he made fast work of it himself. Stepping out of his tailored pants, he stood in all his glory, hidden only by a small pair of briefs that left nothing to the imagination.

Jane swallowed the lump in her throat.

He was so wild, filled to the brim with masculinity. His touch was greedy, yet his kisses were as gentle as butterflies.

He laid on top of her as they feasted on each other. Feeling her bare flesh pressed against his, Logan felt a jolt of need that threatened to over power him. He had to force himself to take things slow. Her moans were a song to his ears.

Her fingers dug into his shoulders as they became one.

When they finally exploded, the rush caused them both to collapse into a sweaty heap.

She fell asleep in his arms, listening to his chest beating against the sound of the waves lapping on the shore below.

26

She was lying on a soft pillow of bliss, her body spent.

Bright sunshine as sunny as her mood poured into the room, drenching her with its warmth. She could still feel Logan's mouth on her, as he kissed and nibbled, until it had driven her wild with abandon. She could even feel him licking her cheek now, panting heavily into her face.

This seemed… odd.

She forced her eyes open and was met with the full force of Loki's exuberant love. Having finally managed to climb his way onto the bed, he couldn't have been more overjoyed. She pushed his wet nose from the side of her neck.

"That tickles!"

Her response only made him tackle her again until she was forced to move him onto her chest. He laid down on her, nose only a dangerous inch away from her face, delighted by this full-on attention.

The bed beside her was bare, though still warm from

the heat of Logan's recent body. She could hear the jets of the powerful shower going. Steam billowed from the bathroom, curling along the carpet toward her. Sighing happily, she stroked Loki, letting the sound of the shower and sea outside relax her.

For the first time since she could remember, she felt like a real person and Logan had given that to her.

The shower stopped. Logan's feet padded to the doorway. When he emerged clad only in a towel, his body gleaming and surrounded by steam, she felt a tug inside and was surprised by the need in her.

Seeing that she was awake, a slow, sexy grin appeared on his face when the sun decided to dip behind a cloud, casting his face in shadow.

And for a split second Jane saw a flash of another man's face instead.

One that filled her with utter terror.

It was gone in a moment, but those eyes… they had looked at her with such a seething rage that all her nerves screamed out. Those eyes had gone now, but she could still feel the hatred they held for her.

She sat up, sending Loki tumbling with a whine of protest.

Her face was a study in shock that left Logan's heart hammering. She looked as if she'd seen a ghost — one that had driven the fear of God into her.

"What is it?"

He crossed to the bed, wrapping a wet arm around her. She was as tense as a drawn bow.

"It wasn't your face. For a moment there, I saw someone else. A man. I've seen him before and… God, why am I'm so scared?"

He rubbed her back, his mind racing at the possibilities. "Was it a memory?"

"I don't know. Sometimes, I think I remember things, but then it turns out that it's just part of a movie I've seen. It's not clear."

"Like the eggs?"

She nodded, blonde hair tumbling around her face. He brushed away the strands that had fallen into her eyes. "Yes."

"I might know of a way that can help you to get your memories back if you're willing to try? I didn't bring it up before as I didn't think you were ready, but, it seems too important to wait any longer."

She chewed on the corner of a lip, unsure where he was going with this.

"If it's not clear to you by now, Jane, I'm crazy about you. Whatever we discover about your past, we'll handle it together."

Her heart did a happy dance. Up until this moment, she hadn't been truly aware how alone she had felt, even with his help. They'd both had that wall between them, though for very different reasons, but just hearing those words from him now. It was everything. She had him now: he would be there for her.

"What were you thinking?"

"I know of a hypnotist. She's popular with celebs for losing weight or getting clean. I think we should get in touch and see if she can help you."

She didn't hesitate to answer. "It's worth trying."

"I'll get dressed and make the call."

Nerves fluttered in her stomach. "I'll feed Loki while you do that."

She looked for something to wear, but her charity dress was unsuitable for the task ahead and the pool house was all the way across the property. Snatching up Logan's shirt from the carpet where it had been tossed last night, she put it on, rolling up the sleeves to her elbow. The shirt was too large and hit her mid thigh, but she'd be mostly decent, in case she came upon any of the help.

In the kitchen, she filled two metal bowls, one with kibble and the other with water, and presented both to Loki. He dove in with abandon, though he seemed to flick more food out of his bowl than he ingested.

She fried eggs and bacon, made toast, poured juice and coffee and arranged all onto a tray. Someone — Kitty, most likely — had stacked the day's newspapers on the counter. Jane picked up the top one.

As expected, their faces were all over the cover. First, a shot of the two looking regal and happy as they emerged from their car. The camera had captured her mood perfectly, while the careful lighting of the host flattered everyone who appeared beneath those lights. Her skin was radiant, eyes bright and sparkling with life, and all her joy seemed to have been directed at Logan. An air of happiness wrapped around him like a cloud.

They looked like a couple madly in love.

The next picture included Mandy and Stonewall, as they laughed and chatted. There was even one of Mandy and Jane conversing together, looking for all the world as if they were friends. It surprised Jane that in that dress and with all the work that had been done to her, she didn't look as out of place as she had felt at the time.

Her eyes moved down to the last picture. As luck would have it, it was a perfectly timed shot of Logan with his fist flying through the air as he went for Jon. A snarl had distorted his face, causing him to seem more savage than he was.

Jane braced herself for the headlines, steeling herself for the worst. As her eyes took in the words, her breath hissed out in one big release.

They explained Logan was only protecting his lady from the unwanted advances of a drunk. There were witnesses who corroborated the story, other celebrities and guests. Words like 'HERO' and 'WARRIOR' peppered the article.

Relieved that she had been the cause of some good publicity for once, she carried the food to the sunroom and set it down onto the table.

"That shirt looks far better on you than it ever did me."

Logan came up behind her, planting a kiss on the back of her head. He was dressed in a pair of lounge pants and nothing else. His eyes slid up and down her bare legs, liking what he saw.

"You made us breakfast?" He sat down, admiring the spread before him.

"You're not the only one who can cook."

Nibbling on a piece of bacon, he glanced over the papers. "What's the damage?"

"Nothing actually. They're full of praise for you saving your damsel in distress."

He stopped chewing. "That's all? Nothing about my being a monster?"

"No. You're a real action hero now."

The wicked grin that flashed out of him lit up his whole face. "It's about time reality caught up with the truth."

Jane sat beside him. "And there's that ego again. Amazing you can even fit in this room."

He attacked the eggs with a fork, famished from the activity of the night.

"The earliest appointment I can get with the hypnotherapist is for tomorrow. I'll be stuck on set and won't be able to go with you. Would you rather wait until I can? I should have a free afternoon coming up in my schedule."

Jane went with her first instinct. "I'd rather get it over and done with."

"Why don't you see if Clare can go with you?"

"Good idea."

She called Clare only to discover she couldn't get the time off work at such short notice — her manager seemed to live for being difficult despite her pleas that it was important.

Hearing their conversation, Logan spoke in-between mouthfuls of food.

"Tell her to tell him that I'll put in a good word for their store if he'll let her have the entire day off tomorrow."

Jane didn't think it would do much, but to her shock, the offer was snapped up as Logan had suspected it would. She hung up the phone, turning to face him.

"Are you really going to do that?"

"I always keep my word. It's not actually me who tweets though. Someone on my team deals with that."

Of course. It was another way to cover up the dyslexia.

She was beginning to see how well he functioned with it, given there was an entire team ready to cover the condition for him.

"Do you have to work today?"

"As luck would have it, I'm all yours. I wonder if we can think of some fun things to do?"

And it turned out that they could.

Many fun things that left them each breathless.

27

Marko's face throbbed from the stitches he'd just had removed that bisected the scar on his left cheek. The wound ran only an inch or so long, but even that had been too much.

A burst of renewed rage threatened to spill over and into the room where he sat waiting for his plastic surgeon to return with his jacket.

The man had been surprised when he had arrived over a week ago, demanding to be seen, stitches normally being the work of hospital staff. But Marko took his appearance as seriously as he did everything else.

Everything had to be perfect.

He had to be perfect, which meant, if there was a scar to be left, that had to be perfect too.

He heard voices beyond the door. Another client had just arrived and was wondering if he'd be able to schedule in their daughter for a procedure.

Good luck with that.

The plastic surgeon was highly sought after, with a waiting list of months for his patients. Luckily, for Marko, the man was one of his clients, so the usual wait didn't apply to him.

He'd kept the man on retainer almost as soon as he'd started his business in the city, after all, it was only smart to have someone on his staff who could give him a new face, if one were ever to be needed again…

Drumming his fingers impatiently, he glanced at the tacky tabloids that littered the coffee table.

And his heart stopped.

There, staring up at him, her face more happy, more lovely than it had every right to be… was his wife.

His dead wife.

The one who, he'd thought, was rotting in the bottom of the ocean.

Thoughts of his surgeon flew out of his mind. Marko snatched up the magazine, pouring over the pictures that were plastered over the pages.

How could this be?

How was she not only alive, but thriving — and living with a movie star of all people?

Confusion caused his heart to twist painfully.

In the days since she had left him, she had been all he could think about. He'd barely been able to drag himself out of bed, surrounded by so many reminders of their time together. The only time he'd even left the house was to come here, to have the stitches put in when it was clear that he'd needed them.

He couldn't eat.

He couldn't sleep.

Every time he closed his eyes, he could see the loathing on her face as she'd jumped into the water as vividly as if it were happening right before him.

He hadn't been able to resign himself to the thought that she had actually believed that he would hurt her!

Yes, there had been times he had been a little rough, but it was only because he'd been driven insane by his love for her. He'd only ever wanted the best for her, so her betrayal, her leaving him like that, was like a dagger to his heart.

He couldn't understand how she had survived that storm, being the terrible swimmer that she was. How was she alive and living with Logan Steel? And why had the authorities not come for him?

His head hurt as he tried to make sense of it all.

His eyes raced across the page, the words searing into his skull.

She was introduced as Steel's girlfriend, but there was nothing about who she really was. They called her Jane Smith, said the two had met on the beach one day while he had been walking his dog. There were pictures of her around town, getting stopped by a policeman when her car had broken down, and some of her shopping for clothes on Rodeo Drive — and Steel was in *all* the damned pictures.

There were even pictures of the three of them on set, playing happy families with the dog.

He could feel the bile rising in his throat.

She had always wanted a dog, though he couldn't abide the awful things. The fur they left everywhere, and the smell. Dirty creatures, not fit to clean his shoes.

He looked for a mention of her previous life, of him, *her husband*, but there was nothing.

It was as if she had not existed until now.

As if their lives together, their marriage, had meant nothing at all.

The door opened as his surgeon returned with his jacket in hand.

"Here. If there is any sign of an infection, call me, otherwise you're as good as done."

Marko could barely hear his words over the pounding of his own heart.

"Good."

He needed to get out of there. He needed to think. Grabbing his jacket, he hurried out of the room.

The walk back to his car was a blur.

He might have pushed past a housewife and her brat who had gotten in his way. She had shouted at him, full of indignant righteousness, until she had seen the expression in his eyes and felt the fury that was only held back by a thread. Pushing her brat behind her, she'd backed away.

At least she had known her place.

Arriving back to his car, Marko searched Google furiously for what information he could about his wife, but there was nothing except that same story that had obviously been created for her, recreated almost word for word.

No site ever mentioned where she was truly from or her real name, constantly referring to her as that ridiculous Jane Smith, which begged the question, why?

What on earth was happening here?

The more he thought about it, the more confused he

became. He grabbed his head, squeezing it until tears pricked his eyes and the noise dialed down. Only then did one thought became abundantly clear.

If his wife was alive, he was going to get her back. And no movie star, or anyone else, was going to stop him.

28

On a recommendation from Logan, Jane and Clare feasted on Eggs Benedict and fruit salads as Loki lay by their feet at a booth in Musso & Frank Grill, the city's oldest restaurant pre-dating even the Hollywood sign. And it wasn't only the food that made it special: industry veterans — several with their handprints in the Hollywood Walk of Fame — could still be seen holding court as they thrashed out their latest movie deals behind them.

When Jane had told Logan that she would be meeting with Clare before the session with the hypnotherapist, he had booked them a table under his name, which might be the reason they were experiencing such VIP treatment.

Unable to join them himself, he'd wanted the two to experience a little of the city's magic, knowing that the appointment ahead might cause some distress.

He was, as she was rapidly learning, a most thoughtful man.

Looking unconsciously chic in high-waisted pants and

a sleeveless camisole, Clare was making easy work of keeping her nerves at bay.

"People seek hypnosis for anything in this town, I'm sure he's only recommending the best. You've got nothing to worry about."

Jane's fork pushed around a piece of melon on her plate.

"I'm more concerned about what it might dredge up. I called Summers again, before I got here, but he still had nothing to report. It's like I didn't even exist before I came here."

Clare hated to see her so worried.

"Well, you've certainly arrived with a bang, haven't you? And can we please discuss this glow around you today, that, despite all your concerns, you can't hide."

She looked over her plate, a knowing look on her face.

"You two have been doing the nasty haven't you?"

The blush that stained Jane's cheeks was answer enough. Clare laughed, dropping her fork to reach across the table to grab her hands.

"Please tell me it was amazing."

"It was. It is," Jane admitted, unable to stop the goofy smile from appearing. "He's nothing like they say he is."

She picked up a piece of bacon, passing it to Loki. Wolfing it down, he bathed her fingers with his tongue until no trace of them remained.

"You don't have to tell me. I've already experienced the man's generosity, and look at how he gave you a place to stay… unless, it was always his plan to get into your pants. Then that would be pretty bad, actually. The #MeToo crowd would have a field day."

"He wasn't interested in me in the beginning. It all grew from us spending time together."

"Then it's the real thing?"

"I hope so," Jane admitted.

Clare squeezed her hands. "Then I'm really happy for you. God knows you could do with some happiness."

Struck by how much of the conversation she had monopolized already that morning, Jane changed the subject.

"How about you: anything new to report? I swear there was a pep in your step today, too."

Clare's eyes widened. "I'm that transparent?"

"Only because you can't seem to stop smiling too."

"I might have met someone." She grinned, pushing her plate away, no longer interested in the food no matter how delicious it was.

"Tell me everything."

"I met him at my store. He came in to find a gift for his mother, isn't that adorable? Hopeless about women's sizes, though. I had to use a line of staff members for us to figure it out. We got chatting and when he paid for the goods, he asked me out for a coffee."

Her eyes had taken on a glow as she relived the moment in her mind.

"That's great! When are you going?"

At Jane's question, Clare looked embarrassed.

"We actually went already. The end of my shift was approaching, and he didn't mind coming back to the store for me. Does that make me desperate? I've been out of the game for so long I don't have a clue what the rules are."

"The rules are that you do whatever you feel like," Jane

was pretty firm on this. She hated that their society decreed games should be played in a relationship, especially in the beginning stages. Honesty was best. It let both parties know where they stood at all times.

"Then that's OK then." Clare took her hands back and interlaced her fingers, holding them girlishly to her chest. "He's so lovely, Jane. He's handsome, dresses well, and dotes on his mother. I think he must have money too, given how he dresses."

"Sounds like a winner to me." Jane shared her friend's grin, happy they were experiencing romance in their lives at the same time. "When are you seeing him next?"

"Tomorrow. He's taking me to a classy restaurant for a real date. I can't wait! It's been so long since I've felt special."

Her words struck a chord in Jane. She smiled.

"Maybe we can double date in the near future, wouldn't that be fun?"

Clare's laugh tickled the air.

"I'm not sure about introducing him to a famous super star just yet. I think even the most well-adjusted man would feel inadequate against that."

"In a few weeks, then. I'll wait until you've cemented the deal, then we'll fix something up." Jane smiled, eyes full of mischief.

"IF YOU'RE SITTING COMFORTABLY, WE CAN START."

The therapist sat opposite Jane, legs crossed in a wide armchair. He had a round face with wide, honest eyes that were only half hidden by the thick-rimmed glasses he wore. He spoke with a smooth, easy cadence that put her at ease.

Beside him, he kept a notebook and pen, though neither were in use right now. Soothing ambient sounds played from the walls. The blinds were drawn but angled so that some light still slanted in.

Clare and Loki sat in the waiting room outside, within "shouting distance" as Clare had put it, so if by chance she felt at all uncomfortable, she had only to let it be known.

Her hands rested on either side of a matching armchair, her head cushioned by the headrest. She was as comfortable as she could likely be, given the situation.

"I'm ready."

It wasn't a lie.

Despite the nerves dancing a tango in her stomach, she needed to know who she was. With her relationship with Logan developing as it had, it was more imperative than ever to learn her truth, whatever it might be.

"Let's focus on your breathing. Breathing in through your nose and out through your mouth. Allow your mind to drift… to silence the chatter. All we're concerned with, is the air coming in, then out of your body."

Her chest rose and fell as the air entered and left. He paced his words to match the rhythm of her breathing.

"When you are nice and comfortable, I will begin counting down from twenty. Just keep breathing and listen to my voice as you start to feel yourself letting go. Twenty… Nineteen… Eighteen…"

The room was like a womb, cradling her in warmth and security. Whether it was the ambient sounds or his gentle voice, she soon found herself drifting into another place.

"Where are you now? What can you see?"

His voice was omniscient, coming from all around her. She was comforted by it, assured by its safety.

"I hear water. The ocean." Although she had answered, she wasn't aware of her own voice. There was only the hazy vision that appeared in her mind. She wasn't in her own body, her spirit floating through glimpses of a possible past.

"Where is this ocean?"

She frowned, unable to put a location to it. "I don't know. I'm in a marina."

'What is the weather like?"

"Sunny, but I'm cold."

She shivered, the therapist caught the reaction.

"How are you feeling other than cold?"

Jane twisted her hands. "Anxious. I need to be perfect."

"Why?"

The question made her face fall. Her entire demeanor changed. She seemed to shrink before his very eyes.

"I can't talk about it," she whispered in a scared voice. He noted it down, feeling the first flicker of concern by her reaction.

"Let's move on then. Other than the ocean, what else is there at the marina?" It was important not to put words into her mouth.

"A building. A glass square cube. I don't like it. I've never liked it."

"Do you know why that is?"

Her head shook from side to side, a frown on her brow as if the question was too difficult to answer.

"What else do you see?"

"A yacht."

"And who's there at the marina, do you see any other people?"

There was a sudden thudding in her ears. The world swam, a black fog clouding her mind. She heard a faint hissing sound that sent terror spiking into her heart.

"No!" She gasped, lurching up in her seat. "Stop!"

Seeing the abject terror that had taken over her, the therapist had to stop the session. It wasn't safe to continue any further.

"Breath Jane. You're not really there. You are here in my office with me. I'll count to three and you'll start to regain consciousness. On three, you will be fully awake, do you understand? One… two… three… Wake up, Jane. Come back."

Her eyes flew open.

She blinked, her vision returning. Her fingers dug into the arms of the armchair until they hurt, but she welcomed the pain. Pain meant that she was still here.

Locating her therapist's face, she held onto the concern she found there, but even though she was safely in his office, it would be some time before the terror of her vision would fade.

"THAT SOUNDS HORRIFYING. DID HE SAY WHAT HE THINKS IT all means?"

Jane sat in Clare's Prius, holding Loki in her lap. They were on their way to set to visit Logan. More than thirty minutes had passed since her hypnosis session, though Jane was still reeling from it.

"That something important happened there, but my mind isn't ready to remember it fully yet."

Clare shot her a sidelong glance. "And that's it? We just leave it?"

"No. I'll go back again, but he said I need to give myself a few days to recover, the mind being more fragile than we realize."

"Well, he is the expert. At least we're starting to get somewhere. That's a breakthrough."

She was trying to sound positive, but she couldn't hide the doubt that had crept into her voice. Loki licked Jane's chin, trying to comfort her in his own little way.

Suffering through the downtown traffic, they pulled into Universal Studios an hour later. Knowing that Clare would never have been to a movie set, much less a major Hollywood production such as this, Jane had thought it a nice way of rounding out the day, giving them some fun to take away the chill of the morning.

As they drove through the barriers and made their way to the soundstage, Clare craned her head every which way, taking in the sights with as much excitement as a child on her first visit to Disneyworld. She and Loki made quite the pair as they both stuck their heads out of the window.

Clare oohed as they passed a group of extras dressed as futuristic warriors who didn't have much use for clothing if their leather loincloths were any indication. She'd snapped several pictures of them before Jane could stop her.

"You can't post those up anywhere. Anything you see in here is confidential. You signed an NDA, remember?"

"They're for my personal education."

Jane had to laugh at the stubborn look on her friend's face.

They arrived on Logan's set to find the man himself, standing offside, receiving a last minute touch-up while the powerful HMI lights that provided the set with artificial sunlight were adjusted. Luckily for them there was a pause in proceedings, as Loki started barking the second he spotted Logan, his tail whipping against Jane's leg.

At her appearance, his beam seemed to light up the space better than all the specialist lights combined. He made his way to them, and in front of everyone, kissed her so deeply that cat calls came from the crew. When he finally stopped for breath, she found herself a little shaky on her feet. He stooped to pet Loki as the small dog lost his mind by their reunion.

Clare enjoyed the show with a twinkle in her eyes. "A simple 'Hi' will do for me, thanks."

Logan's smile fell on her. "Hello, Clare. Good to see you again. Thanks for taking the time to accompany Jane this morning."

"Aren't you going to interrogate me again? We had so much fun the last time." She grinned to take away any sting from her words.

He looked suitably chastised. "I don't normally behave like that—" He started only for Clare to wave the apology aside.

"That dress you gave me is worth more than any apology you could ever give. Thank you. It was very kind of you."

"It was the least I could do, really. No thanks necessary."

He pivoted to Jane, eyes turning cloudy with concern. "How did it go this morning?"

She ran through the session quickly, detailing all that had occurred. He listened without comment, though his expression grew more serious the longer she talked.

"What scared you like that, have you any idea?"

She shook her head as a chill blossomed between her shoulder blades.

"Do you think it might be that man you've had flashes of before?"

She didn't want to admit it, but it seemed the most likely answer.

"Places, everyone," the AD called, cutting short any further conversation. The lights and cameras were ready. All that remained was for the actors to take their marks.

"I need to go. You're both welcome to watch the scene or maybe Clare would like to see the rest of the production?"

"Oh, don't worry about me. I can entertain myself," Clare assured him.

He jogged back to the set as the two moved out of his eyeline where they might distract him.

"The man is besotted with you," Clare grinned, happy for her friend.

Jane blushed, but that chill was still with her, growing its icy fingers around her heart every time she thought of the man whose face had sent her into such a tailspin.

"Is it what we just learned? Is that why you look so worried?" Clare seemed to peer straight into her soul.

"I feel completely out of control, like I'm not in the driving seat. All this time, I had thought that getting my memories back would be a good thing, but now, I'm not so sure. I'm actually worried about what I might find out about myself. Then there's what's happening with me and Logan. He's this big movie star. I mean, how can this possibly work?"

Clare smiled. "How does any relationship work? No one can ever be sure of anything. Take me, I thought, I knew my man. I was very secure in our relationship. But he cheated on me at the first sign of success."

"At least the two of you were from the same world. I have nothing to offer him."

"Oh, Jane," Clare sighed deeply. "What nonsense. You can offer yourself. People get together all the time. Sometimes there's an age gap, sometimes the two are from different cultures. Who knows why one couple works and one doesn't? All I know is, if he makes you happy and you trust him, throw caution to the wind and live! Think how many celebrities have gotten together only to split up? It makes no difference how much fame or money you have. It's what's inside that counts. And obviously, Logan can see that. Besides," she continued with a wink. "I've decided to develop an expensive dress habit so if nothing else, you should consider your friends."

"You have quite the way of thinking there."

"I've always thought so." Clare slipped her arm through Jane's and then all conversation was silenced as the scene unfolded before them.

They spent the next few hours watching scenes being shot, chatting and playing with Loki in-between the long gaps as crew reconfigured lights and cameras to cover the same scenes, but from different setups.

When Logan was done for the day, he took the two on a tour around the studio. They drove to other movie sets, dropped in on other famous actors as Clare took a million selfies with them, but the most excitement came from watching a stunt sequence.

It was a complicated scene that involved one car smashing into another, then barreling through a shop front that required multiple cameras capturing the action from various angles. Logan explained that it was better to film dangerous and costly stunts like these using more cameras, rather than to recreate the stunt several times over.

After the footage was in the can, Logan's stunt double, Nathan — the driver of the vehicle that had crashed into the store — came over to introduce himself. Jane noticed the physical similarities between the two, but Nathan seemed bigger and tougher, with scars that ran the length of his arms, revealing just how much he had put into his work throughout his life.

Clare and Nathan seemed to hit it off instantly. He joked around while Clare found everything he uttered either hilarious or apparently, the most interesting thing she had ever heard.

When it was time to leave, Jane couldn't resist giving her some of that sass that she usually experienced from her.

"I couldn't help but notice all the chemistry flying between you too."

"He was just being polite." It wasn't like the Clare she knew to play coy. Jane found it all very interesting.

"What's your excuse then?" Jane shot back, not buying it at all.

"So, I am particularly receptive to a good-looking, confident man. Shoot me."

She was a full-blooded woman, and if the last few days had shown her anything, it was time for her to come out of hiding. She'd been divorced and alone long enough.

"I thought you were a taken woman now?" Jane couldn't help teasing.

"Maybe I am, but a girl can still look."

"Yes, she can," Jane laughed. "Yes, she can."

29

The chatter of the ET news channel sounded from the television.

Wearing only a robe, Jane sipped coffee at the breakfast table while Logan got ready for another day of work. Having eaten a breakfast of pancakes and fruit salad that Kitty had rustled up for them, Loki lay by her feet. She entertained him by wiggling her toes now and then so he could stalk them. It was a game that he never seemed to tire of.

It was a blissful morning that had begun at first light when Logan had woken her with his urgent need. Over the crashing waves and the pink sunlight that bathed their bodies, they had made love until both had been spent.

Everything was almost perfect.

She took another sip of coffee, allowing the heat to melt away the fears that lurked at the corners of her mind like a shadow.

Last night she had dreamed of the marina.

She had been standing in that same place as the cold

wrapped around her like a snake. Ahead of her bobbed a moored yacht, though try as she might, she could not make out the name that was painted on its hull: a blur obscured the letters as if her mind had censored the word.

She heard voices, a desperate, pleading voice, then an answering one that seemed to carry no emotion. That second voice made her heart thump painfully, but she didn't know what they were saying.

All the while, an icy fear seeped into her blood.

She felt as if she were being pulled toward that yacht, though every instinct in her body was telling her to run. Something terrible would happen on that boat. She couldn't allow herself on it, yet even as her mind screamed at her to run away, she was being pulled closer.

Then suddenly, she was surrounded by black water.

It was in her lungs and over her head.

Lighting flashed, the heavens rumbled, but she was sinking. Drowning in that dark, dark water.

When Logan had woken her, she was still trapped in that nightmare.

Driven by a desperate need for it to go away, she had kissed him with an urgency that had startled him. But when she had straddled him and her hips began to rock against him, all thoughts had vanished.

There was only the two of them and the passion of the moment.

Jane was brought out of her thoughts when her own face flashed up on the television. There she was with Logan and Clare on their tour of the set yesterday. The three looked so happy, yet she was dismayed to hear one of the anchors comments.

"Well, there's 'natural' and then there's making a bit of

an effort," the other anchor said bitchily as a close up of Jane came onto the screen.

She set down her coffee, flushed with the shame their comments had caused.

She paused the show and studied her reflection on the screen. Her hair was loose around her shoulders, make-up kept bare with only mascara and some lipstick. Knowing that she had her appointment with the hypnotherapist, she hadn't felt like plastering her face with make-up beforehand. Regardless, she thought she looked good — maybe even more than good. She glowed with the happiness of a woman in love. How could they not see that?

The cell phone Kitty had organized for her, vibrated on the table. As soon as she answered the call, Clare started speaking.

"I was just having some of my no-carb breakfast when these two idiots on my television started talking nonsense about my friend, so I thought I'd call in the hopes that she hadn't seen it."

"Do I really look that bad?"

"You looked lovely. They're only picking on you to justify their salary: unfortunately, being nice in this town doesn't pay half as well as being spiteful. You shouldn't care what they think of you — you should only care about what you think of yourself, what Logan thinks of you."

A muffled sound came over the phone. Clare spoke away from the handset.

"Coffee's over there, help yourself. I'm just on a call."

Jane checked the clock on the television display. It was still early, only seven thirty in the morning — far too early to be entertaining guests, unless they were still there from the night before.

"Is that your new man? Are you with him now?"

The laugh that came over the line carried more than a hint of embarrassment.

"He stayed over last night, but in the living room! I think I must have had too much to drink over dinner and passed out. Luckily, Ken was the perfect gentleman. He brought me home and slept on the sofa, just in case I needed him."

Jane could just hear a low male voice speaking to Clare. Her friend laughed at whatever it was he said. "Of course I'm singing your praises to my friend. How many men would have done what you did last night? Come and say hi to Jane."

Seconds later, she came back on the line to her, laughing even more. "He won't. He's too shy to speak to a celebrity."

"I'm not a celebrity. I'm no one."

"Then why are you all over my television? I think you need to get used to this new fame of yours."

The chime of the doorbell interrupted their conversation, followed by Loki's excited barking as he ran off to greet whoever it was that had arrived. "I've got to go, there's someone at the door and Logan's still in the shower."

"Just remember to only listen to the opinions of people you actually care about. Talk later!"

The sound of approaching heels coincided with the arrival of Logan, returning from the shower with only a towel wrapped around himself. Kitty had brought in their guest, but it wasn't any of Logan's team as Jane had suspected it would be.

Instead, the petite brunette who stood before them

carrying Loki in her arms bore more than a striking resemblance to Logan. She had his eyes and lips, though that's where their looks converged. Her curves had extra padding now, though she was as lovely now as she must have been in her younger years. The only sign of her advancing age were the silver streaks in her hair that she did nothing to disguise. Wearing a simple but classy twinset number, she oozed a quiet grace.

Logan's eyes had gone as round as his mouth.

"Mom! What're you doing here?"

She kissed both of his stunned cheeks, an amused if annoyed smile on her lips.

"Well, I thought I'd come and meet this new woman in my son's life, particularly as he seems to have neglected to mention her himself. There is nothing quite like finding out these things in your morning newspaper."

Jane felt the sting of her words, even though she was sure the woman hadn't meant anything by it. She knew how close Logan was to his mother, so why hadn't he mentioned her at all? What did that mean?

Unaware of the turmoil his mother's words had caused, Logan shrugged helplessly. "It's just been one thing after another."

The look she gave him said what she thought about *that*. She lowered gracefully into a chair as Loki flopped against her, laying his head on her lap, apparently so in love that Jane was taken aback.

Traitor.

"Can I get you something to drink, Miss. Stanton? Maybe a light breakfast?" Kitty asked.

"It's Delia, Kitty. I've told you a million times before, have I not?"

"Yes, Miss. Delia," Kitty replied, bowing her head.

"And no thank you, I can just help myself if I'm hungry."

"Yes, Miss. Delia," Kitty echoed again before making a discreet exit.

"This is Jane. Jane, my mom." Logan finally had enough wits about him to introduce them to one another.

"Delia, yes. Nice to meet you," Jane took the hand that was offered to her, cringing inwardly at her lack of clothing. What a way to meet his mother!

"And you, Dear. Would you like a moment to put some clothes on? I can entertain myself with this little angel while you're gone."

She scratched Loki behind the ears, sending the puppy squirming. He shoved his head against her hand, unable to have enough of her attention.

"Thank you. I'll be right back."

Jane returned moments later with her hair brushed and loose, wearing a simple gypsy skirt and a sleeveless shirt. The woman had already seen her in next-to-nothing. It seemed ridiculous to dress up in anything more.

It could have been her imagination, but there seemed a tiny look of approval in Delia's eyes when she saw her outfit.

Logan had also pulled on a pair of those lounge pants he favored, but he remained topless, torso still damp and gleaming.

Jane forced herself not to look at it for fear of the feelings that would rise.

Loki sat at Delia's feet now as the woman fed him large pieces of bacon that he gobbled up, and Jane knew instantly why the dog loved her so much.

It was simple bribery.

"Logan has explained how the two of you met. What an extraordinary story." Delia eyes were sympathetic as she looked over Jane.

"I've told her the truth," Logan explained. "How I found you, how you came to stay here because you had no where else to go, and how we subsequently found ourselves drifting toward each other."

But nothing about the contract. She guessed it wasn't something his mother would be particularly proud of.

"And you really can't remember anything from before?" Delia couldn't imagine how awful that must be.

"Just small bits here and there. We had a breakthrough yesterday. It was the first time I've really been able to recall something more tangible than the odd dream, when it's difficult for me to tell what's real or not."

Delia showed Loki her empty hands, so the dog changed tactics, licking her fingers in place of getting more treats. "And that Detective, Summers? He hasn't been in touch?"

"Not lately, though I guess he will only call if he has news. I should actually update him on my session yesterday…"

"I've already done it," Logan replied, surprising her. "I didn't want you to worry, and you were having fun with Clare so I called him myself."

"When? You were filming yesterday?"

"In between scenes. I'm pretty good at multi-tasking… for a man," he shot a grin at her as a vivid memory of the morning's love making — and how he had done precisely that — made her look away, for fear that his mother would be able to read the truth in her eyes.

"Logan takes good care of those he loves," Delia said, not realizing the effect her words would have.

Love? Logan had never said the words before, but was it possible? Could he really be in love with her?

And did she love him back?

The thought sent her reeling.

Logan's phone chimed with a reminder. He cursed, looking trapped. "I've got to get to work. Do you want to come with me? It's not a heavy day, though it might still take a while before I'm done."

Delia shook her head.

"Honey, you know I love you, but visiting you on set is so dull. Nothing but waiting, waiting, waiting. I have a much better idea. Why don't I take Jane out so we can get to know each other better?"

Jane couldn't tell who was more startled by the suggestion. She and Logan stole a panicked glance at each other.

"I think Jane might have plans already..." Logan began, but at the crestfallen look Delia gave, even Jane could feel herself caving.

"But we've only just met. Seems very unfair that the world knows more about your girlfriend than I do. People keep asking me about the two of you, and it's so embarrassing to have to say that I know nothing. You, being my only son and all."

She bowed her head as if to hide the glint of tears, but Jane was starting to see that Logan wasn't the only actor in the family. Delia seemed quite the character, and she was itching to know the woman who had single-handedly raised Logan.

"I can cancel them."

The beam Delia gave could have lit up a nation. "Oh,

that's wonderful! You go off to work, Dear, and don't worry. Jane and I will have a lovely time. Go on… go now."

The woman was practically shoving her 'only son' out of the door. Jane had to hide her own smile. Logan dropped a chaste kiss on her forehead, grabbed a hoodie and left, looking somewhat shellshocked.

As soon as he was gone, Delia pivoted round to Jane, hands clasped together. "Don't worry, I'm not as frightening as I might seem. I do have an ulterior motive for being here, however… did you know it's Logan's birthday tomorrow?"

"No. He never mentioned it."

"He never does. My son might be in the limelight all the time, but deep down, he's a simple soul. I must confess that what with one thing and another, I haven't got him anything yet. Why don't we go shopping together for his present?"

It seemed an innocent enough request, though Jane suspected that nothing about Delia was as she seemed.

Still shopping with his mother.

What could possibly go wrong?

TEN MINUTES LATER, THEY SAT IN DELIA'S MERCEDES, LOKI sticking his nose out of the tiny crack of Jane's open window. Even with her fingers looped around his collar, she was afraid to open it any further in case he somehow fell out of it.

Delia was a calm and considered driver, not taken to being affected by whatever madness surrounded them on the streets. Jane found her presence calming, which was a surprise given the situation warranted any other feeling but that.

"I suppose we should start at Rodeo Drive?" Delia asked, looking to Jane for agreement.

Jane considered her suggestion. "I can't imagine him needing any more clothes or accessories, not with the amount of designers who keep gifting him things. Besides, he doesn't seem to care too much about what he wears as long as it's comfortable and well made. Why don't we look for something fun he can use in the kitchen? He told me he learned how to cook from you, maybe we could find him some gadget or other that he doesn't have yet?"

Her answer seemed to have taken Delia by surprise. She didn't reply immediately, but when she did, it was with a sidelong glance that she caught.

"Sounds like a plan."

"The Grove should have some good stores for that," Jane suggested. And it was true. It was also just about the only place she knew other than the clothes stores she had previously frequented.

They spent a few happy hours ambling around the shopping center, with Loki's antics keeping them entertained. Today, he'd decided to carry one of Logan's shoes with him, something which seemed to amuse everyone who saw him. Jane had attempted to wrestle it from him, but the look he had given her had been enough for her to stop.

It was only a shoe, and Logan had plenty of others.

Despite her picture being displayed on the tabloids and entertainment channels, Jane was able to walk around without being noticed much. Here, she was just a woman shopping with her dog and her boyfriend's mother.

The conversation steered away from anything intense. Mostly, Delia chatted about the products they were considering as gifts, though Jane had no doubt in her mind that questions *were* coming up. Logan's mom seemed a patient woman who was able to bide her time.

They went into a pet store where Jane picked up some treats and a ball that bounced around on its own, hoping it would come in handy when they were too busy to entertain Loki. Then they perused several stores, contemplating the goods on display. While in a pretty homeware store that made her think of Martha Stewart, Jane finally decided on a sous vide machine.

Reading the label, Delia turned her confused eyes to Jane. "I'm not even going to pretend to pronounce that. And what exactly does it do?" Her cookery lessons hadn't amounted to using one of these high-tech looking machines.

"It's pronounced sue-veed. It's French. It means "under vacuum" and isn't half as frightening or difficult as it looks. You just simply put whatever you are cooking, meat or fish, for example, vacuum-seal it in a bag then immerse it into a very precise temperature in the water bath. The process cooks things perfectly every time with no burning, retaining any juices and moisture. When it's done, you can broil, sear or fry to brown it off."

Delia looked far from convinced. "Seems like a lot of trouble to go to."

"Oh, it's really very simple. I can't live without mine."

To moment she said the words, the ramification of the words hit home.

"I had a sous-vide machine! I've just remembered something else!"

"That's wonderful, Jane. Now that the floodgates have opened, I'm sure more and more things will come to you."

"I hope so. It's a strange feeling, not remembering who you are or where you came from. Almost as if I'm only half a person."

She didn't see the sympathy that dimmed Delia's bright green eyes.

"Do you think I might have been a chef? I mean, what normal person would have one of these at home?"

"You were just thinking of getting one for Logan," the older woman replied.

"But he's far from normal."

Delia nodded. "That's true, even if I do say so myself. Well, since you're getting him that, I'll go for this Air Fryer. It's wifi controlled apparently, whatever that means. I hardly think anyone would need to surf the internet while using one."

Jane fought to contain a laugh. "I think it just means that you can control it using your phone."

"And why would that be any less ridiculous than what I suggested?"

They started laughing as they went to pay for their goods when Jane's attention was caught by something.

"Give me one moment. I just need to check if something's available."

Delia turned her focus to some crockery that had taken her fancy. Like handbags, a woman could never have enough coffee mugs. "Take your time. I'll be over here, buying more cups that I don't need."

Jane knew exactly what it was she was looking for and

went straight to the audiobook section where she hoped one particular title would be available.

There was only one copy, nestled between the other "Based On A True Story" titles.

It was My Blood, My Right, the book she had found in Borders, which she had wanted to gift to Logan. After learning of his dyslexia, she now wondered if maybe an audiobook might suit him better. It was only a small thing, and maybe presumptuous of her to even think that he'd want it, but there was just something about the story that she thought might appeal to him.

She paid for the audiobook and rejoined Delia.

WITH THEIR GIFTS WRAPPED AND SAFELY IN THE TRUNK OF Delia's car, the woman sat at a restaurant terrace, contemplating the menu as Loki watched the world go by beneath the table. Their waiter had set a bowl of water on the ground, which the dog was busy drinking up.

It was a popular place judging by the line, though not exclusive in the way that required a booking system. Delia had offered up some more exclusive options for lunch, but Jane had decided on this. It was a popular choice with diners, so why should they drive across town only to wait longer and pay more?

Their waiter waited for their order and smiled. "What can I get you both?"

"I'll have the seafood linguine with a side salad and an ice-tea for me, thank you," Jane ordered.

Delia blinked, thinking she'd heard wrong. "Carbs for lunch? And no champagne? You really aren't from this town, are you?"

"I like food and I'll never understand people who don't."

"Hear, hear!" Delia laughed, turning to their waiter. "I'll have the same but I'll have a sparkling apple juice instead of the iced-tea."

"Of course. I'll be back with your orders soon."

"I saw you picked up something else from the store? Was it anything fun?" Delia asked, referring to the audiobook.

"It's just an audiobook. I actually got the physical book thinking Logan might like it, before I learned of his dyslexia. I thought I'd offer him both versions so he can decide how he'd like to read it."

A knowing glint appeared in Delia's bright green eyes, the same eyes she had passed on to her son. "I'm sure he'll appreciate the thought."

With the natural pause in the conversation, Jane figured now was as good a time as any to ask her own question.

"So… have I passed?"

The older woman's expression became guarded. "Why? Whatever do you mean?"

"This has all been a test, hasn't it? To see what you think of me?"

Delia was saved from answering as their waiter returned with their drinks. When they were alone again, Delia smiled broadly and reached across to pat her hand.

"I think you and I are going to get along just fine."

It was with no small sense of relief that Jane accepted her blessing.

"But is it his birthday? Was that part true?"

Exasperated, Delia pulled a face. "Of course it is, Dear.

You think I'd make us go through this entire exercise and lie about something like that?"

Time flew by over delicious food and wonderful conversation. Now that she had passed her tests, Delia was an open book, while the walls Jane held seemed to crumble in her presence.

Delia had a way of listening, of conversing, that made it easy for Jane to spill her thoughts and fears… even if they applied to her own son. They'd talked of Logan's fame, how he had started in the industry — by slogging his way up from the bottom in unpaid roles on indie movies and short films. And how life had been as a child with learning difficulties. But there was one subject Jane hadn't been brave enough to broach until now.

"Logan hasn't mentioned his father before. I don't mean to pry, but can you tell me a little about him? Nothing that would anger Logan if I knew. I would just like to know something so I have some context."

Some of the sparkle left Delia's eyes.

"I'm happy to talk about him, as I'm sure Logan won't. It's only that I haven't done so for quite a while now. Logan acts as if he doesn't exist, but he does. He's living in California actually, but Logan won't have anything to do with him."

"He only briefly mentioned that his dad left, and you had to work three jobs to raise him."

The look Delia gave was piercing. "Well, that is telling in itself. He usually doesn't even say that much."

She sipped her sparkling apple juice and set the glass onto the table. Her hands fidgeted with the napkin in her lap.

"Logan was young when I discovered that my husband

was sleeping around. Somewhere between 'till death do us part' and Logan's eighth birthday, my husband decided I was too boring for him, that I hadn't been enough for him for a while. He'd slept with several women that I knew of, though it could have been many more. After the first few, I simply stopped looking."

Her eyes took on a distant look, though the hurt was still raw, even now, so many years later.

"Like a stupid woman, I put up with it as I didn't want to break up our home. I wanted Logan to have both parents, but one day, I came home from work to discover that all of my savings — including Logan's college fund — had been cleared out."

The gasp Jane expelled couldn't contain her shock. Delia continued, her voice growing hoarse as she recalled those painful memories.

"He had decided to start a new life with someone else and was using the money I had saved to do it. He left, and we never spoke to him again. The last I had heard, he had cheated on his new wife and left her for someone else."

A bitter laugh escaped. "A leopard never changes his spots."

"So you had to work all those jobs to get by?" Jane couldn't imagine what a toll that must have taken to do that *and* raise a child alone. It certainly spoke of her determination.

"I wanted Logan to have everything he deserved, so I saved every penny so he could go to acting school. We lived a very frugal life for a long while which is why Logan appreciates the smaller things. As much as he can be lavish, he can also appreciate a home cooked meal, made in a sous vide machine."

She said it with a smile.

"With all the trouble he's been having in the press, why doesn't the public know these things about him?" Jane asked. "Logan only recently revealed his dyslexia to me, which only makes his success more commendable. I'm sure the rest of the world would think the same if they knew."

Delia's eyes turned hard. "It's all those people he hires, those so-called experts. Somewhere along the way, they decided the truth would emasculate him, so they turned him into a bad boy. Spun stories about his wild partying, but you live with him, how often has he done any of that?"

Aside from the charity ball which had been work related, not once that she could think of.

"What about the women?"

"Well, the woman have been true I suppose, but not usually in the way they ended. He always went for models or actresses and yes, they were beautiful, but you can't make a life with only looks. There has to be a soul underneath."

She smoothed out the napkin in her lap.

"My son isn't a saint, and he has made many bad choices in his life, but he isn't the bad boy they paint him to be. He has worked so hard to get here, which is why he was crushed when it all started going wrong. I keep telling him, I can live somewhere else. He can sell my cottage and I'll be happy with a smaller place, somewhere else less expensive. But he won't listen. Stubborn to the core. He gets that from me."

It took a moment for her words to sink in. When they did, worry gnawed at her chest. "Is Logan having financial troubles?"

It was hard to imagine it, living in the house that he did.

"When his last few movies didn't do well, he lost a lot of money. A lot of money. He had invested in them with his own cash, slashing his rate, expecting a big back-end payment which never came. Though he does make good money, he also pays out a lot. The agents, lawyers, managers, publicists, household staff... every one of them takes a big cut. If he just sold the cottage he bought me, he would be in the black again, but you can't tell my son anything. He has to come to the decision himself."

"So he really needs this job, is that why he was so stressed when I met him?"

"I assume so. Everything is riding on this. And now, on top of his mother, he has another woman he loves who he needs take care of."

"That's the second time you've said something like that."

"You mean, love?" Delia asked, smiling. "A mother knows, Dear. And it's written all over your face too."

And with that simple sentence, Jane knew the woman was right.

She was madly, head-over-heels in love with Logan. Why, then, was there a pulsing fear behind her heart?

What was causing her so much concern that she couldn't relax into this new love of hers?

30

The timer ticked over so agonizingly slow, that Jane wondered if she'd be staring at it for the rest of her life.

Having arrived home several hours ago, she'd spent the rest of the day frantically throwing together a carrot cake, after Delia had revealed it had been Logan's favorite, growing up.

His mom had offered to help, but Jane had wanted to do this on her own. Now that she'd had a chance to see just how much he had been taking care of all those around him, it was important for her to give something back, however small this might seem compared to his lavish gestures.

She knew she had made the right decision when Delia kissed her cheeks as she left, vowing that it wouldn't be long before they would see each other again.

Standing on the doorstep, those green eyes of hers shining, she had confided, "You are the first woman Logan has introduced me to that I approve of."

It was a moment after Delia's car had turned down the drive before Jane was able to compose herself.

Logan was due home in less than two hours. She needed the cake out of the oven and cool enough that she could frost it without the frosting melting.

Kitty hovered close by, picking up on Jane's anxiety. "I'm sure it'll be ready in time. Miss. Delia's recipe has never failed to deliver."

"I haven't baked anything since I've been here. I have no idea if it's something I do well or not. I should have just bought one from the store." Jane paced the kitchen as Loki regarded her with one big ear flopped over to the side. He was carrying yet another of his toys into the new bed she had picked up for him. They surrounded the bed with their rainbow of colors, but he still wasn't satisfied. He dropped the rubber bone that was in his mouth and padded off — presumably to bring more toys back.

"You followed the instructions perfectly. I'm sure it'll be fine. Have some faith in yourself."

But Jane couldn't stop from over-analyzing every aspect. When had baking a cake become so important? "I'll bet none of his other girlfriend's have ever worried about a cake like this."

Washing the mixing bowl in the sink, Kitty paused as she considered her comment. "No. Then again, you are the first to make him one."

Wiping down the marble island, Jane's hand froze. "None of them have ever baked him a birthday cake?"

Kitty's eyes were a well of sadness. "No. That's why, he will love this one, no matter how it turns out."

Jane couldn't resign herself to what she'd just been told. Logan — who looked after everyone, and in particular, the women in his life — had never had a cake baked for him other than by his mother.

What kind of women had he dated before her?

It was even more important that this cake be perfect. She stole another glance at the clock — the hands had barely moved in the few seconds since she'd last checked. She busied herself by cleaning the kitchen, almost incurring Kitty's wrath in the process as the woman kept insisting that it was her job to do. When the buzzer finally sounded, Jane was ready with the oven mitts. Kitty had cleared a large space for the cake and had set a rack for it too.

There was a moment of panic as, intoxicated by the smell of the cake, Loki tried to snatch it out of her hands until Kitty had to chase him off with a towel. His howls of displeasure could be heard inside the house, but both women ignored him. With the cake waiting in front of a fan, and Kitty to keep an out on it, Jane persuaded Loki to forgive her and took him into the gardens for a game of catch.

The two raced and chased and tugged in battle, weaving in and around the gardeners at work, laughing at their antics. The gardeners didn't even seem to mind when Loki stopped by that particular flowerbed that seemed to be his arch nemesis and promptly undid all of their work at fixing the last arrangement of flowers he'd dug up.

Under the crystal sky, with a happy anticipation of the surprises she had in store for Logan, Jane was able to forget her worries of yesterday.

As far as she was concerned, her life was here and now, with this amazing man and his adorable dog.

And she was determined for it to stay that way.

LOGAN DRUMMED HIS NAILS ON THE CAR DOOR, FOOT TAPPING an impatient beat in the footwell.

All day he'd felt a pressure on his chest, pushing down just enough that it was noticeable, though not something he'd need to see the medic about.

He knew what the cause of it was and it had nothing to do with the trying scene that was being shot, or his charmless, antagonizing co-star.

Neither of those worried him as much as this other thing.

He loved his mother more than anyone else in the world, but that didn't mean he was blind to her ways: the woman could be as sneaky as they came.

But somehow, when she had suggested she spend the day with Jane, Logan hadn't the wits about him to come up with a suitable excuse. It had been far too early in the day for him to think straight.

And, having raised him, she had known that would be the case.

God only knew what the two of them had been discussing all day.

He felt literal footsteps treading over his grave, and the feeling didn't disappear even when he arrived home. Jane greeted him with a delightful kiss, though he didn't allow the delightful feel of her body pressed against his to sway his attention. He stepped away from her, and kept one eye peeled, looking for any sign of his mother.

Jane gave him an impish smile. "Don't worry, she's gone."

"I'm not worried. Why would I be worried? Unless... should I be worried?"

There was amusement in her sea-blue eyes. "I don't know... Is there a reason you might be concerned?"

He growled, low in his throat, the sound sending Loki — who had finally been persuaded to leave the bed that he had made his new home — wild with excitement. "You are a devil woman."

She laughed, a delicious, bubbling sound. "If that were the case then why would I create this lovely dinner for you?" She inclined her head at the kitchen where tantalizing smells of cinnamon and orange wafted toward him.

"Don't try to distract me. What did the two of you get up to all day?"

To stop Loki from barking, he picked up the bundle of fur and scratched him under the chin. Loki's face sagged, turning blissful. His tongue fell out as if it wasn't attached to anything. He leaned into Logan, placing a big paw on either of his shoulders as if he were hugging him, and tucked his head under his chin.

For someone who constantly said he didn't like dogs, Logan seemed to have a mighty strong bond with this one. Jane knew well enough not to comment on the matter.

"Oh, nothing much," She milked it for as much as she could, enjoying the slightly desperate expression on his face. "We just walked around The Grove, then had a bite to eat. She's a lovely lady, your mom."

"Uh huh." He looked a little green around the gills. Jane almost took pity on him, but she couldn't break now, not if she were going to stick with her plan. It was partly why she had chosen to cook a Moroccan Tangine, knowing the strong smelling spices would cover over any lingering scent of the cake.

"So… what *did* you talk about?"

"That would be telling, wouldn't it? I can't possibly break the female code." Her nose wrinkled in an impossibly cute way.

"Not even if I torture it out of you?"

Setting Loki onto the ground, he went for her and started tickling her under the arms. Completely unprepared, peals of uncontrollable laughter burst out of her.

"Stop it!" She gasped, trying to get away from him, but Logan was a man on a mission now. She thought she could tease him and get away with it? Two could play at this game!

Chasing her all the way to the bedroom, Loki yapping at their heels, he tackled her onto the bed, both of them laughing between breaths.

His hands were everywhere. Tickling her under her arms, behind her knees, dancing along that tender spot on her side. She twisted and bucked, trying to crawl away, but he grabbed a bare foot and attacked the sensitive sole.

Squealing, light dancing in her eyes, hair akimbo, she looked glorious. The air became charged. Their laughter faded.

The thin strap of her top had slipped off one creamy shoulder, the sight of which made him want to see more. Crushing her lips to his, his hands made quick work of removing their clothes.

"But… what about dinner?" She asked, eyes playful and light.

"I'm hungry for something else."

He went on to feast on her body for hours until both lay satiated in each other's arms. Jane glanced at the clock, waiting for the digits to turn over into the next day.

A second after midnight, she crept out of bed.

Logan was fast asleep, one arm slung over his eyes. Hearing her movements, Loki's head lifted up from his paws where he was curled up by his usual position in front of the fireplace, but she shushed him.

"Good boy," she whispered, hoping he wouldn't wake Logan. The dog's eyes drooped sleepily. Sensing there wasn't going to be much excitement, he lowered his head back onto his paws.

Stealing the sheet from the bed, Jane wrapped it around her sarong style and tip-toed to the kitchen where she retrieved the frosted cake that was hidden in the refrigerator, all ready with candles.

Palming a box of matches, she hurried back upstairs and set the cake onto the table on the outside terrace where plates, cutlery and a bottle of champagne had already been stashed earlier in the day.

She lit the candles carefully, sending a quick prayer to the heavens for the lack of sea breeze this evening that would allow the candles to stay lit.

Stealing back to the bed, she woke Logan with a kiss.

"Wakey, wakey."

A smile appeared on his lips before he even opened his eyes. "You are insatiable."

"As if you can talk. Anyway, that's not why I was waking you."

Taking his hand, she guided him to the terrace. At the sight of the cake, and the effort she had gone to, his eyes went dark, overcome with feeling.

"A little birdie told me it was your birthday so I baked you a cake."

She darted back into the bedroom, to his walk-in closet, reappearing moments later with a large gift-wrapped box and a smaller package. "It's not much — and certainly not if you compare all that you have done for me — but I hope you like it."

Logan's heart thumped.

No woman had ever gone to so much trouble for him. They would sleep with him and please him in that way, but outside of bed, the women he had been with tended to require that he make all the effort, and usually in the form of increasingly more lavish gifts.

Not one had ever baked a cake for him.

Opening the box, his breath caught.

Not one had ever gotten him something that he'd wanted, either. The sous-vide machine gleamed under the light of the full moon. Jane stood against a spectacular backdrop of stars, shifting nervously from foot to foot as she waited for his response.

He opened the smaller package to find two editions of the same book. Somewhat nervously, she explained why she'd bought the two versions.

It had been a good few minutes since he'd last said a word, something that was giving her major anxiety. Unable to help herself, she asked, "Well, do you like them?" She really needed to hear that he did.

"I love you."

She laughed, taken aback by his comment, but was

pleased. "I was hoping for a 'thank you' so I think I overshot it a bit."

He knew his words and their meaning had not sunken in. Setting down his gifts, he took her hands in his. He drew her close so that she was forced to look into his eyes.

"I mean it, Jane. I love you. And not because of the effort you made, or the gifts — which, I love too — but because of you. This industry, the lifestyle I lead, it has all tainted me, given me a shell that no one has been able to penetrate before. But with you, I can be myself. There is no acting, no pretence. You accept me for the person I am, and not who I pretend to be. I don't know what heavenly powers brought you to my shore, but I'll be forever grateful they did."

Her eyes misted over. She gazed at him with an intensity that matched his own.

"I love you too," she whispered.

He took her lips in his, claiming this woman that he loved. Her heart beat against him, their rhythm mingling into a duet that only they could hear. They only pulled away when they heard a strange lapping sound.

It was Loki. Perched precariously on a chair, he was licking the cake. Jane launched herself away from Logan and bolted over to Loki…

But not to save the cake, as he'd thought.

"Loki! Be careful not to burn your nose!"

She blew out the candles, removing them so that their curling smoke wouldn't bother him. She gave Logan an apologetic smile.

"Sorry. I hope you made a wish."

"I've already gotten it."

Happy tears brightened her eyes. They didn't bother

cutting the cake, eating it using the forks that were already on the table. Loki wasn't left out of their celebration too: they fed small chunks of the cake to him, much to his delight.

"If you never decide what to do with yourself, you should open a bakery. This cake might be the best I've ever tasted."

"I think you might be a bit biased since this is your mom's recipe."

His brow raised. "Just because I get to see you naked, doesn't mean I'd be the least bit biased. I'm a professional, Jane, and your bodily delights would never sway my opinion."

"I think the sugar is getting to your head," she laughed.

He grabbed hold of it, pretending to be hurt. "You're right. I need to go to bed… STAT. And you need to join me."

Only a whine from Loki stopped them in their tracks. He looked up at them, agitated.

"He needs a bathroom break."

Logan made a move to get up, but she stopped him. "No. Wait for me in bed. I'll be back with him when he's done."

Taking the remains of the cake with her, she opened the back door as Loki darted out into the night. While he did his business, she covered the cake and put it away. Then she set the kettle to boil, thinking some of Kitty's special peppermint tea brew would be nice.

She moved in a happy daze, still trying to reconcile their declarations of love in her mind.

When the kettle finished boiling, she poured the teas

and set the cups onto a tray. Seeing a vase of pretty roses that one of the gardeners must have brought in earlier, she picked the biggest one and set it on the tray too. She almost started out the kitchen before she realized that Loki hadn't returned.

Moving to the door, she called out to him. "Loki? Here boy. Come inside."

His barks of excitement sounded far away. The dog never strayed too far, so this was a surprise. A slight knot appeared in her stomach. She wondered if she should have accompanied him and not let him dash off alone.

She stepped onto the stone patio. "Loki? Come back, Boy."

His barks came at her again, closer.

"Come on, Loki. It's bedtime," she encouraged. When his little face appeared, the anxiety she had felt faded away.

He ran up to her, a quivering bundle of love, wildly excited as if it had been weeks since he'd last seen her. She cuddled him, holding him close.

"Don't run off like that, you hear? You had me worried for a moment."

He cocked his head at her, trying so hard to understand her words.

She went back to Logan. Neither of them complained when Loki jumped up between them, burrowing into a ball like it was the greatest thing on Earth to be in bed with them.

They drank tea then fell asleep, the three of them entwined, with Logan thinking this was the best birthday he could remember having.

. . .

Pained cries woke them a few hours later.

Logan snapped awake, blinking fast to clear the sleep from his eyes.

Loki sprawled on his side beside him, panting heavily and whining. His eyes were unnaturally bright, as if he were trying not to cry. Jane sucked in a shocked breath as Logan felt Loki's neck.

"What's wrong with him?"

The pulse beneath his fingers seemed to be racing, but he had no idea if that was the case since he had nothing to base it on.

Jane's gaze landed on several piles of vomit on the carpet. She pointed. "Look. He's been sick."

Logan's face turned serious. "We need to get him to a vet."

Wrapping him in a towel to keep him still and warm, they hurried out to the garage, not even bothering to change clothes. Jane simply pulled on a sweater over her night-dress, while Logan wore those lounge pants and a hoodie.

Loki was young, and that meant he was more fragile. Whatever had happened, both knew that time was of the essence.

While Logan drove, Jane called ahead. Thankfully, the veterinary hospital was open 24/7. At this time of the night, traffic was scarce, and they made it there soon after.

Having anticipated their arrival, Loki was rushed into examination as Logan and Jane waited, nervous as any pet parent.

"I shouldn't have let him out on his own. He must have eaten something bad. Are there any plants in the garden that could be toxic to him?"

Logan's eyes had drawn a blank. "There are plants that can be toxic to dogs?"

"And cats," Jane replied, having no idea how she knew any of this. "I know lilies are incredibly toxic to cats. Even just the pollen from them can kill a cat."

She couldn't sit still, jumping up to pace the room.

"I'm sure there wasn't anything in the back yard. He's been out there a hundred times before."

"But never on his own." She stopped, her thoughts diverting to a different tangent. "Maybe it wasn't even that. What if it was the cake? Maybe he reacted to something in there?"

She tried to run the ingredients through her mind. What had they been? Flour, eggs, butter…

The guilt was torturing her. Logan had to do something to bring her back down.

"Stop blaming yourself. It won't help anything and will only make you feel worse. Come sit by me. The vet will be out soon. Until then, it's pointless to keep guessing when it could literally be anything."

But soon didn't come until two hours later, by which point, Jane was pale with exhaustion, her nerves frayed. The vet had dark circles under his eyes. He looked at them both, gravely.

"I think Loki has eaten something toxic. We have induced vomiting and flushed his stomach with fluids. We've also given him activated charcoal to stop the toxin from getting into his blood."

"Will he be OK?" Jane's voice sounded alien to her own ears.

"I think so. We have him on an IV right now to replace

the lost fluids, but he is already better, though missing mom and dad." The vet smiled.

"I fed him some cake that I'd baked earlier. Could that have done this?" Jane asked, her mouth dry as the desert.

"Did it have chocolate or raisins? Citrus maybe?"

"No. It was a regular carrot cake."

"With raisins?"

"No," Jane shook her head.

"Then no. Human foods aren't great for dogs, but nothing in your cake should have caused this. Your quick action might have saved his life. At the end of the day, it's hard to pinpoint the cause, and dogs do love to eat anything and everything they can get their paws on. But you did the right thing in bringing him here so fast."

"Can he come home with us?"

"I'd like to keep him on the IV a while longer, but you can take him home soon. Are the two of you fine to wait?"

"Yes," Logan answered immediately, speaking for the both of them.

"I'll be back when he's ready to be discharged. By the way, I'm a big fan of yours, Mr. Steel. I hope you don't mind my saying."

Logan flashed him a small smile. "Of course. Thank you."

His response was polite but automatic.

The relief that came from knowing that Loki would be fine had Jane shaking. She sank into a chair, letting her head drop against Logan's shoulder.

He held her hand as their fingers entwined, and they waited.

31

The drive to the beach house was easier than Marko had thought possible.

Getting the actual address had proven to be the most difficult task, though when you were as smart as he was, there was always a way.

The famous Logan Steel didn't think enough about his security as he was able to park his rental vehicle — a flashy Porsche so he wouldn't stick out in this neighbor-hood — only a few blocks away. Then, it was a simple case of jogging the rest of the way to the house.

He wore a hoodie and sweatpants and looked for all the world like a jogger on his evening run. He'd even passed a police cruiser that he'd waved at, thanking them for their tireless work. The clueless cops had grinned, puffing up their chests like the baboons they were, before leaving, probably heading to the nearest Dunkin Donuts.

The eight-foot-tall steel fence that surrounded the property was more of a problem.

It wasn't electrified, but despite walking its circumference, he hadn't found a weak link in the entire thing. If only he'd known ahead of time that the property stretched right onto the coast. He could have swam or used a jet-ski if the noise of one wouldn't have reached the house.

At least the fence — with its half a foot gap between the posts — afforded a view into the property.

The movie star couldn't be that bothered by privacy if he was happy to let just anyone have a view inside. This only confirmed what he thought about him: the man was full of crap.

In all the interviews he had read in the days leading up to this, Steel had talked about how private a person he was, how he didn't like the paparazzi that pursued him endlessly. Yet, he hadn't bothered with a simple screen that would have stopped anyone from peering in and seeing his disgusting hands all over his wife.

His Emily.

His blood boiled with such heat that it was a wonder he didn't implode right then and there. His fingers flexed, curled into a ball, wishing for something he could connect his fist to.

It wasn't a dark night, not with that enormous pale moon casting silvery light around the area, yet he wasn't concerned that he would be spotted. He'd chosen a section of the property that was hidden in the shadow of a row of tall oak trees, which protected him from being spotted while affording him a direct view into the back of the house.

Lit up like a Christmas tree, he'd been able to spy on her as she flitted around that enormous kitchen, cooking a vast meal that they hadn't even eaten. It had stabbed him like a knife in the heart, seeing her so happy as she prepared food for another man when he had taught her everything she knew.

How could she do this to him?

How could she forget him so easily when he had been tortured by her face every minute of every day since she had jumped into that ocean?

Especially when, until the moment she had turned up at the marina and seen the unfortunate events that had come to pass, they had been blissfully happy.

Hadn't he given her everything she could have possibly needed?

Designer clothes, an expensive house, even a membership to the most exclusive spa that was only ever offered to celebrities. She'd never had to work a day in her life while living under his roof.

Apparently, none of that had been good enough.

Not the way he had cultivated her from the backward hick she had been when they'd met, into the beautiful, polished woman she was now.

And Logan Steel was reaping all the benefit of his hard work.

He'd suffered for years, dealing with some of the most despicable scum to have ever walked this Earth, just so she could live a life of luxury.

The hours ticked on, though in typical Californian fashion, the temperature never went below comfortable. Marko was perfectly fine, seething with rage as he stood in his hiding spot, watching his wife fornicate and cheat on him with the night-vision goggles he had purchased online.

The wild abandon on her face as the scumbag kissed and touched her most intimate of places was almost too much to bear. But he forced himself to keep watching as his mind began to formulate a new plan.

Coming to LA, this Godforsaken, smog-filled cesspit, his intention had been to find out exactly what was going on, why there was no mention of her real identity, and why there was no mention of him.

But now that he had seen her face again, he was reminded of all she had ever meant to him. He had grieved her death, and those two weeks had been the worst of his life. Now that she was alive again, a new spark had been lit inside. She was his world, his light, and he didn't care that she had left him once before.

All he cared about now was getting her back.

There was movement on the terrace outside the bedroom that caught his eye.

What was happening now?

Why was his wife sneaking out there?

When she lit the candles on the cake with such an effervescent smile, something snapped inside.

He was desperate to see her bestow that smile on him. He needed it. Craved it. He knew they could return to their previous happiness if he could only get her to see him again.

When the dog had come into the back yard, it was easy to lure him close with the dog whistle he had bought.

He hadn't had any prior motive with the whistle when he'd bought it. Just as he wasn't sure how and if he ever need to use the handcuffs, rope, hunting knife and gun that was in the bag that sat in the trunk of the car.

But he was a man who liked to prepare for any eventuality, and the whistle had come in handy at just the right time.

The stupid mutt had raced up to the fence without a care in the world.

It seemed obvious to open the bar of chocolate he had brought with him as an energy source. Seeing it, the fleabag became excited, barking and yapping in anticipation of a treat…

A treat that Marko knew would be poisonous to him.

He broke the bar into several pieces and tossed them to the dog. The dumb mutt gobbled them up, then barked for more.

Dirty, disgusting things. He glared at the puppy, channeling all the hate he felt for his owner to him.

He would have gotten the entire bar of chocolate if his wife hadn't called for him.

"Loki? Here boy. Come inside."

The dog cocked his head, one ear pricked in the direction of the house.

Marko knew that time was running out. If his wife came out here, she might see him.

And that couldn't be allowed.

This wasn't the time.

He had to get her away from Steel first and take her somewhere quiet where he'd be able to convince her to come back to him.

By the time she called for the dog again, Marko was already returning to his car.

32

Jane had barely slept a wink all night.

After they had returned home with Loki, who was pale around the gums and much quieter than normal, they had kept turns keeping watch on him.

Instead of his place by the fire, they'd had him on the bed between them, which had sent the puppy's tail wagging until he'd quickly run out of energy.

Though the vet said he should make a full recovery, Jane wasn't able to shake the feeling that it was her fault he was sick. She wasn't able to relax, her nerves shrieking at her that something was very wrong. Even with the fire burning, she wasn't able to shake the chill that had entered her body.

When six o'clock came, Logan got up reluctantly. Dark shadows ringed his eyes.

"Are you sure you can't call in sick?" She didn't want to cause issues with the production, but she would feel much happier if he stayed home with them today.

Reluctantly, Logan shook his head. "I wish I could, but I have to go in today."

Swallowing her disappointment, she looked at Loki, sleeping by her side. "I'm supposed to see the hypnotherapist again today, but I can't leave Loki. I know he shouldn't take a turn for the worst, but I'm not willing to risk it."

"I'll arrange for him to come here for your session."

There wasn't a doubt in her mind that he'd be able to do that.

"Thank you."

She went to hug him, but Logan seemed distracted. There was a distance in his eyes that hadn't been there during the night.

There was trouble on the horizon.

She couldn't say how she knew this. Call it intuition or her gut, but she knew it as sure as the sun rose each morning.

Something was coming.

They walked into the kitchen to find Kitty, having cooked another breakfast for them. Today, she'd made waffles and eggs, with freshly squeezed orange juice and an exotic fruit salad.

"Can Loki eat anything yet, or should I wait?" Kitty asked, bending down to fuss over him as followed them inside. "Poor boy."

He whined up at her, still as adorable as ever, though the little pep in his step that was usually there was nowhere in sight this morning.

"Let me check with his vet," Logan said.

A quick call to the clinic as the vet was wrapping up the night shift, and he confirmed, "We can give him bland food like rice and chicken, and lots of water, but nothing else until his system stabilizes."

"I'll get right on it and steam him some chicken. I'll mix the chicken juice with the rice. He should like that," Kitty said, casting the puppy a concerned look as he crawled into his bed in the kitchen.

Grabbing a banana, Logan stroked Loki on the head. "Don't give us any more problems, understand? I'll be back later."

Loki managed an answering thump of his tail.

He kissed Jane. "I don't have a big day today, so I should be home before too long. Thank you for the birth-day. And if I forget to tell you later, it was the best one I've ever had."

His words should have instilled warmth, though she couldn't get rid of that churning that had been in her stomach since they'd arrived home from the vets.

He waved goodbye and left, leaving Jane nibbling on a croissant even though her stomach recoiled at the very thought of food.

She had to eat something so she wouldn't crash and burn, particularly when the therapist arrived. Even though she wanted to crawl back into bed, she forced down the rest of the croissant, finished her coffee and took a quick shower while Kitty kept a watchful eye on Loki.

When she was dressed, she spent an hour with Loki to make sure he was recovering. Despite how good the food Kitty had made for him smelled, Loki needed encourage-ment to eat, his stomach still somewhat sore.

It wasn't until Jane fished up one of the pieces of chicken with her fingers and held it to his mouth that his tongue snaked out to lick it. Once he tasted it, it seemed to kick-start his appetite. He ate the entire bowl, which made her feel a little better. It was about as much as they could have hoped for at this point, but it did show he was making progress.

When the doorbell chimed, Jane went to greet her therapist.

WATER LAPPED AT THE MARINA. THE BITING COLD WIND rattled her bones.

She shivered from the cold, wrapping her arms around herself to keep it at bay.

Why wasn't she better dressed for being by the water?

Goose pimples ran up and down her arms. Her shoes pinched her feet. She glanced down to see the new stilettos that adorned them. They seemed a strange choice for being out here, too fussy and impractical.

Her legs were smooth and glowing in the way of recent pampering, her newly polished nails, buffed.

But more than the cold, there was a pain in her arm that lashed out each time she moved. She looked down and found a discolored patch of skin.

It was make-up.

A layer of foundation that someone had used to try to hide the marks beneath.

What had caused her arm to hurt like this?

And why would she need to hide the marks?

Who was she hiding them from?

Her mind went over the night before. Snatches of memory flashed up, ones that painted a scene.

A messy kitchen after a meal had been cooked. The dining table overlooking an immaculate back yard laid with food. Candles were lit, napkins folded, cutlery arranged for two. Mellow music played, setting the mood.

But moments later, the food covered the floorboards. The tablecloth curled around the legs of an upturned chair. Red wine spilled out of the bottle that had been chilling in an ice bucket.

And there she was, cowering as a dark, overwhelming shape seized her arm in a burning grasp.

The memory changed, morphed back to the marina.

She let out her breath, relieved to be away from that dark place.

She took a step forward on those new heels, her legs shaky and unsure.

There was a boat in front of her now, a luxurious yacht that was familiar, but the outer edges of the vessel were clad in darkness.

Her mind was still only allowing her to see parts of her memory.

What was going to happen that her mind didn't feel safe enough to reveal all?

Her question went answered.

Tap, tap, tap went her heels on the concrete ground, each step more ominous than the last. All the while, the waves crashed, creating a tense soundtrack that echoed in her mind.

When she arrived at the yacht, a high-pitched buzzing sounded in her ears, like millions of hornets flapping their wings.

Then suddenly everything vanished.

The yacht, the shoes, the waves.

There was only pain that she could feel on her head, a terrible, suffocating cold, and a world of darkness.

She couldn't breathe.

She clawed at her neck, catching it with her nails, but still the breath wouldn't come. She would drown out here and no one would ever know.

"Open your eyes now, Jane."

The voice was gentle yet commanding.

She turned in the inky blackness, tried to follow the sound of it, knowing instinctively that it led to safety.

"Come on, open your eyes now. You are safe, Jane. Breathe."

Her eyes flicked open.

Black spots clouded the edge of her vision but she was able to recognize the stunning house, the white leather armchair she sat on, and the adorable Australian Shepherd puppy who lay beside her, watching her every reaction with his ice-blue eyes.

She sucked in a greedy lungful of air even though she didn't need it.

"How do you feel?"

"Shaken." Jane admitted, wrapping her arms around her to ward of the chill of the memories. "What do you think happened to me?"

"I'm not entirely sure but the answers lie on that boat and with whoever that man is."

"I couldn't see his face at all, not any identifying feature."

"I'm sure that's your mind trying to protect you, but it will come back to you, and sooner than you think judging by our progress today. You're coming along in leaps and bounds."

Jane wished she could share his enthusiasm, but there was only a deep apprehension in her heart.

. . .

LIGHT EMITTED FROM THE GIANT PLASMA TELEVISION THAT covered the end of the wall, though the sound was muted. Nestled under the covers in bed, Jane cuddled with Loki. Exhausted after her session and the stresses of the night, an afternoon nap seemed the best way to go.

But, try as she might, she hadn't been able to fall asleep without those vivid glimpses of her past assaulting her mind. For what must have been the twentieth time today, she checked her phone, hoping that Logan had called or sent a message, but her notifications were empty.

She wished she had something to do, but everything here was taken care of, even Loki's meals for the next few days. Kitty had gone into overdrive, prepping more than enough for the dog.

She reached for the remote, flipping the channels in her search for something to take her mind off things when Logan's face flashed up on the screen. It was footage of him at a coffee shop. It wouldn't have been of any interest to her until she caught a glimpse of the clothes he was wearing — they were the exact clothes he had left for work in today.

Frowning, she glanced at the scroll bar at the bottom of the screen, which announced that the footage had been captured only minutes ago on Santa Monica Boulevard.

But what was he doing there, when he was supposed to be at work?

She unmuted the television to hear the anchor discussing who Logan's mysterious — and very good-looking — companion might be.

Jane didn't see who they were talking about, as Logan

sat alone at the table, but within moments, a striking brunette appeared with two coffees.

Long-legged and lithe with the kind of curves most women would wish for, the woman wore giant sunglasses on her face, but they did nothing to hide the stunning, pouty lips or the perfect cheekbones that only great genetics could bring.

Logan sat close to her, their heads bowed together as they spoke in intimate fashion.

A hammer smashed into Jane's heart, breaking it into a million pieces.

It was his birthday today, but rather than spend it with her, he had snuck off to meet with this other, very stunning woman.

What a fool she had been to trust him, to believe that he could love an ordinary woman like her!

Tears stung her eyes as she dialed Clare's number. Her friend picked up after a few rings, sounding out of breath.

"Jane? You OK?"

She didn't want to get into the whole sordid tale on the phone.

"Are you free today? I was hoping that I might be able to see you?"

"Oh, I can't. I'm sorry. I'm with Ken right now. It's our second date this week," she couldn't help revealing. Her happiness was palpable and Jane knew she couldn't bring her friend down, not when she'd had so little of it in her life.

"That's great. I'm sorry I interrupted you."

"No… never apologize for calling. You know I love to hear from you."

"I don't want to keep you, do you think you could meet me tomorrow?"

"Sure, I'll swing by the house after work? Say five o'clock?"

"No, I'd prefer we go somewhere. I'll probably have Loki with me. He was sick last night but getting better today."

"Oh no. What happened to him?"

"We're not sure. He seemed to have eaten something that was toxic to him. I think it's coming out of his system though. He certainly seems much better this morning."

"Well, that's a relief. Poor little guy." She thought for a moment. "How about Silver Lake Dog Park? It's near where I live so I can get there pretty fast. Will that work?"

"That'll be perfect. I'll see you then."

They signed off as Jane spent the rest of her day feeling sick to her stomach, searching the internet for whatever mention she could find of Logan and his mysterious date.

33

Dinner came and went, but there was no sign of Logan.

The meal of Chicken Parmesan Jane had prepared, sat drying in the oven and would probably end up inedible by the time he finally arrived home, but she kept it there as a form of torturous reminder.

She checked her phone again, but there was still only the one message from him today.

"Work is running late and might even go on through the night. I won't be home for dinner, so eat without me. Sorry about this. L x"

If not for the "x" at the end, it could have been written for Kitty or any other employee. For the woman he purported to love, the message was so impersonal and rushed, it cut her to the quick.

Her stomach churned with a mixture of hunger and nerves. She hadn't been able to eat anything other than that croissant all day, not with her mind endlessly going over every little detail of this morning.

Did his coolness have anything to what happened last night?

She closed her eyes, letting the memories of his touch, his words and the promise of new love washing over her. It was less than twenty hours since they had declared their love for one another — how, then, was he lying to her already and spending the day with that gorgeous brunette? And on his birthday, of all days? The woman must mean a lot for him to devote the entire day to her.

Her eyes flicked open as Kitty entered the kitchen. Jane sat at the marble island in the center of the room, hands wrapped around a coffee that had long grown cold.

The older woman didn't have a hair out of place, even after a full day of work. Nothing ruffled her, not even the sight of an anxious woman driving herself insane with her own thoughts.

"How is the puppy doing?" Kitty asked, nodding toward Loki, who napped in his new bed. In what seemed his favorite sleeping position, he was upside down, tummy exposed to the world.

"Better. He had a small snack a few hours ago, and he's been drinking. He even wanted to play a little but got tired out fast. I think he'll pull through."

A wide smile broke out, causing wrinkles to appear over her weathered face.

"That's a relief. Logan loves that dog, even though he pretends otherwise."

"He's very good at looking after everyone. Dogs, women... He's quite the hero."

There was a hint of bitterness that underscored her comment. Kitty's hands hesitated over the kettle as she reached to refill it.

"Logan is misunderstood by many, but in my experience, he is the best person I know. He is kind with such a big heart."

Too bad that heart and his love needed to be spread around.

The second the thought came, Jane mentally shut it down. It wasn't fair to talk to Kitty like this. The man had saved her entire family and was still looking after them now. Whatever issue she had with him had nothing to do with her, and she shouldn't be putting the woman in the uncomfortable position of defending someone she obviously cared greatly about.

The timely ring of her phone made her jump out of her seat. She reached for it eagerly, answering the call.

"Hello?"

"Hey! Is this a good time?"

It was Clare. At the sound of her warm voice, Jane's blues lifted a little.

"I actually have nothing to do and was just considering my options for some mindless binging of television shows I should know better than to watch."

"I've called just in time to save you then?"

"It would appear so."

"Well," Clare continued, sounding excited. "Ken has been called to work, so I have the evening free. I felt bad I wasn't able to talk much earlier, didn't want you to think I was blowing you off. So, on the off chance that I can steal you away from Logan, do you want to meet for an evening walk? You can bring Loki still. The park stays open until late."

"I'm fine to meet you, but let me check with the vet to see what he thinks. If it's fine, I'll bring him. Either way, we can still meet there."

"You're sure? I'm fine to come to you instead if you want?"

But that was the last thing she wanted. She'd never feel as if she could speak freely with Logan's staff running around, discreet as they were.

"No. I haven't been out of the house today. I'll meet you there after I've checked in with the vet."

"Sure thing. I'll be there in twenty or so minutes."

They ended the call. The vet was happy with Loki's progress. The fact that he hadn't been sick again and was now eating was a good sign. He warned that Loki shouldn't have much exertion as his little body would still be fighting any toxins that might be working through his system, but a short trip where he didn't have to walk much, would be fine.

After her police scare, Jane knew not to attempt driving again. But, not wanting to trouble Kitty, she summoned a car from the service Logan had an account with, and arrived at the park. A few minutes later, Clare's Prius parked close by. She appeared with a bright smile and two cups of Starbucks' coffees.

"Thought you might like a hot drink," she said, handing one to her as they hugged. "It can get chilly out here at night."

"You are fab, thank you," Jane replied.

Loki planted himself beside Jane and refused to budge, wary of the other dogs he could see, although none were close. His tail wagged when Clare bent down to greet him, but he returned to his watchful sentry, refusing to play. Jane had never seen him like this.

"I think he's feeling vulnerable," Jane explained.

"So would I if I'd had the night he had. What a brave little trooper for coming out."

"We're barely out," Jane laughed. "The car dropped us off a few feet away and we've pretty much sat here since."

Clare shrugged. "Well, it's something. Little steps, right, Boy?"

Loki's ears pricked up and twisted round to her, though he kept his eyes on the other four-legged visitors.

"So, how are things with you and Ken?"

At the mention of his name, Clare smiled happily.

"At the risk of jinxing it all, really well."

"That's wonderful, Clare. What's he like?"

Clare stared across the park, contemplating the question.

"He's extremely courteous, an old-fashioned gentleman. You know, opens doors for me, pays the bills instead of expecting to go Dutch like most of the guys I've come across on dating apps. He's also a great listener and actually interested in what I say: I swear he listens to every word. And he's so respectful. Can you believe he hasn't actually made a move on me? We've only kissed so far and held hands, and in this town, that's so unbelievably rare."

She hugged herself. "He makes me feel so special, like I'm the center of his world and the only woman he has eyes for."

The moment she'd said the words, Jane felt her smile crack. She ducked her head, hoping Clare wouldn't see the glimmer of tears that threatened to spill over. But she was too late.

"What's wrong? Did I say something to upset you?"

Jane brushed aside her tears, angry at herself for being

emotional when Clare deserved this moment of happiness. "I'm sorry. It's not you. I'm really happy you've got Ken now, it's just… Logan said he loved me last night."

Clare's concerned frown deepened in confusion. "And that's terrible because you don't know who you are?"

"No… I mean, yes, that's one thing I'm concerned about, but that isn't what's got me so worked up."

She pulled up a screenshot of Logan with his mysterious woman on her phone and showed it to her.

"He told me he had to work today, but then he was caught with this woman. They're obviously on a date."

Clare studied the image quietly, the emerald in her eyes almost glowing beneath the light of a streetlamp.

"I'm not sure we should jump to conclusions…"

"He said he had to work. That it was important for him to go."

"Maybe there's a simple explanation. I think you should try not to worry too much until you can at least talk to him about this."

"You're not worried about this?" Jane looked back at the woman, at how perfect she was and could feel her insecurities starting to suffocate her.

"I admit it doesn't look great, but you're forgetting one thing: I've seen the two of you together. I know that man loves you. And he's even told you now, why on earth would he do that only to cheat on you the very next day? Does that sound like something he'd do?"

"No," Jane admitted. "But… it's his birthday today. Why else would he spend it without me unless this woman was important to him?"

Clare studied the image in the phone again as if it

would offer new clues. "Maybe it's family. Does he have a sister?"

"He's an only child."

"Then you've got me. I don't know."

She set her coffee onto the bench, reached over and squeezed Jane's ice-cold hand.

"Thing is, you won't know either until he gets home and you actually speak to him about it. It's pointless to torture yourself. The whole thing could be entirely innocent for all you know — which, I'm willing to bet money it is. Don't forget that this is the same man who was so protective over you that he interrogated me! Me, Jane! And I'm about as nice as they come."

Jane could feel her panic receding. She smiled a wobbly smile. "I know I'm being ridiculous. I just..."

She couldn't finish her words with the frog in her throat.

"You love him." Clare finished for her. Jane nodded, not trusting herself to speak. She lowered a hand to stroke Loki. He relaxed and pressed into her, warming her cold legs.

"Letting yourself become vulnerable is a frightening thing for everyone, not only those who have lost their memory. You need to not be so hard on yourself. Whatever you're feeling is justified. Just allow yourself to feel it so you can get through it. You'll feel better when you come out on the other side, I promise you."

"When did you get so wise?"

Clare laughed wryly. "After years of being a doormat and putting up with a jerk for a husband, I guess I had to learn sometime."

Clare's phone rang, interrupting their conversation.

"It's Ken, hold on." She took the call, smiling into the phone. "I guess you just can't stop thinking about me?"

Whatever Ken said had her eyes flaring open with alarm. "Oh God. Are you alright?"

Ken spoke rapidly. Jane couldn't understand his words, though his tone sent a chill through her body. Clare got to her feet, clutching her handbag as she ended the call.

"He's been in an accident. They've rushed him to Cedars Sinai, but I need to get going."

Jane stood up with her, shocked by the shade of pale her friend had gone. "That's awful. What happened?"

"A car ran into his. His airbag deployed and broke his nose, but they need to run some other checks on him, make sure he's OK internally."

"Do you want me to go with you?" Jane tugged Loki's leash, forcing him to stand.

"That's really kind of you, but no. I'd rather you go home and straighten things out with Logan. I can take it from here. Do you need a lift home?"

Jane waved her considerate friend away, touched at how, even in a time of such great distress, she could still think of her safety. "I'm fine with Loki. I'll call for another car. You go, he needs you."

"Thank you." Clare hugged her tight before sprinting to her car.

"Call me later and let me know how he is!" Jane shouted after her.

"I will!"

Gunning the gas, Clare peeled out of the parking lot, leaving Jane to sit back down onto the bench. The shock of

Ken's accident had jolted her out of whatever misery she had been feeling.

This was ridiculous!

Here was something real that actually threatened Clare's relationship. Logan said he loved her and his actions had proven that. Shouldn't she give him the benefit of the doubt? Shouldn't she go home and be there waiting for his return with open arms?

"I'll call us a ride, Boy," she told Loki, whose tail thumped a response.

She summoned the car using the app on her phone and was told the car would be there in ten minutes. "Not long now. We'll be home soon and you can see your dad."

Loki's tail began to wag when he suddenly tensed. A growl came from deep within his throat.

"What's the matter?"

She started to look over her shoulder, to where Loki was staring, when someone grabbed hold of her, dragging her off the bench and away from the circle of light that she sat under.

Loki went crazy, barking and leaping toward her, but his leash got caught on one of the planks of wood that formed the bench. He wasn't able to break free. He howled into the night, trying desperately to reach her.

Terror had turned Jane's blood to ice.

Her head snapped back as she tried to get a look at her attacker when a piece of cloth came over her face. The smell that hit her was overly sweet, like Vodka mixed with sugar.

Her head started to feel light and her body, limp.

Her last thought as she fought to remain conscious was that she recognized the eyes that held her in their grasp.

She knew the hate that lay within them and that dark wickedness she had forgotten about, but which now seared its memory into her heart.

Before she could scream for help, the world faded away.

34

Clare drove as fast as she could.

Her heart was in her throat and even though Ken had sounded OK, she knew he was downplaying his injuries so she wouldn't worry. But, if there wasn't any concern, he wouldn't have called her in the first place.

She blew past traffic, her small car coming uncomfortably close to its neighbors at times. She prayed that he would make it. She wouldn't accept any other outcome, not when she'd just met the man of her dreams.

After the longest thirty minutes of her life, she hurried to the front desk of the hospital.

"I'm here to see my boyfriend. He was brought here half an hour ago. A car accident."

Her sentences ran into each other and she couldn't quite get her breath.

The receptionist, a mature woman with a no-nonsense yet calming air, gave her a reassuring smile. "Let me check the system. What's his name?"

"Ken Blackwood," Clare replied, relieved that he had

given his full name early in their relationship. She remembered it clearly, having searched Facebook for his profile that night only to have come up empty. That hadn't been all that surprising: he had already revealed how little he thought of social networking sites.

The receptionist pushed her glasses up her nose and peered into the computer screen with a frown. "I don't have a listing for that name. Could it be under something else?"

"No. That's his name, I'm sure of it."

The receptionist spread her hands in apology. "I'm very sorry, but it's not listed here."

Clare blinked, trying to think. Someone had obviously entered his name incorrectly into the system. Of all the luck…

"Can you just search for Ken then, in case someone spelled his name wrong."

She wasn't sure how that could be since it was a pretty standard name. "Maybe there's an 'e' at the end of 'Blackwood'?"

The woman tried several variations, then just under the name "Ken," but the screen came back empty.

Clare tried to fight the rising irritation. She did not need this right now.

"Can you just check for car accidents in the last half an hour then?"

The receptionist hesitated only a second before she replied.

"Well, that's the problem. I've already tried that. We haven't had any car accidents in the last four hours. Are you sure he said he was at this hospital?"

Clare's heart started thumping in her chest. "Yes, I am. Let me try calling him."

She found his number on her recent callers list and dialed, but his phone was turned off.

She ran a hand through her hair and tried to think it through.

He was in a hospital, so his phone might need to be turned off. As for the hospital name, he'd just been in an accident. Maybe he'd hit his head, or gotten confused. Or the ambulance crew could have changed hospitals at the last minute and forgotten to tell him.

But wouldn't he have known where he was when they took him there?

"Ma'am? Is there anything else I can help you with? I can give you a list of the other hospitals that have emergency care in the area?"

The receptionist was being polite, but there was already a few people behind Clare waiting to be seen.

She moved away. "No... Thank you. He must be somewhere else."

There was a gnawing in her stomach. An anxiety she had no idea how to handle. Not knowing what else to do, she called Jane's number.

The call rang and rang, but there was no answer.

She waited a few seconds before trying again, only for more of the same.

It was an unfortunate coincidence. Jane was likely already home and making up with Logan, but something in her gut didn't sit right.

Jane knew she was rushing to the hospital. She'd even said, very clearly, to call her as soon as she had any news.

There was no way her friend would not answer her phone at a moment like this.

Something did not feel right *at* all.

Without any way of locating Ken's hospital, she drove back to the park, hoping that maybe her friend was still there and just hadn't heard her phone ring. She parked in almost the same spot — the park wasn't busy, tonight being colder than normal.

There was something on the ground by the bench, lying in a pool of dark liquid.

The sight of it sent chills down her back.

It was the coffee she had given Jane. She could see the name "Jane" written on the side of the Starbucks cup.

Right next to the bench sat a trashcan.

If she knew anything about Jane, it was that the woman wouldn't leave her trash on the ground like that. She approached the cup slowly, unsure what to do.

A whimper sounded close by, so timidly that if there was any other noise in the park, she might not have heard it.

"Hello?"

She called out into the night, senses on full alert. The sound that came this time wasn't so much a whimper as a whine. Ducking down, she met Loki's fearful blue eyes from where he had been hiding beneath the bench.

"Loki! What're you doing here all alone? Where's Jane?"

She untangled his leash from the bench, encouraged him out. The puppy trembled from fear and cold. She hugged up to her chest, warming him up even as fear took hold of her.

"Let's try calling her again."

She didn't know if she was talking to calm the dog or herself. She found Jane's number and hit 'call'. The phone started ringing almost immediately...

As did another, very close by.

The rings echoed hers so closely that they could have been synchronized.

Her heart plummeted to her stomach.

Holding onto Loki, she approached the sound of the ringing phone and found it coming from the trashcan. Peering over the top, she saw a handbag lying on top of the trash — Jane's brown slouch bag. The lights from her phone screen could be seen through the material of the bag.

She fished out the bag and the phone, fingers trembling to see "CLARE CALLING" on the screen.

"Jane? JANE?!!!" She shouted suddenly, eyes darting every which way in the hope of seeing her friend. "WHERE ARE YOU?"

But of course, there was no answer.

Only the ringing of the two phones.

Holding tightly to Loki, she ran for her car, carrying Jane's bag and phone. Once inside, she locked the doors and took off, not wanting to stay in the dark park a moment longer.

Her heart was threatening to burst out of her chest. Something terrible had happened to Jane, she knew it for sure. Although she was still concerned about Ken, he was being taken care of. But Jane... she was on her own.

Clare had to get help, she had to speak to Logan.

Keeping one eye on the street ahead, she tried to activate Jane's phone but it asked for a passcode or fingerprint to unlock it. Flinching at a pain in the middle of her head, she suddenly came up with the solution.

"Hey Siri?" She asked the phone, hoping desperately that the automated service had been activated and would consider her voice a close enough match to Jane's.

"Go ahead" the automated male voice answered.

Such relief surged through her that she almost burst into tears. "Call Logan" she instructed.

Immediately, the system started to call him. She gripped onto the wheel, fingers dead to the world as she waited anxiously for the call to be answered. It was finally picked up on the sixth ring.

"Hello, Logan's phone."

The sultry female voice clearly wasn't his.

"I need to speak to Logan. It's an emergency." The terror in her voice brokered no argument.

"Is this Jane?" Asked the concerned female.

"No, it's Clare, her friend. Something terrible has happened to her. Please, can you just put him on the phone?"

"Of course. One second."

There was the muffled sound of the phone being handed over to him before Logan's voice came down the phone.

"Clare?! What's happened?"

The explanation spilled out of her in-between tears of fright. She felt awful for calling her friend out then dumping her at the park. This was her fault. If anything happened to Jane, she'd never forgive herself.

Logan listened as she explained, his breathing becoming terser and terser as he barked out the occasional question. When she was finished, the strain cracked his voice. It was the voice of a man out of his mind with worry for the woman he loved.

"Are you calling the police? I don't know what to do," she admitted, wishing she could be more helpful.

"We're going to call them on the way to the station. Can you meet us there?"

"Yes."

He gave her the address of the closest LAPD, but as she went to hang up the call, he stopped her.

"Clare? Please be careful. Don't get out of your car for anyone, understand? Not anyone but me. Just come straight to the police station."

She promised and hung up before his last words sank in… and then she couldn't get them out of her mind.

Why had he stressed that?

What on Earth was happening here?

THE WORLD WAS SPINNING.

There was a thumping inside his head that threatened to collapse his skull. A woman's voice spoke to him, calm and soothing, trying to cut through the pressure building inside, but she might as well have been a world away for all the good it did.

All he could think about was Jane and what could be happening to her right now.

"Logan. I'm going to need you to snap out of this if we're to have any chance of saving her."

A pair of elegant fingers snapped loudly in front of his eyes and it seemed to do the trick, shocking him out of himself. He looked at the woman beside him in the car, driving with such expertize that she could have been one of the stunt team on his movie.

Except she wasn't.

Yanking on the wheel, she took a sharp turn that sent the manilla folders on the backseat sliding into the footwell. Notes, records and surveillance photographs spilled out, colliding with a state-of-the-art digital camera with its wide zoom lens.

A MacBook Air that was used to download evidence captured by the camera, teetered on the edge of the seat but stopped short of toppling over.

The woman's curtain of gleaming chestnut hair swung over her shoulder, revealing delicate features that were the envy of many a model, yet which had proved impossibly useful in her line of work.

Westler was one of the best Private Investigators in the city.

Trained by her father, and his father before him, when Westler decided to carry on the family's line of work, no one was more surprised than her parents who had expected her to go the usual route chosen by girls whose beauty was out of this world.

Westler hadn't been interested, however. Having grown up idolizing her father and even attending the odd stakeout with him — when he was sure there was no risk — she wanted to be just like daddy. She had trained hard and learned how to use her looks to her advantage: neither men nor women could help underestimate a beautiful woman.

And she was pretty fine with that, having amassed a fair fortune through her set of unique skills.

She worked the big cases where millions — even

billions — were on the line. Lately, she'd had a swath of sexual harassment cases to deal with where she'd gone undercover to see what proof she could gather on the men suspected of the crimes. Unfortunately, nearly all had been guilty.

She even performed honey traps. In the most recent one, she had been hired by a wife who suspected her director husband of infidelity. Westler had gone undercover as a sweet young thing straight off the bus from the Mid-West, with more boobs than sense. One look at her wannabe actress and it wasn't long before the director had requested much more than was normal for an audition.

If it wasn't for her beloved family, Westler would have moved somewhere nice and wholesome a long time ago. Montreal sounded nice plus they had Mounties, and Westler loved herself a man in uniform.

Logan's glazed eyes stared blindly ahead.

She felt for him, knowing what had likely happened to Jane. Still, they couldn't do anything until the friend arrived at the station and the cops were involved. As tough as Westler was, a kidnapped woman wasn't something she was willing to handle alone.

"We're almost there," she assured Logan. "Summers has been informed. He's gathered a team and we can start briefing them as soon as we're all together."

A curt nod was the only answer he trusted himself to give. Westler focused on getting them there while Logan silently prayed for her to hurry.

When they arrived, Clare was waiting in her car with Loki as he'd instructed. Seeing his arrival, she burst into tears of relief.

"I don't understand what's happening! Have you

found Jane? Can someone please tell me what's going on?"

"We'll explain everything inside."

They went in as Summers and Westler nodded a greeting to each other, having crossed paths before. Westler handed Summers a thick manilla file and a memory stick.

"Thanks. Come this way," Summers instructed, leading them into a room where a photograph of Jane's wane and pale face peered back at them from the center of a whiteboard.

Feeling her tremble beside him, Logan took Clare's hand and squeezed it. The gesture made her feel slightly better. Her arms tightened around Loki, who sat on her lap, looking almost as overwhelmed as she did. It suddenly came to him that, much as he had been doing, she had been blaming herself for Jane's disappearance.

"It's not your fault." His voice sounded alien, with none of the charisma or personality it usually held. She turned to him with eyes that said she didn't believe him.

"It's true," Westler offered suddenly.

"Who are you?" Clare asked.

"She's the PI I hired to look into Jane's past," Logan answered.

"What?" Clare gasped. It wasn't what she'd expected at all. "Jane saw the two of you having coffee. She thought you were cheating on her."

The stricken look on Logan's face made her wish she hadn't spoken.

"Is that why you met up today?"

"Yes. She wanted to see me, but I had plans with my boyfriend, except he then had to go into work so I was free to meet her. She'd been upset all day but didn't have anyone to talk to. She said… she didn't understand why you would lie to her about going to work when you were with her instead."

She pointed a finger at Westler, apparently finding it hard to believe the woman's profession.

"When Jane started getting glimpses of her past, when she started recalling things, I knew something had to be done. No offence," he said to Summers and his team of cops standing around them. He shook his head.

"None taken. Please continue."

"I was falling for her and I knew I had to find out who she was to protect her, if not myself."

"Why would she need protecting?" Clare asked, confusion clouding her green eyes.

"The way she was when I first found her, and the little quirks she had… I study body language all day long in my line of work so it seemed obvious to me that she had been abused before… By a man, her ex we think." Logan explained.

Clare's horrified gasp echoed around the room. She gripped onto Loki tighter until he whined.

"It made sense in the way she kept apologizing, kept blaming herself for things that weren't her fault. It would also make sense why no one has come forward for her. And we can't forget the way in which she was found."

"Abuse victims are often isolated from family and friends, which might explain why no one has been in touch to report her missing," Summers explained. "It could be that Jane was alone with only her abuser for company."

"Are you sure it's her ex? It all sounds too horrific."

"Yes," Westler replied. "Because I've almost found him."

"Remember when Jane went to the hypnotherapist, and she mentioned a marina and a yacht and a glass cubed office?" Logan asked. "Using those clues, Westler was able to narrow it down to one particular marina that has all of those things."

"Right," Westler continued. "I gathered information on every single person who has regular access to one of the yachts in the marina, but that still leaves us with almost forty suspects."

"We can check out each of them, but that would entail having teams to investigate some forty places of work and their homes, and the yachts themselves, which would be an enormous production. If we could narrow it down, it would be so much more helpful. Timing is crucial in a case like this." Summers stuck the memory stick into a nearby computer and activated the folder Westler had helpfully named "SUSPECTS."

Faces flooded the screen.

"But, we haven't got anything else to go on," Logan replied.

"No. So, I guess we'll have to send those teams out. I'll start with the marina myself," Summers said. "And we can liase with some other stations to put together the actual teams."

While they talked, Clare had been studying the men and women who were projected onto the screen. She wasn't expecting to recognize any of them, but when she came to the fourteenth photograph, the blood drained from her face.

"No... it can't be."

She pointed at the man on the computer screen, her ears rushing with sound. The world began to tilt on its axis. She could feel herself growing faint with shock.

"That's Ken, my new boyfriend. That's the man I've been seeing."

35

She was parched, her mouth was so dry that it hurt. A dull thud in her head made it hard to hear well, but she could still tell that the waves sounded different today.

They weren't lapping gently against the shore but hitting against something hard.

Why was the world moving around like it was?

The rocking motion made her stomach lurch, bringing a wave of nausea to the fore. She felt strange, groggy, as if there was a fog wrapped around her head, and instead of the heavenly cushion that she had slept on the night before, the bed now felt uncomfortably hard beneath her.

She rolled to one side, hoping to ease the pain along her spine only for her hip to jut against the hard surface.

She flinched.

What on Earth was she lying on?

"Where am I?"

Her voice croaked out the question.

"Sweetheart, you're awake."

The male voice that spoke sounded excited, yet there was an undercurrent of danger that she couldn't miss. Something about the voice was frighteningly familiar, but she couldn't place it, not with her head still in that fog. Even so, her body was starting to wake, and with it, her senses began to shriek in alarm.

Something was very wrong.

She pushed up with her hands, trying to get into a sitting position only to discover that they were tightly bound with rope.

The fog lifted immediately, replaced by a terror that left her gasping.

The man bent over the wheel of the yacht was tall and muscular and of a similar build to Logan, but that was where the similarities ended.

This man had hair the color of tar, and where Logan's eyes were a warm green, his was so dark that they looked as black as the night that surrounded them. A thin scar covered his left cheek that hadn't quite healed yet.

Her mind crashed back to another time, when her ring had caught this man's face as she had flailed against him. She hissed out a panicked breath that left her hollow.

She knew this man.

More than knew him.

She had been married to him.

Images assaulted her then, memories and flashes of their previous life together. She saw their whirlwind romance when she had thought he was Prince Charming. When she had been so desperate to leave her sleepy, unloved, and uneventful life, that she had reasoned away the early warning signs.

Mistaking intensity for love.

Controlling behavior for care.

Misogyny for old-fashioned charm.

He had known how vulnerable she was, how much she had craved love that she fell into his open arms, blindly and willingly…

Only to pay for it later, many times over.

He was so good at ripping away her last vestiges of self-esteem that Jane never even realized that she wasn't the problem. Brainwashed from his mental beatings, and isolated from anyone who could have helped, she'd had no one, not even herself. She never blamed him even when she had been doubled over with pain, especially when he was always so sorry for it, the day after.

For that was how abuse worked.

He would hurt her, then shower her with so much love that all of her resolve to leave him would melt away. She would believe his promises, and life would be wonderful for a time, until the next thing would set him off…

The moment she saw him murder another man, she had woken up from that daze, and would have reported him to the authorities if Marko hadn't gotten to her first.

Marko.

Just the name sent chills racing down her back.

Jane blinked, eyes darting around to record the details of her surroundings. If she could somehow get out of this alive, she'd need to remember as much as she could for the law enforcement.

"I can't believe you are alive, Emily. I thought I'd lost you."

Emily.

That was her real name, though it felt alien in this moment. Emily was a lifetime ago. She was Jane now…

she wasn't the abused and frightened wife Marko had turned her into. A picture of Logan flashed into her head, filling her with love.

This wouldn't be the end of her story.

Not if she could help it.

"Who are you?"

She asked the question, hoping to throw him. If he believed her, maybe it would stall whatever plans he had for her.

Marko's head snapped to her, his eyes turning hurt.

"How could you ask me that? I am your husband! We have been married for almost ten years. How could you pretend to be dead when all the while, you were here, living with that *man?*"

He sneered at the word 'man', like it disgusted him.

Jane shook her head, allowing her eyes to soften with confusion. "No. I don't know who you are. I don't remember anything from the time I woke up on that beach and Logan found me."

He froze at her words, lips tightening into a thin, white line. "You're lying. You can't have forgotten me, not after all that we have meant to each other."

"It's the truth! You can talk to Detective Summers at LAPD. He was assigned to my case. He'll be able to verify my story. Just call him and ask! Tell him you want to know about Jane Smith, that you think you might know who she is."

His dark eyes glittered with indecision. Jane took this as a good sign that she was getting through to him. She reached out to him.

"Please… You don't have to do this. Whatever has happened was in the past — and I don't remember it, anyway. You can just leave and we'll both get on with our lives. You can't still want me now that I've been with another man."

He flinched as if she'd physically struck him. Remembering how territorial he was, she had known he wouldn't like that. Wouldn't be able to stomach the thought of another man touching his property.

"I'm sorry if I've hurt you, but I didn't know I was doing it. The doctor said I had amnesia that was caused from blunt forced trauma. I must have been in an accident."

"You fell… from this yacht."

His answer was calculating as he started to spin a variation of the truth, one he thought he might get away with. Jane forced herself to nod as if he had just revealed a big secret that she had been trying to uncover.

"That makes sense. If you can cut these ropes, I promise I won't run. There's nowhere for me to go anyway, not while we're on this boat."

"True. And you always were the worst swimmer."

He smiled at her. The scumbag actually smiled as if they were sharing a joke! She got up to her feet, started toward him. When he flicked open a switchblade knife, she fought not to flinch, keeping a pleasant smile on her lips.

He took hold of her hands, moving to slip the knife through the rope when the whir of approaching helicopter blades sounded. Spotlights hit the choppy waters, churned up by those spinning blades.

A siren shrieked, lights gyred into the night.

Marko's reaction was immediate. Instead of cutting

her loose, he grabbed her, pulling her to shield his own body, and sliding the knife to her neck.

"What're you doing?" Jane cried as the cold steel bit into her neck.

"You were trying to trick *me*?!" His voice rose on the word 'me', stunned that she would try to pull a stunt on him.

"Of course not. I don't know who they are! How could I have called them when I only just regained consciousness?"

But common sense had left the boat and was heading fast for the shore. He dragged her to the top deck where three helicopters hovered in the sky and several dark shapes waited on the water surrounding them.

It was the Harbour Patrol, with their distinct white on red sign sprayed onto each end of the boat. The knife pushed against her throat. Feeling the pressure of the moment, he felt panic grip.

"The knife. You're hurting me!"

The spotlights suddenly swung toward them, centering until they stood in a halo of light. A commanding voice called out of a loudspeaker.

"You are surrounded Marko. Release Jane and we can talk about what's gotten you so upset."

It was Detective Summers. Hearing his familiar voice, some of Jane's terror receded. He would know what to do. She wasn't alone with Marko anymore. All these people were here to help her.

Marko glared defiantly into the lights, shifting constantly in case they had any weapons trained on him, making it impossible for them to land a hit.

"Her name is Emily! And she's *my* wife!"

"She goes by the name Jane, now, Marko. Please release her so we can board. You won't be harmed as long as you do what I say."

Jane felt his rage grow tenfold at the detective words. The hope that had flared in her chest began to sink.

"You don't tell me what to do. She belongs to me!"

"But you are surrounded Marko. There's nothing you can do, so let her go and we can see that you will be fairly treated."

She could see faces peering down at them from the helicopters, but none of them clearly enough to discern who they were. The choppy waters sent the yacht yo-yoing unevenly beneath her feet. The sound of the blades were drowning out everything around her.

Among the madness, she found herself growing quiet. In her mind, Logan's face appeared. She smiled wistfully, wishing that they could have had more time together.

She could feel that her life was coming to an end.

Marko would never let her go.

He was too twisted, too controlling to let her out of his grasp.

He pushed her toward the edge of the yacht, fingers digging into her arm.

One of the helicopters lowered, coming as close as it could. The door slid open, and Jane looked through the group of cops inside to find Logan staring back at her, his terror palpable.

A thrill went through her.

He was here!

She was so happy to see him this one last time, she took a step toward him. Marko spun around. Spotting

Logan in the helicopter, his face twisted with ugliness, his fury combusting.

"No! She will never be yours!"

He shoved her hard, sending her over the side of the yacht.

She crashed into the black water.

The frigid cold stunned her. She felt her lungs catch as she held her breath, only to realize that she was free! Marko hadn't used the knife on her — too chicken to end her life that way. All she had to do was swim to the surface, and she'd be safe.

She'd be reunited with Logan.

She swung her hands through the water before remembering with a sudden, thudding horror that they were still tied.

With all the nonsense Marko had spouted, one thing had been true — she was a terrible swimmer at the best of times, but with her hands tied like this…

She shook off her fear and kicked her legs, moving her arms in a downward stroke, giving it everything she had. Instead of rising closer to the surface, she sank lower into the ocean.

It wasn't working.

She couldn't get enough momentum to propel herself upward. Her eyes flicked toward the surface, at the last of the light that was rapidly being swallowed by the inky black water.

Her lungs were burning.

She had maybe a few seconds before she'd exhale her last breath… Before her world would fade away.

The edges of her vision began to turn fuzzy. She

recalled an image of Logan in her mind, needing to hold on to a last happy memory before the dark took her.

She saw him gliding toward her, grim determination like the steel in his name, on his face. He looked so real that she reached her fingers toward him.

He snatched hold of her hand, pulling her to him.

Her last breath hissed out of her in shock.

The fogginess that had started to occur vanished instantly. It wasn't her imagination at all: he was there!

Snaking one arm around her chest, he held her in a solid grip as he swam upward like a dolphin. She kicked her feet, helping him as much as she could until they burst through the surface.

She gulped in a lung full of air as Logan turned onto his back with her pressed firmly against his chest. They swam that way until they reached the closest patrol boat. Someone threw down a rope ladder as several cops jumped into the water to help.

Jane found herself pulled into the safety of the boat as Logan climbed up after her. Seeing the love reflected in his eyes, she sank into his arms as he crushed her to his chest.

Across from them, on the yacht where Jane could easily see the name AMELIA that was painted onto it, Marko was thrown to the deck and his hands cuffed behind his back. He raged and kicked at the cops that held him, but all that resulted in was a cuff to the head as they pinned him down harder.

Logan kissed her cheek, speaking into her ear.

"It's over. He will never touch you again."

A familiar bark sounded close by as Clare and Loki emerged from one of the helicopters and ran toward her.

And all the emotions she had been holding inside, burst out in a flood of tears.

AFTER SHE WAS CHECKED OVER AND DECLARED FIT IF SHAKEN, they were air-lifted to the LAPD.

Jane had so many questions, and they tried their best to explain, filling in the empty gaps until she was mostly caught up.

Her head was reeling from it all.

"So my ex husband," the words stuck in her throat, thick and cloying, and utterly unbelievable to her. "He was the man you were dating? He was Ken?"

Clare bit her lip, hanging her head. "I'm so sorry, Jane. I didn't have a clue who he was. He was really good at hiding his true intentions."

Jane took hold of her friend's hand. "Don't apologize. I of all people know how persuasive he can be. He's an expert manipulator, Clare, and very good at targeting decent, kind-hearted women."

Logan had kept his arm around her the entire ride back, and even now, sitting in Summers' office, he pressed against her as if needing the physical reassurance of her body. Loki's head lay on her bare feet — her ballerina pumps now lost to the ocean — his eyes tilted up to stare at her adoringly. Their love could have filled the room.

"That's right," Summers confirmed. "We went through Marko's records, but it turns out, he's been living under an alias this entire time. A new face too."

"What?" Jane drew in her breath, shocked to the core.

"His real name is Paul Lyman. Born and raised in

Chicago. After several of his previous girlfriends filed charges against him for assault and battery, he disappeared before he could be arrested. He must have resurfaced a few years later as the man you knew, Jane. He's been targeting women all of his life, and when he saw you reappear from the dead, he wanted you back. Men like him never let the women go. Losing their control over you sends them over the edge. He came to force you to go back with him."

"That's ridiculous! The bastard tried to kill her!" Logan's jaw clenched tight. He radiated fury.

"We're logical people, so we can see how it really is. But, Marko, rather, Paul, isn't like us. He's very disturbed and belongs behind bars."

"But how did he even know about Clare?" Jane had been running this through her mind but couldn't come up with any answers.

"He saw several pictures of the two of you together. The first time, outside the Armani store, and then again, on the set of Logan's movie. He must have used facial recognition software to locate her somehow."

"I'm on the Nordstrom website." Clare's green eyes were stricken. "They did a story recently about its staff and they used a photograph of me on the main page."

Summers nodded, the final missing piece falling into place.

"He simply walked into the store when you were working and chatted you up."

"One thing I still don't understand," Jane brought up, not wanting Clare to feel a second more of guilt. "How did you tie him to me in the first place? How did you find us?"

Logan cleared his throat. "When you started to recall pieces from your past, I hired a private investigator. I needed to protect you... a great job I did of that." His laugh was bitter.

"I'm only here now because of you. You saved me, in more ways than one. All of you." She glanced at each of the caring faces that surrounded her. "Because you all cared about me... I still have breath left."

A striking woman came into the room, tall and lithe with the kind of face and body that stopped even Jane in her tracks. It took a moment before she could place why she looked so familiar.

"You're the woman Logan was having coffee with."

The 'woman' flashed a brilliant grin at her, reaching over to shake her hand. "I'm Westler, PI. Really great to meet you. I'm so glad you're safe, now. Logan has been out of his mind with worry."

"Thank you," Jane replied simply.

"I barely did anything. Not for nothing, this man you have here didn't think twice about leaping out of a helicopter some thirty feet in the air, into the depths of the ocean to save you. Turns out, he's a real-life action hero after all."

Logan looked at her with such love in his eyes that Jane felt suddenly incredibly foolish.

"I told you there would be a logical explanation," Clare winked.

A wave of exhaustion hit her hard then, leaving her reeling. She swayed against Logan and only managed to stay upright because of him.

"If we're done here, I'd like to get her home. We can follow up with everything else once she's had a chance to recover." His tone gave no room for argument. There was no doubt in anyone's mind who was calling the shots now. Summers stood up, nodding.

"Of course. Jane, we'll be in touch later for your statement but for now, get some rest. You too," he turned to Logan. "You've more than earned the right for some R&R."

"Clare, will you stay with us for now? We've plenty of room. I don't like the thought of you being home by yourself," Logan surprised them all with his offer.

Jane's heart swelled with love for him. He really was the perfect caretaker.

Clare smiled a warm, wobbly smile. "That'd be great. Thank you."

He was right: the thought of going home alone was beginning to fill her with dread.

They said their goodbyes. The four of them stepped out of the station, only to be blinded by a row of paparazzi and their cameras.

Logan grabbed Jane's hand, shielding her from view with his jacket as he escorted her into the waiting car. Clare and Loki followed closely behind. The little puppy growled and snapped at the photographers, not liking or understanding all the attention.

When everyone was in the car, Logan rapped on the partition to let Daryl know he could go. There, nestled in his arms, Logan held onto Jane as if he would never let her go.

36

SIX MONTHS LATER

JANE STARED OUT OF THE STRETCH LIMO, MARVELING AT A night sky that was lit up by floodlights.

The atmosphere was electric.

She could almost taste the excitement that hung in the air.

Cinematic music blasted outside Grauman's Chinese Theatre on Hollywood Boulevard, its distinctive mint green roof glowing from thousands of blinking LED lights that cascaded down.

A large crowd had gathered, screaming and chanting for the stars they were hoping to see, though most were likely there for Logan.

The past few months had seen an extreme upturn for the movie star. His heroic rescue of the woman he had loved — captured on a body-worn camera by one of the rescuing team — had been repeatedly shown on channels around the world causing the public to fall in love with him all over again and gaining him new fans in the process.

He was now THE hottest actor in demand, besieged by studios and television stations alike, yet, after production of his latest movie completed, he had ignored every offer that was flung at him.

Jane had needed time to recover from her ordeal, and he had been determined to be there for her every step of the way.

He took a long-overdue hiatus from filming so they could spend their time together, cooking delicious meals and taking long walks on the beach with Loki. With his gardeners help, they created the organic vegetable garden Jane had always dreamed of having, though they'd had to test out several options before they found a solution to stop Loki from destroying it every opportunity he had. They even listened to audiobooks, starting with the one Jane had gifted him.

As Jane had hoped, the book connected with Logan in a way that he'd never expected. Although Logan had never had kids, he had spent his life taking care of the ones he loved. It wasn't difficult for him to see himself in the main character's shoes, as he fought to keep his family from being taken away from him.

Logan was so affected by the real-life story that he optioned the book. It would be the first movie his production company would make. He planned on producing the movie as well as star in it and had brought studio mogul Stonewall Jones — the man who had turned him into a star — on as a partner.

The new venture and being able to be his own boss, was liberating for him.

With Logan and Clare by her side, and Loki providing much entertainment as well as unconditional love, the three helped Jane to recover.

She kept up the appointments with the therapist as they worked together to fill in any of the remaining gaps in her memory. She had recovered most of her memories now, though it all caused a tremendous sadness when she understood how unloved and isolated she had been. With no support system around her, Marko had found her easy prey.

Jane thought about the first time she had worried that maybe she had gotten herself into a dangerous situation. It was the only time she had ever asked for her parents' help.

They tended to speak only at Christmas when Jane, still trying to salvage some part of their relationship, would call. She had barely begun to explain about her complicated marriage when they had cut her off. As far as they were concerned, marriage was a onetime thing.

She had chosen her bed, now she needed to lay in it.

After that last conversation, Jane never called them again. She tried not to let it upset her that they had never reached out to her of their own accord. Even with everything that had happened of late, they hadn't shown any interest in participating in her life.

And she realized that she was finally fine with that. Those terrible, dark days were a thing of the past and if that meant leaving the parents who had never loved her behind, so be it.

She smoothed down the material of her dress, another

stunning creation by Armani, a dress that dripped with pear-shaped diamonds that made her look and feel like a literal princess.

She looked across at Clare, resplendent in the emerald gown Logan had gifted her, having finally had a real occasion to wear it. Clare smiled at her date, Nathan, Logan's stuntman, who she had hit it off with on that first set visit of hers.

The two had been dating for several months now and she couldn't have been happier for them. Nathan was a great man, and the four had spent many a happy evening together, laughing, drinking, and playing board games. Under Nathan's loving attention, Clare had blossomed, even finding a way to forgive herself for what she considered her part in Jane's ordeal.

Delia, Logan's mom, sat beside them, glorious in a sea blue sequined dress that emphasized her timeless beauty. She was on babysitting duty tonight, looking after Loki, who lay on the floor wearing a designer bowtie. He was almost six times the size he had been when Jane had first met him. Hyper active and dangerously smart — and still with that fetish for Logan's shoes — they referred to him as if he were their child and spoiled him outrageously, accordingly.

These were her people now. The family who cared about her. The family who loved her and had her back no matter what.

A happy sigh escaped her lips that Logan caught. Wearing a platinum suit that showed off his tightly honed physique, his dark hair was styled with Ivy League waves. He'd grown a designer goatee recently, which accentuated the square cut of his jawline.

But it wasn't only how he looked that took her breath away.

With the truth of their relationship exposed, the shackles that had held him captive for so long were released, and with it, he was finally able to be himself. Imbued with this new freedom, he had flourished as a man.

And she had been the sole recipient of this.

She'd been with him every day since that fateful night, but the novelty never went away.

She was head over heels in love with him and couldn't imagine being happier.

The car stopped by the red carpet. She waited for Logan to open the door. Instead, he turned to Jane.

An expectant hush fell over the car.

"I know we've discussed this issue of your name before, but you never made a decision. I think now might be the perfect time to decide who you want to be for the rest of your life."

Jane was taken aback by the odd timing and couldn't hide it.

"Now? You want us to resolve this, now? But we're just about to step out there. The whole world is waiting for you."

"They won't mind waiting a little longer. This is more important. I've been thinking about this for a while. I don't think they should call you Jane Smith anymore. It's not the right name for you."

Her eyes were as confused as they could be.

"I'm happy with Jane, though. I've gotten used to it. I never want to go back to Emily. Emily is gone."

"Yes, she is," Clare smiled at her. "But we do need a

better surname than 'Smith.'" Her eyes twinkled as if she was hiding a delicious secret.

"What about Smithington? That's very regal, like a British duchess?" Nathan suggested, only for Delia to frown.

"Absolutely not. It's far too stuck up for our Jane."

"What about Ford, then?" Nathan tried again.

"Classic. Like the car," Clare grinned mischievously, rolling her eyes.

"I think I'll pass on being named after a car," Jane laughed.

"I've got it," Logan said, looking at her with a sudden intensity. "What about Steel? Mrs. Jane Steel? Don't you think that has a nice ring to it? Speaking of…"

He slipped his hand into his pocket to retrieve a stunning diamond ring that he presented to her. Jane's eyes went as round as an owl. She looked from the ring to him, to the others, all beaming with breathless anticipation. Even Loki seemed to be holding his breath.

Logan kneeled onto the floor, taking her hand in his.

"From the moment I met you, you have changed my life. I don't care where you came from, or even what name you want to go by, so long as I can call you my wife. Marry me, Jane. Make me the happiest man alive."

"Of course I'll marry you!"

He slid the ring onto her shaking left hand as tears of joy misted her eyes. The brilliant 18 carat diamond flared dramatically from the flashlight of Clare's phone as she snapped a photograph to immortalize the moment. Logan dove in for a kiss that left Jane breathless, as cheers erupted, spurring Loki to howl in excitement.

"We could just skip this, you know?" Logan suggested,

inclining his head at the chaos outside. "Go straight to celebrating our engagement privately?"

"I did not hear you say that," Delia opined in a stern mother voice that didn't belie the sparkle in her eyes.

"Somehow, I think you'll be missed if we do that," Jane replied even though there was a tug in her body that hoped for it to be possible.

Going straight home and foregoing the craziness to celebrate in bed did sound even more fun than walking the red carpet, but for one thing.

"You've worked hard on this movie, Logan. You deserve this moment. Besides, we can celebrate them both at the same time."

The smile that spread over his face made her weak at the knees.

"That is a wonderful idea." He flung open the door to instant mayhem.

The crowd roared with excitement, surging against the barriers that held them in place. Jane was blinded by a million flashes, her vision momentarily lost to them.

Logan climbed out and helped her from the car. The second she emerged in a cloud of cream, in a full skirted silhouette with material that shimmered like the stars, the crowd went wild.

She wore her hair loose tonight, styled in prominent waves to match his in a shout-out to the time period of the movie they were celebrating. Her neck was bare. Other than her new ring, the only jewelry she wore was a pair of classic cut diamond earrings.

She was a vision that Logan couldn't wait for the world to see.

He stood beside her, heart swelling with love and pride as he watched his fans admire the woman he worshiped.

Normally reserved when it came to his relationships, Logan stunned the world by dipping Jane low to the ground — just as he'd done that night at the charity ball — and kissing her long and deep.

When they came up for air, Logan took hold of her hand and made a show of presenting the crowd her stunning engagement ring.

The place erupted into absolute pandemonium.

Fans screamed, the ones on the frontline sobbing, overcome with emotion. Paparazzi yelled for Jane to move closer so they could get the money shot of the newly engaged couple.

The pair of ET anchors Jane had seen before — the famous ones who had said spiteful things about her appearance — came toward them, a cameraman in tow, but Jane turned away, not wanting to grant them this big moment.

Instead, she gestured at an anchor from a lesser known station who seemed to be struggling to gain the attention of the stars, and offered her full attention to the young woman.

And as the anchor congratulated Logan on the success of his new movie, he waved the topic aside, interested only in speaking about the woman he loved, and the glorious life they were going to live.

A NOTE FROM THE AUTHOR

. . .

If you've got this far then hopefully you've liked this book, maybe even loved it (yay!) in which case can you please take a few minutes to review this book and the series?

I'm an indie author, which means I write on my little computer from my little rental home (London is *expensive*).

The websites, paperbacks, advertising, even the book covers… everything is done by me so if you love my books and would like to see me become successful as an indie author, and you know, maybe finally be able to have my own happily ever after by bringing my fella to the UK or by joining him in the US (we've been in a long distance relationship for six years now!), please help by leaving your reviews.

The more people that know about my books, the better they will do and the more time I will have to write you more books!

—Joanne

UNTIL THE LAST LEAF FALLS

SILVER SCREEN SECRETS 3

After a landslide crushes half of her home, private and agoraphobic Eden, a screenwriter who lives with three cats, is forced to employ the services of a popular builder, but he comes with a nosy team of family members - and an equally nosy dog - and they're determined to fix not only her house, but her broken heart as well. Just when she starts to trust again, one mistake threatens to destroy them all.

Eden never leaves the beautiful home she has created for herself in Montecito, CA. Disciplined and intensely private, Eden's only company are the three adorable cats she calls her fur-children, and the best friend she speaks with daily, but she considers her life full due to her work as a screenwriter. Over half of Netflix's Original romance movies have been written by her. The pay is great, more importantly, she can work from home, something that's essential due to the agoraphobia that leaves her housebound. Having escaped from a mysterious past that she has never discussed with anyone, Eden holds the world at bay so that she can keep her life intact.

Matt is *the* builder to the stars. Having inherited the company from his father who says he has retired - though no one can stop the man from turning up at every job - Matt works with his large and boisterous family. He has five siblings: two brothers who work on-site with him, and three sisters who manage everything from the admin, to their accounts, and the landscaping, while his mom provides the team with their daily lunches.

Then there's his beloved gentle-giant rescue dog, Bear, who seems to be a cross between a Malamute and a St. Bernard, though no one really knows what he is. Known for their high-quality craftsmanship and smalltown family values, Matt loves his job... if only his personal life was as successful. Matt isn't on the lookout for love, but when he meets Eden, he can't stop thinking about her. It doesn't help that his family seem determined to break down the walls she has built around herself.

Eden and her cats aren't happy by the intrusion into their lives, while Bear - who has no idea how big he is - finds himself at the mercy of the much smaller cats. Despite how they seem to be polar opposites, Matt and Eden find themselves falling for each other. Believing he can help her out of her prison, Matt digs into the mystery of her past only for his actions to put not only their love, but their lives, at risk.

Can Eden brave the world again to save the life they have built together?

Heat level: a hint of steam - nothing graphic.

This book also covers billionaire themes and deals with anxiety and agoraphobia issues.

This is a standalone book with no cliffhangers though you'll get the best experience by reading the series in order!

Preorder the book HERE!

Continue reading for a free preview of Joanne's much-loved, award-winning thriller trilogy.

IF YOU LOVE THRILLERS AND DOGS, READ ON!

What would you do if you found an exceptionally intelligent dog only to discover he had valuable information inside his head that could change mankind forever?

** **Gold Medal Winner of a Readers' Favorite Book Award 2018****

"If you loved Dean Koontz's " Watchers," you're going to love this book." - Kindle Customer

The first time I saw him, I had no idea he had recently escaped from a mysterious lab. That he had been created there. I'd been living on the streets which was tough, but preferable to home. Then one day, I stumbled upon this mangy dog being attacked.

I saved him, but then he saved me, and I realized that Muttface wasn't a normal dog. He was crazy intelligent. I'm talking Mensa levels. It wasn't only his cleverness that I fell for, however. Bandit happened to be one of the sweetest, most purest souls that ever walked the earth. Also, who knew that a dog could have such a goofy sense of humor?

When we sought help from a grieving veterinarian named Sully, his clinic was attacked and destroyed by mercenaries. So now here we are, the three of us. On the run across the country against a powerful enemy.

Who are they and what do they want with us?

Through the danger, terror, and pain, one thing was becoming clear to me: I have finally found the family I always wanted, and I will do anything to keep them safe...

Even if it means risking my own life.

With over 300 5-star reviews across retailers, Jo Ho's award-winning debut novel is an action-packed thrill-ride that readers love, describing it as a "Must-Read" and "Unputdownable".

If you're a fan of heartwarming stories about dogs (and people) in desperate need of family and love, you will love *The Chase Ryder series.*

Turn the page to read your special free preview —>

PROLOGUE

NEW YORK CITY, NY

He had been running now for days.

The hot asphalt stung his cracked soles and the burning sun pounded onto his thinning frame, but he knew he couldn't stop. He had to get away.

A battered blue truck thundered past, and he flinched. No matter how often it happened, he still wasn't prepared for the rush of sound that roared into his ears. Where he was from, there were no cars. No vehicles of any kind.

He lifted his nose to the wind and welcomed the heady sensation of another new smell to add to his collection. Juicy, with a hint of smoke. He licked his lips, mouth watering in anticipation. Crossing onto the sidewalk, he moved towards the aroma, to where an overweight man in a greasy apron cooked on a stand. Meat patties sizzled on the grill.

He hadn't eaten since the escape, and now his stomach protested painfully. He padded up to the man and gave him a hopeful look, but clapping eyes on him, the vendor grabbed a broom and started shaking it in warning.

"Get lost, you filthy beast!"

Red from the heat of the flames, perspiration slid down his wobbly chin and landed with a plop an inch away from the meat. When his target failed to move, he glared down at the optimistic hopeful and—

WHAAM! Steel-capped boots lashed out onto his rump.

The sharp stabbing pain shocked the brown and white dog who had never felt anything like it in his life.

He blinked back tears and howled.

THE CEO

The CEO wasn't pleased.

Though considered an attractive man by many, The CEO had an eerie way of smiling that never reached his blue-gray eyes. Of slim build, he took great pains with his appearance, which showed in the Saville Row tailored suits he'd had shipped in from London. Custom made, a single suit could feed a starving African nation for a week — not that he ever would, abhorring charity as he did.

Deceptively soft-spoken, The CEO's calm exterior masked a ruthless streak that terrified men twice his size. Any who failed to do his bidding had a way of vanishing, never to be seen again.

The CEO stood by his desk in the glass office overlooking The Facility. Pouring himself a glass of Cognac, he sipped at the drink, letting the warmth of the liquid slide down his throat.

For all intents and purposes, The Facility was a high-tech laboratory where secretive experiments were being conducted on a daily basis. White-coated scientists rushed around below conducting wide-ranging research, but few knew the real reason for The Facility's existence. Only The CEO's most trusted advisors had the key to that secret, which essentially included only two people: the muscle, and Dr. Elora Robins, the brain.

After years of research, they had finally created the perfect specimen, only for him to escape. The CEO frowned, remembering the ineptitude of the staff member who was ultimately responsible. His name was Julio, and he was one of the night janitors.

Julio had worked at The Facility for close to twenty years when its number one focus was genetic engineering and DNA splicing. An illegal immigrant, The CEO had hired him specifically (as he had done with all low-level staff) as he knew Julio couldn't afford NOT to keep quiet about what went on in the lab. As an added bonus, Julio also worked for below minimum wage. The CEO had never understood anyone who paid higher rates to such low dwellers unless they liked flushing company profits down the drain.

On the night of the escape, Julio had been suffering from a bout of food poisoning. It seemed he'd left out some food at home that had been visited by houseflies. On his fourth trip to the toilets, when nausea and diarrhea had almost forced its way out, Julio had left a security gate unlocked.

This was all the opportunity that the resourceful dog had needed. Sticking to the air shafts and lesser used walkways, the dog had snuck out of The Facility before the alarm was even raised.

Needless to say, when it was discovered that Julio was

to blame, The CEO had had him disposed of. His family is still searching for him to this day.

The CEO fingered his sleeve now as he waited for the call to be patched through. *The Mercenary wouldn't let him down. He knew what was at risk.* They had lost the dog for a few days, but a new sighting had pinpointed him in New York City. Feeling the beginnings of a headache, The CEO took another sip of his drink, a three-hundred-year-old brand of Cognac that cost the same as a small car.

Finally, Suzanne, his assistant, spoke through the intercom.

"Sir, he's on one."

The CEO activated the speakerphone and spoke one quiet word.

"Well?"

The Mercenary's voice was strained.

"Alpha escaped."

The glass slid out of his hand, smashing onto the granite floor. Shards of glass flew in every direction. Almost immediately, the office door flung open and Suzanne bustled inside. In her forties, she was his right hand and prepared for every eventuality. Including this, it seemed. Suzanne had entered carrying paper towels, which she now used to mop up the spilled liquid. He watched her in silence before issuing The Mercenary's next command in a voice loaded with threat.

"Find him, or don't bother coming back."

CHASE

GREENWICH, FAIRFIELD COUNTY

Everyone loved sunsets. Everyone, that is, but me, Chase Ryder, to whom sunsets signaled that yet another hard night was approaching.

In the leafy upmarket park surrounding a man-made lake, wealthy couples strolled hand-in-hand admiring the mottled orange sky. I stirred, waking from my nap beneath a towering oak. Oaks were best as they provided plenty of foliage to protect against sudden showers and prying eyes. There was also the added bonus of load-bearing lower branches that someone nimble could scramble onto should trouble come calling... and you should know, trouble had me on speed-dial.

I stared at my reflection in the water. The face that stared back at me was fourteen but looked younger. A button nose and blue eyes gave the illusion of innocence. My mouth was plump; a little bigger than I'd like, but at least I'd never need collagen. The shoulder length hair would be a glossy chestnut if it weren't hanging in one big, greasy streak. Despite my current condition, I knew I was above average, but I'm not exactly what you'd call vain, usually choosing to hide my face rather than show it.

My stomach emitted a low rumble. I slipped a hand into a pocket and retrieved the last of my money, a hundred bucks or so. All that's left of my stash. It might seem like a good amount, but I'd already been on the road for eight months. In that time, I learned to only spend when I absolutely had to. *If only I was rich, I wouldn't be in this mess.*

I looked around at my surroundings. Yummy mommies with Pilate's-honed bodies bouncing designer-clad babies on tanned knees. The only hunger they knew was self-inflicted. I compared my figure to that of a passing cyclist, frowning when I realized that the only difference between us was our ages.

Originally from "The Paper City" Holyoke in Hampden County — one of the poorest cities in Massachusetts — I'd come here thinking I would receive more charity in affluent Greenwich, which had seen Mel Gibson and Meryl Streep among its wealthy residents, but these people, so caught up in their self-made dramas, barely noticed me. I'd totaled less here than if I'd stayed home.

I frowned as a shadow fell over the water, obscuring my face. *Strange.* The shadow didn't encompass the whole park, just me. Too late, the danger signs came into my head as a hand clamped down on my shoulder. The nails were ripped and blackened with dirt. I noticed the smell next, pungent, like raw sewage mixed with a brewery.

"Spare some change?"

I spun around to find myself gripped, vice-like, in the arms of a guy who was maybe seventeen. His glazed eyes focused on the money in my hands. I looked at his arms — yup, mottled with needle tracks. I scanned the area quickly, searching for help, but help wasn't coming. *Note to self: if trees are leafy enough to shield you from prying eyes, they'll also shield the nasty druggie who has you in his grasp.*

I froze in terror.

The druggie eyeballed the money in my hand and snatched it from me. He hesitated then, doubt clouding his eyes, but when he realized we were isolated from the rest of the park, they narrowed shrewdly.

"That it, or you holding out on me?"

Without waiting for an answer, his hands started patting me down. Here's something you should know about me: no one, but no one touches me without my consent. Instantly, a surge of white-hot fury broke through the fear. I screamed into his face.

"Don't you touch me!" and struggled like a wildcat. He was startled but much stronger than he seemed and moved like I was nothing but a mild annoyance. As he reached into my pockets, I saw my opportunity and plunged two fingers into his windpipe, slamming the palm of my other hand under his nose, snapping the weak cartilage there. Eyes wide with shock, he released me instantly.

Groaning in pain, he sank to the ground, hands around his now bloody nose. Fallen, he looked much younger. Not much bigger than me and nothing like the terrifying beast I'd thought he was. I swooped in and snatched my money back.

Shooting a quick prayer to the YouTube gods of Krav Maga, I grabbed my backpack and got the hell out of Dodge.

SULLY

ELLINGTON, CONNECTICUT

I tossed aside the thin sheet that covered my body and glanced at the bedside clock's digital display: 1:47. Those seemingly innocuous numbers filled me with a sudden, though expected, weariness. I stared up at the ceiling and sighed.

Every night, the same goddamn thing.

As I rolled over to stare out of the window, a stray beam of moonlight caught the wedding band on my finger. The ring glinted, a tiny spark in the inky blackness, but I ignored it, the same way I ignored the framed picture that was currently lying face down on the vanity table. I didn't need to see it to know what it contained; the image was seared into my brain.

Taking care not to disturb the empty side of the bed, I picked up my watch, absently running my fingers over the engraved inscription on the back. "To Sully, with love and thanks from the Bauer family". The watch was a gift from a grateful family whose beloved cat I had saved.

Although my actual name is Jake Sullivan, no one but my father calls me that, and anything that helped distance myself from that tool was a good thing in my mind. I slipped on the watch, grabbed a pair of tracksuit bottoms from the floor, and tugged them on.

Moments later, I jogged out into the dark. With my mussed brown hair, week's facial growth, and sweat encrusted gym clothes, I knew I wasn't quite the poster boy this prestigious neighborhood insisted upon, but to hell with it. There were extenuating circumstances.

The barren streets were silent, but in their own way, welcoming. Out here, in the dark, I could let the full range of my emotions run riot.

And tonight it was anger.

They say grief comes in seven stages, but for me, they alternated each night. Days were tough, especially the sunny ones that taunted me with how life could have been. On those occasions, I stayed away from parks and beaches, anywhere that might prove too nostalgic. The memories would flash up, stabbing like a knife in the chest even now, almost a full year later.

Things were changing, though. I was beginning to find the odd moment to be grateful for: the scent of freshly cut flowers, a traffic-free Route 83 during an emergency call-out. Little by little, I was learning to cope… but as soon as my head hit the pillow, the demons would come.

Placing one foot in front of the other, I stared up at the stars and wondered how much longer it would be before I would get used to sleeping alone.

CHASE

The sun had barely risen, but I was already on the hunt for breakfast. Like they say, it's the most important meal of the day.

It had taken me all night to shake off the druggie incident. I knew I was lucky this time, but I couldn't afford another slip-up. In the future, I would stay away from trees, bushy or otherwise.

From experience, I knew Monday mornings were the most fruitful, with restaurants tossing whatever hadn't sold from the week before. It was with this promise of delectable treasure that I jogged into the back end of a strip of restaurants and climbed into the dumpster behind The Blessed Palace, a popular Asian establishment. The place was kinda tacky looking, covered with gold and red dragons that looked more like a distorted fish than those epic mythological characters, but they do a weekend buffet that never failed to impress, judging by the length of the waiting line that curved around the block on a regular basis.

Sadly for me, Lady Luck hadn't just left the building, she'd taken a slow boat to China, as a deep dumpster dive only delivered some decomposed fish heads *(seriously gross)*, half a fortune cookie *(semi-gross, and empty, so no good fortune for me — figures)* and something I'd prefer not to examine in closer detail. All you need to know is it looked like Swamp Thing's illegitimate lovechild with a roach.

Enough said.

I sighed with irritation. *Damn greedy staff must have taken the leftovers home with them.* That's the problem with Asians. Never waste a thing.

Shoving the cookie into my mouth, I picked my way over the remaining mess of empty cartons and boxes. As I grabbed hold of the skip to haul myself out, I heard a sound and froze. Someone had just yelped. Loudly. In a that-really-hurt kind of way.

I raised my head and peeked over the edge of the dumpster. A mangy dog, some kind of collie mix, was backing away from a man. There was a bone in his mouth, but the guy had one hand on it. He wore the uniform of The Blessed Palace and struck repeatedly at the dog with a wet dishtowel.

THWACK! The towel made a whipping sound as it connected with the collie's flank. The dog whimpered but didn't let go. He didn't attack either, just kept backing away. It's like the thing didn't know he had two rows of sharp teeth.

My eyes narrowed into slits. From the collie's thin frame, I could tell he was starving, maybe even more so than me. It could have been my own lack of food or the injustice of it all, but I felt a sudden rage building.

Stealthily, I crawled out of the dumpster and dropped silently, landing behind the guy in my Kmart sneakers. He twirled the towel, readying another strike. Neither of them had noticed me yet, so I took full advantage of the situation. I reached for the nearest trashcan, snatched the lid off, and HURLED it at the guy's head. The dull sound it made on contact made us all wince. He dropped like a hot spring roll. I looked at the dog. "RUN MUTT!"

And took off. I only glanced back when I reached the end of the block, so it was a shock to see the dog panting right behind me.

"Shoo! Scram!" I waved my hands at him, but he just cocked his head at me. Seeing that we were alone, I slowed my running to a jog. Clearly Angry Chinese Man wasn't after us. Which, come to think of it, was weird.

I suddenly stopped. What if I'd hit him too hard? Heads are pretty soft and not the best defense against steel. What if I'd... *killed* him? My life didn't flash in front of my eyes so much as my mugshot.

Muttface suddenly dropped his bone. That alone was shocking enough, but then he clamped his jaws around my wrist and started tugging.

"Hey, dufus! I just saved you! What kind of gratitude is that?"

And then I heard it. Furious shouts. Furious *foreign* shouts. I glanced back and saw Angry Chinese Man was not dead after all, but alive and kicking — and he had brought friends. *With cleavers.* The dog and I stared at each other, the same expression mirrored in our eyes... holy crap.

Muttface tore off, stopping a few yards ahead of me. He looked at me and barked once before tearing off again.

Didn't need a membership to Mensa to figure out what he meant. Having no Plan B, I sprinted after him.

The dog ran fast, but never in a straight line. It was like he had experience evading capture. Already light-headed, I was becoming dizzy with all the twists and turns we were taking. *I* had no idea where we were any more, so Angry Chinese Man and chums had no chance. I followed Muttface down a side street.

And suddenly I collapsed.

One minute I was running, the next I tasted tarmac. I felt a wet, sandpapery tongue on my face.

And then there was darkness.

SULLY

Staring moodily into a mug of black coffee, I stifled a yawn. I sat at a kitchen table, eyes staring blankly at a newspaper open in front of me. My next client was due any second, but I found it difficult to care. While the late-night workout sessions meant my body was in its prime, my mind felt groggy, and I wished I could sleep the day away. But duty called.

"Your eleven thirty canceled," came a shout from the next room.

Or maybe not. It was Florence, my elderly, no-nonsense receptionist-come-assistant. This was a small practice that didn't require much staff, so multi-tasking Florence was a Godsend, though her domineering attitude wore me thin on occasion. Her long floral dress made slapping sounds against her legs now as she marched into the kitchen. An image of Florence doing a Hitler salute flashed into my mind before I shook it guiltily away. When I caught the determined look on her face, however, I steeled myself, ready for trouble.

"Since there's nothing in the diary until three, now would be a good time for you to do some spring cleaning. Clear out anything you don't need," she suggested. She gestured upstairs at my house above the practice. Her eyes bored into me, but I refused to take the bait, lowering my gaze to the paper.

"Another time. I'm busy."

She glared at me, but not without some sympathy. It was quite the feat and a Florence special. With a sigh of impatience, she snatched the paper away, grabbed my chin, and raised it to meet her gaze. But when she spoke again, it was unnervingly soft.

"It's unhealthy, dear."

I swallowed. I knew she was right, but just the thought of clearing *her* things away caused my chest to constrict. Experience meant I knew Florence wouldn't be dropping this anytime soon, however. With no energy for a fight, I nodded meekly.

"I'll make a start," I conceded and made my way slowly up the stairs.

At the top of the stairs, I shut the door that separated work from home and walked into the living area. The room was decorated eclectically, the result of many happy weekends perusing the local flea market, but right now, it seemed as if a tornado had left its devastation in its wake, with empty microwave trays and beer cans littering the floor. I stepped over them and turned the television on, finding comfort in the inane infomercial chatter. Tossing a crusty pizza box from the sofa, I lay down and shut my eyes. I'd get to it, but first I needed a snooze...

CHASE

I don't know how long I was out for, but it was the smell that woke me. My mouth was as dry as parchment, and my eyes felt like they were stapled shut, but I forced them open. I had to see what was causing the delicious aroma wafting towards me.

There was a something on the ground. It took a second for my vision to clear, but when it did, I thought I must still be in La La Land. There, in front of me, lay a carton of STEAMING DUMPLINGS! I blinked. The dog sat next to them patiently, as if waiting for me to react. When I gaped stupidly, he nudged the carton towards me and *grinned*. I spotted the Blessed Palace logo on the side of the box and pulled what can only be described as a comical double take.

No way…

I forced myself into a sitting position, dusted the street scum from my face, and reached for the food. My fingers closed around the edge of the box.

It felt real enough?

Muttface woofed and pawed the ground as if to say get a move on. I needed no further urging and shoved a dumpling into my mouth. Holy taste bud explosions! Turns out, those lines were onto something! I inhaled the box of deliciousness, even giving a few pieces to my new best furry friend, surprised to see how delicately he ate them. Clearly, I could learn a thing or two. Together, we *woofed* them down. In no time at all, the carton was empty. I tipped it upside down, just in case there was another sucker hiding in there, but nada. C'est finito. I looked at the dog.

"That was the best meal I've had in… just the longest time. If only we had some fritters too, huh? I could die and go to foodie heaven." Muttface cocked his head like he was actually considering my words, then suddenly took off without a backward glance. I felt a pang of crushing disappointment. "Thought we had something going here," I called after him — but I was talking to thin air. Littlest Hobo was long gone. Feeling kinda bereft, I thought about how I was humanizing the dog. Me. Miss. Anti-Dolittle. Eight months on the streets could sure change a person.

As a kid, the only pet I'd ever had was a baby duck, and that lasted for all of a week. One day, as a treat, I decided to let him swim in the gutter (The Paper City = Poor = No Paddling Pool for Ducky), only he got swept away by the current and into a drain. I'd lain on the side-walk, ear pressed to the drain, listening to his cries until they were all but swallowed by the gushing water. I cried for months after. OK, I was five, but still.

Back to my present situation. Muttface is just a dumb animal. So, somehow, he brought me food from the same restaurant we ran away from. Ironic, but hardly rocket science. Maybe he'd already stashed them some place when Angry Chinese Man caught him. And while I was having my tarmac nap, he'd fetched provisions. It made sense. Kind of.

I could stay here waiting for Big Trouble in Little China to happen, or I could move on and find a bed for the night. It was a no-brainer. I staggered to my feet, swaying a bit, my blood sugar still low despite the recent meal. I'm one of those annoying girls who can eat whatever she wants without putting on a pound, but that also meant my high metabolism required more sustenance than the average girl of my size, which, being homeless, sucks big time.

I made my way back onto the main street and spotted a bus shelter on the other side of the road. It wasn't great, but it might do. I just needed to check if it was watertight — nothing worse than waking up to a mouthful of rain.

Expensive cars roared past, not in the least concerned by my bedraggled state. Car-jacking was low in this part of town, but these guys weren't going to risk a higher insurance premium just to test out that statistic, especially for pungent moi. I wasn't counting, but it had been at least five days since my body had seen any water, and that was even before the dumpster dive. I waited for a break in the traffic.

"Woof."

The sound came from behind. I took an involuntary gasp and spun around — but a bit *too* fast. Balance and co-ordination fled me as my foot slipped from the curb. I caught a brief glimpse of my furry best friend before I felt myself tumbling backward into the sea of cars.

Time slowed to a crawl.

When you're about to die, adrenaline pounds through your body and details fly out at you in what can only be described as supersonic vision. Like Muttface's eyes, which I only just noticed were an emerald green with gold flecks. And the see-through plastic tub he gripped in his mouth containing banana fritters, covered in sesame seeds that formed the initials BP.

While I was in slo-mo, the dog, conversely, seemed to be moving at super speed. In one quick motion, he dropped the fritters and lunged for my chest, snagging a mouthful of T-shirt. I hung there, suspended over the road, just inches away from my demise, anchored only by this animal's teeth and a prayer that the cheap polyester fabric wouldn't give out. A car horn blared to tell us to quit messing around. As if.

And then the dog pulled me to safety.

I sank to my knees, shaken, gasping for the breath I hadn't known I was holding. I couldn't believe it. I wasn't dead. I was alive. The dog had saved me.

Muttface tapped his paw on the tub of fritters, which had landed unscathed on the sidewalk, and chuffed softly like he was inordinately pleased with himself.

My jaw hit the floor.

CHASE

I admit I was freaked.

Too much was happening, and I wasn't prepared for any of it. A million questions swam through my already taxed brain. I found myself eyeballing the dog constantly. There was no other logical explanation than the conclusion I'd come up with for his talents, and trust me, I'd exhausted all the possibilities in the hour since my near miss with the reaper.

Muttface was an alien disguised as man's best friend.

Which was kind of brilliant, if you think about it. What better way to spy on a different species than to camouflage yourself as the number one pet in America? Just look at him: head swiveled around, sniffing his butt like a real dog. He couldn't be more disarming. Or gross.

We'd discarded the bus shelter idea due to both our discomforts of it being so overlooked *(well, I'm assuming Muttface had objections; he was definitely restless)* and we were now camped out in a shopping mall's mother and baby room, which to me felt like The Hilton.

I was trying to ignore Muttface — who had suddenly taken a great interest in sniffing each of the toilet stalls — and turned my attention to the room instead.

There were marble walls, a glass-domed ceiling, and hanging baskets overflowing with dried flowers. Opposite the stalls stood a floor-to-ceiling mirror etched in gold, while the far wall was covered with posters of upcoming movies in steel frames. An entire area of the room was kitted out with sofas and bean bags. *I mean seriously, why would anyone put sofas in a restroom?*

I was hoping the security guards would forget to check this place so we could stay the night. I'd gotten lucky previously once or twice, though they were never as nice as this. I was pretty sure I could fit on one of those gigantic baby-changers if I rolled my legs up. Could probably fit on there *with* the dog. I figured that along with mansions and cars, rich people must have bigger babies.

Feeling uncustomarily light-hearted, I plucked a flower from a basket and tucked it behind my ear. Turning to the mirror, I meant to mock my own reflection. Instead, I was shocked at how I'd taken dirt to a whole new level. Quickly, with Muttface guarding the door, I gave myself a flannel wash (one of the things I always carried in my trusty backpack) and dried off using an air blade dryer thingy. There was even a classy hand cream dispenser—

—Which promptly disappeared into my bag. It's not like I condone stealing, but this place wasn't going to miss it. Besides, it smelled like *coconuts.* Then I turned to my furry friend, who was busying himself with his own version of a bath. I'd put things off for as long as I could, but I knew it was time to get some answers, whether I was ready for them or not. I perched on the edge of a baby changer and cleared my throat.

"Hey, dog. Could you stop that? We need to talk."

Muttface immediately ceased licking and fixed his intelligent eyes on me. Then he waited, head tilted. It was disconcerting, to tell the truth.

"I'm going to ask some questions. I'm assuming you can't actually speak?"

He barked. I heard the chastisement in his tone.

"Correction, you can speak. I just don't understand what you're saying."

He barked again and wagged his tail.

"We're going to need to establish some rules for this to work. How about I take one bark as yes and two for no?"

"Woof." His butt shook with excitement. I grinned in spite of myself, pretty sure we were making history here. Shame about the restroom though, nice as it was. Maybe, in years to come, they'll rewrite this whole event and make the setting more palatable. I heard they change things all the time.

He pranced on his feet before settling back down.

"Let's begin. Are you... an alien?" I waited expectantly, but he said nothing. I suddenly realized the possible flaw of my questioning. "You know what that is, right? Creature from outer space? Not of this Earth? Little green man? Or furry in your case?"

One bark.

"So, you're not an alien, but you know what one is." I felt the need to clarify, for my own sanity if not his.

Another bark. Hmmm.

"But clearly you're super intelligent."

The resounding "WOOF!" was obviously something he was very proud of. And who could blame him?

"Were you born that way?" The question was greeted by two barks. Our first no. I tried to decipher what else it could be. My eyes landed on one of the movie posters. Some sci-fi thing to do with DNA splicing. I felt the hairs raise on the back of my neck.

"Did someone make you like this?"

"Woof."

This time, his bark was somber, like he was remembering something deeply sad. The ramifications of this hit me pretty hard. If he was made, it was for a reason, and I don't think it was to perform at Rocco's Traveling Circus. I reached out and stroked his head. He leaned into me, pink tongue hanging out in a goofy expression. Honestly, you'd think he'd never been petted before.

"Did you run away from the people who made you?"

Another bark. This one more determined. He stared at me and tensed his body as if how I responded would determine his next move. I thought about what he'd just revealed and realized we had more in common than I'd initially thought. I dropped down from my perch and cupped his face in my hands.

"Just because someone made you, doesn't mean they deserve you. If that was the case, I'd be back in Massachusetts. If you're worried I'll send you back, don't. I wouldn't do that to you."

He regarded me solemnly. Then his tail twitched suddenly, swinging from side to side in the biggest wag I'd seen to date. When I smiled, the dog leaped up, and I got my first whiff of doggy breath as he licked my nose to my forehead. Not an inch of my face escaped unscathed. It wasn't the most pleasant experience of my life.

"Stop that! Rule number 1, no licking!" I wiped my face on my sleeve, trying to rid it of any excess saliva. "So," I asked nonchalantly, "are you planning on sticking around, or is this a flying visit?"

"WOOF!"

I managed not to smile, but honestly? I felt a huge sense of relief at his answer. It kind of surprised even me.

"Then we need to call you something other than Muttface. I should warn you, Lassie and Hooch have been used to death." Several other possibilities ran through my head; Beethoven, Bruiser, and Bingo, but none of those felt right. And then I was hit with a spark of genius. And the cherry on top? It was still a B name!

"How about... Bandit? That means outlaw, in case you don't know, except you probably do, seeing as you seem to know a lot for your type…" I was babbling, suddenly nervous, surprised by how much it mattered to me what he thought of my choice.

Next thing I knew I was on the ground, the wind knocked out of me as a giant tongue slobbered over my face again.

We probably needed to run through our rules of engagement a few more times.

SULLY

The hands on the antique brass clock revealed it was a little after six in the evening. A freestanding monolith that took up the whole of one wall, it was the one luxury I kept in the practice. A little ostentatious for the simple surroundings of the workplace, but I didn't care. Besides, there was no room for it upstairs. It was a family heirloom passed down from my father and had sentimental value. That we both treasured it was the only thing we had ever agreed upon.

I sighed at the time. I had thought I'd be done with work by now. The Red Sox were playing tonight, and I had planned on watching the game, but instead, here I was, rifling through the cabinets, compiling a medicine list. Really, this fell under Florence's job description, but after our earlier altercation, I had avoided her for the rest of the day. Childish, I knew, but I was the boss. I was almost done when the doorbell rang. Irritated by the interruption, I growled down the hall.

"Unless someone's dying, we're closed. Come back tomorrow."

"Sul, it's me," a familiar voice said. "Open up."

I frowned but put down the list and unlocked the front door. Mark Armstrong stood outside. All chiseled jaw line and broad shoulders, he was a regular hit with the ladies, though, unlike me, Mark was a player who cherished his freedom. We had been firm friends since college. Mark worked as a consultant down on Wall Street. I never really understood what his job was, only that it involved ridiculous amounts of money and offshore accounts. Mark had the kind of lifestyle most people envied. And the icing on the cake? He only worked three days a week. Today must have been a work day, as Mark was still dressed in an Armani suit in lieu of his usual shirts and slacks, and instead of a briefcase, he carried a perspex tray of lasagna.

"Figured you could do with some home cooking."

I pulled a face. "Like I haven't been through enough already."

Mark sidestepped smoothly past me, not waiting for an invitation. "Relax," he said. "I didn't say it was *my* cooking."

I closed the door as Mark made his way up the stairs. "Then I hope you gave her a good time at least. First, there's mothering, then comes the smothering. That's your saying, right?"

Mark ignored me. He stood in the living area, taking in the empty junk food wrappers and general mess. I felt some embarrassment, but I knew Mark wouldn't make this into a thing. "I keep asking to borrow your cleaner…" I cleared a space on a chair for Mark, but he shook his head.

"I'll heat this up, get some beers going. You, my friend, are heading for the shower." He moved into the open-plan kitchen. Once a safe distance away, he tossed a look back at me. "You're pretty ripe."

I sniffed under my arms and had to agree that I wasn't at my best. Mark set the dial on the oven and placed the dish inside.

"Instead of food, I'll bring you a case of Axe next time."

I grabbed a tennis ball from a shelf and aimed it at Mark's head. Anticipating a comeback, Mark side-stepped. The ball went wide, sailed over his shoulder, bounced off of the kitchen tiles and rolled into the sink.

"If you could only score like that the rest of the time," Mark quipped.

I mumbled something unintelligible as I stepped into the bathroom, slamming the door behind me.

When I stepped out of the bathroom fresh from my shower, dressed in a pair of jeans and a cotton shirt, I had to admit I felt almost human again. The rich aroma of the reheating lasagna caused my stomach to flip-flop. *Real food,* I thought. *Not something out of a box.* I padded barefoot into the kitchen but was surprised to find it empty. Two beers and place settings were neatly laid out on the table, but Mark was nowhere in sight. Hearing a sound across the hall, I followed it to my bedroom… where I froze in the doorway.

Having erected several removal boxes, Mark was

rifling through the closets at a rack of women's clothing. He had an armload when the floorboards beneath my feet creaked, revealing my presence. Mark spun around guiltily.

"What the hell are you doing?" My eyes glittered angrily.

Mark dropped the clothes onto the bed. "You can't avoid this forever." He stepped towards me, palms held outwards, placating. "We hoped you'd arrive here yourself, but it's been ten months. You needed a push."

"We?" My breath caught as it came to me. "Florence."

"She's worried about you. We both are."

"So you thought you'd *ambush* me?"

Mark took a step back, sensing my building rage.

"Sully, come on. I only want to help. Let me help you."

A range of conflicting emotions flickered across my face. Anger, fear, and then pain. Mark made an attempt to continue when his leg knocked against the pile of clothes, sending them tumbling to the ground.

I reacted like a man possessed. Darting forward, I scrambled around, snatching the clothes from the floor as if they were made of a precious material that would disintegrate if left there a second too long.

"Sully." Mark's voice was pained, struggling to watch his friend's desperate behavior. He cleared his throat. "They won't bring her back. Nothing will."

But I was beyond hearing, now methodically sorting the clothes into a neat pile. My touch was gentle, reverent.

Mark steeled himself. Clenching his fists, he braced himself.

"Emma's gone," he said flatly. "You need to accept it."

I suddenly rounded on him.

"You think I don't know that? There isn't one second of any day where I haven't thought about her cold body lying in a box instead of with me. I can't sleep, I can barely function, but her things keep me sane. Having them here keeps her close to me." My voice cracked, raw with pain.

But Mark refused to bend.

"You're holding on when you need to let go." He slipped a business card from his wallet, offering it to me. "Look, just... call them. They're expecting you."

I didn't move. Sighing, Mark set the card onto the table. Unbidden, my eyes roamed over the typed lettering. *Dr. Philip Grass, Psychologist. Specialist in grieving.*

"Get out," I said softly.

Mark hesitated. Then placed a hand on my shoulder.

It was the wrong thing to do.

ROARING, I flew at him, shoving him back through the hallway to the top of the stairs.

"Jesus, stop!" Mark cast a startled look over his shoulder at the fast approaching steps, but my rage knew no bounds. Mark reached for the banisters, fingers closing around the sturdy wood. He held on, anchoring himself even as I continued to push.

"I want you gone! Leave us alone!"

Unable to withstand my fury and at a disadvantage beneath me, Mark stumbled down the steps, all the while pleading with me.

"Can you hear yourself? There is no more 'us'."

With a determination built of desperation, I forced him through the hallway and out of the practice. No sooner had Mark's foot landed outside than I slammed the door on him.

Mark walked slowly back to his car. I waited until he unlocked the car, then I slid open the upstairs window. The lasagna flew at Mark with unnerving aim, landing inches from him. Hitting pavement, the dish smashed into a thousand pieces. Meat sauce and glass splashed onto his pants.

"Nothing wrong with my aim now," I said.

Gritting his teeth, Mark climbed into his car and drove away.

CHASE

I woke to find dog hair in my mouth and the smelly beast stretched out by my side. At some point during the night, he must have crawled onto the baby changer with me. He must've been cold and needed the added warmth. *Note to self: Give him a blanket, or at least a towel, next time.*

I yawned and stretched. Light streamed in through high set windows, showering the bathroom in iridescent sunlight. I blinked, somewhat taken aback. The place was practically sparkly. I was entertaining the possibility of this being our nightly stay when Bandit suddenly sat up and cocked his ear.

"What is it?" I asked.

Bandit looked towards the door, gave a low warning growl, and bolted into a toilet cubicle. I scrambled after him and had just enough time to climb onto the toilet before a cleaner entered, pushing a cart. Tacky salsa blared out from her cheap headphones. I peeked through the crack in the door to see a Hispanic woman wielding a mop, dancing to her phone. Good. At least she wouldn't hear us over that racket. I waited until the cleaner entered the first cubicle and signaled Bandit to follow. Quickly, we snuck out, darted around the cart, and escaped into the mall outside.

A scattering of early morning staff was trickling in. I knew we had to get out before we were spotted - a girl and her dog would stick out like a sore thumb. Seeing a sign for the exit, we started for it, when a gorgeous smell assaulted our nostrils. Practically drooling, Bandit sighed and gave me a pleading look.

I craned my head for the source of the heavenly scent and found it just a few feet away; a pastry stand, being looked after by one lone worker with his back to us. I was figuring out how we could sneak some goods when Bandit darted ahead. I watched in amazement as Bandit slunk closer, always keeping out of sight. Within seconds he had reached the stand. He snatched three pretzels into his mouth and made it back to me before anyone had seen a thing. I beamed at him.

"You sneaky little thief!"

I swear he grinned at me.

Shoving the stolen goods into my bag, we bolted for freedom and didn't stop until we were at least two blocks away. I found a nice spot by a green and handed a whole pretzel to Bandit. His eyes went so wide with happiness I thought they would explode out of his head.

Stupid dog.

After breakfast, we headed downtown. My newfound companion's special abilities had got me thinking. Like me, Bandit knew a thing or two about survival. Also, like me, he had sticky fingers — or paws — and could lift things better than anyone. Clearly, we could survive just taking what we needed when we needed it, but I realized we should aim higher. Here was a goldmine waiting to happen!

Having been broke my entire life, I had always craved money. And right then, I considered the various ways we could utilize Bandit's skills. Obviously, there was street performing, but that was just one step away from begging, which I draw the line at (there was that small matter of pride). I could enter him into a dog competition, but that would bring too much attention to us. I doubt my mom would care enough to find me, but Bandit's real owner, that was another story. I knew I still needed the full lowdown from the dog, but somehow I kept putting it off. Some sixth sense told me he or she was way bad news.

I looked at him now, padding next to me. His tongue lolled out in a sign of contentment, and he seemed for all the world just a normal dumb dog, but I could see he held his posture differently to other mutts. No matter what he was doing — goofing around, resting, or eating — Bandit was constantly aware of danger.

In my experience, there were only two types of people in the world: one's who had suffered by the hands of others, and one's who hadn't. Bandit fell into my camp.

We arrived outside a grand stone building with an ornate welcome sign that read: "Welcome to Ashdale Library."

Perfect.

I reached up and unwrapped my scarf, then tied it around Bandit's neck. He cocked his head at me in question, but I didn't elaborate. As I headed inside, I called back to him.

"Come on boy, time for some schooling."

At the word "school", Bandit pricked up his ears and bounded after me.

I let out an impressed whistle.

The old stone facade disguised a thoroughly modern interior. A glass ceiling hung over the central chamber. Shelves filled with books formed a maze across the floor. I could make out some familiar-sounding titles — The Hunger Games, Harry Potter, Twilight — but I had no interest in those.[1] My gaze swept the room until I found what I was looking for… a bank of computers. Happily, there were only a few other web geeks around. I started towards them when a voice stopped me dead.

"Young lady, there are no dogs allowed in here."

This had come from a prickly looking librarian. I casually studied the name on the badge pinned to her chest. Miss. Thorne. *How apt.* I stared over Miss. Thorne's shoulder and allowed my gaze to drift to one side.

"Even guide dogs? I'm partially blind." The lie came with no effort at all.

Miss. Thorne blinked at me behind wide-rimmed glasses, her expression horrified. What a terrible faux pas she had just committed! Her face flushed an ugly red. She took a step back and stammered.

"I'm sorry… I didn't know."

I smiled sadly at thin air.

"No worries. I get it all the time. Glaucoma," I

explained helpfully. Miss. Thorne took another step away from me as if to keep my eye disease at bay.

"Can I assist you with anything? Our braille texts are on the next floor up?"

So someone who couldn't see would have to stumble up a flight of stairs all on their lonesome? Whoever designed the layout of this place should be given an award. I shook my head.

"That's very kind of you, but my dog is trained to look after me."

Miss. Thorne cleared her throat.

"Excellent. Well, I'll be here if you need me. You just have to call."

I waited patiently for her to go, and after a few moments, she finally got the hint. Spinning on her heel so fast it was a miracle she didn't snap her ankle, Miss. Thorne walked stiffly to the check-out desk.

Stooping down, I clutched hold of the scarf around Bandit's neck and spoke into his ear. "Lead the way, fella." Bandit snapped to attention and — quite literally — pranced to the computers, enjoying the charade. I rolled my eyes at his antics. Someone had to teach this dog, less is more. Happily, the computers were out of Miss. Thorne's line of vision, so we wouldn't be getting any questioning looks sent our way.

The computer was already on, so I pulled up Google and searched for some money-making schemes. Windows popped up with helpful banners like: "Earn $1000 a day working from home!"; "Get paid for surveys!"; and my own personal favorite, "How to gamble your way to a fortune!" While I was pretty sure I couldn't get into a casino for that last one, the gambling thing struck a chord in my brain. Poker!

I looked at Bandit by my side, his back ramrod straight. He was taking this acting thing very seriously. If I could teach him to understand poker, he could be my spy on the inside. I could have him perched somewhere inconspicuous and he could spy on the game for me. I'd just have to teach him a few basic signals… Excitement flooded my body. This could work!

I cleared the unhelpful pop-up windows and opened YouTube. I honestly don't know what I would have done without this site. I've learned self-defense, the best techniques of dumpster diving, and even how to collage. Yes, I'm an artist. Surprised?

Although I'd drawn the short straw in most everything else, one thing I had going for me was my photographic memory. Didn't matter what I saw, heard, or read. Once it went into my brain, it would stay ingrained in there forever. Hence the glaucoma reference.

I loaded various how-to videos and hit play.

"Boy, pay attention. You're getting a quiz later."

A whine of excitement escaped his lips.

Seriously.

What a freak.

We had been walking now for hours.

The day had long since disappeared, having been swallowed by the night, taking along with it the green lawns, flower displays, and coffee shops of Nicetown, Connecticut. Here, the streets were littered with trash. Run down properties were boarded up and covered with graffiti. Others fared little better, as decaying stoops and overgrown, over-junked, front yards battled for attention. Scantily clad women crawled the curb, attempting to flag down passing cars.

Yes, folks, we'd arrived in Ghettoville.

My foot lashed out at an empty Coke can. It flipped over three times before landing into a blocked gutter with a splash. Bandit had to stifle his urge to chase after it. I gave him an apologetic look.

"Sorry. Wasn't thinking."

He shot me a look — he couldn't understand the sudden need to pursue the can. The need left him uneasy.

"You're a dog. Dog's chase. Deal with it."

He woofed, and I could tell my answer displeased him. Earlier, when we'd left the library, his tail was alert and wagging; now it barely even twitched. We'd only been together a short while, but already I was starting to read his body language, and man, was he dog tired.

After Bandit had digested what seemed like every poker video under the sun, we left the library for a jaunt in Walmart[2], where we obtained our own pack of cards. Then, in a nearby park (gotta love Greenwich for the amount of square parkage), I proceeded to teach Bandit sign language, Chase Ryder style: a cocked right ear meant I should raise, both ears facing behind means I fold, and a cocked left ear, call. I knew this amounted to cheating, but you try eating days-old meat crawling with maggots then get back to me.

A couple of shady looking guys walked past. I gave them a wide berth, but they paid me zero attention. They headed towards a dive of a place where a flashing neon sign above the entrance read "McCall's". The guys strolled inside. I was about to move on when I spotted the poker chip one of the guys was tossing in his hand.

This was it, I thought to myself. *This was the place.* No fancy doorman, no dress code. No one would notice a girl and her dog… I hoped.

I waited for a few beats, and when the coast was clear, I slipped in with Bandit.

Like I figured it would be, the place was dimly lit. Tables littered the room in a haphazard fashion, where a dozen or so customers sat drinking amber colored beer. Despite the rock music emanating from a jukebox that had seen better days, the dance floor was empty. A baseball game blared from an ancient television set overlooking the bar — which was lucky really, as the sole barman had his full attention on it. There was a distinct air of despair in this place, and I didn't need Bandit's nose to smell it. I felt a pang of sympathy for the drunk drowning his sorrows in the corner. He looked like how I usually felt. Beaten.

I moved quickly to a cigarette dispenser, pretending to study the brands inside. Bandit stuck close by my side, but we didn't need to be so cautious. The patrons were so deep in their alcohol-induced stupor that there wasn't even one curious glance our way.

From the central bar, two corridors lead off: one to the restrooms and the other some sort of private room. I watched as the shady guys marched up to a closed door and knocked three times. The door was opened by a man whose giant head seemed to float on a cloud of heavy cigarette smoke. When the smoke cleared, I saw the poker game that was in progress beyond. I stared down at Bandit and grinned.

"This is it. You ready?"

He pawed the ground, and his butt shook with excitement.

Despite the lack of attention thrown our way, we kept to the shadows as we crossed the bar and made our way to the closed door. I gave Bandit one last look, then before I could chicken out, I knocked three times. As before, the door opened, but this time, a guy with a patch over one eye shot us a startled look.

"This ain't no nursery. Get outta here, kid."

He turned his back on me, figuring I would heed his words, however, I shoved my foot in the door and forced my way inside. Eight grown men zeroed in on me, including the guys we had followed.

"I'm here to play." I'm sure I would have sounded more convincing if my voice hadn't wavered at the end of that sentence.

Patch grinned at me, revealing a gaping set of black teeth. I cringed and mentally affirmed I would take better care of my own molars in the future.

"This is a private game, young lady."

I gave him the best glower I could manage.

"I have money," I said. Then I pushed past and marched up to the surprised table. I gestured, and Bandit immediately took his position behind the other players. But he couldn't keep still. I think he was nervous, picking up on my vibes.

A big guy with the dealer's pin smirked at me.

"You're pretty gutsy for a kid."

"And you're pretty chirpy for a guy who's going to lose it all," I shot back. Dealer continued to smirk at me, though there was now a hardness in his eyes. Guess he didn't like being shown up.

"Alright kid. Show us what you've got or get out."

I tensed. This was it. Bandit must have sensed my sudden indecision as he stole back to my side. I reached into my backpack, withdrew my carefully saved stash, and slammed it onto the table with as much force as I could muster.

"Here." I kept my eyes level with his. *Show no fear,* I chanted to myself.

Dealer broke his gaze to take in the money I had slammed down… and burst out laughing. One by one, the men around the table joined him in laughter until the whole room was in an uproar. Except for me. I kept my face a mask of defiance, refusing to show my confusion.

"A hundred and twelve dollars?" he choked out in between laughs. "A hundred and twelve?"

Patch left his position by the door. His grin wider — and even grosser — than before.

"What's so funny?" I demanded.

Dealer leaned back against his seat and pointed to the current betting pot on the table.

"See that? That's just the starting bets for this hand. We open with fifty which means, you wouldn't even last one round." He smiled a slimey smile before continuing. "While I do find your naivety charming, I think it's time for you and the fleabag to leave."

Patch grabbed my shoulder and started steering me to the door, but I twisted away from him, dived towards the table and grabbed my money. The other men made as if to stop me, but Dealer held them off.

"No. Let her take her hard earned cash. We are men of honor."

At that, the room erupted again. Bandit, not understanding what was happening, whined unhappily.

I shoved the money into my pockets, then tore out of there with Bandit close at my heels. To my fury, I felt tears pricking at the corners of my eyes. Determined that none of them would see me crying, I found a door marked FIRE EXIT and pushed it open. We stumbled out into a back alley.

"I can't believe those jerks!"

Bandit circled me and shoved his nose into my hand. I petted him without thinking and automatically started to feel a bit better. I remembered reading an article on how pets were great stress relievers in a copy of Reader's Digest before. I took several deep breaths and calmed down. *Oh well. Not all of my plans were winners, but at least we didn't lose our money. Could've been worse.*

Bandit bared his teeth at me and growled.

I snatched my hand back, confused by the complete change in him. And then I smelled it. Hard liquor breath.

Breathing down my neck.

I spun around to find the drunk from earlier standing behind me — only now he didn't seem so pitiful. He staggered towards me, reeking of desperation and whiskey. Bandit growled warningly again, baring his sharp white teeth.

"I don't want to hurt you, just give me the money," he pleaded.

Here's the thing you should know about me. I'd managed to make four hundred bills last eight months. You do the math. With a hundred and twelve still left, that meant I'd used roughly a dollar a day to live on, which I think you'll agree is pretty hardcore. I could go four days on what you spend on a coffee. I take nothing more seriously in life than cash. So was I going to hand it over to this drunk? You bet I wasn't.

Seeing the determination on my face, he looked almost apologetic.

"You don't understand. I need that money. It's a matter of life and death."

I almost snorted in his face.

"Welcome to my world, scumbag."

OK. Here's another thing you should know. My mouth shoots off before I even know what I'm doing. It's one of my worst traits and something I really should work on.

All niceness faded from his face, and he lunged for me. Bandit started barking like a crazed thing. I tried to run, but he snagged hold of my backpack and wouldn't let go. Then I tried to elbow him, but my bag got in the way. He must've slipped as I felt his crushing weight land on top of me. We tumbled onto a crate of empty bottles.

I managed to twist around until I was facing him. I kicked out, getting him on his side. It must have hurt as he suddenly shrieked and backhanded me across my face. My head snapped back as stars clouded my vision. There was a metallic taste in my mouth — blood — and I realized I must have bitten my cheek. His hands went for my pockets, where he must have seen me stash the money when a ball of fur suddenly flew towards him.

A scream of agony pierced the night. I watched with fascinated horror as Bandit clamped his fangs around the drunk's right hand — the hand that had hit me and was about to strike again. The drunk was frantically trying to shake him off, but Bandit wasn't letting go for no one. I felt a moment of deep pride. *Go, boy!*

I was pushing myself up when I saw the drunk reach for a bottle that had had its base smashed off. Jagged edges glinted, caught by an overhead streetlight. It took a split second to realize what his intentions were, but by then I was already too late. I flung myself forward at the same time the bottle flashed through the air and stabbed into Bandit's stomach. He yelped and dropped like a stone.

The drunk stood over him with the bottle raised high, preparing to stab again. Blood pounded in my ears as I realized Bandit wouldn't last another round. I screamed.

"Here! Take it! Leave him alone!" I threw the money at him. A cloud of paper bills rained onto the ground. He scrambled on all fours for the money. When he had taken every last bill, he disappeared down the alley without a second glance.

I bolted to Bandit's side.

There was so much blood.

My hand pressed tightly against the deep wound, but it barely stemmed the flow. Bandit whined, his whole body trembling in pain. He panted loudly, the white of his eyes showing. Did that mean something? Was he dying? My encyclopedic brain ran through everything I'd ever learned on first aid, but it was no use - the data filed up in there applied only to people.

"Hold on, boy. You'll be OK," I choked out.

Bandit looked at me like he knew I was lying. Cold panic ripped through me. *No God, please, please let him be OK.* My heart was thumping so loudly I thought it would explode from my chest. There was a high-pitched ringing in my ears that dulled the world around me. Abruptly the ringing died down and I could hear with crystal clarity: nearby cars screeching to a halt as the drunk skidded into traffic, followed by car horns blaring, and screeching tires. In a white rage, I hoped for the resounding thump that would signal a collision, but it never came. Why do the bad guys always get away?

Unwrapping the scarf from his neck, I turned it into a tight bandage and tied it over the wound, but I'd barely finished the knots before his blood seeped through, blossoming over the thin material and staining it red. I had to get help. He wouldn't last much longer like this.

I wrapped my arms around his body and tried to lift, but he was so heavy, my legs started to buckle from the effort. A whimper escaped his lips as I tried unsuccessfully to lay him down again gently. I spun around, taking in the junk in the alley: there were multiple trash cans, some boxes, and something half hidden behind a doorway. I jogged forward a few steps and had to stop myself from bursting into tears of relief. It was a little worn, but there was no denying the Whole Foods shopping cart!

Quickly, I grabbed a box, flattened it, and shoved it inside the cart. Shrugging out of my denim jacket, I lay it on top. It wasn't much, but it was the best I could do to soften what was going to be a very bumpy ride. With a strength I didn't know I possessed, I maneuvered Bandit onto the makeshift gurney. He flopped loosely in my arms and barely made a sound. This I knew was a very bad sign. I slid a hand under his nose and felt a weak blast of hot air against my fingers. Still breathing.

"Hang on, I'm getting you help."

Seizing the handles of the cart, I thundered out of the alley.

ALSO BY JOANNE HO

ROMANCE

Silver Screen Secrets Series

A heart-warming suspenseful romance series for dog lovers!

If you like Nora Roberts and our four-legged friends, then you will love this series!

Until The Stars Don't Shine, Book 1

Until The Sea Runs Dry, Book 2

Until The Last Leaf Falls, Book 3 (June 2020)

Until All Color Fades Away, Book 4 (Fall 2020)

YOUNG ADULT

The Chase Ryder Series

Read this heart-warming thriller trilogy to learn the story of a mysterious dog who has escaped from a sinister lab, a lonely homeless girl surviving on wits alone, and a grieving veterinarian still haunted by a past that he can't let go of.

Can they keep their new family together while fleeing from the army of a ruthless billionaire? Will they even survive?

Gold Medal Winner of a Readers Favourite International Book Award

Wanted, Book 1

Haunted, Book 2

Hunted, Book 3

Twisted Series

Between her bizarre roommate, standoffish new friends, and overbearing father who's followed her to campus, Marley's first year at Blackville University is off to a rocky start. But when a strange night out leaves her with magical powers, college starts to look a lot more exciting…

What Doesn't Kill You, Book 1

Beware The Signs (Book 2)

See No Evil (Book 3)

The Blood That Binds (Book 4)

When Trouble Comes (Book 5)

Bad Habits (Book 6)

Left Behind (Book 7)

Hell Hath No Fury (Book 8)

In Her Skin (Book 9)

First Date Jitters (Book 10)

Grave Matters (Book 11)

Plus more to come!

Standalone Books

Who is the boy next door? A thrilling mystery that will keep you guessing until the very last page!

The Boy Next Door

See them all including her special discounted boxset deals at:

www.johoscribe.com

ABOUT THE AUTHOR

A champion of complex protagonists, Joanne writes well-crafted, heartwarming suspenseful romance with characters that get under your skin. She writes romance books under Joanne Ho and YA books under Jo Ho - most of her books feature dogs!

A hopeless romantic, Joanne writes stories about lost and lonely people (and dogs!) who are in desperate need of love... even if they themselves don't know it. Weaving compassion, humor, and suspense, Joanne creates worlds filled with characters who will take you on an emotional journey that can be heartbreaking at times, but always end with a happily ever after.

Her debut novel WANTED, Book 1 of the Chase Ryder series - about a genetically engineered dog who has run away from the sinister lab who created him, and the homeless girl who saves him only for the two of them to find themselves on the run across the country against a powerful enemy - won a Gold Medal at the 2018 Readers' Favorite Book Awards.

Joanne lives in London with three adorable cats and hopes to move to the US to be with her fella once they can figure out a way around her MCS (Multiple Chemical Sensitivities), a debilitating condition she has developed over the last few years which has left her mostly housebound. Unfortunately, it is still not officially recognized in the UK despite the World Health Organisation listing it as a physical disability. There is currently no help for sufferers of MCS in the UK.

Sign up to her mailing list for updates, book release details and offers at www.johoscribe.com

facebook.com/johowriter
bookbub.com/authors/jo-ho
twitter.com/johoscribe
instagram.com/johoscribe

DON'T MISS ANOTHER RELEASE!

SIGN UP

to Joanne's mailing list and be the first to her about her news, book releases, gifts, competitions, and exclusive offers at

www.johoscribe.com